THE ICE PRINCESS

BOOKS BY JAMES WALKER

Husbands Who Won't Lead and Wives Who Won't Follow

THE WELLS FARGO TRAIL
    The Dreamgivers
    The Nightriders
    The Rail Kings
    The Rawhiders
    The Desert Hawks
    The Oyster Pirates
    The Warriors
    The Ice Princess

THE ICE PRINCESS

+ + + + + + + + + + +

JIM WALKER

BETHANY HOUSE PUBLISHERS
MINNEAPOLIS, MINNESOTA 55438

Published by Bethany House Publishers
A Ministry of Bethany Fellowship International
11300 Hampshire Avenue South
Minneapolis, Minnesota 55438
www.bethanyhouse.com

Printed in the United States of America by
Bethany Press International, Minneapolis, Minnesota 55438

Library of Congress Cataloging-in-Publication Data

Walker, James, 1948–
  The ice princess / by Jim Walker.
    p. cm. — (The Wells Fargo trail ; 8)
    ISBN 1–55661–703–8 (pbk.)
    I. Title. II. Series: Walker, James, 1948- Wells Fargo trail ; bk. 8.
PS3573.A42533I27   1998
813'.54—dc21   97–45448
                                            CIP

This book is dedicated
to the woman who prayed at the side of my bed
when I needed it most—

my mother.

JIM WALKER is a staff member with the Navigators and has written *Husbands Who Won't Lead and Wives Who Won't Follow.* He received an M.Div. from Talbot Theological Seminary and has been a pastor with an Evangelical Free Church. He was a survival training instructor in the United States Air Force and is a member of the Western Outlaw-Lawman History Association. Jim, his wife, Joyce, and their three children, Joel, Jennifer, and Julie, live in Colorado Springs, Colorado.

A GLIMPSE
INTO THE
FUTURE

✦ ✦ ✦ ✦ ✦ ✦ ✦

JENNY SHIVERED, HER BREATH ESCAPING into the cold, sharp air in clouds of steam. A dull, thudding pain on the back of her head was all that reminded her of the blow. It had been sudden and without warning; just how long she might remain shut up in the dark hold of the ship she could only guess. The pitch-black stillness was broken only by the sound of ice grating and cracking against the hull. The ice snapped and buckled with each swell of the waves, sending a sharp series of reports like a ripple of gunshots.

Jenny blinked to become accustomed to the charcoal interior of the confined space. Reaching out with her hand, she felt the cold, abrasive hull of the vessel. The icy shelf on the other side of the heavy oak hull slid by with a slow groan.

Oh, God, she thought. *What have I gotten myself into? Why am I here?*

She sat up slowly and slid her hand along the hard wooden plank of the bench she was lying on. Her fingers quivered in the cold, stretching out to feel something, anything that might be familiar.

A sharp sting lanced at her finger and sent a stinging pain up her arm. A screeching rat hung on to her hand. She screamed out in pain and shock as she shook the creature loose. It scampered away, squealing as it hit the floor. She was not alone.

Clasping her hand under her chin, she made out the glowing pink eyes of her furry guard. The creature moved around the base of the wooden floor, stopping to glance back in her direction before darting under the far timbers. The noise of its claws on the surface of the wood and its sharp screeches cut through the cold stillness.

Jenny quivered inside, responding more to the horror of the bite than to the below zero temperatures of the ship's belly. The smell of fish combined with smoldering charcoal rammed into her nostrils as she sucked for air.

She wrapped her hands under her arms and shook uncontrollably. "Lord, please send Zac," she murmured under her breath.

The dark hold of the ship seemed like a grave, its tight space closing around her. The low beams made it impossible to stand upright and she huddled on the plank, beating her arms for warmth. *Where is Zac?* she wondered.

She heard muffled footsteps in the distance. The thought of another human being brought mixed emotions to her belly. At the moment, all she wanted was to be out of the darkness, even if it was at the hands of the men who had put her here.

The steps came closer, stopping outside the inner wall of the ship. She heard someone lifting what must be a bar across the door. The door swung forcefully open. Jenny blinked in the sudden flood of light from a lantern. She could make out the shadowy forms of two massive men.

"Let's pick her up and take her on deck," the man with the raised lantern said.

Each of the men grabbed one of her arms and hauled her into the faintly lit hallway. They pulled her down the dim passage, her feet sliding along the wooden planks. They seemed to be in a hurry, not even taking the time to see if she could get her feet settled underneath her.

On deck, they stood her upright, doing their best to make her stand straight. She could barely make out their features through the icy black beards on their faces.

The northern lights fell across the darkness, curtains of brightly colored beams, a soft glow in the night sky. The stars shone overhead and the ice around the ship seemed to glow.

"Take off her coat."

It was the sound of a woman's voice that Jenny knew well. There was no mercy to her, none at all. Her sagging head throbbed.

"She won't last long without that coat."

It was the familiar voice of the man, the man she had met in the forest.

"Good," the woman said. "We don't have much time."

Jenny lifted her head to see the woman who was talking. Her eyes widened.

CHAPTER 1

✦ ✦ ✦ ✦ ✦ ✦ ✦

THE BISHOP LIFTED HIS EYES in a moment of silent prayer. The black cone-shaped spires of St. Michael's Cathedral rose in the pearl-gray sky, and a fog rolled out of the harbor and crept up the bank. The blossoming mist brushed the trees and settled down into Swan Lake. At times like this, Sitka seemed more asleep in the middle of the day than it did at night. The fishing boats were gone, and the men of the lumber mill were out of sight and hard at work.

An unlikely-looking group wound their way up the hill to the bishop's. A dark-haired young woman dressed in the traditional Tlingit garb of skins and whale bone took her steps with a steady rhythm in mukluks made of sealskin and reindeer fur. Her long black hair fell well below her waist and swayed on her back as she walked. Her hand was held by a gray-haired bearded man in a black suit. His white starched shirt was emblazoned down the front with a bloodred silk tie. He clutched the young woman's hand tightly, a grim expression on his face.

The other two young women were blond, the smaller of the two with more strawberry highlights. The larger woman had bright yellow hair and a square jaw. Her blue eyes danced with her legs as she skipped ahead up the path and stooped down to pick flowers. She giggled and squealed as she pulled them up, pausing to inspect each one as she added them to the bouquet. Though she looked old enough to be in her twenties, her actions deceived her age, giving the impression of a young girl.

Along the path was a field of what looked like doghouses, catching the dim sunlight with an array of pigment that would be the envy of any artist's palate. Pink, green, yellow, and stark white slats covered the tiny houses. Some had striped roofs and others were adorned with colorful, pointed studs. A few displayed slanted orthodox crosses, while others were garnished with fresh flowers. Only the fact that these tiny enclosures had no doors would cause a passerby to realize that they were, in fact, the graves of the devoted.

The bishop stood next to his house at the top of the hill. His ebony robe cut a straight line to the tops of his shiny black boots. A white flowing beard cascaded over his thin chest and curled at his waistline in ringlets. Sapphire blue eyes set off his face of parchment, and he clutched his small prayer book and rocked back and forth slightly on the balls of his feet.

Bishop Veniaminov held out his hand as the group approached. "You are welcome here to my house, all of you."

The man with the gray beard nodded. "Thank you, Bishop. We do appreciate this."

The woman clutching her flowers seemed to never stop dancing. "We're here for Risa's wedding," she said. Her eyes gleamed with playfulness. "I like weddings, don't you?"

"Yes," the bishop said. "I like weddings."

He turned and walked up the stairs, followed by the group. Opening the large, carved door, he stood aside and allowed them to enter. The group walked into the parlor, where an older woman was seated by a piano. She placed her hands on the keys, but the bishop held out his hand to stop her. He turned back to the group.

"Ian, you know what you're doing here this day, don't you?"

The old man smiled at the young Indian woman and patted her hand. "Yes, Bishop. I'm about to marry myself off to the woman I've dreamed of all my life. No man could want more."

"And, young lady, do you know what you are about to do?"

The dark-haired woman smiled, her black eyes beaming as she clutched the arm of the old man. She nodded. "Yes. I marry the man who loves me."

"And we have the witnesses?" the bishop asked.

"Yes," Ian said, "my daughter, Dolly, and my niece Naomi will be our witnesses."

"You know, then, what this union will bring about?"

Ian lifted his chin, his eyes riveted on the bishop. "Yes, peace between two peoples and a family."

Dolly handed the fresh-picked flowers to the Indian woman. "Here, Risa, I picked your bouquet for you."

Risa smiled and took the flowers.

"I'm just sorry Jenny couldn't be here to see this," Naomi said.

"She'll be here shortly, girl. This just couldn't wait."

The bishop finished the ceremony a short time later. "The Lord has made you to be one." He made the sign of a cross in the air and, taking up the incense, swung it back and forth, the sweet smoke curling around the faces of the couple.

Ian leaned down and kissed Risa. Dolly squealed in delight and clapped her hands.

"We best get back to the house," Ian said. "Umqua is putting on quite the spread for us."

The bishop walked them out onto the porch and down the steps. He placed his hand on Ian's shoulder. "You are a brave man, Ian Hays. This land belongs to such men as you."

"Thank you, Bishop."

Halfway down the hill, beside the grave houses, Ian called a halt to the parade. He turned to shake the bishop's hand. "Me and mine appreciate what you done for us—"

A boom in the distance interrupted his words of appreciation, followed by the shattering of a cross on the top of a grave box next to Ian. The wooden cross exploded, peppering the group with brightly painted shards and splinters.

Ian pushed Risa to the ground and fell on top of her. The rest of the group took cover behind the grave boxes—all, that is, except Dolly. She ran up and down the path, trying her best to see where the shooting was coming from.

"I see it!" she cried. She pointed and stood erect. "There's smoke over that way."

✦ ✦ ✦ ✦ ✦

The wheels of the prison wagon carrying the iron cage stirred up a cloud of dust, and Zac reined his horse around the vehicle and trotted forward. One of the two men inside the bars glared at him, hatred in his eyes. The other was slumped to the floor and seemed only too happy to be alive. The driver crushed out his cigarette on the seat and slapped the backs of the mules with the reins, sending the team lurching ahead. The angry man grasping onto the bars tumbled backward. He moaned slightly as he hit the rear of the cage.

San Luis Obispo was starting to wake up. Passing the restaurant where he knew Jenny would be cooking breakfast, Zac spotted old Zeke. Shirtless, wearing the same bib overalls he always seemed to have on, day in day out, no matter what the temperature, Zeke was selling strawberries out of the same wagon he used to haul manure. From the look of it, he hadn't taken the trouble to clean it out before loading it with the fruit.

They had traveled through most of the night because Zac hadn't wanted to camp. He was anxious to get home and see Skip and Jenny, and the thought of one more night camping with men in irons made him push the others extra hard. He'd have to put aside the urge to have coffee across from Jenny, at least until he had his prisoners safely deposited in Bridger's jail.

The driver pulled the team to a dead stop in front of the sheriff's office. Zac swung down from his saddle and tied the dun up to the hitching rail. He grinned as Jeff Bridger, a mountain of a man with blond hair and a large mustache, stepped out of the door. His shoulders were broad, and he carried himself fully erect, his six-foot-four frame filling the door. He cracked a smile at Zac, his sea blue eyes shining in the morning light.

"I wasn't expecting you till tonight."

Zac stretched himself and leaned back to try to soften up the knots the time in the saddle had produced. "I wasn't about to spend one more night with what I'm hauling."

He stepped over to the wagon while the driver climbed down and produced two leather saddle bags. He tossed them at Bridger. "You'll find everything there—everything, that is, except two hundred twenty-five dollars. I'm afraid we didn't catch up with these two before they'd had themselves a night of it."

"I don't suppose that'll come out of your bounty money." Bridger chuckled, his eyes flashing.

"You can rest assured it won't." Zac took the keys to the cage from a loop through his belt and, walking to the rear of the wagon, turned the lock. "All right, this is where I leave you."

The iron chains on the men's legs rattled as they stepped down from the wagon and shuffled their way to the door.

"Let's get the papers signed," Zac said. "I got places to be."

"If you're thinking about the Apple Tree Cafe back there, I wouldn't be in no all-fired hurry."

Bridger stepped aside and followed the men through the door. Zac fell into line behind them.

"Now, why is that?" He handed Bridger the keys to the leg irons, perched himself on the edge of the sheriff's desk, and watched Bridger unshackle the men and lead them to an empty cell. He raked his hand across the stubble of six days' growth of beard on his face. "I suppose I should clean up and use a razor before I go."

"No need for that. That's what I'm trying to tell you. Jenny's gone."

"Gone where?"

"She left for San Francisco three days ago, and from there she was headed up to Alaska."

"Alaska?" The idea of Jenny being gone was a strange one, and Alaska was the last place he could imagine her going. Their wedding was in six months, and Jenny had talked of nothing but that.

"She had a lawyer feller come and fetch her. I guess she's got an uncle up there in Sitka and, come to find out, a sister too."

Jenny had always felt bad about being without family. She had little idea of her sister's whereabouts, and the thought of actually seeing her would have been enough incentive to have Jenny drop everything. Zac knew that much about her.

Bridger turned the key on the cell door. "She did leave you a letter." Walking over to the desk, he opened the drawer and pulled out an envelope. He dropped it on the battered desktop. "She said for you not to worry. This here letter is supposed to explain yer ponderings. I reckon this lawyer fella, David Cormia, just couldn't wait around for you to bring in two prisoners."

Zac pushed the envelope into the inside pocket of his buckskin jacket. He figured anything it might say would be best read away from other people's eyes. He liked Jeff Bridger but didn't care to let anyone into his head while he read a private letter. "Just let me sign the papers for these two, and you can wire Wells Fargo and tell them to hold my money."

"You planning on going after her?"

"Right now, I'm just planning on some hot food and a bath." Zac spun around on his heels and walked to the door.

"Well, you just let me know what your intentions are."

Zac stood by the open door, his fiery brown eyes locked onto Bridger.

"Do what yer a mind to. You always do. I'd just like to know where to forward anything from Wells Fargo."

"I'll let you know . . . when I know."

Zac marched out the door and wasted no time. He swung his leg over the big dun and pointed him west. He'd be in Morro Bay by noon and home to Cambria before it was time to quit the chores.

Any other animal would have been played out, given the all-night ride, but the dun had plenty of bottom to him and took to the street with the expectation of a barn up ahead. Even though there were people on the sidewalk already, the place seemed deserted without Jenny. He'd been thinking about her smiling face for days, and now it was a thought he'd have to push out of his mind.

The sun was directly overhead when he rode up on the bluff overlooking Morro Bay. The massive rock that gave the place its name was a nesting ground for sea birds, and he never tired of watching them circle and call out to passersby.

Two ships were tied up at the dock, and one of them was busy loading cattle. The brutes were skittish when it came to being driven aboard something that wasn't dry ground. They stumbled and balked, only to be driven with the crack of a whip. This vessel was headed to San Francisco, no doubt. The cattle couldn't stand to go much farther than that.

Zac rode up next to three sailors who were watching the cattle stagger up the gangway. "You headed north?" he asked.

A burly redhead in a black watchcap pulled a corncob pipe from his mouth. "We sail for San Francisco on the morning tide."

"Taking any passengers?"

The man scratched his long beard. "We might, if you can stand the smell of them things." He pointed with the stub of the pipe to a man in a gray coat who stood at the top of the gangway. "Yonder be the captain. You'll have to speak with him."

Zac got down and tied the reins to a post. Grabbing the outside rail of the gangway, he leaned back away from the line of cattle and cat-walked around the guardrails, one foot over the other. It was awkward with his rear hanging over the water, but he was soon at the top.

He stepped off the gangway and nodded to the man in the gray coat. "Name's Zachary Cobb. I hear you're sailing for San Francisco."

"You hear right."

"Then I might just want to book passage."

The man lifted his cap and scratched the back of his head. "We're not rightly equipped for passengers."

"I can sleep anywhere, if I sleep at all."

"You say you might want to book passage."

"Haven't quite made my mind up."

"Well, we sail on the morning tide." He nodded in the direction of the second ship tied alongside. "The *Western Star* over there won't be leaving for a week."

"If I go, I won't wait that long."

"Then you be here before first light and bring forty dollars in gold with you. We'll have you in San Francisco in four days' time." The man grinned. "You can sleep in crew's quarters, but you'll have to put up with our four-legged passengers."

"I raise them, so I put up with them all the time."

"They're gonna be mighty uncomfortable, and I speck you will too."

Later that afternoon, as Zac rode up to the gates of the hacienda, Skip spotted him right off. The boy set down two buckets of water he was carrying and ran to meet him.

"Zac! Zac!"

There was an eagerness in Skip's eyes that Zac had become addicted to, a sense of hope that Zac liked to think he'd help put there. He swung down off the dun and squatted down to be at Skip's level. He opened his arms. "Good to see you, boy, mighty good."

Skip fell into his arms and hugged his neck. The boy's giggles were accompanied by squeezing.

Zac lifted him up and, turning around, put him on the back of the dun. He picked up the reins and began the slow walk to the barn. "So tell me, sport, you done any fishin'? Old Hans take you out to the rocks?"

"We done lots. We went down there this morning, and Hans is cookin' what we catched. We dug up some of them clams too."

"You boys have had a day of it, then."

Stopping outside the front door of the big adobe house, Zac untied his bedroll and slipped the Sharps out of its boot. "Why don't you take the dun into the barn? Strip the saddle and give him a wash and a good rubdown. Make sure when you put him into his stall that you give him some oats. He's been going hard for a while, and I figure him to be plenty grateful for the oats. Then you can come on into the house and see what I brought you."

"You brought me something?"

"'Course I did. I never want you to think I go anywhere without thinking of you."

Skip grinned and turned and kicked at the sides of the dun, anxious to get the big horse put away.

Later that evening, Zac got up from the table and made his way to the big leather chair that looked out the open window. The sun was low, blanketing the golden grass with an orange haze. Reaching into the jacket he hung on the rack next to his chair, he pulled out the envelope. He sat down heavily into the leather, the air rushing out and the thing enveloping him with a familiar, soft feel. It was the one place in life where he seemed to allow softness to intrude. He drummed the unopened envelope in the palm of his hand.

"Are ya gonna read that thing or not?" Hans bellowed.

Hans had been Zac's cook for years. The Prussian army had taught him all he needed to know about cooking and had added to his already military view of life. He always had a way of breaking into Zac's mind, often when he least wanted or expected it. Zac had told him about Jenny being gone and the letter. Hans had been clearing the dishes, but it was plain to see that he was as much interested in Zac's plans as anything else.

Zac opened the envelope and read silently.

My dearest Zac,

I had hoped to see you first before I did anything, but this just cannot wait. A Mr. David Cormia, my uncle Ian's lawyer, has been sent to bring me to Sitka, Alaska. My sister, Naomi, is living with my uncle there, and they have been searching for me. From Mr. Cormia's tone, all is not well, and Uncle Ian wants me to come at once. I plan to be gone for only two months, maybe three. I shall miss you and Skip very much, but please understand why I must go. Naomi is my only family, and I hope to bring her home to be my maid of honor. I will write to you from Alaska when I know more.

You have all my love, darling. Not a moment will go by without you being in my thoughts.

Jenny

Zac put down the letter and picked up his violin as Hans continued to clear the dishes away. Zac thought best with the violin in his hands. It made him feel more in control of his emotions, and the music seemed to allow him to express himself when words couldn't. He carefully tuned the strings and, placing it under his chin, drew back the bow. The sweet melody of *Flow Gently, Sweet Afton* curled around the rafters of the big room and snaked out onto the grounds.

A short time later, Hans walked up and stood quietly beside his chair. Zac lifted his chin from the violin and handed the letter to Hans. While Hans read, Zac began to play again.

"Will you be goin' to Alaska?"

He stopped playing. "I reckon I will."

"I figured as much when I read that all was not well up there. 'Course, if there was any real danger, wouldn't she say so?"

"Maybe she didn't know."

"When will you leave?"

"There's a cattle boat leaving Morro Bay at dawn."

"I'll pack some things for you and Skip."

Zac cocked his head and squinted his eyes.

"Listen here," continued Hans, "being a father is serious business. You gallivant around enough as it is. Being gone from dat boy for two or three months is just too much to ask. 'Sides, I got myself a life of my own. I signed on here as a cook, not a nursemaid-teacher. Dat's yer job."

He turned to tend to the packing but stopped and swung around. "Alaska might be a good edgycation fer the boy. He'll see all kinds of things there, and you'll be 'round to make some sense of it."

Zac couldn't argue since he knew Hans was right. Skip was his responsibility. Still, there was something about this that Zac didn't like. It gave him no peace to think of Jenny facing whatever her uncle's troubles were alone. He couldn't just sit back and wait, and it sent a chill up his spine to think about taking Skip. Loving a woman and having a boy who looked to him as a father had become the greatest joys of his life. There were times like this, though, when his greatest joy was also his greatest fear.

CHAPTER 2

✦ ✦ ✦ ✦ ✦ ✦ ✦

JENNY SAT IN HER CABIN, studying the letters that David Cormia had brought from her uncle Ian and Naomi. Being below deck didn't sit well with her stomach. The rocking motion of the boat made her queasy. Her uncle's letter had asked for her help and hinted at the danger he faced without someone he could trust. But he was a grown man. Regardless of his circumstances, Jenny knew he couldn't expect rescue from her. It frightened her to think he might need help that she couldn't offer. Perhaps she should have waited for Zac, but it was too late now. When she arrived at Sitka and sent a letter to Zac, it might be weeks before he even received it.

What truly brought her on this journey was knowing her sister was there. Tacked onto the end of Naomi's separate letter was a plea for help. Jenny knew that whatever it was that was wrong in Sitka, she was not about to leave Naomi there.

She put down the letters and tried to remember the last time she'd seen Naomi. When their parents died, Jenny had gone west and Naomi had given her a tearful good-bye. Naomi was sent to live with her aunt and uncle. At the time it was the right thing to do; it allowed Naomi to have a home and the proper schooling. Nonetheless, Jenny regretted the decision, especially since she had lost track of them. They had moved with no word as to where they were going, and even now it made her angry to have been clueless as to Naomi's whereabouts for so long.

She tucked the two letters into her purse and made her way to the gangway that led above deck. The wooden stairs were slippery with the wash of the waves, and she gripped the handrails as she pulled herself up.

As she stuck her head out of the door, the wind whipped at her hair. The bright sunshine burned her eyes, causing her to blink into the stark blue sky. A cold spray blew across the deck.

The bow of the small ship rose in the air, the waves arching it skyward. It slammed back down into the cold sea with the sound of a small

19

cannon. The impact rocked the deck, and Jenny held on tightly to the rail. She could see the cliffs of San Francisco's golden gate, and the mere thought of dry land warmed her heart. Still, getting there would still be a chore since the afternoon winds were against them.

David Cormia stood at the rail of the ship, hanging on with both hands. He had pulled his black bowler hat down over his ears, and it cut tightly across the tops of his cheekbones, creating a somewhat comical look. He was a quiet man, and he struck Jenny as someone who always had something to say about a matter but preferred to keep to himself. He had a dark complexion and black hair with a spotting of gray at the temples. His Italian ancestry showed in his smooth features and brown eyes.

He turned and spotted Jenny, leaving the rail to take her hand. "You must be careful, my dear. This deck is slippery."

"Thank you."

"We wouldn't want any bruises on the future bride."

"No, we wouldn't."

He smiled. "This fiancé of yours, he works for Wells Fargo?"

"Yes, he does."

"And just what does he do for that company?"

Zac's job had always been a touchy subject. She knew of its dangers better than most and never liked to make it seem too interesting for fear it would prompt even more curiosity. "He does whatever they ask him to do. Sometimes he travels," she answered evasively.

"Does he normally bring in prisoners?"

"Very little he does is of a normal nature."

She could tell that her answers didn't satisfy him, but it was all she would say.

"He may just decide to follow you to Alaska."

"I don't think so. He gets much too busy to be gone for that length of time."

Cormia rubbed his smooth chin. "Well, I know if you were my fiancée, I wouldn't want you out of my sight."

"You say my uncle Ian is married now?" Jenny did her best to change the subject. The man's sudden attention and his curiosity about Zac made her feel uncomfortable.

"Yes, and a sweet girl she is."

"Girl?"

"She's twenty. That's plenty old enough for marriage. An Indian girl, but one that brings a lot of land along with her dowry."

"Uncle Ian's got to be sixty."

"Sixty-five."

Jenny shook her head.

"That's part of his troubles," Cormia added.

"I can imagine."

"Risa is the daughter of the old chief Yakta. The Tlingits have a lot of that land up there, and a pretty fair piece of it comes with her."

"Are you saying he married her for the land?"

Cormia laughed. "No, mercy no. If you saw that girl, you'd never think that. She has long black hair that falls below her waist and a face that's as pretty as any postcard I've ever seen. He dotes on Risa and treats her like a princess, and she just adores him. Risa and your sister, Naomi, have become friends too."

"I'm glad."

"Of course, that doesn't mean everyone's happy about this marriage of his. Your uncle has a lot of enemies in Sitka, and they see this marriage as just giving him a better position. Envy is a terrible thing."

"Why does he need me?"

"You're kin. He's been looking for you for over a couple of years now, ever since he and Naomi became settled in Alaska."

"He moved away from his place in Maryland and said nothing, left no word."

"I think it was the death of his first wife. Men in grief don't do rational things."

"He should have left word. Naomi is my sister."

Cormia shook his head. "I expect your uncle has a trunk full of things he should have done."

Jenny clenched her fists into two small balls of fingers. "He can keep those things, but this one involves me."

Cormia sighed. "He *has* been looking for you for over two years now. He hired the Pinkertons. That cost him a bit of money, I can tell you that."

Jenny stared into the wind, bracing herself. "He could have saved himself trouble and money just by being thoughtful and leaving word in Maryland. My letters were all returned."

"You'll have to take that up with Ian. I can defend him in a court of law, but I can't begin to defend him to a niece who's got her feathers ruffled."

Jenny swept the blowing hair from her face. "Wouldn't you be irritated with someone who took your sister and then dropped off the face of the earth?"

"I suppose I would at that."

"And now he finds me just when he needs me."

Cormia threw his shoulders back and lifted his chin. "Well, like I said, his troubles didn't really start until his attachment with Risa. He was going to send for you anyway—that is, as soon as he could locate you. It just happened to work out this way. You'll be someone he can depend on, and right now he needs that in the worst way."

Jenny watched him as he looked off at the bay. She could tell that he was holding something back. "Are you telling me everything?"

Cormia continued to stare at the choppy bay while he seemed to be thinking the question over. "Not quite."

"I don't scare easily. If there's more, I need to know."

"Someone wants your uncle dead. He was shot at on his wedding day, and since then he's lost three dogs."

"Three dogs?"

"Yes, they died after eating food intended for him."

"Someone is trying to kill him?"

"That's about the size of it."

"Well, I'm not about to taste his food for him." Jenny turned away and looked at the high bluffs. Helping her uncle was one thing, but putting herself and Naomi at risk for this newfound romance of his was quite another.

"He just needs another pair of eyes that he can trust."

"Well, Mr. Cormia, I will be in Sitka only long enough to arrange for passage for Naomi and myself back to California. My uncle Ian's troubles are his to solve, not mine or my sister's."

✦ ✦ ✦ ✦

The house on the hill stood in the cold fog as a blanket of milky gauze lay over the bay. The trees on Aleutski Island rose up into the early morning sky like the hairs on the back of a frightened dog. Ian leaned over the balcony and gazed at the fog that bled from the tops of the trees and curled gently into the bay below. The distant sun shone through the mist. It would be bright when it climbed overhead during the day, but now it was no more than a glowing illusion.

A light rap at the door was followed by the sound of Bubba Dean's feet shuffling over the oak flooring. "Mistah Ian, is you ready for the morning?"

Ian swung around, leaning his elbows back onto the railing of the balcony. The old black man held a silver tray in his hands. A silver pot of black coffee teetered on the oak tray and along with it Ian's usual bowl of grits. "I'se jest gonna set dis down right here. You'd better come get it now whilst dis mess is still hot."

Ian hitched up his pants and stepped back into the bedroom. Bubba Dean was in his usual attire—red flannel shirt stuffed into black trousers, with boots worn down at the heel. The man insisted on wearing his hat, a gray fedora, flattened out at the brim and pulled down over his head where the edges of his ears stood out and bent toward the front. His large, flat nose seemed to take up all the space on his face—except for the sharp, piercing, widely-spaced eyes.

Ian swung his leg over the chair in a nonchalant, boyish fashion and, ripping out the white cotton napkin, smoothed it over his lap. "Why do you insist on wearing that hat indoors?"

Bubba Dean's mouth spread out into a grin that showed a beautiful set of white teeth. "Why, Mr. Ian, you knows you done give me dis here hat." He chuckled a bit. "If'n I was to take it off, I'd feel next to undressed."

Ian poured out a cup of the coffee. "I hope you take it off at night."

"Why shore. Y'all don't think Umqua would let me crawl in next to her with my hat on, now does ya?"

Ian took a sip of coffee. "I hope not. I can only hold out that she keeps working on those manners of yours. We ain't in the back country, you know."

"Oh, yes, sir, I'se surely knows dat."

Picking up his large spoon, Ian shoveled the warm, buttery grits into his mouth. He dabbed with his napkin, although with the whiteness of his beard, it was doubtful any of the grits would show.

"Mr. Van Fleetwood is downstairs waiting fer you."

Ian held his spoon back. "Why didn't you say so? Is it that late already?"

Bubba Dean scratched the back of his head, lifting his hat slightly. "I reckon it is. You is losing track of yer morning time, I reckon, given yer wedding and all."

Ian smiled. "I suppose I am. A young woman can do that to a feller."

"Yes siree, dey sure can now. I knows dat fer sure."

"Where is Risa this morning?"

"She done gone with Miss Naomi and Miss Dolly. Dey is pickin' berries."

Ian crammed a few more mouthfuls of the warm grits into his mouth and then washed them down with the hot coffee. Wiping off his beard, he dropped his napkin onto the tray and got to his feet. "I guess I better see to the old coot. We're heading off to the mill this morning."

"Yessah, y'all had better do dat."

Ian buttoned the top two buttons of his shirt and shrugged on his brown corduroy jacket. He liked to think he still cut a manly figure in the jacket in spite of his age. Risa had that effect on him. The first time he saw her, he had felt ten years younger, and marriage to her had made him feel twenty years younger at least.

He stepped out into the candlelit hallway, followed by Bubba Dean and the tray. Walking out onto the balcony that overlooked the great room, he spotted Fleetwood below. The room was massive by Alaskan standards, with overhanging wrought iron chandeliers. Fleetwood stood on a bearskin rug in front of the fire, sipping a cup of coffee and making conversation with Umqua.

"You seem bent on disturbing a man's beauty sleep." Ian's voice roared into the open room.

Fleetwood cocked his head up in Ian's direction and laughed. "You plan on getting beautiful, you best never wake up, you old coon."

Ian started down the stairs. Fleetwood was wearing his usual fringed rawhide jacket. He sported a white shirt and tie, and his peaked campaign hat sat smartly atop his shoulder-length white hair. The man's white mustache blossomed out from his upper lip and cascaded down the sides of his mouth, and his pointed beard had been freshly waxed.

"You look fit to die," Ian said. Ian had a tendency to talk to people in a way he thought might please them. To a teacher, he could be proper to a tee, while he could speak the language of a teamster with equal ease. "Why you wanna get all gussied up for? We ain't going to no dance."

Fleetwood let his jacket fall open, placing his thumbs under his red suspenders and stretching them out. "I figure when I come to the house of the richest man in Sitka with the prettiest durn wife to be found, I best get myself all slicked up."

"Don't you go to tellin' no lies. You just do yer best to shame me, that's all."

Fleetwood's blue eyes twinkled. "From where I stand, that don't take much doing."

Umqua took the man's cup while Fleetwood buttoned his jacket. "You sleep well, Mr. Ian?" she asked.

"I always sleep well."

Fleetwood laughed. "I bet you do these days. If you ask me, you sleep too well. You said seven o'clock and it's already seven-thirty."

"Just hold your horses. That lumber mill ain't going no place."

Ian reached up and pulled down his favorite rifle, a long-barreled Sharps. Unslinging it, he wound it around his shoulder. "Never can tell. We just might do a little huntin' on our way to the mill."

Fleetwood picked up his rifle and sneered. "Only if we have to. I sure ain't plannin' on skinnin' no bear before lunch."

Ian patted him on the back. "You taste the lunch I plan on feeding you at the mill, you might wish you had." He turned back to Umqua. "Don't figure on us before supper. I plan on getting the old coot here to stay fer that, though. He ain't got nothing better waiting for him at home."

With that, the two men stepped out the door and onto the porch. Ian stopped to breathe the morning air deeply while Fleetwood walked down the path to the road below. He stopped and looked back. "You coming?"

Ian grinned and hurried to join his friend. The trail that led to the mill was covered with fireweed. The tall stalks, some seven feet high, were dotted with pink blossoms. Old timers said they could predict the winter by how soon the fireweed disappeared. From where the blossoms now stood, it promised to be a mild one by Alaskan standards.

The sloping hills were covered with greenery that was unlike anything seen in the lower states. At times the grass appeared almost translucent, as if a man could see through it. It sparkled with the dew, and the droplets of water glistened like a million diamonds scattered over a green drop cloth in the store of the world's richest jeweler.

It took the two of them just over an hour to climb the low hills that led to the mill. The mill itself was a hodgepodge of lumber, badly weathered by the winters and the years. It didn't take long in Alaska for buildings to show their age if people didn't live in them. The absence of paint allowed the snow and bitter cold to bleach the wood into a dull, austere gray.

The fast-running stream and waterfall sent a plume of steamy water into the air. It provided the power for the saw, but it was always a wonder to stop and just look at. The green grass and bright flowers tumbled down the sides of the slope and onto the well-worn path below. Everything was seasonal in Sitka. The mill only had six months of life at best until the river would be frozen over. After that, it was just a matter of a man hunkering down and shivering his way through the long, dark months.

The two friends stood looking at the scene and listening to the sound of the distant ripping saw. Even from where they stood, they could hear the harsh noise of the steel as it tore through the logs. Wagons were being loaded by several Indian laborers, their bare backs gleaming with sweat in the morning sun.

They ambled down the hill and climbed the steps to the mill office. The door was ajar, and a stiff breeze blew the tattered oilskin that draped to the floor to keep the bugs from joining the swarm that was already circling the desk. Several lamps glowed in a smoky haze, and Ian sat down at the desk and pushed aside the papers that were covering it. He pulled out a large ledger from the drawer. "I'll show you what we been doing so far. It ain't bad."

Fleetwood picked up a ladder-back chair and placed it beside the open book. "I hope it ain't bad. You got the only game in town."

"It's only going to get better as this area grows. People got to build and they're gonna get mighty tired of haulin' logs. 'Sides, they got too much else to do. Folks spend so much time making a living. They don't need to worry about how to build the places they're living in."

"And you figure this parcel of land that done come with your wedding is gonna supply you with enough lumber?"

"Shoot, man, there's more trees in that stretch of land than a man could cut down in a thousand years."

Fleetwood squinted his eyes at him. "If a man hadn't seen that woman of yours, he'd figure you done up and married her fer what come with her."

Ian leaned back and pulled on his beard. "Something to be said about marrying a Tlingit princess. I s'pose if a man's got to give his heart palpitations, that's the best way to go."

Ian turned the pages of the ledger, pointing out the healthy bottom line when he could. When it came to making money, Ian loved to impress people. He closed the book when the door into the mill area opened and a tall, dark man stepped in. He had a clean-shaven, handsome face with high cheekbones and dark eyes. "We heard you were coming up this morning," he said.

"Good to see you, Cole. Van and me were just looking over the books."

Cole Pressley's face dropped slightly, and he shot Ian an icy stare from his cold black eyes. He walked over to the pot-bellied stove and, lifting up the pot of coffee, poured himself a cup. "We're having a good yield this year. I'd say with all the building going on, we'll do pretty well."

In spite of the good news, there was a distance in his voice. It struck Ian as odd. He might have thought Cole was delivering a death sentence and not a healthy business report. "That's what I like to hear."

Pressley took a drink and set down the cup. He made his way slowly to the door. "I best get back to work."

"Fine," Ian said. "We won't be long here. We're almost done."

Ian noticed Pressley was studying both him and Fleetwood, almost as if he were trying to read their minds.

Pressley turned his back to the two men and, lifting the oilcloth, stepped outside.

Ian got up and poured a cup of coffee for Fleetwood. "Something's got a burr under that man's saddle."

"I wouldn't worry about it. He's probably got a lot on his mind."

"I should show you the timber yield figures we've been getting. They ain't bad, but them fresh new stands ought to make them books shine."

Fleetwood's head jerked up. "You smell something?"

Ian's back stiffened.

Fleetwood dropped his cup to the floor. "Fire!" he yelled.

CHAPTER 3

+ + + + + + +

THE FLAMES ERUPTED AT THE DOOR to the office, sending sheets of crimson lapping at the oilcloth that hung over the window and door. The two men watched as the crackling blaze crawled up the sides of the door and lapped onto the ceiling. It flowed like a stream of red ribbons billowing in the wind, licking the old wood that formed the ceiling of the office. They could hear the saw as it continued to buzz in the mill. The men stared at each other, sharing the same thought. The noise of the mill might prevent anyone from hearing them until it was too late.

Fleetwood pointed to a barrel of water that stood in the corner. "We better grab that bucket."

Ian grasped his arm. "Nonsense, there's no time for that."

Reaching over to the back window, Ian ripped down an oilcloth that had formed part of a dingy curtain and plunged it into the water barrel. Glancing at Fleetwood, he shouted, "Take that bucket and fill it."

Fleetwood dipped the bucket into the water, filling it to the brim.

"Now, wet yourself down."

Fleetwood blinked at him, unable to understand just what the man had in mind.

"Just do as I say! Get yerself plenty wet."

Fleetwood poured the bucket of water over his head, and Ian turned around and wrapped the soaked cloth over the top of the man's head and down his back.

"What are you doing?" Fleetwood asked.

Ian grabbed the bucket and, plunging it back down into the barrel, poured the water over his own head. "We're busting out of here and pronto."

"Bustin' outta here?"

"That's right. We try to fight that thing and we're gonna get ourselves cooked fer sure."

Tearing down another of the sooty cloths from the window, he soaked

29

it and wrapped it around his head and shoulders. He motioned toward the flaming door and the window beside it. "You follow me. We're going out that window there." Reaching down, he picked up the ledger.

With that, he started on a full run toward the window. Turning his shoulder toward it, he shattered it with a crash. The window exploded, sending shards of glass and splinters of flaming window frame in all directions. Tumbling down the flaming stairs, he hit the ground rolling.

He looked up in time to see Fleetwood dash through the rising flames and jump headlong off the porch, hitting the ground with a groan.

Ian slowly got to his feet. He stomped out the flames on the cloth and beat out several smoldering embers on his jacket. Walking over to where Fleetwood still lay on the ground, he bent low over him. "Are you all right?"

"Just leave me lay fer a spell. I think I might want to count my bones."

"You came offa that porch right nice for an old man."

Fleetwood rolled over and got to his knees. "Old ain't got nothing to do with it. A deaf, dumb, blind man of a hundred woulda done the same durn thing." He put one foot underneath his body and slowly got to his feet. "Ain't nothing like a fire to put a spring in a feller's step." Bending over, he worked at rubbing life back into his legs.

The flames finally caught the attention of a number of the mill workers. They gathered in groups at the corner of the blazing building, pointing and shouting. Several men came around the building with buckets, and they formed a line to pass water up from the river.

"Good thing that office shack ain't attached to the mill," Ian said.

"I'd say." Fleetwood looked over at him. "You don't suppose that fire was set for us, do you?"

The sight of Cole Pressley brought them both to a moment of silence. The man rushed over to them. "You two all right?"

"We ain't bad fer a couple of codgers," Fleetwood shot back.

"Just a few bruises."

"Good, I'm glad to hear that."

"You are?" Ian asked.

Pressley gave him a silent look.

"How do you suppose that thing started?" Ian asked.

Pressley pointed over to the burning building. "We do keep our oily rags under the porch there. Maybe somebody tossed a cigarette."

"That has to change," Ian said. "You find a better place to put burnable material. Lumber mills are a bad place for a fire."

"Ain't no worse spot for one," Fleetwood added.

"I'll check it," Pressley said. He turned and walked back to the line of men that were pouring bucket after bucket onto the burning fire.

It was too late to save the office. Ian knew that. The only thing they could do now was try to prevent it from spreading. Fleetwood nudged Ian and pointed to a tall Indian standing near the middle of the line. The man was simply staring at the two of them, his coal black eyes riveted on them. "Who is that?" he asked.

"That's Puka. He's in charge of our Indian labor."

The man was tall, over six feet. He had long, shoulder-length, jet black hair, high cheekbones, a high forehead, and a long nose that swooped down toward his pointed chin. His corduroy pants covered his black boots, and the white beaded vest over his red flannel shirt showed him to be a man of some importance among his people.

"He don't look to be none too happy," Fleetwood observed.

"I reckon not. He's had his eye on Risa ever since she was small."

+ + + + +

The trolley car in San Francisco was the first one Skip had ever ridden. It slid along the tracks with a grating noise, the sound of metal sliding on metal. Zac smiled as Skip hung his head out the window, fascinated by the sparks from the wheels.

Noticing they were getting close, Zac reached up and pulled the cord that sounded the buzzer in front to alert the motor man that this was their place to get off.

When the car ground to a complete stop, Zac stepped off. He turned back and, picking Skip up by the waist, swung him around, planting him firmly on the ground. Skip was getting much too big for this, but it was still something Zac enjoyed doing. It also brought a smile to Skip's face.

The two of them strolled down the street and stopped in front of the Wells Fargo office. The brick building was set off by tall green shutters, the same green used on Wells Fargo money boxes. The color seemed to give the boxes an air of distinction. The company wanted no mistake about whose money was in them.

Zac dusted off his buckskin coat. He knew he still smelled of cow manure, but the people inside would be used to that by now. Everybody in the office knew he was a rancher. It was only right that he smelled like one. Bending over, he straightened Skip's cap. "Man's got to watch his first appearance. You never get another chance to cut a groove with some folks."

Skip nodded. "We gonna have lunch after?"

"You betcha." Zac pointed across the street to the hotel. "We'll go over yonder and tie on some grub. Might be they can even find us some ice cream."

Zac pushed open the glass doors and the two of them stepped inside. The red brick building filtered sunlight through elongated, high windows. The bars on the outside cast long shadows over the red carpet and trailed the streaks of darkness up to the polished oak counter.

Zac stepped up and caught the attention of a white-shirted man seated at a desk behind the counter. The man was clean-shaven and appeared to be young. His brown, slicked-back hair was held in place with a green visor. He got to his feet and, rounding the desk, came up to the counter with a broad smile. "Good morning, sir. How can I be of assistance?"

Zac put his hands on the counter. "I'm Zachary Cobb and this here is my son, Skip. I believe you have some money waiting here for me."

The man's mouth dropped open. "*The* Zac Cobb? Zac Cobb from Cambria?"

"Yes, that's right."

Grabbing Zac's hand, the man pumped it vigorously. "I'm Horace Tuttle. I'm so glad to meet you. I've only been working here for a year now, and already I've heard so much about you."

Zac let the man shake his hand and then hastily dropped it to his side. "You can't believe everything you hear. A man's not nearly as good as when he's successful and not nearly as bad as when he's a failure."

"Well, from what I hear, that's not very often with you, Mr. Cobb."

"Just call me Zac."

Tuttle smiled. "Yes, sir, Mr. Zac." The man's chest swelled up with a deep breath and he blushed a bit. "I'm sorry I seem so befuddled. Let's see . . . about your money. Yes, sir. I believe we had a telegram from the sheriff, a Sheriff Jeff Bridger of San Luis Obispo."

"That would be the man."

"I'll go and get confirmation and then pay you. You don't mind waiting, do you?"

"No, I'll be fine. We'll be waiting right here."

Tuttle backed away and then turned and hurried into the back office.

"Looks like folks get kinda excited around here when you come in," Skip said.

"Not much reason for that. I just get the job done."

Skip looked up at him and blinked. "Is that all?" he asked.

"That's about the size of it. There's too many people who stand about waiting for work to get done by somebody else. Man makes a name for himself when he does it right the first time and does it without much help."

"You help me on my ciphers."

"That's just to get you started, though. Once you figure out how to do a thing, I pretty much leave you alone to do it."

Tuttle came back out the office door with a paper in his hand. "I have the confirmation here, Mr. Cobb. I know Mr. Wells would want to see you, but he's out of town.".

"That's all right. I don't have much time for socializing." He looked down at Skip. "We're on our way to Alaska."

Tuttle smiled. "That's nice. A pleasure trip?"

"Could be." He looked down at Skip. "Of course, any trip I get to make with Skip here is a pleasure." Looking back at Tuttle, he pointed to the paper. "We're using that money to travel on."

"Of course. It says here you have thirty-five hundred dollars coming. How would you like that?"

"I'll take five hundred in gold and the rest in greenbacks."

"Yes, sir." Tuttle pulled open the cash drawer and, shuffling through the currency, laid out a stack of hundreds and fifties. "Here you are." He counted the bills on the counter. "Three thousand dollars in cash." Reaching under the drawer, he opened another one and took out a bag of coins. He positioned them on the counter, five stacks of twenty-dollar gold pieces. "There you are," he said.

Zac pulled out a leather bag from his coat pocket and pulled on the drawstring to open it up before setting it on the counter. He raked the coins off the counter and into his large hand, then dropped them into the bag. Taking the stack of bills, he counted them, folded them, and placed the currency into a gold money clip. He stuffed the rather large wad of bills into his jeans.

"You'll need to sign this confirmation letter, Mr. Cobb." Tuttle dipped a pen into an open inkwell and handed it to Zac.

Zac scrawled his name on the bottom of the letter and shoved the paper back in Tuttle's direction.

"I can't tell you what a pleasure this has been, Mr. Cobb. We're so happy with the work you do in bringing our money back to us."

"Well, you just do your job at keeping that money organized in here, and I'll do mine in case some of it gets mislaid. You can tell Henry, though, that I won't be around for a couple of months. If he wants to reach me, I'll be in Sitka, Alaska."

"Yes, sir, I will tell him."

Zac and Skip stepped out onto the sidewalk, then walked briskly across the street to a large hotel that stood on the corner. They stopped on the sidewalk and watched as men and women stepped into the glass compartments of the hotel's revolving door and pushed their way forward like mules at a grinding wheel.

"I ain't never been through one of them before," Skip said hesitantly.

"Nothing much to it as long as you keep pushing forward."

"Can I have my own space?"

"Sure you can. I'll step in first and you can take the one that comes up behind me. Okay?"

Skip nodded.

They inched closer to the brass-framed glass contraption. "You ready?" Zac asked.

Skip grinned. "Yes, sir. I'm ready."

Zac stepped into the revolving door and pushed it forward. It spun around on its axis, and Zac stepped out into the deeply carpeted lobby. Turning around, he watched as Skip passed him by. The boy was smiling as he marched around in the door for one more spin. Skip's smile widened as he came back around. As it opened once again, he stepped out into the lobby.

"That was fun. Let's do it again."

"We will, as soon as we finish lunch."

The maitre d' at the door had a somber look on his face. He was dressed in a freshly pressed tuxedo with black tie.

"We'd like a table for two," Zac said.

"I'm sorry, sir. Our dining room requires a tie."

"You have a loaner?" Zac asked. He could tell the smell of the cattle boat they'd been on was having a telling effect on the man.

"I'm not sure, sir." The man eyed them suspiciously.

"Well, if you don't, we'll just take the one you're wearing. You're the hired help here, if I'm not mistaken."

The man swallowed. "Just one moment, sir."

A short time later he reappeared with two red-and-blue ties draped over his arm. "Here you are, sir."

Zac took the ties. Draping one around Skip's neck, he made a loop and then tied a knot. It didn't look like much in a dressy way, but it was a tie. He curled his own around his buckskin jacket and pulled the end through the loop. Standing to attention, he smiled at the man. "All right. Now we need a table for two."

"Right this way, sir."

They followed the maitre d' into the room, drawing the attention of a number of well-dressed diners. Zac thought it strange the men and women were so dressed up for a meal in the middle of the day. It made him wonder what they must wear for formal nighttime clothing. The two of them were ushered to a table near the far wall, next to the window. Zac could tell this suited Skip just fine. From here he'd be able to watch the passersby on the street and see the trolleys as they clattered past the hotel.

Moments later, their waiter was by their table. The man wore a starched white shirt and a small black bow tie. He passed out menus and stood and watched as Zac and Skip read them. Zac knew it wasn't a normal practice for a waiter to watch as diners read their menus. More than likely, he decided, the man had judged them unable to read.

"What looks good to you, Skipper?"

"I'd like the chicken fried steak." Skip leaned over and pointed to the item on the menu.

"Fine." Zac took the menu from Skip's hand and gave it back to the waiter along with his own. "I'll have the pot roast," he said. "The boy will have milk to drink. I'll have coffee and a glass of buttermilk."

"Very good, sir."

They were in the middle of their meal when Zac looked up and noticed another unlikely customer standing at the door of the fancy hotel dining room. His blond mustache drooped down over the corners of his mouth and onto the sides of his strong chin. He was broad at the shoulder and built like a baby bull. Standing at only five foot eight or nine inches high, he must have been over 240 pounds. He hadn't shaved in a few days and the stubble on his face covered his cheeks and chin. He wore buckskin breeches and a sheepskin coat that was turned up at the collar.

Zac looked over at Skip and noticed the boy had spotted the man too.

"You reckon they're gonna let him in?" Skip asked.

"From the size of that fella, I'm not sure they have much choice."

After a few words, the maitre d' supplied the newcomer with a red tie. With the man in tow behind him, he marched over to the area where Skip and Zac were seated.

"Looks like they're coming over here," Skip said.

Zac smiled. "I'm not surprised. We're in the far corner of the place. They won't have to worry about customers having to pass us and him on their way to a table."

The man walking in their direction was bowlegged with a body that seemed totally out of proportion to the trim limbs that held him upright. When they reached the table next to Zac and Skip, the maitre d' stopped and took the man's sheepskin coat and fur hat. That exposed the man's blond hair with the gray highlights that gave away his age. His open shirt with rawhide drawstrings barely concealed a barrel-sized chest with blossoming hair. The tie curled around his neck and dangled at either side of the open shirt.

When the man took his seat, he smiled and nodded at Zac and Skip, the sour expression plastered on his face suddenly disappearing. "I see you got yerself a tie too."

Zac pulled on the end of his tie. "You bet. I was just hoping to spill some gravy on it, but I'm afraid I'm not quite that clumsy."

"Now that's an idea." The man beamed, struck by the notion of revenge.

The waiter suddenly appeared and laid a menu beside the newcomer. "Would you like me to read it for you, sir?"

"I just want a steak, the biggest one you got."

"Our steaks are very expensive, sir."

The man pulled out a wad of bills from his pocket and laid them out on the table. "You think you can furnish a steak I can't buy, you just have at it."

The waiter picked up the menu and left the table. Glaring over at Zac, the big man cracked a wide smile. "Good help is hard to find," he grinned. "Give a man a suit and tie and he thinks he owns you."

Zac smiled and nodded as the man picked up the cash and stuck it back in his pocket. "I just sold a ship load of Alaskan furs. One more haul like that and I may just buy me this here hotel. 'Course, they probably don't have a bed that's fit to sleep in—buggy, I hear."

"You come in from Alaska?" Zac asked.

"Just yesterday. I'm going back, though, just as quick as I can. Can't stand too much of this here civilization type living. A little bit goes a long way fer a feller."

Zac leaned over in the man's direction and stuck out his hand. "My name's Zac Cobb. My son, Skip, and I are headed up to Sitka."

"Tarnation! That's where I'm going." He shook Zac's hand. "My name's James MacGregor, but you can call me Mac."

"You have a ship in mind that's going our way?"

"You betcha, the *Wild Goose* is sailin' fer Fort Ross late this afternoon. You and that boy of yours wanna go along, I know the captain. I think he'd be happy to find two new payin' passengers."

Zac looked over at Skip. "Well, I think you just found yourself two traveling companions. Sounds like we'll go all the way to Alaska with you."

MacGregor scratched his face. "I might be a while in Seattle. Got to see my second wife. I been married five times now, but that's the woman that's got my three kids. We wuz only together for a little over a year, but I stop into Seattle ever chance I get. You know how that goes."

Zac tried hard not to smile. "No, I'm afraid I don't. I've never been married myself. My fiancée is up in Sitka, though. She's the one I'm going to find."

"There ain't nothing like marriage. I get myself married ever chance I get. Women are partial to a man who'll up and marry them, ya know."

CHAPTER 4

+ + + + + + +

THE WOMEN WALKED ALONG THE HILLSIDE near Sitka with baskets on their arms. Ian had sent his two Afghan hounds with them. The large, long-haired dogs looked like skinny and very playful sheep with extremely long legs. They would often run ahead but couldn't stay out of sight for very long. Like homing pigeons on paws, they'd run back to where they'd left the girls.

The group stopped to watch a couple of otters rolling and turning in the black water. They could see Baronof Castle on the rock that sat in the middle of the bay. Behind it stood the extinct volcano that seemed to dominate the landscape and its older and distinctly more dilapidated sister cinder cone. In the town, the spires of St. Michael's Cathedral marked the end of Lincoln Street and served as a constant reminder of the Russian heritage of the town.

Dolly skipped ahead of Naomi and Risa and stooped down to pick what berries she could find. Her pale face was smeared with the red juice of the berries that neither made it into her basket nor fully into her mouth.

"Wait up, Dolly," Naomi cried out. "Don't leave us behind."

The young woman looked back at the other two and grinned, showing a set of teeth colored with the fresh berries. She giggled with delight and, picking up her skirts, ran down the path. Her blond curls bounced on her shoulders as she ran.

"Go," Risa spoke to the two dogs. "You go get her." Both dogs ran on ahead after Dolly. They were smart. Often they'd be the ones to find her and bring her back.

"You're going to have your hands full with her," Naomi said. Naomi couldn't help but like her cousin Dolly. Everyone liked Dolly. She always had a smile on her face and not an ounce of guile to mar her mind. With Dolly, what you saw was always what you got.

Risa picked up the pace to keep in step with Naomi. "I know. She's twenty-three, but I have to keep reminding myself that she's really only twelve."

"What will become of her?" Naomi asked.

"I pray some nice man will take pity on her and mix it with love. She is quite pretty, even if she's only a child inside. I suppose for some man, that may be enough."

"Until then," Naomi added, "she belongs to God."

Risa nodded. "She belongs to God, and now she belongs to your uncle and me."

The two young women began to trot down the path in hopes of catching up with Dolly and the dogs. While the girl might have a mind to lose them at the moment, they both knew she was easily distracted. She'd soon find a flower that would catch her attention or a fresh clump of ripe berries to stoop down and gorge herself with. Dolly rarely paid attention to any one thing for very long.

As they rounded the bend in the road, they saw Dolly standing at attention in front of an ominous set of carved totem poles. The two Afghans stood beside her, frozen in place. The basket she had been carrying lay on the ground, with what remained of the berries she had gathered spilled out at her feet. She seemed to be staring intently at the carved figures of the birds, snakes, and almost-human heads, each carved in intricate fashion into a tall spruce tree. She wasn't looking at the totem poles, however. As Risa and Naomi approached, it became obvious that Dolly was staring at something else.

Behind the pole, a man wearing a carved mask of a bird's head peeked out and was talking to her. Risa stuck out her arm, bringing Naomi to a halt. "Wait," she whispered.

Both of the young women stopped to take a closer look at what was happening. The man was obviously old. The bird mask that covered his face and head was realistic, complete with sharp beak. He was wrapped in an ornate woven blanket with colorful decorations of orange and blue. He stood bent over at the shoulders with a carved wooden snake in his hand. He was waving and shaking the carved serpent back and forth in Dolly's direction and chanting softly.

"It is Karl-Reech," Risa said. "He is a holy man of mystery. We must be very careful."

"There is no such thing," Naomi shot back.

"In Sitka there is. We must approach him with great care."

"What is he doing to Dolly?"

"She probably surprised him. He is casting some sort of spell or blessing on her."

"That is nonsense."

"It may be to you, but it's not to Karl-Reech, and when he finishes, it won't be to Dolly either."

Risa had been raised in the traditions of her elders. The superstitions and folklore of the Tlingit people meant very little to Europeans, but for her they were an object of respect and fear. She dropped her hands to her sides and stepped out around the bend, followed closely by Naomi. The old man spotted them right away and, lifting his mask-covered head in their direction, suddenly stopped chanting. He stopped waving the carved snake at Dolly and eased his hands to his side.

Risa stepped forward, her head bowed in respect. Naomi followed. As they walked closer, Risa uttered a few words in the Tlingit language.

The old man shook his head. He spoke in his native tongue to Risa.

"Karl-Reech say she is a stolen child of God and he must protect her. He says evil men will want to take her life."

Naomi had very little patience with the native superstitions. "Tell him she belongs to the Lord. He is the one who will protect her, not the man's magic."

"I can't tell him that."

"Then I will." Naomi stepped forward and put her arm around Dolly, pulling her close. Dolly still seemed to be in a trance. "This is a woman who belongs to Jesus. He is the one who looks after her. She trusts in Him."

The old man backed up at the spoken name of Jesus. He shook his head vigorously.

Naomi pulled Dolly closer. "You can't have her. She belongs to Jesus alone. Do you understand?"

The man raised his arms, exposing the trappings he wore underneath the colorful blanket. He bobbed his head forward repeatedly, giving the impression that he was a part of the mask that covered his face. He spoke in broken English. "You have death come to your house. Your family will die." He shook his bony finger at the two women. "You will see. You wait and see."

With that, he turned abruptly and ran away through the fir trees. Within moments, he had disappeared.

Naomi looked at Dolly, who continued to stare in the direction of the man. "Are you all right? He didn't scare you, did he?"

Dolly shook her head. "He didn't scare me. He stopped me from talking."

Naomi stepped around in front of Dolly and took both of her hands. "Are you sure?"

Dolly nodded. "He stopped me from talking and he was going to stop me from breathing. He said I belonged to his god."

\+   \+   \+   \+   \+

Zac and Skip stood beside James MacGregor at the rail the next afternoon and watched as the *Wild Goose* rounded the bend, taking them into Fort Ross. Zac knew Jenny was just slightly ahead of them. He was hoping they might be able to catch up with her.

Old Fort Ross was built by the Russians, and the cannon that bristled from the log stockade that overlooked the bay was mostly for show. A small contingent of American troops manned the stockade, and the sight of the Stars and Stripes was a great comfort. Still, the place was Russian and most of the people who surrounded it were Russian, if not by birth, then by upbringing.

A large schooner rode at anchor in the harbor. The decks were bare except for a few men making repairs on a sail. "That's the *Northern Star*," Mac said. "I was in hopes she'd be gone by now." He frowned, curling his lip.

"Why is that?" Zac asked.

"The *Star* would be headed up to Seattle and then on to Sitka. More'n likely it's just waiting on more cargo, and the *Wild Goose* here will take care of that." As if to remove a bad taste from his mouth, he leaned over the rail and spit into the water. "I just don't like the man who's captain, that's all. He's a Ruskie—name's Zubatov. He's the skipper and the owner of the boat along with it. Thinks he's got a right to all the fur trade that comes south, jest 'cause his folks lived in Alaska first."

Mac wiped his mouth with the back of his hand and grinned at Zac. "If'n you wants to get on his good side, he likes to be called by his title, Count. He struts about and the like. Folks who is uppity like that jest rubs my fur the wrong way. I ain't got no hankerin' fer people what puts on airs." He shook his head. "This is 'bout as far as I go with you two, I reckon. I figure to jest wait on another boat."

Several sea otters were playing in the bay when the *Wild Goose* sailed in. One had an abalone balanced on his belly and was pounding on it with a rock while he floated in the calm water. "What's that?" Skip asked.

"That's an otter," Mac said. "Make fine pelts, they do."

"What's he doing?"

"He fixin' his lunch, I reckon," Mac said. "Them critters are mighty smart. Ya get the feelin' that if somebody left 'em a hammer, they'd figure out a way to build a house."

Zac put his hand on Skip's head. "I guess Hans was right about this trip, Skipper. He said you'd get a good education out of it and maybe you will at that."

"How far is Seattle?" Skip asked.

"It ought to take you ten days or better, if the weather's good," Mac said. He motioned over to the schooner. "One thing I have to say about the *Star* there is she makes good time."

Skip looked up at Zac. "You reckon Jenny's here?"

"She might be."

"I hope so." Skip looked off at the approaching fort. "I kinda miss her. I'm really looking forward to having her for a mother."

Zac put his arm around the boy, pleased they shared the same feelings about Jenny.

"I'd say if'n you is lookin' fer someone bound fer Seattle, the chances are pretty durn good they come here," Mac said. "There's a few ships that head north straight outta San Francisco, but not many."

Zac stared off at the fort. He didn't like the idea of Jenny traveling alone, especially to a place that might mean danger. Women traveled the West alone all the time, and Jenny was good at taking care of herself. Still, there was something about this that didn't seem right. The idea of seeing her sister had maybe caused her to be just a mite too anxious and not wait for him.

The three of them watched as the men trimmed the sails and then listened to the sound of the anchor sliding down the hull of the ship. It hit the water with a splash, followed by the noisy anchor chain settling to the bottom of the harbor.

The captain yelled out from the wheel well. "We'll put a boat aside to carry you passengers ashore."

Minutes later the three of them were clambering down a rope ladder that led to the dory boat the captain had lowered. They waited on the small boat until the men above dropped their bags, then watched as Mac's traps and the supplies he had purchased were swung over the side and lowered by a rope. Two sailors pulled back on the oars, and soon the small craft was sliding in next to the dock.

Mac bounded out of the boat and stuck his hand down for Skip. "Here you go, young feller." With that, he pulled Skip onto the dock. "Now you lay by old Mac. I'll see that you don't go wrong here. Don't let this here clean-cut lookin' fort fool you none. There's every kinda scalawag known to man that plies these waters here. Don't you let none of them get you into no game of cards. That's why I go and spend most of my money on goods in San Francisco. The rest I put in the bank." He grinned at Zac.

"Course, I cut loose for a night or two." Laughing, he added, "Sometimes a week or two."

"Then I'll watch you," Zac said. He grinned. "And Skip here can watch the both of us." He reached out and gave Skip's hair a playful scratch. "So there you are, Skipper. You have the job of protecting a couple of grown men from themselves. You think you're up to that?"

"Yes, sir," the boy said.

Picking up their bags, the men marched up the hill to Fort Ross. They walked through the gates and onto a series of boards that lay across a muddy field. The blockhouses were situated toward the bay with cannons mounted on the catwalk and protruding through elongated slits in the turrets. Two soldiers leaned against the wall, smoking cigarettes. Zac thought right away that this was unlike any fort he'd ever seen. More than likely, it had troops only because a paper on some general's desk said it had to. It had the look of a forgotten backwater trading post.

The three men walked over the muddy boards toward a large log house. Bending down to get through the door, Zac stepped onto the wooden floor. Inside, candles and several sooty lanterns were lit. The flickering flames sent shadows dancing on the blackened walls while a fireplace made from polished stones at the end of the room stood empty and lifeless.

Several men and a woman sat in the corner of the room. A light glowed dimly in their midst. Along one side of the room was a makeshift bar, if one could call it that. Planks were stretched out over a row of barrels with jugs and wooden mugs scattered over the top of it. A large woman behind the bar had her back to them, her black hair covering her shoulders. Even from where the three of them stood, she seemed rough and muscular.

Mac nudged Zac and motioned toward the woman behind the bar. "I speck I'm gonna be sailin' with you two after all. I purely does hate the count, but I don't figure to stay here fer long. That there's my fourth wife, Jane, behind the bar. I wasn't sure if I'd see her here. She ain't laid eyes on me in more'n two years."

"Does she know you have a wife number five?"

Mac shrugged his shoulders. "Can't never figure that. I sure ain't gonna be the one to tell her." He pointed to the group seated at the far end of the room. "The Ruskie's over there. He's the one with the black beard." Mac smiled, stroking his chin. "And he's seated with the woman I'd sure like to make wife number six."

It was then the woman at the bar turned and caught sight of the three newcomers. "Mac!" she screeched. "Is that you?"

Mac slapped a broad smile across his face. "It sure is, honey bunch. Old Mac has come back fer you."

He stepped toward the bar and Zac slowly followed, dragging Skip along behind him.

The woman leaned over, resting her chin on her folded hands and bending the plank with her weight. She wore a low-cut, dirty blouse with puffy sleeves that had once been white. Dimples glinted in the spaces between the dirt on her face, and she pushed her hair back with her hand. "You old he-coon, I thought I'd never see you again." Smiling, she winked her eye. "I been keepin' myself pure for you, though."

"Now you watch yer language, honey lamb." He stepped aside and motioned in the direction of Zac and Skip. "We got us a little boy present here."

She grinned, showing a missing tooth. "And he's pretty too."

"This here is Mr. Zachary Cobb and his son, Skip," Mac said.

She stuck out a large, dirty hand. "Fine meetin' up with you, Cobb."

Zac reached out and tentatively shook her hand.

"They is lookin fer Cobb's woman here. She was to come up this way going to Sitka."

She looked Zac over. "This woman a lady?" she asked.

"Yes," Zac said. He held his hand near his shoulder. "About this high with blond hair and blue eyes."

"Ain't seen her." The woman shook her head. "We don't get too many lady types in here. If one was to pass through, I'd know about it." She laughed, her chest bouncing. "Might want to put her to work."

"She's Cobb's fiancée and a proper woman too," Mac shot back.

The woman gave off a slow and deliberate shake of her head. "A proper woman? No sir, nobody's passed by like that. Could be she went straight on up to Seattle."

Leaning further across the bar, she reached out and took hold of Mac's hand, pulling him closer. "Now, sweet cakes, you and me has got ourselves some catching up to do."

Zac could tell that Mac didn't much want to be left alone with the woman, but he and Skip backed away all the same. "I'm sure you two have lots to talk about. Skip and I will just wander over there and see if we can book passage to Alaska."

He almost felt sorry for Mac as he led Skip to the corner of the room where Mac had pointed out the captain. "I'm looking for the captain of the vessel at anchor in the bay," he announced, interrupting their muffled conversation.

Seated across the table was a wiry man with dark flashing eyes. His hair was curly and the black mustache and beard that he sported covered his entire face. It gave him a fuller look over what Zac assumed were rather hollow features. "I am Count Sergei Zubatov. I own and am the captain of the *Northern Star*. How can I help you?"

"My son, Skip, and I are going to Sitka. I understand your vessel is headed that way."

"And you are?"

"I am Zachary Cobb."

"And what is the nature of your business, Mr. Cobb?"

"I am going to visit my fiancée."

"And who might she be?"

"Her name is Jenny Hays."

The name Hays seemed to register with the man. His eyebrows arched down in a measure of what could only be disapproval. A tall, attractive blond woman was seated next to Zubatov. She had curls that cascaded down the sides of her head. She leaned over to Zubatov and whispered in his ear as he cocked his head to listen.

Zubatov heard her out and then, sitting straight, cleared his throat. "Are you with that man at the bar?"

Zac glanced back in Mac's direction. "If you mean MacGregor back there, we just met in San Francisco."

"Good, I like to know all the trappers that come to our waters in Alaska. My business is furs."

"Well, I'm no trapper. Does that mean we can book passage on your ship?"

"Two hundred dollars in gold."

"Two hundred dollars!" Zac thought the amount was extreme.

"Two hundred dollars each."

"I'm not a man who likes to be taken advantage of," Zac said.

"Have it your way, Mr. Cobb. You can wait for a stage and ride it for a week to Eureka. One should be along here next week. From there you can take the train to Seattle, but by the time you get there we'll have been gone for two weeks."

"You seem to have the only game in town," Zac said.

The man smiled and nodded.

Zac reached into his coat pocket and produced the bag of gold coins. Pulling open the strings, he took out a stack of twenty-dollar gold pieces and counted them on the table. "It seems I also have the lady here to thank." Zac bowed slightly at the waist. "And who might you be, ma'am?"

The woman smiled. "I am Kathryn Jung. It will be a pleasure to travel with you." Looking at Skip, she smiled. "The both of you."

CHAPTER 5

+ + + + + + +

THE CRYSTAL PALACE HAD SEEN BETTER DAYS, but it was still quite the show. The wallpaper was a bit worn, but overhead, the row of four crystal chandeliers that gave the place its name blazed with light. The bar had been shipped around the horn from Boston. It was a dark mahogany with gargoyles carved into the face of the thing. The devilish creatures seemed to stare out at the customers, daring them to take another drink. Clean bar rags hung from polished brass rings and matching shiny spittoons stood along the floor every five feet or so. A polished set of carpeted stairs curved up the sides of the room and led to a balcony above. It was there a man could rent a room, for a week, a day, or an hour.

The music of the Crystal Palace never stopped. A player piano in the corner made sure of that. It clapped out a bawdy tune, the keys clamping down in response to the invisible fingers of the machinery, as Ian and Van Fleetwood stepped into the saloon, raking the bottom of their boots free from mud with the help of an iron dog that stood just inside the doorway. Its back was a straight spine of sharp metal.

"You figure on driving Quinn out of business?" Fleetwood asked, craning his neck to make certain no one was listening.

"Nah," said Ian, tapping his boot on the floor. "I just figure to give the man some stiff competition. This place is gonna grow. I plan on growing with it."

"If you ask me, that lumber you mill is the stuff it's gonna grow on."

"You got that right. I pay them men pretty well too. Problem is, I give 'em the money and they bring it here to spend. If I had myself a place like the Crystal Palace, only bigger, with some live girls in it, they just might take my money and give it back to me."

Fleetwood laughed. "You give it out and then get it back."

"That's about the size of it."

Fleetwood slapped him on the back. "I do admire your spirit, old man. You just never seem to quit." Fleetwood began a low, guttural chuckle.

47

"Guess you want to own the place and change the name to Haystown."

"Sitka will do nicely. I just want to have my part of the place, that's all."

"Appears to me you already got your part, now you want Quinn's."

"Oh, I'm not sure I'll ever stand that tall. I'll do fine though. You just wait and see."

The two of them walked toward an open table and took their seats. They quickly drew the attention of the bartender, a large man with a drooping black mustache and oversized arms. He set down the glass he was cleaning and disappeared into the back room. Moments later, he was joined by an even larger man. The man had close-cut black hair combed straight down over his forehead. His large, meaty face was clean-shaven with a square jaw set tight. He had a wrestler's build with a massive neck set squarely on broad shoulders. He rounded the bar with the barkeeper behind him and made his way to the two older men in long strides.

"Looks like you done caught Quinn's attention," Fleetwood said.

"Ain't much he don't miss."

"Afternoon, gentlemen." Quinn spoke deliberately in a low tone. For a former roughneck sailor, he seemed remarkably educated. Ian suspected that there was more to the man than met the eye.

Ian leaned back in his chair. "Why howdy, Quinn. What brings you over to our table? We're just looking for something hot to get this rain out of our bones. You know how it is with old men." He glanced over at Fleetwood. "We get the chills easy."

"You two won't be old for another twenty years. Funny though," Quinn said, "I thought you might be here for another reason."

"Now, what would that be?"

"Business."

"Business? What business would I have with you? I send you my payroll every week."

Quinn smiled. "And we do appreciate that." Quinn looked around the large room. There were a number of mill workers at the bar and still others at the gambling tables. "We have a few of your folks here. Of course, it's the middle of the day. You come back tonight and we'll introduce you to the rest of your men."

"I might just do that. Then, if you'd like to sell this place, we could talk."

Quinn put his hands on his hips. "You know I don't own the Crystal Palace all by myself."

"Oh yes." Ian grinned. "I forgot. And just where is Miss Kathryn?"

"She went to San Francisco to get us a fresh supply of good liquor."

"That's right, something you buy for ten dollars a barrel and sell for a thousand."

"A man has to make a living."

"And you do that quite nicely, I'd say. When you have Zubatov to bring the liquor in for you, you can pretty much control the price, can't you?"

Quinn shrugged his shoulders. "He's a businessman. I'm a businessman. He goes his own way. You know that."

"You know, Quinn, if you hadn't told me different, I'd think you graduated from one of those fine business schools back East. You know your business and you tend to business."

Quinn nodded his head. "I'll take that as a compliment, coming from you."

"Take it any way you want." Ian tipped his chair back slightly and swung his arm over the side. The last thing he wanted to appear was nervous. "I'm in the land and lumber business and you handle the entertainment. I'd say we both have a stake in growing this town. You and I aren't competitors."

"Not yet, but from what I hear we might be."

"Oh, is that so?" Ian brought the chair down with a thud.

"I hear you been looking at some property on Lincoln."

He leaned forward. "I'm always looking around for a bargain. You know that."

Fleetwood smiled and brushed his mustache aside. "You know how it is. A man has to keep his eyes open to make it these days."

"You know any bargains 'round here?" Ian asked.

"I'm afraid not." Quinn put his hands on their table. They were like two small hams, large and meaty. "Property isn't cheap and it's getting harder to come by all the time. I thought maybe that fire of yours might have set you back."

"You heard about that, did you?"

"A man hears everything in the Crystal Palace."

"Well, fortunately it was contained within the office. We don't do business in there. We just record it."

"Lucky thing for you, I suppose."

"Yes, lucky thing."

"Well, I'll let Hank here take your order. If there's anything you want, short of my share in the Palace, you just let him know." Quinn turned and sauntered back to the office behind the bar, looking very self-assured.

Ian looked up at Hank. The man was smiling. It was easy to see he took his confidence from his boss. "You got any of that good stew, nice and hot, back there?"

"You bet we have. The bottom of the pot is always the best place."

"Good, then scrape some of it up for me, and I'll have some hot black coffee to go with it."

"Sounds good to me," Fleetwood added.

They both watched Hank beat a hasty retreat into the kitchen, and Ian brought his chair down hard. He reached into his coat pocket and pulled out something he left clutched in his fist. "Fleetwood, I'm going to show you something that's going to make both you and me wealthy beyond our wildest dreams and in a very short time. You just got to promise me you won't say a word to nobody. No matter if they torture you with hot coals on your feet, you got to keep that trap of yours plumb shut."

"All right, I ain't sayin' nothing."

"The timing on this thing is very important. That mill of mine is going to be worth lots more and anything we can lay our hands on in the way of street property will go through the roof."

"Well, what is it?"

Slowly, Ian opened up his hand. There in his palm lay a large nugget of pure gold. It had been worn smooth by the action of river water, but it was still as large as a small robin's egg.

"Glory be!" Fleetwood said.

"Pipe down!" Ian closed his hand and dropped the thing back in his pocket.

"Where did you get that?"

"I got it off a man name of Bob Lilly, a trapper who took it from the river that runs through the property that come with Risa."

"You sly dog. You married the world."

"Nah, I married the finest woman this place is ever seen. Weren't my fault if she brought the world with her."

Fleetwood shook his head in disbelief. "I ain't never seen the like of that."

"Well, Bob's gone back into the upcountry, or will mighty quick. I staked him to whatever it was he needed. He won't even be near enough folks to lay sight on fer a year or better. Besides, he thinks I'm the one that gave him the bargain. I staked him out with traps and everything he needed and told him he could have the run of that land. He's gonna be plenty busy. By the time folks hear of this, we'll have all the property we need."

"We will own this town."

Ian grinned. "You bet we will."

Fleetwood's eyes flashed. "You are a dirty dog, ain't you? For an old man, you seem to have eyes that can see around corners."

"What good is age if a feller has to use a young brain?" Ian reached back into his pocket and pulled out the gold nugget. "I'm going to show you just how serious I am about this thing and how much I trust you." He pressed the gold nugget into Van's hand. "You keep this in good faith."

＊　＊　＊　＊　＊

The islands that led into Puget Sound would have been tricky and dangerous even during the day. At night it would take an expert to find his way through them and into the harbor at Seattle. Jenny stood frozen on the bridge, watching the pilot they had taken on as he maneuvered the ship. She and Dave Cormia had found a fast schooner in San Francisco and considered themselves lucky that it was not only fast, but that it was bound directly for Seattle with no stops along the way. To make matters even better, it was a side-wheel steamer. It could drop its sails and move along on steam alone, which was precisely what it was doing that night.

The pilot kept his eyes fixed on the dark water and swung the wheel to port. He stabilized it, maintaining a new course. Jenny watched the man do that several times. It was as if he had eyes that could see through the water. Jenny couldn't take her steady gaze off the man. He was an older man and had a white beard with snow white hair that curled up from under his blue cap and a smoking pipe stem in his mouth.

"That smells nice," Jenny said.

"Never get too much in the way of complaints," he responded.

"My fiancé smokes a pipe. Just the smell of one reminds me of him."

"Odors have a way of doing that. Now me, I smell the birds and the water. Guess it's all in what a man grows up with." He looked back at Jenny and the crease of a smile formed on his lips. "I s'pose love may have something to do with it. I love the water, and you love him."

"Yes, I suppose so."

"How much farther do we have to go until we get to Seattle?" Cormia asked.

The pilot kept his eyes on the water ahead. "I'd say an hour or better, if we don't run into a snag."

"Does that happen?"

"All the time, if a man's not careful."

"How do you know which way to turn?" Jenny asked.

"Do you see those lights?" the man said. He pointed off the starboard bow.

"You mean those three lights?"

"Yes, those are the ones. It's our way of improving on what God leaves us at night. When they line up, I turn the ship in the direction of the lights. I spend most of my time up here just watching the water."

"And when you turn, do you look for three more?"

"That's about the size of it, missy."

"Fascinating." She looked off in the distance to the three lights that were set on a hill. "I think God does that in our lives."

"How's that?" The pilot turned to catch her eye. He was interested in anything that might reflect on his work, and Jenny could see it.

"There are things we already know that are true."

"You mean like the Bible?"

"Yes, it's always the same. Then there's what other people advise you to do. I suppose you could say the last light would be circumstances or just the things that happen to you."

The man puffed on his pipe. "So when a body sees those things line up, he just heads off in that direction."

"Yes, I think so."

"Is that why you're going to Seattle?" the man asked.

"Yes. The only thing I worry about is the fact that a very important person in my life wasn't there to give me his advice, someone I trust."

"I take that to be that man you love, the one with the pipe."

"Yes. I find so much wisdom in him."

The old man grinned. Taking out his pipe, he tapped the dottle out in an empty cup that sat on the window ledge. "Men with pipes seem to be thinkers in my book. They do everything slow and easy after a lot of thought."

"Zac is like that . . . I miss him already."

"I'm certain he'll be along directly," Cormia said. "If you like, we can try sending him another wire in Seattle."

"I'd like that very much."

The ship edged alongside the dock in the wee hours of the morning. Men were still working, loading and unloading the ships in port. The pilot was shouting out orders from the window, and Jenny was sipping on a cup of hot coffee. As far as she was concerned, the night was already lost. She couldn't bear the thought of finding a hotel room and then getting up in the middle of the day. She turned to Cormia. "Can you try and find us a ship tonight?"

"We can't leave tonight."

"I know. I'd just like to know when we can leave as soon as possible. I'd like to be able to wire Zac exactly which ship I'll be on."

"Of course, my dear. I'll see to it right away. I'll have to try to communicate with your uncle too. They'll want to know."

+ + + + +

Jenny found herself seated in a waterfront cafe, waiting for Dave Cormia. Hours before dawn was not the best time for a woman to be alone in raucous Seattle, especially on the waterfront where men were passing by all the time. Most were not in the best of conditions, and as Jenny sat stirring yet another cup of coffee, she could understand why she'd been advised against doing such a thing. The lights had definitely not lined up on this maneuver.

The man at the far end of the cafe had given her some notice, but then went back to his ham and eggs. He was short and stocky with blond hair and a clean-shaven face. He wore buckskins with a heavy wool coat. His inattention gave her some comfort.

Two obviously drunken sailors burst through the door. They staggered to the counter and pounded away on top of it. "Give us some whisky here, mate," one of them shouted.

The other man turned around. It was then he spotted Jenny. He nudged his friend. "Hear me, bucko, looky what we got us."

The first sailor swung himself around, planting both elbows on the counter top. He wobbled slightly and then braced himself. "By jove, you is right. Tonight might not be such a cold one after all."

Jenny nervously fidgeted with her handbag. She always carried a .32 caliber pistol in it, but it was something she never wanted to use.

"Yeah, and she's a right pretty one, she is."

The two men left the counter and headed in Jenny's direction. One man pulled up on his belt, trying his best to bring it above his protruding belly. He was obviously bent on showing his best figure.

The first man, a man with a full black beard, showed a great deal more liquor in him. He bounced into the chair in front of her. His feet flew up and he went down onto the floor, the chair tumbling after him.

The second man put his hands on the table and leaned in Jenny's direction. He had a long, meandering scar down the side of his face that seemed bright red and angry. "Hello there, pretty lady. You lookin' for some company?"

"Not from you. I'm waiting for a friend."

"Well, we is friendly." He looked down at the bearded man climbing back off the floor. "Ain't we friendly?"

The bearded man slammed the chair back into place and once again sat down hard. This time he clung to the table for support. "We can be very friendly. A pretty lady like you could see how friendly we gets."

The man with the scar sneered. "What would it take to show you our friendship, a gold piece?"

"I just want you away from here so I can finish my coffee."

"Now, we can't do that," the scarred man said. "Can we, George?"

The bearded man shook his head in slow motion. "No, we can't go back without something to warm our bed."

The man at the far end of the cafe got to his feet and walked towards Jenny. "Are these men bothering you, miss?"

"They most certainly are."

The two men looked back at the sudden intruder. "Go on about yer business," the man with the scar shouted. "We seen her first."

"And I think she's seen quite enough of you." With that, the stranger planted his hand around the belt of the scarred man standing at the table. He jerked him off his feet and ran him toward the door.

The drunken sailor stumbled, his arms flailing wildly.

When they reached the door, the stranger kicked it open and with one mighty toss, flung the man into the street. Turning around, he marched back to the table.

The bearded drunk wove in his seat, trying to make up his mind whether to run or fight.

Reaching down, the stranger grabbed the man by the ear and yanked him to his feet. "You're gonna join your friend where you both belong— in the street."

The man reached into his belt and pulled out a long knife. In a rush of blinding speed, the stranger grabbed the man's arm, slamming it down hard on the table. The knife flew out of his hand, sending Jenny's coffee and what remained of the tableware onto the floor.

Once again taking hold of the drunk's ear, the stranger moved him swiftly to the open door. Jerking him straight up at the door, he stepped back and planted a foot on the man's rear, kicking hard and launching him headlong into the street.

He closed the door and made his way back to Jenny's table. "I'm sorry I spilled your coffee, miss. Let me buy you another one."

Jenny breathed a sigh of relief. "It's I that owe you, sir. I owe you my deep gratitude at the very least."

"My pleasure, ma'am. Women shouldn't be treated that way, not in this town or any other for that matter. Do you mind if I sit with you until whoever it is you're waiting for shows up?"

"Not at all. Please sit down." She stuck out her hand to the man. "I'm

Jenny Hays, and I'm on my way to Alaska as soon as we can book passage."

The man shook her hand. "My name is Mike Wass. I trap in Alaska and I'm headed that way too."

"It is a great pleasure to meet you, Mr. Wass."

CHAPTER 6

+ + + + + + +

THEY HAD ALREADY PICKED UP THE PILOT who would guide them into Seattle when Zac pointed over the bow of the ship to several large black dorsal fins.

Skip raised himself up on his tiptoes and looked over the side. "That's got to be the biggest shark I've ever seen," he said.

"No shark." Mac spit over the rail. "Them is killer whales. They'd tear apart a wounded or baby whale in a minute." He put his hands side by side and then widened the gap between them a little. "I seen teeth on them things yay big."

Zac pulled his pipe out of his pocket. Reaching into the flap of his shirt, he removed a bag of tobacco. "You seen those things kill before?" Zac asked. He began to stuff his pipe bowl with the mixture.

"I sure have. Saw a whole passel of them critters attack a sperm whale outta Petersburg. There was blood in the water," Mac moved his hands to show the direction of the blood slick, "blood that seemed to go on fer hundreds of yards."

Zac turned his back on the stiff breeze and, striking his thumbnail on a match, fired it to life. He raked it over the surface of his tobacco mixture and puffed the briar pipe into a smoldering mass of embers.

"Then the sharks, whew-eee. I thought I'd never seen so many sharks." Mac became more animated as he went on.

Skip's eyes were wide. James MacGregor was a good storyteller, and he had Skip's full attention.

"Then what happened?" Zac asked.

"I come back the next day. There was a flock of birds big enough on that thing to cover an island. You ain't never seen the like."

"You tell a good story," Zac chuckled at the amazed expression on Skip's face.

When the *Northern Star* slid into its berth on the Seattle docks, the street was a bustling barrage of people and hand-drawn carts. Men scampered over the docks, shouting orders and barking out their demands to transport cargo and luggage. There must have been some order some-place, but for the life of him, Zac couldn't make heads or tails of it. The place was like a giant anthill, with men carrying materials and stepping over one another. Horns honked and whistles blew.

"Where do we go?" Skip asked.

"Well, our luggage stays to the ship," Zac replied. "That's one good thing. I wouldn't want to look for it in that mess."

Mac squashed the fur cap down over his ears. "Guess I better go look fer the wife and kids." He pulled out and shook a bag of coins. "Them kids eats a whole lots better after I been through Seattle."

"Nice to hear you take care of them," Zac said.

"Why wouldn't I? They're all mine. Emma's a good woman too. She'll want to put a spread out for dinner, and we'll both want you two there."

"We could handle that." Zac looked down at Skip. "Couldn't we, boy?"

"Yes, sir."

Kathryn and Zubatov climbed down from the bridge, and Zubatov shouted out orders for the lines to hold the *Northern Star* fast.

Kathryn was dressed in a bright yellow outfit. Her hair shone all the more in the brilliant daylight. An enormous hat with white feathers swooped down over her face, and several large pins held it in place. "Will you gentlemen be leaving the ship?" she asked.

"You better believe it," Mac answered. "A man's got to feel the dirt under his feet for at least a little while."

"Skip and I will be staying on board tonight," Zac said. "With what we paid for that cabin, we'll want to put it to use."

She smiled at him. "You have no girl to see in port?"

"No," Zac said. "The only woman I have an interest in is the one I'm going to see."

She chuckled at the idea. "Mr. Cobb, it's been my experience that when the woman in a man's life isn't handy, he prefers one who is."

Mac let out a loud laugh at the idea. It was obvious he shared her sentiments.

"I'm not like most men. It's taken me years to find this one," Zac said firmly.

Kathryn leaned next to him and put her arm through his. "A hand-some man like you . . . I should think you'd have many a woman's heart all atwitter."

"I can't speak for what the women I've known have thought. I just know my own mind." He stepped away from her, put his arm around

Skip, and they both moved several steps to the rail.

"That's a shame," she chuckled. "And here I am all alone in Seattle without a man to protect me."

Zac looked back at her with a suspicious stare. Few women threw themselves at a man without wanting something in return. "You and Zubatov seem to get along fine. I'm sure you won't lack for company."

She glanced back at the captain. "He and I are in business together, but I find it much better if business and pleasure are never mixed." There was a twinkle in her eye. "A girl has to keep her wits about her."

When Zubatov finished issuing his orders, he clamped his hands to the back of his jacket and stepped toward the group. "We will leave on the tide tomorrow night," he said. "That ought to give us plenty of time to load cargo."

"We'll be ready," Zac said.

"See that you are. Paying passengers or no, the *Northern Star* will not wait."

"Can you tell me where to find the Wells Fargo office?"

Zubatov leaned over the rail and pointed straight up the hilly street that stood in front of them. "You go three blocks up and then two over. It's a red brick building. You can't miss it. Are you going there now?"

"Might be a couple of hours," Zac said. He put his hand on Skip's shoulder. "I figure me and the boy will look around here for a while. We might get ourselves an education." Smiling, he looked down at Skip. "We might get ourselves some ice cream too."

"Good," Zubatov said. "This is a splendid idea."

Zac, Skip, and Mac stepped onto the dock a short time later. "I'm gonna go find Emma. Where 'bouts can I meet you?"

Zac looked up and down the waterfront. "We'll just knock about here for a spell and meet you up at the Wells Fargo office."

Mac slapped him on the back. "Emma and me will get you a nice salmon dinner. Ain't no better eatin' fish than that."

"I like the sound of that."

"Me too," said Skip.

+ + + + +

Back aboard the ship, Zubatov and Kathryn watched the three of them walk off the docks. "Do you think they'll be all right?" she asked.

Zubatov smiled. "For two hours they will be fine."

"I hope so. They seem like such nice people." She continued to watch Zac, Skip, and Mac parade down the street. "And I know Ian Hays must be counting on that tall, lean fellow."

"Da, it would be a shame if something happened to them."

"And I'm sure you'll look after their welfare, won't you, my dear?"

Zubatov stepped away and walked back to where three of his men were spooling in extra line. He spoke to them, and they listened with interest. Reaching down into his pocket, he produced a wad of bills. Stripping off several of the greenbacks, he handed them over to the men. They tipped their hats and raced down the gangplank and onto the dock.

Zubatov put his hands in his pockets and walked back to where Kathryn was still standing. "I have just looked after their welfare."

"Your men might be recognized," she said.

"Oh, they won't do the job. I've seen to that. There are plenty of men in Seattle that can be called upon for matters like that, and those men of mine will know just where to find them."

Kathryn looped her arm around the captain's and patted it with her hand. "Fine. You're such a man of action, my dear Count, and a bright man too. It's one of the things I like best about you."

"Why did you insist on me taking them as passengers?"

A cold look crept its way into Kathryn's eyes. "I always stay close to my enemies. This Cobb fellow strikes me as a very dangerous one."

+ + + + +

Zac and Skip followed Mac through the marketplace. They watched as he picked through the fresh catch of salmon brought in that morning. "I'll take the king here," Mac grunted to the shopkeeper. "Wrap it up." He turned back to Zac. "There ain't nothing like fresh king salmon taken in these waters. You and Skip here will like it."

Moving through the stalls, Zac watched as Mac spent some time buying the necessities of life: bread, some fresh potatoes, a bottle of wine, a red top, a pair of skates, and a doll with golden hair. "You think of everything, don't you?"

"Got to keep folks happy. I spent me a lot of time keeping this bunch smiling, and I ain't about to stop now."

"It must be tough to juggle all those families."

"Only got one family. Got four wives, had five. They is the ones that squalls the most, though. You know how women folk is about their pretties and such."

"No, I'm afraid I don't."

"Well, you is about to find out," Mac smirked out of the side of his mouth. "You give yerself enough time with a woman and you gots to do things to keep her attention. You keep her attention and she'll keep yours."

"Where does love fit into all of this?" Zac asked.

Mac stopped beside a stall that featured women's hats. "I ain't never thought much about love. Fer me, a woman is to have around, not to talk to." He pointed to the hat the woman was modeling. "What do you think of that?"

"Seems fine to me," Zac said, "on her."

Mac motioned to a large white hat with red ribbons dangling from it. "Let me see that one on you."

"You know," Zac said, "if I couldn't talk to Jenny, I couldn't be with her. We're best friends first."

"Best friends? I ain't never had a best friend who didn't put on his britches and set traps with me."

"Jenny could do that, if she needed to."

Mac nodded at the sales lady. "I'll take that one. Can you put it in a box?" He turned to Zac and shook his head. "The kind of woman yer talking about is strange to me. I just ain't never thought of them in that way."

"I need a woman I can live my whole life with," Zac said, "not just a piece at a time. I need someone who can listen, someone who can think, someone I can laugh with."

Mac paid for the hat. "I'm gonna have to spend some more time with you, Cobb. Maybe you can help me decide which one to settle down with. You already met wife number four, and today you're gonna meet number two."

"Where's number one? I'd say she's the one with the most claim on you."

"She's dead, Cobb. Number five's an Injun woman in Sitka. She give me claim to my trappin' area. Number three's some place in California. I lost track of her."

"You've been a busy boy," Zac said.

Mac threw the hat box over his shoulder, hanging onto the strap. "I'll say I have. Now, let's get on to Emma's place and you can meet my family."

It was a short time later when the three of them mounted the stairs to the building Mac had pointed to. They went up several flights of stairs before Mac stopped at a door and put down his bags. He twisted the knob and stepped inside. "Emma, your honey lamb is home."

As Zac and Skip stepped through the door, they could hear the sound of a woman's squeals from the other end of the house. She came rushing out the back of the house, followed by three children. She was a heavy-set woman with dark curly hair. The bright smile on her face showed a set of sparkling teeth. She threw her arms around Mac as he lifted her off her feet.

He spun her around. "Am I ever glad to see you," he said. Setting her down, he turned her in the direction of Zac and Skip. "Let me spread this love of yours around, honey bunch. This here's Zac Cobb and his son, Skip."

"Pleased to meet you, ma'am," Zac said.

She nervously repositioned the dirty white apron that had bunched up at the waist of her blue dress. "You are welcome to our home."

Mac scampered back to the door and, picking up the packages, lifted them for all to see. "I brung you all something. Old Zac here helped me pick it out."

Zac was a bit nervous. Being at a man's homecoming made him feel out of place, especially as infrequently as Mac visited this home. "I think Skip and I will be about our business and leave you folks to catch up."

"Zac here is coming for dinner. I brought you a king salmon to fix."

Zac and Skip edged their way to the door.

"All right, Cobb, I'll come and find you two at the Wells Fargo office." He walked with them out the door, followed by the doting Emma. "Now, don't you go getting into trouble, at least without me."

"You can count on that."

With that, Zac and Skip bounded down the stairs. "I think he's in enough trouble all by himself," Skip said.

They climbed the steep hill to the streets that hung above Seattle's waterfront, looking for the Wells Fargo office. Zac was hoping it was the one place Jenny might have left him a message, but when they found the office, there had been no word from her. He still had a notion he might catch up with her, but that was dwindling fast. In all likelihood he was on a wild goose chase. And he still couldn't shake the dark feeling that something wasn't right.

Zac and Skip started across the alley that ran up the side of the Wells Fargo office, but the sound of a fight brought Zac to a halt. There at the end of the alley, two men were roughing up a lone sailor. Zac looked down at Skip. "You better go find a policeman. I'll go see to that."

The boy dashed off, a look of panic on his face. Zac turned and walked slowly toward the confrontation. He could see the two men kicking the sailor who was on the pavement. It wasn't pretty. "All right," Zac said, "That's enough."

He fully expected that at the first sign of a newcomer, the men would turn tail and beat the streets. They didn't, though, and that surprised him. They swung around in his direction and stared. One man was bald with a dark blue pea coat. The other, a larger man, wore a striped shirt and hobnailed boots. His shirt was rolled up to the elbows where his muscles bulged. "What business is it of yours?" the man in the pea coat asked.

"I'm making it my business," Zac said.

"Oh, is that right?" the large man said. "Then come ahead on." He motioned Zac forward and railed his fists. The two men separated to either side of the alley while the man on the ground moaned and rolled over in obvious pain.

"Looks like you take your odds in a lopsided way," Zac said. "How are you with two men?"

"Thar's jest one of you," the bald man said.

Zac stopped and knelt down beside the man who had been kicked. "You gonna make it?" he asked.

The man nodded, his eyes slightly glazed.

"You get up and lend a hand when you can." Zac said. Zac got to his feet. "I'd have brung my boy, but then you'd be outnumbered. Maybe women and children would suit you better, though."

The bald man stepped forward and took a swing. Zac ducked the roundhouse and came up with a solid blow to the man's middle. He followed the body blow with a right cross to the man's jaw that sounded like a pistol shot. The man stumbled backward and landed on the wall of the adjoining building. Shaking himself, he stepped back into the alley. He was a bit wobbly, but he stayed on his feet.

Seeing the larger of the two men circling behind him, Zac stepped back to keep the big man in front of him. It would be the dickens to pay if one grabbed him from behind.

"Let's go, boys," Zac said, motioning them forward with both hands. "Get on with it or get out."

Suddenly, Zac felt two massive arms grab him from behind. The man on the ground had gotten to his feet, and instead of lending a hand in the fight, he had clamped a full nelson on Zac, holding him fast.

"Here he is," the man said. "Mister Zac Cobb?"

The sound of his name sent shock waves through Zac. This was no beating of an innocent man—they'd been waiting for him.

"Oh, blast it all," the bald man said. "It's him all right." With that he drew out a long knife.

The large man who had circled Zac picked up a wooden club. "Let's finish him," he said. "Let's finish him now."

CHAPTER 7

✦ ✦ ✦ ✦ ✦ ✦ ✦

THE MAN GRIPPED ZAC CLOSELY, flexing his muscles to create a tight hold. Zac was as much stunned by the ambush as he was bound by the arms of the man behind him. The stranger's hold drove the Colt Shopkeeper special into Zac's ribs. He liked to carry it in his underarm holster, but now, instead of it being a comfort, it was a means of painful torture.

The two men approached Zac. He'd have to deal with the one with the knife first. The big man with the club could wait. Zac launched a hard kick into the groin of the bald man with the knife. He dropped the knife, doubling over.

The big man swung the club, rapping Zac's leg. Zac winced as pain shot though him. Electric charges of anguish rushed through his leg, throbbing like a hammer into his brain.

Rearing back, Zac lifted his legs and clamped them around the big man's head. He squeezed his knees down hard, pulling the man into a stranglehold. Swinging and twisting his body, Zac pulled the big man down, bringing the man behind him down on top of the two of them.

Tumbling out of the man's grasp, Zac rolled free. His heart beat wildly, sending a charge into him.

The bald man launched himself at Zac again, driving him into the wall and knocking the wind out of him. He hit the ground, gasping for breath that wouldn't come.

The man held up the knife, and Zac kicked his foot forward, catching the man on the ankles and knocking him to the ground. Zac rolled over and got to his knees. He looked back as the man who had been holding him drew a pistol. Zac held up his hand. "Hold on there," he said. "You don't want to do that."

The man took quick aim with the revolver and squeezed off a round. It spattered on the wall, sending shards of the red brick into Zac's face. Zac could see the noise of the shot had sent a note of warning to the three men, even the one who fired the pistol. The alley would soon be filled with people, and they all knew it.

A police whistle cut a sharp note in the air.

"Kill him and let's be done with it!" the bald man yelled.

Zac reached under his arm and jerked out the little .45. It was something his attackers hadn't figured on, that was plain to see. For Zac, it was an equalizer no matter what the odds were. He lifted it and fired off a round into the man's wrist. The man dropped the revolver and clutched his hand in great pain.

The two others, sensing they were out of time, scrambled to their feet. "Let's get outta here. I don't like this." They grabbed their wounded accomplice and as a group dashed for the uphill end of the alley. Zac watched them run as he let his arms drop to his side. There was no need for further gunplay. The last thing he wanted to do was have to spend a day in court to explain a shooting. He had to get on to see Jenny. There was simply no time to waste in Seattle.

Moments later a policeman ran up the alley, followed by Skip. Staring down the barrel of his own weapon, the policeman pointed his gun in Zac's direction. "Drop that!" he called, eyeballing Zac from under his polished cap.

Zac cocked the hammer and set it back down on the chamber gently. He stooped over and laid the gun at his feet.

The constable picked up the gun and stuck it in his pants. "Did you fire those shots?"

"I fired one of them, nicked the feller too."

Skip edged around the policeman and made his way to Zac. "This is my father," he said.

The cop looked down at Skip. "The boy here says you came upon a robbery."

"Something like that."

"We don't allow firearms to be carried in Seattle."

"Didn't seem to bother the sailor who took a shot at me."

The policeman took out a notebook and scribbled a few notes. At the same moment Mac came walking up the alley with a big grin on his face. "I leave you alone and you go and get yerself arrested," he said.

"No arrest here." He looked at the policeman. "At least I don't think so."

"What happened?" Mac asked.

Zac smiled. "What I thought was a robbery turned out to be an ambush."

"Can you describe the men?" the policeman asked.

"Can I have my gun back?"

The policeman closed his notebook and shook his head. "Like I told you, we don't allow firearms to be carried in Seattle."

"I'm a special officer for Wells Fargo. I have a license to carry deadly weapons. Do you mind if I show you my identification?" Reaching into his coat pocket, Zac produced his badge and the letter from the company that vouched for his employment. He handed it over to the officer. "You can come with me to the office if you like. I was just in there and they can identify me."

"I'll do just that."

+ + + + +

The kitchen in the Hays household had always been a busy place. Umqua had managed it for a year, since her marriage to Bubba Dean. Not everyone approved of the fact that Bubba Dean was a black man and she was an Indian. And while most people didn't approve of mixing the races, at least both of them were from outcast groups. That seemed to smooth the ruffled feathers of Sitka. It also had an intriguing effect on the couple. Umqua believed she was moving up in society by gaining a place in the Hays household, and Bubba Dean considered himself a lucky man to have a younger woman and one that pleased the eye.

Bubba Dean stepped into the large kitchen, smelling the fresh bread Umqua had in the oven. Ian's two large Afghan hounds trailed in behind him. Several trays of fluffy biscuits lay spread out on a stone-topped counter, and he tiptoed over to them and picked one up.

A wooden spoon caught him in a blow across the knuckles. Umqua shot him a glance and then waved the spoon. "You supposed to wait, like the rest."

"Aw, sugar pie. You're driving me crazy with this here good smellin' stuff. Tell her, Risa. One flour dumpling ain't gonna hurt nobody."

Risa smiled and nodded. "I think it's okay. He's been working all morning."

Umqua pulled the biscuit out of the old man's hand and set it back on the counter top. "You not special just because you sleep with the cook. You go sit down, and we will feed you like all the rest of the field hands."

Bubba Dean's eyes looked sad, and his bottom lip drooped out like the fallen cone on the head of a once proud rooster.

Umqua muttered to herself as she patted the veal with bread crumbs. "There's food that turns up missing in this house. I never seen the like. A woman buys just enough then turns 'round," she swiveled her head to look back at Bubba Dean, "and it's gone." Squinting her eyes at the man, she sneered. "Now, how do you suppose that happens?"

He hunched his shoulders over and shuffled out of the kitchen and back into the great room. He went quietly like a beaten foe too tired to moan or howl.

"I really don't see the harm in that," Risa said.

"He no different than the rest. Nobody takes his meal before the time." Looking down at the two dogs that had refused to follow Bubba Dean out of the room, she shouted. "You two get your nasty faces out of my kitchen!"

The two dogs jerked their heads, almost in startled surprise. They slunk from the kitchen, their tails dangling between their back legs.

Risa bit her lip and continued stirring the pot of boiling berries. The large pot rumbled with the red mixture, sending out a steamy aroma that mixed well with the odor of the baking bread. She was making jam out of what they had been picking. She didn't much enjoy intruding on Umqua's domain, but it was something she was determined to do. At the time it seemed like the lesser of two evils. She didn't want to add more work to the woman. Umqua didn't do well with something she hadn't planned on. But Risa also didn't want the berries to sit around until they spoiled. Picking up the sugar container, she scooped sugar out with a measuring cup and added it to the bubbling mixture.

Risa gave the pot a stir and shifted it slightly off the flame. Reaching over, she picked up the biscuit Bubba Dean had tried to pilfer and slipped it into her apron pocket. "I have it going now. I'll be back in just a minute."

"You better be back. I got enough to do to get the supper ready." Umqua continued to work without so much as a backward glance at Risa.

Risa wiped her hands and walked out the door into the great room. Bubba Dean was moving the couch to the side. He leaned over and, with a long broom in his hand, busied himself with sweeping up the freshly exposed floor. "Bubba Dean, I've got something for you," Risa whispered.

The man straightened himself up. He put his hands on the small of his back and leaned away from Risa to stretch. "What you got, Missy Risa?"

Reaching into her apron pocket, she pulled out the biscuit. "I brought this out for you. Just don't tell your wife. I could get into a lot of trouble."

"Lawsy sakes, Miss Risa." His eyes lit up. "Dis place is yours. How is you gonna get into trouble?"

He held the biscuit in his hand and bounced it once or twice. A broad smile spread over his face and he reached down and scratched a dog's ear.

Risa glanced back at the door. "You and I may think it is, but there seems to be some dispute about certain parts of the house."

Bubba Dean nodded his head. "Yessum, you got me quiet fer sure." He took the biscuit and broke it in two. "Sometimes I can't rightly think what got into dat woman's head. I brung her outta dat hut of hers and put her here, and now she acts like she been here forever."

"She certainly takes ownership of the kitchen."

"Yessum, she does that all right. Dat woman can jest take over when she's a mind to. Now don't you worry. I is good 'bout keepin' secrets."

Risa turned and walked quickly back into the kitchen. Pushing the door open, she stopped in surprise. Her father was seated at the counter, talking to Umqua. "Father, what are you doing here?"

"Yakta was just passing by," Umqua said. "He smelled the biscuits and the pies I've been baking."

Risa's eyes widened. Not only had Umqua laid out a plate of biscuits for the old man, but she'd pushed one of the hot pies in his direction and given him a knife and spoon. He'd already dug into the pie with the spoon, and he lifted his head in Risa's direction, exposing a blotch of red berry juice dripping down the sides of his lower jaw.

"It good," the old man muttered. He pointed to the pie with his dripping spoon. "Me like."

Umqua stepped back to admire her work. There was a look of satisfaction on the old chief's face, and that obviously gave the woman a great deal of pride.

Yakta waved the spoon in Risa's direction. "I hear about dis house." The old man was stocky, his legs folded under the chair. Long gray scraggly hair hung down the sides of his face and was held in place by a red-and-white bandanna. His face was a mass of wrinkles, and his puffy eyes looked like slits carved into a plum pudding. "I hear death come to it."

"We saw Karl-Reech the other day. He was scaring Ian's daughter, Dolly."

Yakta scooped up another bite of the steaming pie. He blew on it and pushed it into his mouth. "Karl-Reech see things and tell what he see."

"How can he see that? Dolly is a girl with little mind. She knows nothing about our ways."

"But he know her and he know this house."

"We are perfectly safe here, aren't we, Umqua?" Risa did her best to drag the other woman into the discussion, especially since her cooking had already made such a favorable impression.

Umqua backed away. "This between you and your father."

Risa's jaw tightened. "We are safe here, Father. This is a Christian house, a Jesus house."

The old man squinted. Risa knew he was the kind of man who thought he knew everything. Most of the time he did. The Tlingit people came to him to solve their problems not just because he was chief, but because most of the time he knew the right answers. But this was something different. For Yakta to admit there was anything to this Jesus thing, he'd have to agree to the fact that he was ignorant about something very important. No, it was just easier for him to cling to the old ways and believe Karl-Reech. He'd already let go of a lot when he allowed her to marry Ian, a white man only slightly younger than he was. It would be too much for him to come to faith in Jesus.

"You must leave before it too late," Yakta said.

"This is my home now, Father, and Ian is my husband."

+ + + + +

When supper was completed, Ian pushed himself away from the table. Umqua and a servant girl busied themselves with clearing the table. The sun was still bright. The fact was, this time of year it might not get very dark until the wee hours of the morning.

"That was a very good meal, Umqua," Risa said. It was hard for Risa to know how Umqua felt about a compliment. To say nothing might be an insult and to say something would communicate that it was Umqua doing the cooking, not eating at the table with the family.

"Yes, it was good," Naomi said.

Dolly clapped her hands wildly. "I like the bread."

Umqua looked over at Ian for a compliment, but it didn't come. Risa watched the woman. It was as if she expected something from the man, and Risa could tell there was a lingering look from Umqua in Ian's direction, a look that wasn't returned or even acknowledged.

Ian took out a cigar from his pocket and rolled it back and forth between his thumb and forefinger.

Bubba Dean came through the dining room, bringing the breakfast dishes in his arms. It was their usual practice to set the table for the next meal just as soon as the last one was finished. When Ian was hungry, he just wanted to sit down and have at it. He seldom had patience with waiting on the food and none at all for waiting on dishes.

Bubba Dean began to lay out the dishes. He glanced out the open window as he put the plates down. "A body needs the dark sometimes," he said.

Naomi stared at the light filtering in the window. "These days get so long in the summer. It almost makes me want to go down to the basement and sleep."

"You stay out of that basement," Ian said.

The sharpness of Ian's comment made Risa curious. It was unlike the man. She was used to not making her feelings known, however, but from Naomi's look, she could see the girl was equally inquisitive.

"What's wrong with the basement?" Naomi asked.

"That area is private. I have some of my old important papers down there, don't want nobody snooping round. 'Sides, a body's liable to get lost."

"How can anybody get lost in a basement?" Naomi asked.

Ian pushed back from the table and got to his feet. "They just can, that's all. You'll have to take my word for that." He turned to Risa and immediately changed the subject. "I hear your father came over today."

Risa shot Umqua a glance. There was no way to keep a secret around this house. "Yes, he was here. Umqua fed him a pie. He liked that a lot." She could tell the idea of having Yakta at the house stirred Ian's interest.

"What did he want?"

"Nothing much," Risa said. She shot a glance at Umqua. The woman was setting out fresh flowers on the table, but her eyes were riveted on Ian. "I think he just came by to pay his respects."

Ian paced to the window. "I'm sorry I missed him then. I kinda like the old fella. He tells some good stories."

"Yes, he does," Risa agreed.

"Next time you invite him to stay for supper." He turned to Dolly, and stooped down next to her. "Why don't you go for a walk with Papa? It would be fun."

Dolly looked up at him, her face breaking into a wide smile. "Yes, Daddy, let's do it. It would be fun."

Risa and Naomi got up from the table, and Risa picked up a book of Shakespeare's plays. It was a book she didn't much care for. She found it a poor substitute for the stories she'd heard around the campfire as a child. It did teach her English, however. Many times she'd find herself keeping her finger on a word until she could track Ian down to tell her what it meant.

Ian took his jacket off the hook and pulled down the yellow one Dolly liked to wear on their evening walks. Dolly had laid her dolls aside and picked up a piece of paper and a pencil. She fancied herself an artist. The characters in her drawings were hard to make out, but they were hers. She knew who they were and she always knew what they meant. She could point to a picture she was drawing and create a story out of the figures in it.

"What ya got there, lamb?" Ian asked.

Dolly continued to scribble with her pencil. "This is you, Daddy, and this is me."

"Who's that in the corner?"

Dolly looked up at Risa and smiled. Risa liked Dolly's smiles. There was only love behind them, unlike some other people whose smiles contained a secret desire for underhandedness. What you saw with Dolly on the surface was what there was underneath. The girl made no attempt to hide her feelings in the least.

"That's Risa. She's in the corner 'cause she just came in."

"And who is this?" Ian asked.

"That's Mommy in her box."

The idea that Dolly still thought about her mother and even saw her in some kind of coffin made Risa shudder. Ian told her the woman had been dead for a year before they all moved to Sitka. Ian had come first and built his house, followed by Dolly. Naomi came when she finished with boarding school that year.

Dolly held back the drawing and frowned. "I'm not very good." She wadded up the paper and threw it against the wall.

Ian knelt down and picked it up. He unwrapped the twisted picture and smoothed it out on the floor. "Why are you throwing this away?"

"I'm not good." The girl got up and, crossing her arms over her chest, walked to the other side of the room.

Ian got to his feet and put his arms around her. "You are good, Dolly. You're good in special ways."

She looked back at him, blinking the tears back from her eyes. "What special ways?"

"Sweetheart, so many things a body sees are just the same as everybody else. You see one man on paper, you've seen them all. You're not like that. When I see something you've done, I see you on the inside. That's a gift, my dear, and not everybody has it."

He handed the paper back to her. "When we get home after our walk, I want you to finish this. I bet it'll turn out to be pretty special, just like you."

She nodded and took the paper from his hand.

"Now, just set it down on the table there and you put on your jacket. We'll go take our walk."

She laid the paper down on a side table, and as Ian held the jacket out for her, she stuck her arms in, one at a time. Ian stepped aside and Dolly danced to the front door. She pulled it open.

Risa jerked her head up as Dolly let out a shrill scream. Ian came running to the door behind Dolly and was unnerved by what they saw. "Risa," Ian yelled. "Come here and look at this."

Risa dropped her book and ran to the door. Ian pulled Dolly back into his arms, and Risa stepped forward. Hanging from the top of the door by a rope was an Indian doll. It was hanging upside down with a blindfold tied around its eyes. Risa reached up and pulled it down.

Ian swung Dolly around so that she couldn't see. "What is that?" he asked. "What does it mean?"

"It's a Tlingit death sign," was all she said.

CHAPTER 8

+ + + + + + +

NAOMI SAT IN HER BEDROOM. The window that looked out on the garden was open, and the bees that Bubba Dean kept were making lazy circles over the flowers. She could almost hear the buzz of their wings. They swooped and flitted from blossom to blossom; in a way, Naomi envied them. They had a purpose. Each one knew what he was doing and went about it without wasted effort.

Naomi thought about Jenny. The picture of her sister in her mind was a distant one, but she could remember the look of kindness on Jenny's face. That kindness was something she longed for, along with a feeling of belonging. Jenny was family, close family. Right now she just wanted to talk to her, to put her head in Jenny's lap like she used to.

Being in Sitka, a town of total strangers, made her feel cooped up, no matter how wide open the look of the mountains were. In a way, she saw herself on an island, a very small island. Instead of the ocean around her there was the forest and the strange faces in the town. She couldn't have been any more trapped.

Getting up from her bed, she walked over to the bookcase. Pulling down first one, then another, she came upon a book of Byron's poetry. She ran her hand over the rough cloth cover of the book. The pages were wrinkled and worn. His work was familiar to her, and all of it seemed somewhat sad at the moment. The last thing she needed was to be sad.

She put down the book and walked to the door. Opening it up, she stuck her head out and looked both ways down the hall. Ian's insistence that his basement area was not to be disturbed made her intensely curious. Even if he did have important papers there, at least they would be something she hadn't read. Ian had gone for a walk, so she could go down and look around. No one would know. She would have plenty of time.

The danger of disobeying made her heart race, and the excitement made her all the more willing to test the boundaries. Reaching over to the table beside her bed, she picked up a box of matches. It was still half full. She used one each night to light her bedside candle and read just before falling asleep.

Stepping out into the hall, she closed the door behind her. Moving toward the basement door, she listened intently for the sound of anyone who might be coming, ready to hurry into the great room at the slightest sound. She turned and pushed open the door with the iron doorknob. The door gave off a slight whine from the iron hinges that held it in place.

As she felt for the first stair with her foot, she reached into her apron pocket for the match box. She'd have to get the first one lit before she closed the door. Fumbling, she struck the match. It sizzled and sparked and then burst into flame. Her hand was shaking, and the small flame wiggled in the darkness. There was no reason to be so nervous. She knew that. As she pushed the door closed, the same small creak sounded from the hinges.

A candle sat on a table at the foot of the stairs. Moving quickly down the stairs, she had almost reached the bottom when the match died. The air smelled musty and dead, and the darkness was total, not a glimmer of light to be seen. Sliding open the matchbox, she pulled out a second one and scratched it across the side of the box. As she touched it to the candlewick, the thing radiated sparks, sending a glimmer of light into the basement area.

Naomi stood for a moment, taking in what she was seeing. The massive room looked like it had been built for storage or to be used in case of a disaster or attack. On one wall, a rack was studded with an assortment of twenty or thirty rifles. Naomi wondered if Ian was preparing for a war after all. She could make out the faint odor of the oil that covered the guns and just a whiff of gunpowder.

The look of the place sent a strange feeling into the pit of her stomach. She realized there could be things she didn't know about her uncle. She had spent most of her years since her parents' death at boarding school. It wasn't until she moved to Sitka that she'd spent any real time with him. What if her uncle was hiding his past from them?

Holding up the candle, she peered toward the back of the big room. There was another door, but where could it lead?

Stepping over several coils of rope, she made her way across the basement. She twisted the knob, opened the door, and moved into an inner hallway. Holding the candle above her head, she could see a long hall with doors on either side. Light peeked out under one of the doors at the end of the hall. Naomi breathed deeply. Unlike the musty smell of the basement, this area almost smelled fresh, like there was or had been a fresh breeze blowing though it.

The first few rooms she passed seemed dark and unused. She opened one of them and, pushing the candle in front of her, looked inside. Paintings were hanging on the walls, a large ornate bed stood in the middle of the room, and an unused fireplace with golden candlesticks on the mantel filled one wall. Several brass fireplace tools leaned against the white bricks. They gleamed at her, twinkling in the candlelight. An oak hutch stood next to a closed window. She could see her reflection in the glass doors of the hutch along with the blue glint of expensive Chinese porcelain.

She backed out of the room, closing the door behind her. Moving to the room next to it, the one near the end of the hallway, she again spotted a light from under the door. Gently she tried the knob, ever so slowly turning it. It was locked. Placing her hand on the door, she felt the wood. It felt warm to the touch, almost as if there were a fire in the room.

Placing the candle on the floor, she lay down to try to see into the room through the crack under the door. The room had light in it. That was plain to see. There was no flickering to the light, and Naomi guessed it to be the light from a window. But why would the curtains in this room be open and the others closed?

Pushing her eye closer to the bottom of the door, she could see the legs of a bed, but a much smaller one. This was an area of the house that stood on the cliff overlooking the harbor. The windows on this side of the house could not be approached from the ground. Even if she'd wanted to do so, she rather doubted she'd be able to climb the cliffs to see inside.

She pressed her eye closer. There was a flickering shadow, but was it the curtain? She wasn't sure. The thought made her heart beat all the faster, pounding in her chest like a herd of caribou stampeding across the open tundra.

She got to her feet. This seemed to be the only locked room in the basement area and there had to be a good reason for it. Moving past the boxes that sat on the floor, she approached the door at the end of the hall and twisted the knob. It opened.

Stepping through the door, she was surprised to find herself outside in the sunlight. An ocean breeze carrying the smell of saltwater blew across her face and extinguished the candle. She sat it on the ground. There were several chairs set in a circle, and an iron sofa with padded pillows laid over it. The area was closed off with a high wooden fence. That would have made it impossible to see from the harbor, or any place else for that matter. Flowers were blooming in neat little rows around the base of the fence, and the grass that covered the area was obviously well cared for. On one side a large honeysuckle bush bloomed. It sent its aroma over the entire lawn area. This appeared to be a place of retreat, but who was it for? Did Ian come here to think, or was this his meeting place for someone else?

Behind the flowers were a number of berry bushes. The ripe berries hung from their thorny vines, ready for the picking. They were large and inviting, making Naomi's mouth water. In Naomi's mind, they also served another purpose. They would tear anyone to shreds who tried to climb the wall.

Looking up she could see that the wall was over ten feet high and the wood was strong and polished. It would take an act of God to scale the thing. It could serve only one purpose, and that was to keep someone in the little garden from ever getting out.

Naomi moved back to the house, to the place where the fence joined the wall. There was a small space. She pressed her face between the wall and the house and could just make out the window of the mysterious room. She could also see that iron bars covered the window. That's odd, Naomi thought, her mind filled with more questions. No one would be able to get to it, so why put iron bars over it? Why were there no bars on other windows in the home?

She shook her head. There was so much she didn't know about this house—or Ian, for that matter. Suddenly, she longed for Jenny to arrive, and the quicker the better. Jenny could help her make sense of all this.

Naomi picked up the candle and opened the door to go back into the house, but once she was back in the basement hallway, she froze in her tracks. There was another light at the far end of the hall. She squatted down behind some boxes piled up near the door and held her unlit candle next to her.

She hoped someone was just getting something from the basement and soon would be gone. But the light got brighter. Obviously, the person with the candle was heading her way. She could hear the steps, but they were not the steps of someone walking deliberately. They were like hers, soft and tentative. They were stopping to see what was there and opening the rooms to look inside.

Her heart beat faster. She began to pray. "Oh, Jesus, please get me out of here. Don't let that be Uncle Ian."

When the footsteps got to the other side of the boxes, to a spot close to the locked room, they stopped. She sat stone still and held her breath.

✦ ✦ ✦ ✦ ✦

Van Fleetwood sat in the Crystal Palace sipping a beer and pondering his next move. The air was rank with the smell of cigars. Their smoke filled the room and mixed with the laughter and the mechanical tinny music of the machine in the corner. It pinged out *Oh, Susanna* in a way that almost grated on a man's ears.

Van had spent a lot of time thinking over the matter that Ian had opened up. If Ian was right and this area of Alaska was due to become a boomtown, then maybe he should consider sewing up the deeds to choice property. He was, after all, a businessman. There had been money made in the gold fields, all right, but much more money made by selling the miners what they needed or catering to their desires.

He watched Puka and Cole Pressley walk through the doors. From where he was sitting in the corner, it was doubtful they saw him. They appeared to be looking for someone else. They walked over to the bar and, leaning over it, said a few words to Hank.

Hank nodded at them and stepped into the back office. Moments later, he came back out, followed by Quinn. The three men started what appeared to be an animated conversation. It wasn't until a mill worker stepped closer to them and ordered another beer that Quinn nodded in the direction of the back office.

Van had almost finished his beer when the three men appeared again. Pressley spotted him first and nudged the other two and motioned in Van's direction. They walked over to his table. "Fancy seeing you here, and alone," Quinn said.

"Oh, I get out from time to time." Van wrapped his fingers tightly around the cold, beveled mug.

"We were just talking about a lumber purchase," Pressley offered.

"Lumber now, is it?" Van picked up the mug and swirled the last of the beer around in the bottom of it. He watched it spin around, taking care not to look any of the men in the face.

"I understand you almost got yourself burned," Quinn said.

The fact that Quinn wasn't ignoring the fire bothered Van. Of course, he was still wearing the clothes he'd worn when he catapulted out of the flames. He hadn't washed them, and he smelled like a bundle of sweaty sheets left out to dry next to a campfire. "I got my hide scorched somewhat, but we made it out all right."

"Looks like Ian will be using some of his own wood to rebuild that office," Quinn said. "Man shouldn't have to buy from himself."

"Don't you pay for your own drinks?" Van asked, grinning up at the man.

Quinn crossed his big arms and stuck out his chin slightly. "Part of my keep, I suppose."

"Well, I like for a man to take care of himself," Van shot back. He held the mug up to his lips and slurped out the last little bit that had coated the bottom. Setting the glass down, he wiped his mouth and the ends of his mustache with the back of his hand.

Quinn leaned over the table and put his hands on top of it. "That would be my advice to you, Fleetwood. You just take care of yourself. A man can easily get in the way when he tries to mind somebody else's business."

Van pulled his campaign hat down close to his eyes and stared up at the man. "Sounds like a threat to me, Quinn."

"Oh, no threat, just some friendly advice. Alaska is plenty dangerous without bringing trouble on yourself that belongs to somebody else."

"I'll remember that." Van got to his feet and buttoned up his jacket. He made his way to the door and cast the three men a quick glance as he left. They were still watching him as he passed by in front of the window.

The breeze had put a slight chill in the air, along with the scent of slaughtered fish. It was a familiar smell on the streets of Sitka. Walking down Lincoln Street he passed several people, but the town seemed unusually deserted.

Several times he heard what he thought was the sound of footsteps behind him. Each time he turned to look, a shadowy figure would dart into one of the storefronts. It sent a chill up his spine. He knew those men wouldn't try anything, not on the street. Of course, he had planned to go on up to Ian's house. There would be plenty of chances to take him unaware on the road that led up there.

He slapped his coat, right where the old Colt Navy he carried was holstered. He hadn't fired it in quite a while, but he knew how to use it and he would, if he had to. Taking a few more steps, he turned to see if he was still being followed. Then he raced into the alley beside the general store and backed up into the shadows. He would wait for whoever it was. He reached under his coat and pulled out his gun.

It was only a minute or so later when the figure of Puka crossed the head of the alley. Van spoke up. "You lookin' for me?"

The man froze in his tracks and turned slowly.

"Puka," Van sounded out the man's name deliberately, "is that you?"

The Indian stepped into the alley and walked his way.

Van moved out of the shadows, his hand still at his side. "You didn't say much back there. Maybe you wanted to tell me something and forgot."

Van knew full well that if Puka had anything against him, it was the matter of Risa. According to Ian, Puka had intended to marry her. And since he had helped Ian and Risa get together, it didn't seem far fetched that Puka would be mighty angry at him.

The Indian reached into his belt and drew a long knife. The sight of the gleaming steel in the man's hand sent a rush of hot emotion into Van's face, but his hands were ice cold. Van raised the revolver. The glint of the gun metal caught the faint light and stopped Puka in his tracks.

"I wouldn't do that," Van said. "I wouldn't even think about it." He drew back on the hammer. The action of the gun and the cocking of the thing in place sounded like a small string of firecrackers. It was a crisp, unmistakable sound. "You just stop right there, right where you are. Now, is there anything you'd like to say to me?"

"No, I have nothing to say to you."

"Then you jest put that frog sticker back in its place and go on back to where you come from. We'll just forget all about this."

Puka looked down at his knife. Van could see that thoughts were tumbling through his mind.

"You might throw that thing," Van said, "but I guarantee you I'll get off one bodacious shot. This thing has quite a kick. Even if I winged you, you'd be picking yerself up off the ground with one less arm or leg, and I ain't planning on jest winging you." Van held the pistol out further. It was level with his eye. If the thing actually still could fire, it would do the job. "I may be old, but bullets don't care how old a man is."

Puka returned the knife back to its sheath. He turned and slowly left the alley, headed back in the direction of the Crystal Palace.

Van breathed a sigh of relief. He walked toward the street and stepped out onto the boardwalk and looked in the direction Puka had turned. The man was gone.

CHAPTER 9

NAOMI CLUTCHED THE CANDLESTICK to her chest. If she had to use the thing to defend herself, she would.

"You get out from there." It was Umqua, using a far more menacing tone than she'd ever heard before, even in the kitchen. "I know your naughty ways."

Naomi slowly got to her feet, quivering like a leaf.

Umqua held up a lit candle and was shaking her finger. "You know you not suppose to be down here. What you doing here?"

Naomi thought she heard movement from behind the door, but she couldn't be sure. "I-I just wanted to t-take a look," she stammered.

"You have to learn to obey."

Naomi stepped across the hall from the woman, her hand back against the far wall. She was still shaking, trembling like a dog in the cold rain. She could see the smoke of Umqua's candle rising from the sharp, hot flame. It couldn't possibly match the fire she saw in the woman's black eyes as they peered into her soul. A small drop of sweat formed at the base of her neck and slowly wound its way along her spine.

"You come down here to live? You want to stay here?"

Naomi shook her head vigorously. She was too afraid to speak.

"Well, you just might. I might put you here myself."

"Please," Naomi croaked out the word in a plaintive cry, "I just want to go back to my room."

Umqua smoothed the wrinkles on her apron. She stood erect and tall, almost ramrod straight. Lifting her arm, she pointed into the dark hall. "Then you just go back to where you come from, and you forget anything that you've seen down here. It's not for your eyes. Do you understand me?"

"Yes, ma'am." Naomi nodded her head forcefully. Her heart was beating wildly. She crept along the edge of the wall, taking just one more small step.

The woman jabbed her finger into the darkness. "Don't let me even see you thinking about this place again."

Naomi lifted her skirt and ran into the darkness. The coolness of the basement air rushed against the heat and perspiration of her face and neck. The faint light of Umqua's candle showed her the door to the basement area, and she rushed through it stumbling over a coil of rope that lay stretched out on the floor. She tumbled headfirst onto the hard dirt, the rocks and dirt cutting into her knees as she slammed into it. The candlestick flew out of her hand, sending a rat scurrying in her direction.

She got to her knees, trembling. She didn't want to be anywhere near here when Umqua came into the room. Looking back, she could see the woman's light was still at the far end of the hall. Perhaps she was just as curious as Naomi had been, or maybe she already knew what was there and just wanted to make certain nothing had been disturbed.

Reaching into her pocket, she found the box of matches. She slid it open and fumbled nervously, dropping two of them on the floor. Breathing hard, she tried again. She pulled one out and struck it against the edge of the box. It flared and sparked.

The stairs were left of where she was standing. It would have been so easy to have missed them altogether in the darkness. She quickly ran to the top of the stairs and burst through the door.

Closing it behind her, she stood for a moment with her back to it, breathing hard. *How can I face Umqua ever again?* she thought.

Running for her room, she yanked the door open and slammed it behind her. She slid the bolt into place. Panting, she tried her best to catch her breath. Visions of what she'd seen in the basement tumbled through her mind and her thoughts drifted to her uncle. Everything she knew about him suddenly seemed questionable, but was it right to condemn him for something she didn't know? How could she take his kindness of the past years and throw it away without even asking him about what she had seen? If only Jenny were here. Jenny would know what to do.

Once the fear of the moment began to subside, Naomi grew mad that she had allowed the woman to frighten her so. After all, she was a servant.

She stepped over to the far side of the room, leaning over the books on the small shelf and looking out into the harbor. A small boat was coming closer to the dock. It wouldn't be the one Jenny was on. It was too small, a fishing boat. Still, the sight of the thing caused her heart to soar. Jenny would be here soon. Then she could go. But when? She imagined the two of them exploring the hills around Sitka, picking flowers and talking about the parts of their lives that nobody else knew. She wanted to know about California, and she wanted to know about this man Jenny had fallen in love with.

There was a loud knock at her door, startling Naomi out of her thoughts. "Who is it?" she croaked.

"It's me Naomi, me." Dolly's voice sounded weepy. "Please let me in."

Naomi swung her feet over the side of her bed and pulled back on the bolt.

The young woman burst into the room, crying at the sight of Naomi. She flung her arms around her and, burying her head on Naomi's shoulder, continued to cry.

Naomi wrapped her arms around Dolly and patted her on the back. "It's okay, Dolly, you're with me now. You can tell me what it is."

Dolly pulled back from her. The tears had streaked down her face, leaving a trail of salty tracks that curled over her cheeks. She pointed toward the front of the house. "The doll," she said.

"Did you break a doll?" Naomi asked.

Dolly started crying again and grabbed Naomi, laying her head over Naomi's shoulder. "The Indian doll at the door."

Naomi patted her on the back. "Tell me about it."

"It was hanging upside down with a blindfold over its eyes." The bawling became more intense.

"Just some Indian trick," Naomi said. "You know how they hate us. They just want us to go. There's nothing else to it."

Dolly pulled away once again and, looking at Naomi, shook her head. "Risa said it was a sign. She said it was a death sign." Dolly's eyes filled up once again. "Risa said it might mean a death that I cannot see. I don't want to see death, Naomi."

"There's nothing to be afraid of in death, Dolly," Naomi said, "not for a Christian. You go to be with the Lord and live with Him in heaven, and heaven is a wonderful place."

Naomi reached into her apron pocket and pulled out a handkerchief. She dabbed it at Dolly's eyes, wiping away the tears. Helping Dolly had put her own fear away for the moment. "There. Now we need to wash your face. You're so pretty, but when a girl cries she can look so very awful." Naomi continued to wipe Dolly's eyes. "I'm glad we're friends and that you can tell me what is bothering you."

*   *   *   *   *

The steamer *Tiger Lilly* had made excellent time out of Seattle. With a cargo hold full of goods, it had made a direct trip to Sitka. There, the goods could be sold for much more than the asking prices for the same items in Seattle. The prices in Seattle were far out of sight from the purchase price of the same goods in San Francisco. If a man wanted to, he could make a very good living just by sailing from San Francisco to Seattle. To own a vessel that made the trip to Alaska, though, was like having a license to print money. A man could name his own price and come away rich.

When the engines on the vessel slowed down and began to chug, Jenny could hear the change in her stateroom. She smelled the coal as the smoke drifted out over the water. Bending down, she looked into the mirror. It was set too low, but it was all the small room offered. She hurriedly ran a brush through her hair and then pinned it into place with a large tortoiseshell comb. She had put on her best yellow dress, the one Zac always thought made her look like a sunflower. She picked up the lapis choker with the blue ribbon and tied it into place around her neck. The soft blue of the stone and the azure sash around her waist would pick up the color of her eyes. She pinched her cheeks to put some blush into them.

Jenny stepped out into the gangway and bent over to clear the beams that hung low over the bottom of the ship. She made her way through the semidarkness over the polished wood and climbed the stairs into the sunlight. The rear deck had a cloud of the oily ash floating over it, and Jenny looked down at her dress. She would have to hurry over the passage that led around to the bow of the ship. It was there she could find fresh air and be spared a coating of soot for her yellow dress.

She swung around and quickly made her way forward. Mike Wass was at the bow, looking off at the land in the distance. "You must be looking forward to getting home," she said.

He turned around. His eyes lit up when he saw her. "You certainly are a sight for the morning."

He was wearing blue jeans and a denim shirt with the sleeves rolled up halfway between his wrists and elbows. A white fleece vest provided some warmth from the sea, and his boots were like none that she had ever seen before. Fitting up to his calves, they were made from some sort of animal hide and lined with white wool. They had the very appearance of warmth. All in all Jenny thought he cut a quite striking figure.

"Why, thank you. I wanted to look nice when we came into Sitka."

Wass buttoned the middle button on his vest. "I'd say you left nice in the dust." He grinned.

"Those folks in Sitka will get an eye full," he went on, "probably take you as some sort of entertainer, and heaven knows they could use that."

"Do you like it here?" she asked.

Wass turned and looked at the faraway buildings that surrounded the entrance to the harbor. He shook his head. "No, I don't like it here." Raising his hand, he pointed to the mountains with their snow-covered peaks. "I love it over there."

Jenny edged closer to the man to see just where he was pointing. "Over there? What is over there?"

"The world is over there. Sitka's here, but the world is there. There're places a man has never set foot on before and beauty the eye has never seen. A man hides himself in the filth and squalor of towns like Sitka so he can huddle with other folks just as greedy and dirty as he is, but over there the air is pure and the land is green."

"Don't you ever miss people?"

Wass shook his head. "No, I don't miss people. I do miss companionship, but a man has to go a long ways to find a companion, someone he can place his heart close to. Some of us never do find one, but when we do, we don't want to lose them."

Jenny could see the sudden sadness in the man's eyes. He wasn't just talking and telling her his ideas, he was remembering. She wanted to ask him about his thoughts, but she didn't dare. To ask him about the memory would be to intrude on the deepest part of his life. Jenny knew she would feel like an outsider, a passing spectator. "What makes a good companion?" she asked instead.

He looked back to the distant mountains. "Sometimes I think that when God created a human, He took one lump and split it into two pieces. He fashioned one of them into a man and held the other one back for some time later. When He was sure that the feller would do what he would need, He made the other lump into a woman."

He looked back at Jenny. His eyes glistened. She wasn't sure if it was from the ocean breeze or if tears were forming in them.

"A man spends his whole life looking for that other part. He doesn't know what she looks like, but he does know what she feels like."

"And what does she feel like?"

"She feels like him, the other part of him, the deepest part of him that he's never seen before."

"And what if he never finds that other part?"

"If a man never finds the other part of him, he spends the rest of his life trying to fill up the space. He fills it up with liquor sometimes, or he fills it up with the noise of faceless people. He buys things and thinks that furniture will give his empty soul a place to sit down, but it never does."

He cocked his head, staring Jenny right in the eye. "Me, I fill up the emptiness with miles—miles of beauty, miles of numbing cold, miles and miles of thinking about what's going to fill up my belly. That's the only way for me to stop looking for the most important thing."

"I'm sorry," Jenny said. "I didn't mean to cause you pain."

"No matter." He shook his head. "Pain keeps me alive." A smile creased his lips. "It makes me laugh too."

"Hey, you two."

Both their heads turned to see Cormia coming down the steps from the pilothouse. He was dressed in his customary black suit and white shirt. His shoes had a shine on them, a high polished gloss. They slipped a bit when he headed over the deck in their direction. He stopped to steady himself, holding his arms up suddenly for balance. "Now, you'd both better be careful," he said. "These ships have a way with hearts, and Miss Jenny here is an engaged woman."

Jenny glanced at Wass. The man's face was turning red. She immediately jumped in to defend him. "Mr. Wass was just talking to me about Alaska and how much he loves it."

"Trappers have to love the place. It puts food on their tables. Most of them do quite well at it, if they don't drink their money away."

"And do you do well, Mr. Wass?" Jenny asked.

"I get by. I take my Christmas drink now and then, but nothing that unscrews my head."

"You don't seem to be the type."

"We'll be coming into Sitka shortly," Cormia said. He looked Jenny over. "I can see you're dressed to make quite the impression. I'd say that uncle of yours will throw one fine party."

"Do you think so?"

"I most certainly do. Ought to be one of the biggest affairs Sitka's seen in a long while."

Jenny looked back at Wass. "Would you come to the party, Mr. Wass?"

He shook his head. "I ain't much for dress-up gatherings."

She slipped her hand onto his arm and looked into his eyes. "Please say that you will. It would please me very much."

He looked at her long and hard, then nodded. "All right. If it will please you, I'll come."

"Good." She looked back at Cormia. "I guess Uncle Ian can throw his party. I'll have at least a few people there I know."

"And who would that be," Cormia asked.

"You, my sister, Naomi," she tightened her grip around Wass's arm. "And Mr. Wass here."

CHAPTER 10

+ + + + + + +

THE BOOM FROM THE CANNON in the harbor brought Naomi straight up out of her chair. She almost knocked over her glass. "Is that. . . ?" she started to ask.

"It just might be," Ian replied. He set down his spoon. "Let's go have a look. I have me a telescope up on the balcony off my room. We ought to be able to see if it's Jenny's ship from there."

Dolly clapped her hands. "It might be Jenny." She continued to repeat the phrase in a singsong fashion, "It might be Jenny."

Umqua poured Ian a fresh glass of water. "I don't know why you're bothering. If it's her, she'll be up here soon enough."

Ian got to his feet and dropped his napkin onto the half-empty plate in front of him. Naomi knew he didn't much care for broccoli anyway, and the man had left a plate full of it, the same portion Umqua had spooned up against his protests. *Maybe that was why Umqua was so cross at the idea of Ian leaving the table*, Naomi thought. *Women always like to think they know what's best for a man.*

Naomi was all too glad to leave Umqua down there at the table. She hadn't been able to look her in the eye for a day now, and her hopes were that Jenny's arrival would change all that. She needed courage. Jenny's letters had shown her to be a woman of strength, and Naomi hoped that maybe some of it would rub off on her.

She stopped at the landing above the dining room and looked back down. Umqua was staring up at her. The look unnerved Naomi. Umqua set down the dishes in a huff and walked out the front door. Turning around, Naomi ran down the hallway to join the others.

Ian and Risa's huge bedroom was too masculine for Naomi's taste. The polished tongue-in-groove floor was made from maple, which set off the green and red rugs with its honey color. The bed was massive with a large bearskin that covered the foot of the thing. Naomi shuddered as she looked at it. The jaws of the bear seemed to growl at anyone who might approach as it hung over the foot of the bed. *What a thing to have on one's bed*, Naomi thought.

A fireplace was set into the wall. There was no mistaking Ian's taste and design in creating it. It was surrounded by tiles, each painted with a delicate blue scene depicting a ship. The tiles were each unique and came from Holland. Two sofas of pure white, set off with gold trim, flanked the fireplace. There was a large table in the middle, polished, and with a basket of fruit sitting on it.

The small group had gathered around the bay window that looked out over the garden and onto the harbor. Two soft green chairs faced each other on either side of the open bay windows and on the loft that hung over the garden. Ian had stationed a large brass spyglass on a wooden tripod so he could keep track of the comings and goings of ships putting into Sitka. The sea was, after all, his first love. He was staring into the thing and signaling Naomi with his hand to come closer. "Come on, girl. I got something to show you."

Naomi crowded her way between Risa and Dolly, and Ian backed away to allow her to see. There in the bay was a large steamer. The sailors were gathering sail and Naomi could see the black plume of smoke drift out over the harbor. She stepped up on the small riser that stood behind the tripod and peered into the brass eyepiece. She could make out the name on the vessel.

Naomi squealed. *"The Tiger Lilly!* That might be Jenny's ship."

"It most certainly is." Ian crowded over Naomi's shoulder. He moved the telescope forward slightly. "And who do you see on the bow of that ship?"

"Is that her?"

"I'd bet ya dollars to doughnuts it is. That's her, the pretty lady in the yellow dress."

Naomi pulled back from the device. "Can we go and meet her? Can we go now?"

Ian laughed. "Why, of course we can. Do you think I'd make you sit here in this house while Jenny pulls into port?"

Naomi and Dolly clapped their hands.

It took Bubba Dean almost half an hour to hitch the horses to what was one of the few carriages in Sitka. He also coupled a team to the wagon to help with any luggage. He held the reins of the carriage in his hand and waited as Ian got in. "Y'all be careful going down dat dere hill, Mister Ian. You knows dees animals can run. Ain't no need a leavin' me too far behind."

Naomi climbed into the back, and Bubba Dean helped Risa up front with Ian.

"I'se gonna take Miss Dolly wif me. Umqua told me dat would be best. It'll give y'all plenty of room and me somebody to talk to."

"Fine," Ian said. "You just do that." He grinned. "We'll meet you at the docks." Ian swung the small whip high over his head and sent the team plunging down the road.

Naomi looked back to see Bubba Dean. The man had his hands on his hips, evidently disgusted that Ian wasn't taking his advice. He climbed up in the wagon beside Dolly.

Naomi was alive with chatter about what she wanted to do with Jenny and the things she wanted to show her. It had been so many years since the two of them had laid eyes on each other, and Naomi doubted that Jenny would even recognize her. "It will be funny to introduce myself to my own sister," she said.

She was secretly glad Umqua had chosen to stay home. It would have been most uncomfortable to have this happy moment spoiled by some dire look on Umqua's face.

The horses were running freely, Ian holding and tugging on the reins. They were leaving the slow-moving wagon far behind them. Rounding a curve, the three of them could feel two of the wheels leave the ground. The women screamed, Naomi more out of delight but Risa with a genuine note of fear in her voice. Ian pulled back on the reins, bringing the animals under control.

When they rounded a second corner, they spotted a man as he stepped out of the woods. "Karl-Reech," Risa said.

Naomi leaned forward and took hold of Ian's arm. "Please stop and send that old man away. I wouldn't want Dolly to see him. He scares her."

Ian pulled back on the ribbon-traces, bringing the horses to a dead stop. The man was without his mask, but Naomi didn't think that improved his looks whatsoever. His black stringy hair fell down the sides of his head. It had been coated with bear grease, which gave it a shine along with a powerful odor. To the Tlingit, a man's smell indicated his power, and Naomi thought if that were true, this was one of the most powerful men she'd ever smelled. His skin was a dull olive color, the shade of old saddle leather. There was a glower on his face, lips rising with a scowl that sloped down the sides of his mouth, and the tip of his wide and flat nose seemed to touch his top lip. The robe he wore was brightly painted, and once again he carried the carved serpent. He was shaking it at them.

"We're on our way to the harbor," Ian shouted. "What do you want with us?"

Karl-Reech chanted, swinging the brightly painted snake back and forth across their path.

Ian shooed the old man aside with the back of his hand. "You get out of our way now. We're in a hurry."

"You no go here. Death is here."

"That's nonsense," Ian shouted. "You just leave us be and get on about mixing those herbs for the sick people you tend to."

"Beware!" The old man raised both of his hands. It was a posture that looked like a bear that had been provoked into a kill. "Death will come."

Risa began to speak to the man in his native Tlingit tongue. Just the sound of the familiar words appeared to quiet him, but he seemed insistent. "You will have trouble if you do not listen."

It was plain to see that Ian didn't care to give the man much leeway. He had always said that the Tlingits' only chance of survival was to do business with the white man, and many of his views centered around the notion that their only real hope was in becoming white men. He frowned at Risa in disapproval. Looking back at the old man, Ian growled. "Did you leave that doll on our door?"

Naomi knew that was what was really bothering her uncle. He was very protective of Dolly, and the fact that she had been frightened by the omen, no matter how well-intentioned it might have been, was enough to boil his blood.

Karl-Reech ignored him. Instead, he lifted the snake and began once again to shake it. His chant grew louder, almost as if by raising his voice he could ward off Ian's disbelief. He moved over in front of the horses. Grabbing hold of the traces, he held them steady and continued to chant in the direction of the carriage.

Ian reached into his pocket and flung a silver dollar to the ground. It stunned Karl-Reech, and he momentarily stopped the chanting.

"There now, if that's what you're wanting, you can pick it up and be gone. We're not stopping." Ian swung the whip, cracking it over the heads of the horses. They jumped in their harness, sending the old man to the ground beside the road.

Risa screamed at him, grabbing for the whip, but Ian fought her off. With one more crack of the whip the horses bolted, racing down the hill.

Naomi looked back to see Karl-Reech get to his feet. He never made a move to pick up the coin. He just backed away, all the while staring at them with a sad expression on his face.

"I have no patience with people like that," Ian said. "They act like they are living a hundred years ago."

"You forget," Risa added, "it was my grandfather who led the revolt against the Russians. That hasn't been so long ago."

"What are you saying?"

"I'm saying if the people are not treated with respect, they might do something about it. They are here. They are not dead memories. The story is told over and over, and it's very much alive in their hearts and minds."

Ian shook his head. "I won't have any herb-squeezer scaring my little girl back there, not without me doing something about it." Holding the reins in his hands, he slapped them hard on the backs of the horses. As the carriage rounded the next bend, Ian yanked hard on the right rein to hold it in the road. It broke free.

"What's wrong?" Risa asked.

Ian was fumbling for the brake, jamming it hard. "The rein broke," he yelled.

"Can't you stop us?"

Ian had a look of panic on his face. "I'm not sure."

"This road leads to a narrow spot on the cliff over the bay," Risa screamed. "You've got to stop us before we get there."

Ian continued to pull back on the brake. The smell of the hard rubber burned a sickening scent into the air. As Naomi bounced in the back, she could see the wisps of black smoke rising from the wheels. They were out of control. The horses were running hard with the carriage swinging from side to side all over the road.

"Here," Ian said, "You get next to this brake pedal, and I'll go out there and see if I can't stop them."

Risa gulped. She grabbed his arm. "You can't do that."

"I ain't got time to argue with you, woman. If I don't get out on them traces, we're all going to die." He got up from his seat, holding on to the rail. The footbox was a high one and he leaned over it, watching the back of the horses' hooves fly close to his face. There wouldn't be any second try.

+ + + + +

Van picked up his Colt Navy and stuck it in his holster. He shrugged on his coat and pulled his sleeves to a spot just below the end of the arms of the jacket. Looking in the mirror, he sat the campaign hat on his head and cocked it just a mite. Dabbing his finger into a tin of wax, he twirled the end of his mustache.

He stepped out of the front door of his house on the edge of Lincoln

Street and watched as the street filled with people on the run. A steamer docking from Seattle always had a way of doing that. Folks wanted to know who it was that was coming, and more importantly, what they were bringing with them. He'd heard the cannon boom along with the rest of the town. It was partially the reason he'd decided to make his move now. Even if anyone was up over at the Crystal Palace, they'd be most likely running down to the dock with all the rest. They'd want to get a look at the liquor on board and any women that might be coming in.

He walked slowly as the men rushed on past him. Looking back, he could see that the foot traffic had cleared. There was no one behind him. They'd all run down to the docks to see the ship come in. Taking a deep breath, he darted between the two buildings to the alley that led to the back door of the Crystal Palace.

One door had a knob on it and led to the back of the main saloon. The other one just had a handle and, more importantly, a brass lock in the door. Van reached into his sheath and extracted his Greener knife. It was plenty strong and just might be able to pry open any door in the city. Jamming it into the space between the lock and the door, Van pushed the big knife forward. It splintered the wood on the door, revealing part of the bolt that held the lock in place. Working his way up, he continued to separate the water-soaked wood of the door from the brass works inside. In moments, he had the entire lock exposed and most of the door that held the bolt into place.

He grabbed the iron handle and jerked on it, springing the door open. It was dark inside the office, just what he wanted. Looking for a lamp, he spotted one on the desk. He bent over and turned up the wick. Reaching into his pocket, he pulled out a match and struck it on the top of the desk. It flared up, and Van lifted the globe on the lamp and held the flame to it. As the shadowy light filled the room, he reached back and closed the door tight.

CHAPTER 11

+ + + + + + +

IAN KNEW HE'D HAVE TO WAIT until he could be certain the horses were running straight before making his jump. He watched as they ran, trying to measure their gate. Craning his neck back in Risa's direction, he could see she'd taken the seat beside the brake. "Hang on, girl. You don't pull up on that thing until I get on the back of that wheel animal. Then you grab onto it and pull for all you're worth."

Risa nodded her head.

Ian slung his hat back into the seating area. His gray hair was flying in all directions, and the wind pushed his beard into his face. He took one more look at Risa and yelled. "One thing more."

"What's that?" Risa asked.

"I love you," he yelled. With that he climbed over the box and stood on the wooden T that marked the end of the carriage. He timed his jump so that he wouldn't be kicked by the flying hooves and then flung himself forward. Landing in between the two horses, he grabbed for the traces. His feet fumbled, dangling between the two running horses. One slip would finish him.

Risa and Naomi watched him struggle, trying his best to hang on to the harness and keep his balance. He hauled himself up, struggling hand over hand to pull himself forward.

The trees seemed to whiz by the carriage. Risa pulled back on the brake. With each second they were nearing the narrow spot on the road where they would need the most control over the horses. The problem was, they had none. Risa used two hands. Seeing Ian dangling between the running horses sent a feeling of panic through her. She yanked hard. A grinding sound filled the air as raw metal hit the wheels.

When Ian reached the wheel horse, on the right, he jumped, swinging his leg over the animal and onto its back. Reaching down, he grabbed onto the bridle and pulled back hard. Naomi watched him wrestle the beast, working hard to gain control. The wheel horse set the pace and if its head could be turned, the other one would follow.

Both horses seemed to stumble and break stride. Ian pulled harder, slowing them down still further. Both of the women could feel the change almost right away. In a matter of minutes they were brought to a lathering halt, not more than fifty yards from the narrow spot over the cliff. The horse with Ian on it stamped its feet and swung its head, doing its best to shake itself of this sudden, desperate rider.

Ian swung his leg over the side and dropped to the ground. He held onto the harness as he moved from handhold to handhold all the way back to the carriage.

Naomi listened to the horses' labored breathing. She knew that they had to be walked, but right now she was glad they were standing in one place.

Stepping next to the front seat, Ian stopped. He was breathing hard, too, almost as hard as the horses. He bent over, putting his hands on his knees. Taking his time, he gave off loud puffs of air, slow and deliberate. Standing straight up, he gave Risa a smile. "Maybe I ain't that old after all." He held his hand out, offering it to Risa.

Naomi blinked and watched as he helped Risa step down. She'd never known him to be any other way than what she'd just seen—brave and heroic. She admired him, but the questions about the basement and the locked room buzzed in her head.

"Come on, little lady." He looked at Naomi and clapped his hands. "You get down from there. We're gonna walk the rest of the way and just lead these here horses."

Naomi moved to the front seat and stepped off. Ian grabbed hold of her, lifting her up by the waist and gently setting her on the ground. "There, don't that solid ground feel good?"

Naomi nodded and smiled. "It feels real good."

Risa walked around the horses, patting them. "How did this happen?" she asked.

Ian joined her and moved around the animals, looking for something. Reaching over, he fished out one of the traces. He looked the break over carefully and ran his finger over it. Moving to the other side, he found the trace that led to the second horse. He held it up for Risa to see. "This was no break. A man doesn't lose a harness on two horses at once. These things have been cut. Whoever cut them slashed them just deep enough to not make it apparent until it was too late. One jerk on the reins and the ribbons here would snap like a string of spaghetti."

"Who would do such a thing?" Risa asked.

Ian looked back down the road. "Might be that fella back there."

"You mean Karl-Reech?"

"Who else?"

Risa shook her head. "He wouldn't do this." To most people, Risa might just seem to be blindly defending her people, but Naomi knew her better than that. The woman was an intentional thinker. She would ponder a matter long after most people had shot their mouths off. And Naomi realized full well that Risa knew the Tlingit better than most. What they would and would not do was something she was very familiar with.

Ian went on, not letting the notion die. "Maybe it was his way of fulfilling his own prophesy." Ian scratched at the ground with the toe of his boot. "I suppose I didn't pay him enough."

Risa looked back up the road. They could hear the approaching wagon from around the bend. "Maybe it was the other man up the road."

Naomi watched Ian's eyes. They narrowed, glaring at Risa. It was obvious Risa was talking about Bubba Dean, and for that matter it was a logical choice. He had gotten the carriage ready. Naomi couldn't believe that, though. Bubba Dean was kind. He wouldn't hurt a fly, much less a man he'd been working for all his life.

"No need to stick up for your Injun friends. When a man's wrong, he's wrong. Don't matter what color his skin is."

"And if a man's skin is red it makes him wrong right away, I suppose." Risa turned as she spoke the words and walked off.

"I'm sorry, sugar," Ian immediately retracted his statement and followed after her.

The wagon pulled up moments later. Bubba Dean yelled out. "What's wrong? One of them throw a shoe?"

Ian marched back to the wagon. "No, but I'll have to take the girls on up ahead in the wagon. You walk the carriage down. The traces broke. We'll have to get them fixed in town before we head back. Can you take care of that?"

"Yes, sir, I sure can." He seemed puzzled, shaking his head. "That don't figure none to me. Don't figure a-tall."

"All right girls, let's all get in the wagon. We've got ourselves a boat to meet."

Risa and Naomi climbed into the wagon, Naomi moving to the back to ride with Dolly and the two hounds of Ian's that had come along. Dolly was clapping her hands and smiling like nothing had happened.

Ian gave Bubba Dean a few more instructions on the team, and then, climbing into the wagon, slapped the backs of the mules with the reins. It lurched forward. Risa curled her arm around Ian's, obviously putting their tift behind them. Naomi looked back at the carriage and Bubba Dean as he led the horses. The slower speed wasn't all that welcome to her, even though she did feel quite a bit safer.

It took the wagon almost half an hour to reach the docks, and they were far behind the crowds that had gathered. A number of the merchants had wagons ready to receive goods; still others had hand carts. The crew was in the process of swinging the cargo down onto the loading docks. Several sailors manned block and tackle. They had large nets with boxes filling them. After pushing them over the side, the men on the dock lowered them into place.

One of the smiling merchants, a bald man with a full red beard, had already opened a barrel with his name stenciled on it. He turned to the crowd and gave out a loud yell. "I got me some pickled eggs here. You folks want some, they'll be at my store. They'll cost you fifty cents apiece." There were no moans or sounds of agony from the crowd. Eggs were a rare item in Alaska. Men would have paid almost any amount.

Ian caught sight of Jenny as she came down the ramp on the arm of Dave Cormia. They were followed by another man. Ian waved at her, calling her name. "Jenny, Jenny girl."

Weaving his way through the crowd, he was followed by Risa, Dolly, and Naomi. For all of Naomi's excitement at seeing her sister, she was beginning to feel a little uncertain about the prospect. She was sixteen now, and what if Jenny was dissatisfied at how she'd turned out?

Jenny spotted Naomi from the ramp. Naomi could see the joyful look in her eyes, and relief swept over her.

It took the group several more minutes to wind their way to where Jenny was. Ian took Jenny by the shoulders and stared at her. "You are a picture of your mother, child, the most beautiful woman I ever did see." He glanced back at Risa. "Apart from my own wife, of course."

"Of course," Jenny replied.

He shook Cormia's hand, pumping it like a dry man finding a long abandoned well. "Glory be, Dave, I sure do appreciate this. You don't know how much."

"It's a good thing you sent me." Cormia smiled back at Jenny. "She almost didn't come. Don't think she would have for anybody who wasn't your lawyer. It's hard to tear a woman in love away from her man, you know."

Ian looked behind Jenny and spotted Mike Wass. "And is this your man, my dear?"

Jenny stepped aside to introduce Mike. "No, Uncle Ian. But he is a very special man. He's from here—Mr. Mike Wass."

Ian shook his hand. "I don't seem to recall a Mike Wass," he said.

Mike pointed to the mountains. "Actually, I'm from up yonder ways. I'm a trapper."

"Well, any friend of my niece's is a friend of mine. You're welcome in my house, sir, any time."

Ian looked back, signaling the young women to step forward. "This is my wife, Risa. You remember my daughter, Dolly."

Dolly couldn't contain herself. She threw herself into Jenny's arms. "I remember you, Jenny. I seen your picture lots."

Ian then reached back and took Naomi's hand. He pulled her forward. Standing her in front of him with his hands on her hips, he smiled. "And this is your sister, Naomi. You can't believe how this girl has been living for this day."

Jenny gently pushed Dolly aside. Looking at Naomi, she opened her arms. "I've missed you so much, Naomi, and thought of you almost every day."

Naomi began to cry. She moved forward into Jenny's arms, sobbing.

Jenny stroked the back of her head. "That's all right. I'm here now. You're home, darling."

+ + + + +

The back office of the Crystal Palace was in shambles, which didn't surprise Van. He was only happy he'd never taken a close look at their kitchen. He might not have eaten for a week. A leather sofa stood with its back to the wall. It had long ago lost any notion of what color it should be and now was consumed with keeping its insides from completely falling out.

Van moved to a spot behind the desk. It looked like it had been used to chop meat on. Deep gashes were cut into the top and one of the bottom drawers hung off its rollers, the lower corner of the thing resting on the floor. Van imagined it might still be good to hold pencils in. He pulled out one of the drawers that was still in relatively good shape. Papers filled the drawer; ledger sheets, accounting books, and one marked "loans."

He picked up the loan sheet. It wasn't what he was after, but he figured it might be fun just to find out who had gambling markers out to the Palace. It might explain some of the votes taken in the city council. Looking it over, he nodded. There were indeed some prominent names written on it.

Turning to the back of the office, he spotted a filing cabinet. It was in the shadows, but that would be the place to look. Moving over to it, he noticed that one of the filing drawers had a brass lock built into it. Pulling the trusty Greener out once more, he slipped it into the crack and broke it open.

He fingered through the files until he came to the one he hoped he might find. It was labeled *Property to be purchased*. Most businesses had a limited amount of money to be spent on capital improvement. He knew if he went up against the Palace in some place they had their sights set on, it might cost him a pretty penny. If Ian was right and Sitka was due to turn into a boomtown, then any old piece of dirt would do. He was just interested in any spot the Palace didn't want to buy. It would be the building itself that drew the people in, not so much where it was located.

His head jerked back. He heard some voices close by and one of them was Quinn's. The man would be coming into the office. Closing the file cabinet, he scampered back over to where the lamp was still burning. He leaned over and blew it out, then quickly squatted down behind the desk.

Quinn opened the door and stepped into the room. "Come on in," he said. "I have some really good stuff I'll pour you."

Van was fairly trembling. He was hoping the man kept his liquor in the open where he wouldn't need to use the lamp. To his dismay, Quinn said, "I'd better light the lamp. Man can see to pour better that way."

"Yes, you had better do that." It was Umqua's voice. Van would know the woman anywhere. *What is she doing here?* he wondered.

Van heard Quinn pick up a match from the cup on the desk and strike it. Quinn then leaned over the lamp. He tried to pick up the globe but instead yelped in pain, flinging the match from his suddenly scorched hand.

"What's wrong?" Umqua asked.

"This lamp's hot." He shook his fingers and then stuck them in his mouth. "I blew it out myself late last night."

"Maybe Hank has been in here."

"No chance. I had to wake him up myself, and I sent him straight on to pick up our shipment of liquor."

Quinn took a handkerchief out of his pocket and reached for another match. Van could hear him strike it and then pick up the globe. Moments later, the soft glow of the lamp flickered on the shabby walls of the room. Quinn stepped around the desk and reached for the lower drawer that had been hanging to the floor. He caught sight of Fleetwood and jerked to attention. "What are you doing here?"

Van slowly got to his feet. He dusted himself off as Quinn drew a revolver. "I was just waiting for you."

"On the floor, behind my desk, in the dark?"

"Figured you'd be here sooner or later."

"How'd you get in here?" Quinn stepped back around the desk, moving to the back door to inspect it. "Umqua came here to get some liquor for a party that friend of yours is throwing."

He opened the door and eyed the spot where Van had ripped the bolt from the door. "It seems we have ourselves a burglar here," he said. He cast Van a long look, a gleam sparking in his eyes.

"You better go on back home, Umqua," Quinn said. There was a coldness in his voice. "Mr. Fleetwood and I have some business to discuss."

Van could only imagine what that might mean, but as he watched Umqua disappear, he felt his hopes fading fast. "What business?" he asked.

Quinn grinned at him, the revolver still in his hand. He wagged the gun in the direction of the old couch. "I just figured you must have something mighty important in the way of business with me. A man doesn't break into another man's office unless he's got something that can't wait. Let's just see what you've got on your mind."

Van gulped and moved toward the couch. He should have known better than to come here. He had been trying to get an advantage on property in Sitka, but if it meant explaining to Quinn his business ventures, it wouldn't be worth it in the end.

CHAPTER 12

+ + + + + + +

THE NORTHERN STAR ROUNDED THE CAPE that brought Sitka into view. It was an overcast day with the clouds hanging low over the harbor, but that didn't matter one whit to Zac. Anytime he saw Jenny, there was sunshine.

Zac and Skip stood in the wheelhouse of the big ship, watching carefully as Zubatov shouted out his orders to the men below. The man had been rather closed-mouthed after leaving Seattle, and that suited Zac just fine. Zac had said nothing about the attack next to the Wells Fargo office when he boarded the ship. Were they seeking to rob him, or were they just trying to prevent him from getting to Sitka? He decided the motive must have been robbery, since they didn't know him. They only knew he was carrying money.

Kathryn climbed up the stairs and strutted into the wheelhouse. She was wearing a striking green dress with a fur stole over her shoulders. The dainty hat she had on appeared to be mink. She flashed a smile at Zac and Skip. "There you are," she said. "I didn't know I'd find you two up here."

Zubatov stepped out onto the gangway. Cupping his hands to his mouth, he shouted to the men on the rigging, "Take in the main."

Zac slipped his arm around Skip. "We just came up for the education. Skip likes to see all of a ship and its workings that he can."

She smiled and folded her hands. "And have you been learning a lot?"

"Yes, ma'am." Skip stepped to the window and pointed up at the rigging. "Those are the main sails the sailors are taking down now. When we come into the harbor, the captain wants us to be going slower so we don't ram into nothing."

"And I think that's an excellent idea, don't you?" She stepped over to Skip, next to the window. "It's a fine thing that a little boy learn."

Zac didn't much care for the way the woman talked down to Skip. She had a voice that was all too sweet, like milk with sugar stirred into it. Skip was used to being in the company of adults and didn't need someone treating him like an infant.

Kathryn looked around in Zac's direction. "I think it's wonderful for a man to give his son more than his name. He should give him an education too."

Skip looked up from the window and caught her eye. "A name is what a man makes it," he said. "It's like a suit of clothes. It may look nice enough on the rack, but it's the man inside that makes it really special."

Zac could only smile. He watched as Kathryn's mouth fell open. She seemed stunned. "Yes, I suppose you're right. Where did you learn such a thing?"

Skip pointed over to Zac. "Zac says it all the time. I may have heard the words from him, but I learned the lesson all by myself."

"You are a very special boy," she said. "Your father must be quite proud. And I just hope you like Sitka. Today will be a wonderful day. It always is when a ship docks."

Skip looked at Zac and smiled. "Today's a special day anyway. It's my father's birthday."

Kathryn cast a smiling glance in Zac's direction, her blue eyes shining like the sea behind her. "It's your birthday? How very sweet. And do you have special plans?"

"We haven't made any yet, but I expect we'll be looking for my fiancée."

"Oh yes, that special lady of yours." There was a teasing smile on her face. Zac could see that the woman liked to toy with men, and it all started with her eyes and the hint of a smile she liked to show. "Well, women are very scarce in Sitka. I'm certain she's had quite a bit of attention since she's gotten here. I suppose you should look for her before you find her in the arms of another man."

"I'm not worried about Jenny," Zac said.

"Oh really? Why not?"

"Because we love and trust each other."

"And what is this type of love like?" she asked sarcastically, a smirk on her face.

"I really don't know how to explain love," Zac said. "I only know that I feel good when I'm close to her and that I can be close to her anytime I want."

"You can?"

"Yes. All I have to do is think about her. That's enough to make me feel close. You ever been in love?" Zac asked.

She dropped her eyes and looked out at the ocean. "I was once, but it didn't work out. Maybe we were too much alike."

"People often fall in love with someone who resembles themselves. I suppose they can imagine no greater beauty than their own."

Zac watched the smirking expression change on Kathryn's face. She didn't look sure about what to do with that remark. "Well, I hope you do find your lady, and I trust she's waiting for you. Where will you stay to-night?"

"I'm not sure. We'll look for Jenny and book ourselves into a hotel for the night."

"The hotels are miserable here, I'm afraid. You'd be welcome in my house, though."

Zac looked down at Skip and shook his head. "No, I'm afraid we couldn't do that." The last thing in the world he wanted to do was spend more time with Kathryn Jung. The woman was a piece of work just to stay ahead of, and he didn't trust her one little bit.

"What's wrong? You afraid that lady of yours would find you in an-other woman's house?"

"I'd just rather not, that's all."

"Well, suit yourself. It's a shame for a man to spend his birthday with-out the comfort of a nice place, though."

"We'll be all right, won't we, Skipper?"

"Yes, sir. We'll be fine anywhere we are."

It wasn't long before Zac and Skip had packed up their gear and were waiting on the bow of the ship as it nudged into the dock. Zac had his Sharps Creedmore in hand. It was wrapped in the buckskin case and bal-anced over his shoulder.

"What kinda rifle you got there?" Mac asked.

Zac dropped it in his hand and Mac untied the case. He slid it out and gave off a long whistle. "Land sakes, man, this ought to do the job. We got plenty 'round here you might just need this for." He slid it back in the case and handed it to Zac. "But what you figure to need a thing like that for in California?"

"Targets that are a long way off."

"Well, that would do it, all right. Might work on some of these Kodiak bear 'round here too."

"I'll remember that," Zac said.

Mac gripped the railing and leaned over to get a better look at the gathering crowd. "Thar's my fifth wife over yonder. She's probably out meetin' every boat that come north till she sees me."

Zac surveyed the crowd. A rather hefty Indian woman with long black hair and a deerskin dress was waving and jumping up and down.

"Is that her?" Zac pointed in the woman's direction.

"That's her, good old Dimple Cheeks. She's got an Injun name, but I forget it. Never figured out how to say it anyway. The woman ain't much to look at holdin' up against some of them stateside women, but she sure keeps a warm spot in the winter."

"Will you be going on to your trapping grounds after that?"

"I 'spect I will. It might take me some time to pardner up with a likely sort, though. I can get plenty tired pulling all the weight. A man's got to have a good pardner, and they is hard to come by."

"What happened to your last one?" Skip asked.

Mac scratched the back of his head, pushing his fur cap forward. "Come spring, we split up. We divided up the furs and went our own ways. Me, I went to San Francisco, and him," Mac shook his head, "ain't no tellin' where he went off to."

"I guess people don't settle down like you do," Zac smiled.

"No, I reckon not. Maybe that's why I got me some wives all over. I like to have the feelin' of being settled even if I ain't. If you and yer boy want to find me, though, you can always check the Crystal Palace."

"Is there a place you could recommend for Skip and I to stay?"

Mac curled up his lip, cocked his head, and half closed his eyes in deep concentration. "You'd be best off at the widder McCoy's place. She runs a boardin' house. The beds ain't ticky and the slop's hot and plenty." He pointed at the main street that ran away from the docks. "You just go on down there and ask for the widder's. Folks'll steer you fine."

"We'll just do that," Zac said.

+ + + + +

It took Zac and Skip the better part of an hour to get settled into the boarding house. The woman was the widow of a ship's captain who had been lost at sea. The house was plain but large. They had a room overlooking the main street. It wasn't what Zac wanted because he never liked to have to fight the noise of the night life, but it was all she had left. It did have one bed, and the woman prepared Skip a pallet in the corner. Her hair was pulled into a gray bun at the back of her head. She fluffed the feather pillows on the bed. "How long you two staying?" she asked.

"That's something we're not quite sure of," Zac said. "But you ought to hold our room for tomorrow night too."

She nodded her head and started to leave the room.

"One thing more," Zac said. "Do you know an Ian Hays?"

"Sure, everybody knows Ian, even the ones that don't want to. The man's got money to burn. He owns the lumber mill."

"Do you know where we might find him?"

"You just follow the road the other side of the harbor all the way up the hill. It's a ways, though. You're gonna have yourself quite a walk."

"How far is it?"

"I'd say it was better than five or six miles. He's got himself a big place on the cliff. It overlooks the harbor entrance."

"Thank you."

She turned to leave the room, then stopped. "They got themselves a big party there tonight. Hays' niece came up from Seattle, and I suppose he's anxious to show her off. I hear it's going to be quite the to-do."

"Can we go?" Skip asked. "Please?"

Zac looked down at him. "We're not invited, Skipper."

Mrs. McCoy laughed. "You might as well go. There's gonna be so much food and drink they'd never notice you anyway. Besides, lots of folks will be there."

It was after six when Zac and Skip started on the long walk. Normally, they wouldn't have gone on foot, but from what they had heard about the daylight hours, it wouldn't begin to be dusk until at least one or two in the morning. Zac figured that would give them plenty of time to walk back. They wouldn't be staying for long, just long enough to say hello to Jenny and meet her uncle.

They had to step aside on the road for a number of horses that were evidently carrying riders up to the party. Much to Zac's surprise, he heard Mac's familiar voice from a wagon as the thing pulled up behind them.

"Hey there!" Mac shouted. "You goin' to the party?"

Zac and Skip stepped to the side of the road. "Yes, we are. I guess my Jenny is the guest of honor."

"Sounds good. Ought to be plenty to eat there. From what I hear they been killin' the fatted calf all week." He jerked his thumb in his wife's direction. She sat snuggled up beside him, beaming. "Dimple Cheeks here is some kinda kin to the lady of the house. Old Ian went and married a princess. You two climb on up and ride with us."

Zac and Skip rode in the back of the wagon as it rumbled up the hill. They spent the better part of the time listening to Mac rattle on about Sitka and what the place was like in the winter. To hear Mac tell it, Sitka was the garden spot of Alaska. While it rained a good bit, it never got very cold. Mac pointed over to the mountains. " 'Course, it's a different world 'cross them things. A man could freeze himself to death in no time at all. I wouldn't advise you to go wanderin' off up there, not unless you have to."

"Don't worry," Zac said, "we'll stay put."

When they pulled up outside the Hays house, two Indian servants were there to take the wagon. Mac jumped out and picked Dimple Cheeks up by the waist, setting her on the ground. "Whew . . . eee," he said. "You put on some since the last time I picked you up."

The woman just smiled and giggled.

The four of them strutted through the two massive doors that led into the great room. Even though it was still daylight, Zac couldn't remember seeing more in the way of candles. The chandeliers overhead were a blaze of lantern light. Laid out on a long table were two sides of beef, each with a servant carving off huge chunks to put on pewter plates. Mutton and cheese were arranged on plates along with fruit. The fruit must have been very expensive since very little of it grew locally. In the corner, a small four-piece band was playing a jaunty melody. They were an odd-looking lot. While the dress was somewhat upscale, each of the outfits was different, and the man with the trombone was jacking his slide back and forth with a coonskin cap perched on his head.

"Looks like quite the party, don't it?" Mac said.

"Wow," Skip replied. "It sure does." He looked up at Zac. "I got really tired of the food on ship. This looks real good, though."

Zac smiled and swung his hand out in the direction of the table. "You go right ahead. I don't think our host will mind."

Skip grinned. "Thanks." With that, he dashed off to where they had the dishes stacked.

"I can't wait to find Jenny," Zac said excitedly. "She'll be awfully surprised to see Skip and me."

Mac had been tickling Dimple Cheeks under her chin and seemed for the moment to be totally preoccupied. "What?" he said. "Oh yeah, you better go lay hold of yer sweetie b'fore somebody else does."

Zac moved around the edge of the crowded room. He politely nodded at people, and they in turn nodded at him. Crowds were never his favorite thing, especially crowds of people that he didn't know. He felt a lot like a mule at the races, just a spectator who appeared to be the same species but wasn't.

As he looked out over the floor, he accidently bumped into someone. "Pardon me," he said. "I wasn't looking where I was going."

The girl was young, in her early twenties. She had brown eyes the color of deerskin and curly blond hair. "Silly me." She waved her hand at him as if batting a bar of soap into a tub full of water. "I slammed into plenty of people tonight. I like bumping into some though, like people I don't know." She smiled at him innocently. "Are you a single man or are you married?"

Zac flicked his mustache nervously with the back of his index finger. "I guess you could say I'm single." He started to finish his thought by talking about Jenny, but the young woman wouldn't let him. She clapped her hands vigorously. It surprised him. He never thought about a man's marital status as a cause for celebration one way or the other.

"Good, good, that's good." She leaned into him on her tip-toes, putting her face only inches away from his. "I think you're real handsome."

Zac was stunned, completely at a loss for words. He stammered momentarily before saying, "And you're very pretty too."

She smiled, again not letting him finish his thoughts. "Then let's us marry. I know most of the men here and they're not very nice."

"But I don't even know your name." He tried to keep a good distance between himself and the woman.

She giggled. "I know. That's terrible." She extended her hand. "I'm Dolly Hays. This is my daddy's party and my cousin Jenny's too, I suppose."

"I'm pleased to meet you, Dolly." Zac once again looked over the room. "Where might I find your father?" He smiled. "I'll need to speak to him, you know."

Dolly beamed with excitement. She pointed across the room to where a man with a gray beard and a head of long gray hair was standing. "There he is." Dolly grabbed his arm, tugging him in the direction of her father. "Let's go talk to him."

"Oh, but first I need to pay my respects to your cousin Jenny. Where might I find her?"

Dolly's eyes widened and she looked around the room. "She was here just a while ago." She turned back to Zac. "Why don't you wait right here and I'll go see if I can find her? I want her to meet you. My daddy puts great store in what she says. If she says you can marry me, then Daddy will too."

Zac didn't know what to do with that prospect. He'd have to get to Jenny first and discover what he could about this young lady. Then maybe she'd find a way to calmly drag him out of this dilemma. "Fine, then she's the one I'll need to speak to."

Dolly started to run away on her quest but then stopped. Swinging back around, she slammed her hand into her chest. "I didn't get your name."

"My name is Zac, Zac Cobb."

"Good, I like that."

The girl turned and once again hurried off through the crowd.

He moved around the crowd in the opposite direction that Dolly had taken. He'd have to set her straight the next time the two of them talked. Rounding the far side of the room, he spotted Jenny on the part of the big floor that had been cleared for dancing. She was in the arms of a handsome man who had a rather large grin on his face. The band had switched to a waltz, and the two of them were cutting a most romantic figure on the floor. Zac moved off to the side to watch.

The man held Jenny close in his arms, and they seemed to know the way the dance ought to go. Jenny was relaxed—that was plain to see. She hadn't been expecting to see him. Zac knew that. Still, looking at her in the arms of another man sent a charge through him, no matter how cool he appeared. The man swayed to the music and twirled Jenny. She gave off a big smile. In a way it made Zac proud. He was like the owner of a fine jewelry store looking at his most precious gem in the window. One thing bothered him though. This was a jewel he didn't own, at least not yet.

He shook his head to drive the thought away. It was wrong-headed and he knew it. Jenny was and always would be her own woman. He was the outsider here, not her. If there was anyone who should be stared at and talked about, it would be him, not her. For Zac, there was a world of pride in just knowing the woman and calling her friend. He still found it hard to believe that she'd said yes to the notion of marrying him.

Jenny danced and twirled around the dance floor, then she saw him. She stopped in the middle of the dance, stone still on the floor. Removing herself from the man's arms, she ran in his direction. "Zac! Zac! What are you doing here?"

She fell into his arms and kissed him. Zac thought her kisses were heavenly.

"I couldn't let you go off to Alaska all alone, now could I? I came in on the *Northern Star* today." Zac watched as the man she'd been dancing with stepped over in their direction. "Especially if you were going to find another handsome gentleman to squire you around."

"I take it you are Zac Cobb," Wass said, approaching him with outstretched hand.

Jenny hung on Zac's arm. "Yes," she said. "He came. I thought he might. I just didn't know it would be so soon. And on your birthday, no less. We have another reason to celebrate."

Zac shook the man's hand. "Yes, I'm Zac Cobb. I suppose I just couldn't let her out of my sight for very long."

"I can understand why. My name's Mike Wass, and I for one was hoping you'd spare her a little longer."

Zac laughed. "That was plain to see."

"Well, you have nothing to worry about with Jenny here. She's talked of nothing but you."

"And I've thought of no one but her," Zac said.

It was just at that moment that Dolly spotted the two of them. She came racing across the dance floor, a smile lighting up her face. "Jenny, Jenny, did you meet Zac Cobb?" She latched onto Zac's arm, almost pulling him away from Jenny. "He's the man I'm going to marry."

CHAPTER 13

✦ ✦ ✦ ✦ ✦ ✦ ✦

"I SEE YOU'VE MET MY COUSIN DOLLY," Jenny whispered in Zac's ear with an impish grin.

"Yes, we met just a few minutes ago."

"My, you are a fast worker, aren't you?"

Zac could see that Jenny wasn't about to pull him out of the quagmire he'd gotten himself in. She seemed to be perfectly satisfied with watching him twist in the wind.

Dolly hung on his other arm. She looked up at Zac and giggled. "Isn't he so handsome?" she asked. "I just couldn't believe it when I ran into him." She patted his hand. "And right here in my house."

"I'm afraid . . ." Zac started to say the words, but to his great relief, Jenny interrupted him.

"What Mr. Cobb is trying to say is that he's already spoken for."

"He is?" Dolly swung around to look him in the eye.

"Yes, I am. I didn't have the chance to tell you back there but," he looked at Jenny, "I am definitely spoken for."

"Darn! Of all the luck." Dolly braced the clenched fist of her free hand on her hip. "Who is she? I bet she's not as pretty as me."

Zac looked over Dolly's shoulder at Mike Wass. The man was obviously trying not to laugh, but it was hard. Far from being a total stranger at the party, Zac had evidently become the main attraction in this little group.

"You are a very pretty lady," Zac said. "The lady I'm going to marry, though, is special too."

"Who is she?"

Jenny slipped her arm around Zac's waist, pulling him closer. "Dolly, Zac probably didn't have the chance to tell you, but he's from California."

"You are?" Dolly's eyes lit up at the notion.

"Yes," Jenny said, "and you know I'm from California."

"Yes," Dolly nodded her head.

"And if you remember, I told you I was engaged to be married."

Dolly looked over at Jenny and continued to bob her head up and down in agreement, for the first time taking her eyes off Zac. "I remember. That's why I thought it was my time too."

"And it might be," Jenny said, pulling Zac closer, "just not to Zac. You see, he's the man *I'm* going to marry. I didn't know he was coming, and he surprised me tonight."

Dolly's eyes widened and her face fell. She looked like a puppy whose bone had been taken away.

"I'm sorry, I didn't have the chance to tell you," Zac said.

"But how about this," Jenny interrupted. "You can come to California and be in my wedding."

That idea seemed to brighten Dolly's face considerably. She gave off a huge grin. "California? Me, come to California?"

"Of course," Jenny said, "if your father will allow it."

Dolly began to bounce on the balls of her feet. "Yes," she squealed, her face smiling again.

"You'd like our place in California. It's a ranch with cows and horses, and it's close to a beach you can swim and fish in."

Dolly let go of Zac's arm and clasped her two hands to her cheeks. "That would be wonderful. Can I take my dolls?"

"Yes, you can take your dolls," Jenny said.

Dolly started clapping her hands. It was plain to see she'd forgotten all about the disappointment of not being a bride in waiting. The prospect of being in Jenny's wedding and in California with her dolls was almost too much to contain. "I better go ask my daddy. He'll want to know where I am, you know." With that, the girl rushed off into the crowd in the general direction of the last spot they'd seen Ian.

"You pulled my bacon out of the fire," Zac said.

"Dolly's a sweet girl," Jenny said. "It's just that despite her body being grown up, her mind is still a child's. But when you get to know her, you can't help but love her."

Zac watched as Dolly disappeared into the crowd. "I can see that. I like her already, even though she cost me a year of my life tonight."

It took Dolly only a few minutes to drag Ian in their direction. "Here," she said, "I brought Daddy. I told him about me going to California."

Jenny curtsied to the man. "I'm sorry to spring that on you, Uncle Ian. I can explain it later. I just didn't want Dolly to be too disappointed." Changing the subject, she turned in Zac's direction. "Uncle Ian, this is my fiancé, Zac Cobb. He came in on the *Northern Star* today."

Ian reached for Zac's hand and shook it. "Pleased to meet you. Jenny's told me a little bit about you. I'm surprised, though, you came all this way."

Zac glanced at Jenny. "When I read Jenny's note, I thought I'd just tag along. I brought my son, Skip, with me." Zac waved in the direction of the food-laden table. "He's over there trying to purge his belly of the food served on the ship."

"I can understand that," Ian laughed. "Knowing Zubatov, you probably made out well if you like red cabbage and borsch. Never could stomach beets myself."

"Me neither. That's why Skip's eyes nearly popped out when he saw what you were serving."

"Well, he's welcome to it, and I'm glad you came. We have lots of folks here tonight."

Jenny stepped back. "And this is Mike Wass."

Ian shook his hand. "I remember Mike. Good to see you. Surprised you'd come to a party, though. Trappers like you spend so much time to yourself, people must be an irritant, especially a group like this all at once."

"I'll get by." Mike looked down at Jenny. "Your niece insisted."

"Well, I'm glad she did." He turned to speak to Dolly. "You didn't see Van Fleetwood here tonight, did you, honey?"

She shook her head. "No, Daddy."

Ian put his arm around her. "Dolly here's my little hostess. If she ain't seen someone, they ain't here. She meets up and talks with everybody."

"She does love people," Jenny said.

"Where are you staying?" Ian asked Zac.

"We're at the Widow McCoy's place."

"I'll send Bubba Dean down to pick up your things. I wouldn't want you listening to the drunks. Lots of fishing boats come in during the night, and those boys are done with sleeping when they get into town."

"We'll be fine," Zac said.

"You'll be better here. I won't take no for an answer. You know, when this thing breaks up, I'll go into town with you myself. We'll just bring your kit back with us."

"All right, if you insist. I'll go when you're ready."

"Wonderful, it'll give us a chance to get acquainted. You don't mind if I take your man away from you, do you, Jenny?"

Jenny hung on Zac's arm. "Just don't take him away for too long."

Ian wiped his beard and glanced at Zac. "Got to tell you, Cobb, once these women get a hold of you, a man never shakes loose."

Zac watched as Mac made his way through the crowd toward them. Dimple Cheeks was at his arm, carrying a plate piled high with red meat, cheese, and pastry. She hung on to his shirt for a bit and then poked her finger into the cream-filled pastry puff and stuck the goo-laden finger into her mouth. Her eyes sparkled and she gave Zac a smile over Mac's shoulder.

"I see you found that pretty lady you keep talking about," he said.

Zac stepped aside. "Yes. Jenny, this here is James MacGregor and his wife."

Mac grinned and put his hands on his hips. "I'd say you got yerself a pretty fair lass there, Cobb. You better hang on to her b'fore some rascal like me comes along and snatches her away."

+ + + + +

It was several hours later when Ian found Zac. "Things are dying down a mite. Thought we might want to take that trip into town. When we get there, you can go with Bubba Dean to the widow's and I'll check on my friend. I figure he's got to be on death's door to miss out on a feed like this. Some things you get to know about people, and I know Van. He never misses something free, especially if it's edible."

They walked to the door and Zac picked up his rifle.

"I see you're totin' a long gun. That's good. Man never knows when he's going to need one 'round here. The bears feed on berries, but when there's the smell of food in the air, you can never tell."

Stepping out the door, they climbed up into the carriage that Bubba Dean had gotten ready. Ian slapped the backs of the horses with the traces, and the rig lurched toward the road.

"So what do you do for a living, Cobb?"

"I'm a rancher, horses and cattle." Zac had learned not to discuss his job with Wells Fargo. It was hard to explain it without labeling himself as a bounty hunter.

"That so? Is there money in it?"

"There is if you have enough land."

"And I take it you do." He slapped the backs of the horses once again, sending them into a faster trot.

"I do all right for myself."

"I'm glad to hear that. I wouldn't want my niece starving with no dirt farmer. I done me a share of that in the past and there ain't much to it but sweat."

"Miss Jenny's a real sweet lady," Bubba Dean said. The man was rocking back and forth in the backseat and swaying with the movement of the carriage. "You sure is a lucky man to have her."

Ian bobbed his head back in Bubba Dean's direction. "Both Bubba Dean and I are recently married ourselves. I suppose you've never had the fortune of riding with a couple of newlyweds. The sparkle of the thing hasn't rubbed off yet. You give it time, though, and every man starts to see the cracks."

Ian pulled the team up to a spot close to the Widow McCoy's boarding house half an hour later. He got out and tied a small weight to the lead rope on the wheel horse and dropped the thing to the ground. "There, that ought to hold you." Turning to Zac, he motioned in the direction of the darker end of the street. "You go on in and get your things. I'll be right back, and then the three of us can maybe get ourselves a drink over to the Crystal Palace."

"I can't stay out long," Zac said. "I'm a little wore out."

Ian started down the street. The idea that Van hadn't shown up all evening bothered him. It wasn't like Van to miss the party without telling him.

He turned the corner and stopped in front of Fleetwood's house. The house was dark, except for a light in the back bedroom. Four corner posts surrounded a porch that had seen better days, and several blocks of stone had been pieced together to form a semblance of steps.

Ian walked up the steps and, standing beside the door, leaned over and peeked in the window with the one shutter that was hanging. The front room was dark, but he could see a figure seated in an old chair, hunched over with a blanket wrapped around him. It looked like Van. Ian knocked on the door. "Van, you in there?" There was no answer.

Ian leaned back over to see if the man had bothered to get up from his chair. He hadn't. He was still seated in the same position. He knocked on the door again, this time harder. He called out as he knocked, "Van, it's me, Ian. Open the door!"

Twisting the brass knob, he opened the door and stepped inside. He heard the cock of a pistol. The figure in the chair had raised his hand in Ian's direction and along with it what Ian assumed was a pistol. Ian held out his hands. "Hey, pardner, don't shoot. It's me, Ian."

"What are you doing here?" It was Van's voice.

"You didn't come to the party. I was worried about you."

"I didn't feel well."

"What's wrong? You want me to go get the doctor?"

"No!" Van snapped. "No doctor."

Ian stepped closer. "What are you doing sitting here in the dark? If you're sick, you ought to be in bed."

"I don't want to be in bed. I just need to sit."

"With a gun in your hand? Why?"

The darkness was beginning to bother Ian. He reached into his pocket and pulled out a match. Holding it firm against his thumbnail, he popped it into a flame. "Let me get some light on in here. You're going to trip over something, or I will for sure."

"Put that out!" Van yelled.

Instinctively, Ian shook out the match, but not before he'd caught sight of the man's face. Van had been hurt. That was obvious. There were red blisters all over his face. Ian stepped closer. "What happened to you?"

"Nothing. Nothing happened to me."

"Don't give me that. I ain't no child. I can see something's wrong. I'm going to light a lamp in here. You've got to be tended to."

Reaching into his pocket, he pulled out another match, lit it, and leaned over and lifted the globe on the lamp. He held the flame to it and turned up the wick. The soft flickering light bathed the room in a soft glow. He picked up the lamp and stepped in Van's direction.

Fleetwood's face was pockmarked with red burns. They stood out like raspberries in a dish of goat's milk. Van held his hand up to try to hide the worst of them.

"What the blazes happened to you?"

"Nothing. It ain't important. You just go on back home and leave me be."

"Are those burns?" Ian stepped yet closer, bending over to get a better look at the ones Van couldn't quite conceal. "Who did this to you?"

Fleetwood was frozen. His eyes watered up, like a man haunted by the memory of great pain.

"Tell me," Ian raised his voice. "Who did this? Did Quinn or his boys do this?" Van winced at the sound of Quinn's name. "So it was Quinn?"

"You just never mind. It ain't important."

"It is to me. Nobody does something like this to a friend of mine."

Van shook his head. "It's too late to do anything now." He waved his hand at Ian like he was shooing away a pesky child from nagging at him. "There just ain't no point to it no more. You go on home and leave me be."

"Let me help you into bed." Ian reached down and put his hand under the man's elbow, trying to get him on his feet. "That's the least I can do."

Van pulled his arm free. "The one thing you can do is leave me alone. I just want to be alone here in the dark. I ain't no baby. I'm a man full grown and if I want to sit here in the dark, then you better just do as I say."

"All right." Ian set down the lamp on the table next to the man's chair. "I can't force you to get up, but at least let me get Doc Spence."

"I don't want no doctor. I just want to be left be, that's all."

Ian took a step back, puzzled. "I want to help, but if you won't let me . . ."

For the first time Van's face softened. "I'm sorry. I tried, but I just couldn't . . ."

"Couldn't what?" Ian asked.

"Couldn't stand up to them. I just couldn't take it." He waved his hand. "Now go. Just get out."

✦   ✦   ✦   ✦   ✦

Zac and Bubba Dean stood beside the carriage. Zac had loaded his and Skip's baggage into the backseat and had the Sharps still in his hand. They watched as Ian plodded in their direction.

"Is you all right?" Bubba Dean asked.

Ian turned around and looked back into the gathering darkness, back to where Van's house was located. "I don't know," he said. "That old man looks like he's been burned by something, but he ain't saying."

"Burned by what?" Bubba Dean asked.

"Looked like a cigar or a hot poker to me."

Bubba Dean let out a long whistle. "Dat is bad."

"It's bad all right, but you know him. He's as grumpy as a bear prodded out of a winter's sleep. He ain't saying what and he ain't saying who. I reckon I can guess, though."

Ian noticed Zac's look of interest. "We have us some problems with some of the folks round here. You were with a couple of them on the *Northern Star*. The rest are over at the Crystal Palace, the local tavern." He raised himself up, straightening his shoulders. "You still up for that drink?"

"I take buttermilk," Zac said, "but I'll watch you."

"Buttermilk? Your momma put you onto that?"

Zac smiled. "As a matter of fact, she did."

Ian put his hand on Zac's shoulder. "Well, then, let's go find you some buttermilk and me and Bubba Dean here some brandy."

"Sounds fine to me," Zac replied.

They walked in the direction of the music and laughter. Behind the painted glass of the Crystal Palace they could see a blaze of brightly burning lights. They crossed the muddy street, the gooey wet dirt of the day forming cakes on the bottom of their boots. Ian pushed open the batwing door and stepped inside. Walking up to the iron dog, he raked the mud off the bottom of his boots. Bubba Dean did the same and then Zac repeated the process, leaving a pile of Sitka's streets at the foot of the metal beagle. Ian found a seat at one of the more prominent tables and waved Bubba Dean and Zac toward him. They pushed back their chairs and took a seat. Zac laid his Sharps rifle on the table. The smoke from the room filled the place, and Zac took out his pipe. He figured if they had to smell the stuff, he might as well mix it with something pleasant to the nose.

Ian waved at the man behind the bar, but the only response he got was the man's quick retreat into the back room. "I can't understand that," Ian said. "They normally want to serve you drinks here. Hank's usually quick to pour."

It was no more than a minute later when three men stepped out of the back room, followed sheepishly by the bartender. One man was large, and the other two looked like desperate types: one had a flowing red beard with a red scar cutting through his right eyebrow, and the other was lanky with a half-buttoned denim shirt. The three men made a straight line for their table.

"I didn't think I'd see you tonight," the big man said.

"I'm just showing a guest where he shouldn't eat, Quinn, that's all. He would like some buttermilk, though, if you've got that."

"Buttermilk?"

"Yes, and Bubba Dean and me are gonna have some brandy."

"What did you do, go out and hire yourself a gun from the States?"

"Why would I need to do a thing like that? No, Zac here is my niece's fiancé. He's a rancher in California."

The big man circled around to where Zac was seated. "You're new here, so I might as well tell you. You're keeping bad and dangerous company."

Zac was silent. He watched the man with the red beard move to where Ian was seated. As Ian started to get up, the man put both hands on him, slamming him back into his chair.

"You see," Quinn said, "Sitka ain't a safe spot for a man who tries to own the town but just can't hold on to what he's got or what he knows."

"What are you talking about?" Ian asked.

"I'm talking about you, you and your highhandedness. Did you go see Fleetwood?"

The sound of his friend's name made Ian's eyes burn. He started to get up once again, but the man with the red beard pressed him down into his chair.

Zac glared across the table. "Why don't you just step back and take your hands off Mr. Hays, there."

Quinn laughed, followed by the other two.

"And what are you going to do if I don't," the man said, "rope me and brand me?"

"I wouldn't want to do that," Zac said. "Then I'd have to feed you."

Zac's words froze the man, but Quinn and the lanky man beside him continued to laugh. "Looks like we got us a tough cow farmer here," Quinn said. "You better be careful. He might try to milk you."

The man with his hands on Ian kept staring in Zac's direction. It was a hard look, one with a dare attached to it. "You gonna try to milk me, mister cow farmer?"

"No," Zac said, "I'd just treat you like any other varmint that wanders onto my property."

"You do seem full of sand," Quinn said.

Zac's look didn't change. He'd locked his eyes onto the man with the red beard and he wasn't taking them off. "I just don't like for folks to be pestered. Now, step back and take your hands off him."

The man dropped his right hand off Ian's shoulder and onto his gunbelt. Zac sprang at once. In one sudden movement, he scooped up the rifle and rammed it butt-first over Ian's shoulder and into the man's forehead. It sounded with a crack and dropped the man to the floor, bellowing in pain. Zac spun the rifle over, end over end. Pointing it at Quinn, he cocked the hammer back. The man had dropped his hand to his sidearm. "I wouldn't," Zac said. "The Sharps here only carries one round, but if I squeeze it off, you'll end up with your head next to that spittoon over there."

CHAPTER 14

+ + + + + + +

THE WALK ACROSS THE GLACIER was torture for most men. The two trappers stood on the edge of the trees and looked over the white and blue ice field. It had white powder over the top of it like sugar that had been sifted over a plate of cookies. There were deep cracks and peaks—small, deadly valleys of ice. The crevasses were especially dangerous with freshly fallen snow over them; a man might not see them until it was too late. It was the color of the blue in the ice, though, that attracted their attention. There was nothing like the ice blue color of the glacier.

The men leaned on their walking sticks. They'd carved them that morning just for their walk across the glacier. They could prod the ice in any suspicious area and test if it would hold them up or not. The whiteness of the ice field fooled the eye. What looked like a short jaunt would take them the better part of three hours, and it might take them all day to circle the thing. They hefted their backpacks and started across.

Sam Brewster had been in Alaska for seven years. He was no tenderfoot. His brown beard covered his face, and with his husky build he took on the appearance of a bear. Sam's brown eyes sparkled. He lowered the eye protector he'd fashioned out of rawhide over his eyes. It would cut down on the glare.

Frederick Schmidt had been in the north country for almost ten years. Unlike Sam, he was a wiry man, all sinew and bone. He didn't weigh much, but all that he had was solid muscle, tested by the Alaska winters. His blond hair came down past his shoulders, and he stood almost a head taller than Brewster.

The men had been partnered up for almost three years. That was about two years longer than most men would stay together, but each of them were eager to maintain the partnership. It was hard enough to find a man you could trust without having to look for another one come spring.

They tried to keep to the top of the ridge. To get bogged down in some of the shadowy areas could be trouble. The white snow was deceptive there. It might just be a dusting that covered up a crack, a bridge that would look solid but give way under a man's foot. Out here, no man could afford to break a leg, let alone his neck. They walked in single file, Sam going first.

The sound of a shift in the ice brought both men to a halt. It was a cracking sound, like the noise of a huge tree falling in a dense forest, followed by the noise of the ice rubbing against itself, grating like the popping of a string of firecrackers. The glacier had a way of moving when a man least expected it. One minute you might have a route picked out, and the next it would be gone.

Sam signaled and both men started to walk again. The sun was out and the glare on the ice was intense. They moved ahead, slowly and deliberately.

They hadn't been on the glacier for more than half an hour when Sam stopped stone still, then bent over and peered into one of the cracks in the glacier.

"What's wrong?" Schmidt shouted.

Sam continued to stare down into a crack in the ice. "There's somebody down here."

"In the ice?"

"Not yet, but he soon will be." The slow moving river of ice was dangerous. It swallowed up everything in its path, and if a person found himself caught up in the thing, he became a part of it in a short period of time. Sam bent over and, taking off his pack, pointed to the bottom of a crack. Schmidt shuffled ahead, his snowshoes dragging across the powder. He reached Sam's side and peered inside.

A man lay face down at the bottom of the crack. He didn't move a muscle. He was wearing a buckskin jacket and no hat. His gray hair was matted and his arms stretched out.

"Is he alive?" Schmidt asked.

"No way to tell. But we better go down and get him." Sam stood up and looked over the glacier. "We leave him down there and this ice is gonna close up on him." He reached into his pack and took out a length of rope. Tying one end around his waist, he handed the other end to Schmidt. "I'll go down and tie my end around him. You drag him up and then drop the rope back down to me."

Schmidt nodded his head and took up the slack on the rope.

There was another loud crack in the ice field; Sam's face turned almost white. "Let's get this thing done. I sure don't want to be down there if this thing decides to close up and move on."

With that, he backed up to the crack and, bracing himself against the bare ice, started down. With Schmidt grunting and digging his heels in, Sam worked his way to the bottom where the man lay. He stamped his feet, making sure he was on somewhat solid ice. Unhitching the rope from around his waist, he bent down to feel the man's neck for a pulse. He stood back up and shouted, "He's dead and gone."

"What do you want to do?" Schmidt shouted back.

Sam turned the man over and stared into his face. "You ain't gonna believe this," he shouted. "It's Fleetwood."

"Fleetwood? Van Fleetwood?"

"He's got some burns on his face, but it's him all right."

"We better drag him out then and haul him back to Sitka. We can't leave him out here."

"No," Sam shook his head, "we can't."

Sam stooped down and wrapped his arms under the corpse. He held the man up and wound several turns of the rope around him and grabbed onto the rope. "I'll climb up on the rope and we can both pull him up together. He ain't gonna be the worse for wear."

"Reckon not."

Latching onto the rope, Sam pulled himself up the crack hand over hand. He kicked his mukluks into the ice as he climbed, sending showers of snow and ice cascading back into the crack. When he reached the top, he and Schmidt began to slowly drag up Fleetwood's body. The man was light and wiry, so it wasn't as hard as it might have been with another man. In a short time, they pulled him free from the crack.

Sam circled around the body and then looked off to the trees on the edge of the glacier. "We'll just leave him tied on and drag him over to the woods," Sam said. "From there we can cut some branches and rig up a litter."

"What's he doing out here?" Schmidt wondered. "A man like him don't go wandering off, and he ain't exactly dressed for it neither."

Sam looked down at the man. "No, he ain't. Hard to figure folks' heads, though. He mighta just gone for a walk and went too far." Stooping down, Sam checked the body. "Ain't no gunshot wounds. I'd say the fall killed him."

"Either that or somebody hit him over the head."

"Why would a man want to kill old Fleetwood here? He ain't never been a bad sort." Sam patted down and rummaged around in the man's pockets. He pulled out a roll of bills and held it up for Schmidt to see. "He's got money on him. I'd say he wandered off. Ain't nobody robbed him."

"Don't make sense. Fleetwood here's a townie. He wouldn't walk this far without a gun to his head."

Sam shrugged his shoulders. "I guess that's for other folks to figure out. We better get him back into town so we can get on about our business."

They tied the rope around Fleetwood's arms and shoulders and each of them took an end of it and started the pull back to the tree line. It took them almost an hour to cover the distance they'd traveled earlier in just a few minutes.

It was almost ten o'clock at night when they brought Fleetwood back into town on the litter they'd made.

"Doc Spence." Sam pounded on the door of the doctor's house. "Open up."

They could hear the doctor shuffle to the front door. The parlor in the front of his house served as a makeshift hospital and examining room, and the aroma of alcohol drifted out when the man swung the door open. "What ya got there?"

"It's Fleetwood," Sam said. "He's dead."

"What did ya bring him here for, then? Old man Barns takes care of the buryin' around here."

Sam looked down at the corpse on the litter and then back up at the doctor. "You is the coroner, ain't you? We found him out on the glacier. He didn't have no business there, and we both figured it for something strange. Thought you might want to take a look see."

"All right." The doctor waved them in. "Bring him in and put him up on my table. I'll take a look."

Jack Spence was an old timer, and if he hadn't liked to hunt in his younger days, he never would have come to Alaska. His walls were covered with trophies, and the eyes of deer, bear, sheep, and wolves stared down at the men as they dragged Fleetwood's body into the room and lifted him onto the table. The doctor dropped the small, round glasses he'd been carrying on top of his bald head into position on the bridge of his nose and rolled up his sleeves. "Take off his jacket and let's have us a look."

+ + + + +

Ian and Zac got back to town quickly after they got the message about Van's death. Ian had driven the team hard, sending it on two wheels around the curves on the road a number of times. Zac thought it odd that Ian was in such a hurry. After all, the man wasn't going anywhere, not anymore. Anything worth seeing would be worth seeing just a few minutes later. Still, he hung on for the ride.

Ian opened the door to Doc Spence's house without knocking. The doctor was in the process of examining a baby in the den next to the parlor, but the first thing both Zac and Ian saw was the shape of the body under a sheet on the examining table. Spence heard the men come in and looked up at them from the other room. "Hold your horses, Hays. I'll be with you in a minute."

Ian paced back and forth across the wooden floor, occasionally glancing at the body. Fleetwood's boots were staring at him from under the sheet. Zac could see that every time Ian laid eyes on them, the anger rose in the old man's face. Under that gray beard, Ian Hays had a rather fair complexion. The gray could barely conceal the flush of anger on his face.

Spence pushed the sliding door open wider and stepped out in front of the mother and her baby. He was wiping his stethoscope off with a handkerchief. "You just mix that powder I gave you with some milk for the child the next few days. Give it to her every four hours, then come back and see me the end of the week."

The Tlingit woman and her baby were wrapped in deerskin. She bobbed her head, nodding and smiling.

"She'll be all right. You just do as I say."

Spence watched the woman leave and then turned around to look at Ian. He pushed his glasses on top of his bald head and stroked his clean-shaven chin. His soiled white shirt was halfway pulled out of his brown corduroy trousers, and his well-worn shoes had splits in the bottoms of his leather soles.

"Now, let's see what we can do here." He jerked his thumb back in the direction of the door. "I brought that child into the world two weeks ago and I'm around to see old Fleetwood go." He stepped over to the covered body. "I s'pose that's the way it is with doctoring," he pulled back the sheet, "they come and they go."

Ian and Zac stepped over to view the body closely.

Spence eyed Zac. "Who's this fella?" he asked Ian.

"Oh, that's my niece's fiancé from California." He spoke to the doctor even though he was preoccupied with looking Fleetwood over carefully. "He's come up to take her back for their wedding."

Spence put his hands on the small of his back and leaned away from the two men. He appeared to be working the kinks out of a very long day. After a couple of loud cracks, he leaned back over and motioned toward the body. "Couple of trappers found him up on the glacier. They pulled him out before the thing closed up on him. I figured you'd want to know about it first thing, seeing as how the two of you were so close."

"I appreciate that. How'd he die?"

The doctor circled the body. "Got his head stove in." Reaching down, the doctor turned Fleetwood's head slightly. "See here, blow to the back of the head. He must have fallen on the ice."

"How was the body found?" Zac asked.

Spence crossed his arms and lifted his chin. "Men that found him said he was face down in a crack in the ice."

"Strange," Zac said, "You'd have thought his face would have been damaged by the fall."

"That seemed a mite odd to me too."

"And what about these burns on his face?" Zac asked.

"That's what they are, all right." Spence turned Fleetwood's face back up. "Mighty unusual place for a man to burn himself. There must be a dozen boils over his face. Appears to me it was deliberate. Man don't get that from a grease fire on the stove. They're pretty fresh too. I'm surprised he never came to me. They must have smarted him some."

"Did they find any personal effects on him?" Ian asked.

Spence pointed a finger in the air. "Yes, they did." He stepped over to a side table and slid open a drawer. Taking out an old cigar box, he flipped open the lid. Stirring the contents with his finger, he began to call out the items. "Here's a rabbit's foot for good luck." Reaching down, he pulled out a wad of bills. The currency was bound in a silver money clip with a twenty-dollar gold piece embedded in it. "And here's his money. I counted it. There's three hundred and forty-eight dollars there." He handed the box to Ian. "Now what's a man doing wandering around a glacier with nothing to do but die?"

"Whoever took him out there didn't do it to rob him," Zac said.

"I'd say not," Spence agreed, "or they didn't look too close."

"Did you find anything else?" Ian asked.

"Like what?"

Zac watched Ian as the man worked on a thought, obviously uncomfortable. "Uh, Van had something else he liked to carry for luck, but I don't see it."

"And what would that be?" Spence asked.

"A large gold nugget he got from someplace, probably California."

Spence shook his head. "No, he didn't have nothing on him like that. I'd say for a man who carried a rabbit's foot and this lucky nugget you mentioned, his luck wasn't too good. Remind me not to carry things like that."

"How are you going to list the death?" Zac asked.

"If I were to hazard a guess, I'd say it's a homicide. The man wasn't robbed, even though for a skinflint that was a large sum of money he was carrying around. Maybe that's why they didn't bother to look. You know Fleetwood here. If he ever had any money on him, he might have to buy the drinks. Might have been somebody who knew that. Anybody who knew Fleetwood here would never check him over for money. Only a stranger to the man would do that."

"And he wouldn't go just wandering off on that glacier and fall," Ian added.

"No," Spence said, "I reckon not. Whoever it was that left him there figured the thing would just close up on him. If them two trappers hadn't come along, we never would have found the body."

"I s'pose not," Ian said.

The doctor flipped the sheet back over Fleetwood. "I'll talk to Barns about preparing the body and setting up a funeral."

Ian reached into the cigar box and pulled out the wad of bills. He took them out of the money clip and handed the money over to Spence. "You better take this. Take out what your fee is and pass the rest on to Barns. Tell him I'm good for whatever else is needed until we can settle up Van's affairs."

"All right, I'll do that." He nodded his head, his glasses on the top of his head falling back into position. "I'm sorry about Fleetwood here. I know how much he meant to you."

"I am too."

"You all right with this?"

"What do you mean?"

Spence stepped over to the door and opened it. "I mean you ain't about to go off half-cocked and do something foolish, are you? You're no gunman, and I don't want Fleetwood here just cooling down my table for you. You don't even know who did this."

"I got a pretty good idea," Ian said. There was a hardness to the man's voice that Zac didn't like.

"Well, you just leave well enough alone until I can talk to the magistrate. He ought to be back in town next week, and we'll get to the bottom of this then."

Zac followed Ian as the man silently walked out of the doctor's office. Spence just stood at the door and watched. "You mind my words, Hays. Leave this be until we can bring the law into it."

CHAPTER 15

+ + + + + + +

THE DINNER AT THE HAYS HOUSE was a quiet one, partly because they'd spent the morning at Fleetwood's funeral. Ian sat slumped at the table, brooding. Zac watched the man. Some men had a way of going off with a head full of fire when they had an empty heart, and Ian had tried to do that the night he'd seen Fleetwood's body. Zac knew if he hadn't stopped him, they'd have been burying Ian this morning along with his friend.

Umqua swung into the great room with a plate full of cornbread muffins and butter. It was a favorite of Ian's, and it was obvious that Umqua wanted to do what she could to break the cloud of despair that hung over the man. She was dressed in the red dress with the full skirt that she'd worn at the funeral. It seemed totally out of place to the whites in Sitka to see a woman in red at a funeral, but for her culture, it was just the thing to put on for a burying.

Umqua set out the plates. "I have some stew in the kitchen," she said, waggling her finger at her husband. "Bubba Dean, you help me bring it out. I want to see it gets served hot, and I ain't going to have you standing around."

As Umqua turned around, the ruffles on her dress made a noise like the wadding of paper. She marched through the double doors to the kitchen.

Bubba Dean took his cue immediately and followed Umqua into the kitchen. He dropped his chin and shuffled forward.

The sound of Dolly laughing at Skip at the end of the table caught their attention. Dolly and Skip had become fast friends, in spite of their age difference. Dolly had someone to play with, and it was an opportunity she wasn't about to pass up. She looked across the table at Skip. "You wanna go outside and play hide and seek for a while?"

"Sure, I guess." Skip looked at Zac for approval. They still hadn't eaten supper, but they had crammed several strips of smoked salmon

131

into their mouths while waiting for the stew.

"Go ahead," Zac said. "You can eat later."

Dolly didn't bother to look for Ian's approval. The man was far too lost in his own thoughts to even notice her. She slid out of her seat, grinning all the while at Skip. "Let's go then. You can be it and try to find me."

Zac turned to Jenny. He spoke quietly in a husky whisper. "I guess the decision making doesn't change when it comes to men and women, no matter what the age."

"You have your own mind, Zac, and I have mine," she said. "And when I fell in love with you, I fell in love with your mind too."

Dolly looked over at the two hounds seated in their usual spot under the table. The dogs always seemed to be lurking there when the smell of food was in the air. "Hobo and Sissy, you come with us," she said. She grinned at Skip. "The dogs can hide too."

The Afghans slowly got to their feet and reluctantly followed Dolly and Skip to the door, unconvinced about parting with the smell of the dinner table. The dogs turned back for one last look before Dolly latched on to their collars and then steered them out the door.

Zac looked at the kitchen door. "Umqua's going to be surprised when there's no one left to eat her stew."

"I suppose cold stew is the price of play," Jenny said.

Zac was right; when Umqua came back out the door with two bowls of stew in her hands, she frowned. "Where did the children go?"

"They're playing," Jenny replied.

"Fine, just fine." She stomped toward the table. "I spend my time making this and they can't eat it hot." She slapped the two bowls down at the empty places and, turning around, went back into the kitchen for another. When Umqua brought in the last of the bowls for Ian, they started to eat.

The meal was a quiet one, with Ian only stirring the contents of his bowl and drinking an occasional sip of hot coffee.

"Eat your food," Umqua said.

"I ain't very hungry," he replied.

She shook her head and mumbled under her breath, "I don't like to fix meals for folks that don't eat them."

Ian ignored the woman, looking up at Zac as Umqua turned and raced back into the kitchen. "You should have let me go into the Palace the other night."

"And do what?"

Ian sipped his coffee. "I just wanted to see Quinn's face. That would have told me all I needed to know."

"And then what would you have done?" Zac asked.

Ian shook his head. "I don't rightly know. Somebody's got to do something, though."

"It's been my experience that when a man carries a gun, he has to be prepared to use it. I'm not sure you wanted to go up against those odds, not then and not there."

"You're probably right." Ian looked at Jenny. "You got yourself a smart man here, girl. You best hang onto him."

"I plan to," Jenny said, reaching over and patting Zac's arm.

Ian brushed the coffee off his beard. "How'd you like a trip through the country, Cobb?"

"What you got in mind?"

"I need to go up the river a ways and find a trapper I know, a Bob Lilly. I know where he is and I need to have myself a talk with him. I already told Risa I was going, so she knows not to expect me for a few days. We're gonna come on to some bear country, though, so you'll need that cannon of yours."

"Can we take Skip with us? He might like to see that."

Zac could see the man was turning the idea over in his head. There wasn't instant agreement, but finally he nodded. "Sure, I don't see why not."

"All right, then, count me in." He looked over at Jenny. "I suppose Jenny can be without us for a few days."

"Just don't make it long," she said. "I've been without you enough already."

"All right, then, we'll leave tomorrow morning," Ian added. He got to his feet and straightened his vest. "I'm going down to the basement, and I don't want to be disturbed for a while."

They watched as he turned around and made his way to the lower bedrooms. Jenny had told Zac that Ian often disappeared there, sometimes for hours on end. It was a retreat of sorts for the man, a place where he could get away with his thoughts, and it was plain to see that he had plenty to think about.

✦ ✦ ✦ ✦ ✦

Risa and Naomi had been walking for hours, and while the Tlingit village wasn't a long ways off, it was more than Naomi had expected. "When will we get there?" she asked.

Risa moved ahead of her and ducked under some low-hanging fir branches, holding them back for Naomi to pass under. "It won't be long now. If you listen close, you can hear the river."

Naomi's face brightened. She cocked her head. "Yes, I can hear it."

"My village is about a mile upstream on the other side. The people will be fishing now. The salmon are many. There will be plenty to eat for dinner."

Naomi stooped over and plodded under the branches of the tree. "Your people eat a lot of salmon, don't they?"

"Yes, and we smoke enough for much of the winter too. Our dogs eat it too. In fact, it's most of what we feed them."

Naomi chuckled slightly and shook her head. "That's funny. I never thought of fish as dog food. Cats like it, but I didn't think dogs did."

Risa caught up with her. "Up here, people and animals eat whatever they can find."

They broke out into a clearing beside the river and started walking down the slope. The water sparkled in the sun, bright rays bouncing off the smooth stones and glistening river. When they got to the bottom, their ears suddenly perked up at the sound of grunts and growls. In front of them, beside the river, two bear cubs were rolling in the grass. The cubs somersaulted over each other in a wrestling match, each lost in a world of play. They looked up the stream, and there in the middle was a large bear. It was standing in the water and swatting at passing fish.

Risa grabbed Naomi's coat sleeve and twisted her fingers into it. "We're in trouble now."

"We are? Why?"

Risa nodded in the direction of the large bear. It had turned around in the stream and was now eyeing them.

"Why would we have trouble?" Naomi asked. "The bear's catching fish."

Risa pulled Naomi back. She pointed to the cubs. "She is the mother and these are her cubs. We're much too close to them."

Naomi took another step back and watched the large bear open its mouth. A roar that seemed to shatter the sky came from the bear's outstretched jaws. It stepped closer in the river and paused slightly while it sent out another bone-chilling bellow.

Both Risa and Naomi took another slow step back. Naomi's heart began to pound.

"We better move back slow," Risa said. "If she charges us, we're in big trouble, but if we can make it back to the trees and out of sight, maybe she'll just tend to her babies and leave us alone."

Naomi gulped. "Let's hope so."

"Just move back with me, one step at a time."

The bear in the river took several steps forward, the fast water rushing through its paws. Naomi saw a large fish splash in the water, practically in front of the beast. It didn't draw the slightest attention from the bear, however; its beady eyes were trained on the two young women.

They took one more step back. Their movement sent the bear into a rage. It roared and ran across the stream in a rambling dash for the shore.

"Let's go," Risa screamed, pulling on Naomi's sleeve.

"Where?"

Risa began to run and Naomi followed. They could hear the bear as it cleared the river, heavy breathing punctuated by low moans.

They ran up the slope that led to the trees, running for their lives. Suddenly, Naomi tripped over a small rock. It sent her sprawling to the ground. "Help!" she screamed.

Risa stopped and turned. She stepped back and took hold of Naomi's arm, hauling her to her feet. The bear was closer now; they could see the fury in its eyes and a snarl on its lips.

"The tree!" Risa yelled. "We've got to climb it!"

They ran to the base of the fir and watched as the bear cleared the top of the ridge. It was almost on them now. Reaching up under Naomi, Risa shoved her up to the lowest branch. "Climb, climb now!" she screamed.

Naomi reached for the next branch and swung her foot up. She pulled with her arms and dragged herself up. Looking down, she could see Risa climbing. The woman's face was twisted with terror.

"Go on," she yelled. "Keep climbing."

Both women started up the tree, one limb at a time. They were only ten feet high when the bear stopped at the base of the tree and stood up. It shot a glancing blow at Risa, raking her shoe off and sending it to the ground.

Naomi climbed higher and Risa scrambled up behind her. The tree was not one of the largest ones, and soon the bear was shaking it, roaring out in fury.

Risa climbed to Naomi. "Keep going. We can't stay so low."

Naomi looked up. The branches were getting thinner and more sparse. "We can't go up too high," she said.

"We better," Risa shot back. "Bears can climb."

The very idea of being pursued up the tree caught Naomi off guard. She had never imagined such a thing. Reaching up, she grabbed hold of the next branch and, letting go of the trunk, pulled herself up.

The bear gave the tree another shake. Naomi felt her grip loosen. "Help me!" she screamed. "I'm going to fall."

Risa extended her hand and caught hold of Naomi's wrist. "You're not going to fall, not as long as I'm here. Now hold on and climb."

The women began the careful climb into the higher branches as the tree continued to shake. Soon they were in the branches near the top of the fir. They could see that the limbs above them couldn't possibly hold their weight, and they clutched at what they could find, their eyes fixed on the beast below them.

The bear clawed and scratched at the tree, tearing off a few of the smaller branches. Roaring loudly, it scrambled up the lower limbs, breaking several of them off in its furious climb. Inching closer, it swatted at the two women.

Naomi lifted her feet. The bear was getting much closer than she ever imagined possible. She could see the hatred in its eyes, a burning that seemed to radiate like two red-hot pokers. She could almost feel the heat of its breath as it snarled and roared.

Suddenly, a shot rang out, followed by two more. The bear looked down and then dropped to the ground with a thud. It got up and started to run back toward the river.

Risa pointed out of the branches. "Look over there," she yelled. "It's three men, men from my village."

Naomi looked out over the branches. She could see three men standing on the other side of the river. They had their rifles lifted and were firing shots into the air. The women watched as the mother bear rejoined her cubs. The three of them went scampering up the river and away from the men with guns.

Risa touched Naomi on the cheek. "I think we're safe now. We can get down."

It took them several minutes before they could recover enough to climb down, but soon they were both standing at the base of the tree, holding on and shaking.

The three Indian men in buckskin pants and brightly colored shirts were climbing the hill to where they stood. The man in the lead was tall with long black hair, sharp features, and a peaked nose. He smiled at Risa. "You make yourself bear meat today," he said.

"That wasn't our plan," she said. She turned back to Naomi. "Naomi, this is an old friend of mine. He goes by the name of Puka. He's a foreman at your uncle's mill."

"Your *husband's* mill," Puka added, glancing pointedly at Risa.

"Yes." Risa bowed her head slightly. "My husband's mill."

CHAPTER 16

✦ ✦ ✦ ✦ ✦ ✦ ✦

THE TLINGIT VILLAGE LAY NESTLED alongside the river, rows of dark wooden longhouses with smoke curling up from makeshift chimneys. Large totems stood in formation, each telling a story—serpents, eagles, bears, wolves, and men, standing on one another's heads, frowning and sticking their tongues out. Along a path cut through the middle of the village, children were running with a pack of oversized dogs. A number of women were gathered by the river washing clothes. They looked up to watch Risa and Naomi as the group wound its way down the hill. The sight of the young white woman almost froze them.

The most striking thing in Naomi's mind were the lines of salmon drying in the sun. The racks were laced together with rawhide, and threaded between them were row after row of the bloodred fish. Spread out underneath the racks was an enormous bed of hot coals. Several of the Indian women chopped away at large pieces of green wood, forming a pile at their feet. Two young children scooped up the chips of wood and, dancing alongside the bed of coals, scattered them into the glowing embers. This kept a steady column of smoke rising through the rows of salmon without any hot flame to burn the fish. Smelling of salty fish, the smoke snaked its way through the village.

"Does this happen all the time?" Naomi was curious about the way the women lived among Risa's people. There seemed to be no leisure, not the least bit of idleness to distract them from the work at hand.

"When the salmon are running, everybody works."

Naomi caught sight of the tall man. Puka seemed to be amused at the question. Naomi already felt more than a little foolish at how she'd behaved with the bear. Sixteen years old was an awkward age. She felt clumsy, old enough to be a wife and mother among the Indians, but still a child among the white population. She wondered how the people in the village would see her.

It hadn't taken her long to notice that something was wrong between Puka and Risa. He had saved their lives, after all, yet for some reason Risa hadn't been too overjoyed to see him.

Naomi had watched the way that Puka looked at Risa. There was something more there and she knew it.

The two young men who had been with Puka had run on ahead of them, and they came out of one of the lodges followed by an older, stoop-shouldered Indian. His gray hair fell down below his shoulders, and his face was brown and wrinkled like a raisin. He wore a white shirt with smears of brown grease down the front and buckskin pants with fringe.

"That is my father, Yakta," Risa said. "His father, my grandfather, led the fight against the Russians."

Naomi watched as a tall, lanky man stooped down and cleared the low door of the longhouse. The man was wearing a black robe that fell to his ankles and black boots. His hair was a sandy blond, and his light blue eyes seemed to shine with fire. He wore a silver cross around his neck with a bright red stone in the center.

"Who is that?" asked Naomi.

"Missionary." Risa almost spat out the word. "Some of these come for good. I think this one loves only power, though. He is LeBarge, Francois LeBarge. Stay clear of him."

Naomi noticed that LeBarge was watching her. He lifted his pointed chin into the air slightly and spoke a few words to Yakta, words that they could not hear. The old man nodded, taking them in.

Risa broke into a slight run in the direction of her father. She threw her arms around him. "I am so glad to see you, Father. Are you well?"

Yakta nodded his head and smiled. "Yes, daughter, I am well. I hear you danced with the bears today."

"Yes I did, Father, a mother and her cubs. We didn't see them until it was too late." She cast a glance in Puka's direction. "It was good some of the men of the village were close by. The bear was climbing up after us."

Looking back to Naomi, Risa motioned her forward. "Father, I want you to meet Naomi. She is my husband's niece."

Naomi extended her hand to the man and smiled. "I'm so very pleased to meet you. Risa speaks of you often."

Yakta took her hand and, chuckling, looked at Risa. "Yes, our Little Flower is still a child of her people. You will stay for food with us."

"We cannot stay for long today, Father. My husband leaves for the upcountry tomorrow. I must see him before he goes."

Naomi watched Puka's reaction. He narrowed his eyes and cocked one eyebrow slightly.

"We will eat with you, though, before we have to go. Maybe you can send some of your men with us when we return. I think Naomi was a bit frightened by the bear. She would feel better if someone were with us."

Naomi spent the next couple of hours walking through the village with Risa. It wasn't long, however, before she recognized an all-too-familiar face. Karl-Reech had stepped out of his longhouse. He watched the two of them intently. He made no attempt to speak to them. He didn't have to. It was plain for Naomi to see that he had very little welcome for her.

They sat down to their evening meal and Naomi crossed her legs under her. The longhouse was dark, although the sun was still up outside. The smoldering fire in the middle of the room sent out a column of smoke that rose through a makeshift chimney in the roof. It didn't prevent a large portion of the smoke from circling the room, however, hunting for some escape hatch. Naomi picked up one of the freshly made pieces of bread and bit into it. Several women were standing opposite her. They were taking great delight in every morsel she put into her mouth, nudging each other and grinning. Naomi smiled back at them and chewed. The bread seemed like a mixture of cake and shoe leather.

"Your husband go upcountry tomorrow?" Yakta asked.

Naomi watched Puka. The man was seated to the left of Yakta and the missionary LeBarge was on his right. Puka eyeballed Risa intently and then cast a glance in Naomi's direction.

"Yes," Risa said. "I think he wants to look over the timber land that came with my wedding."

"That land belongs to the Tlingit," LeBarge chimed in. "It is not the American's land."

Naomi could see the fire in the man's eyes. He was almost squinting through the smoke, but his eyes were riveted to Risa. There was almost an accusatory tone to his voice.

"It was mine by birth. My father gave it to me and now it belongs to me and my husband." There was a sneer in Risa's voice that Naomi had never heard before. It was plain to see that she had no affection for this man, nor he for her. "Besides, my husband provides jobs for the people. He keeps them warm and filled when the winter comes. That is more than you can do."

"Stop," Yakta said, holding up his gnarled hand. "It is enough." He smiled at Risa, then at LeBarge. "You two not fight. I have heard enough. Little Flower only here for short time. I not have her spitting out her food in anger." He glanced back at the priest. "Ian is good man. He will use the timber well. Our people will make good boards for the houses."

Puka got to his feet. "Yes," he said, "the houses of the white men. More will come and there will be less for us." He bowed his head at Yakta. "I must go on a hunt, my father. I can stay no longer."

Yakta waved his hand at the man. "Yes, go. Hunt well and shoot straight."

Puka started to leave the room but stopped at where Risa was sitting.

"Thank you for what you did with the bear today," Risa said.

He nodded his head and smiled. Turning abruptly, he ducked his head and went out the door.

+ + + + +

It had rained at least part of every day that Zac had been in Sitka. It was the constant moisture that made the place the greenest Zac had ever seen. He rode in the carriage with Ian, Risa, and Jenny, while Bubba Dean drove the wagon to the dock with Skip and the Afghan Hobo. The wagon was loaded with their supplies, most of which would remain on the boat. A man often appreciated a light pack more than a tea kettle on the fire.

Ian had been rattling on about the upcountry. "It's gonna be one long day today, and I hope we can get there before we have to pitch our tent. But you better enjoy the boat while you can," Ian went on. "It's the last riding we're gonna be doing for a while. Everything else is on foot."

"Just so we carry light," Zac said. "I figure all we'll need is something warm and a slicker to keep the rain off."

"A little food, coffee, and ammunition would help," Ian added.

The docks had long since seen the last of the fishing boats for the day. Those men liked to be out before any hint of dawn, and in the summer that came early—almost as soon as the sun set. Ian had wanted to leave earlier, but Risa and Naomi had gotten back late and they insisted on seeing them off. A number of sea birds beat the air with their wings and took off when the carriage arrived at the dock.

Zac took notice of two boats that seemed to have steam up. One was a larger boat with a paddle wheel. It was painted a bright white and had a small cabin sitting on the second deck. Two men were rearranging cargo boxes on board. The older was a small steamer with an engine that shook. "Which one is ours?" Zac asked.

"The little one. That Jung woman owns the big one."

The small steamboat had no cabin, only a tarp spread across the last two-thirds of the boat to give cover to the engine and the wood they would need to keep the fire going. Two eyes had been painted on the bow of the boat; Skip saw them right away and nudged Zac as he climbed down. "What are those eyes for?" he asked.

Ian chuckled. "They'll help us see through the fog so we don't come up on no rocks unexpected."

Skip walked down the dock with Hobo. They had decided to take the dog on the trip, though Ian had at first been reluctant. Skip wanted both hounds with them, but Zac insisted they leave one at the house to protect the women.

Ian had busied himself loading supplies with an older man who took care of the boat. He had on a blue serge wool coat and a cap pulled down over his ears.

"This here's Benny," Ian said. "He's an old salt and a durn good hand. He just got himself sick of blue water."

Zac nodded at the man and he grinned in return.

"Glad to see you fellers b'fore lunch," he said. "I wuz afraid you weren't gonna get much of a start."

"We'll have to camp out one night before we get to where we're going. We'll make it fine though and be back to the boat in a few days."

"Good. Glad to hear it. I gets my bones a mite freezy sleeping on the water." He put his hand on his back and rubbed it. "I ain't what I used to be, ya know."

"You'll do fine," Ian said. He looked at Hobo and clapped his hands. "All right, boy, let's get in." The dog obediently hopped into the boat.

Bubba Dean loaded the supplies, and Ian swung two Winchesters over the side of the boat. "I figured I'd bring the saddle guns along. Seeing as how you got your cannon with you, I won't need a large caliber. Those babies of mine can put out plenty of firepower, though."

"Why would we need to do that?" Zac asked. There was something about the way Ian had been treating this trip that concerned Zac.

"A man can never tell what he might get himself into out here, that's all. There's all sorts of varmints, both on four legs and two."

Zac laid his Sharps in the boat. He turned and watched as the women circled the small steamer, following Skip. "Look, let's get something straight," he said, looking into Ian's eyes. He wanted to make sure the man understood every word he was saying. "It's the two-legged kind I'm worried about. You seem to be short of friends in these parts. I didn't come along to take part in any killing you got in mind. Just because I know how to use a gun is no reason for me to go hunting up another man's troubles, especially with my son along."

Ian shrugged. "What trouble? I'm just going to find an old friend, that's all."

"Then why do I get the feeling there's something you're not telling me? If I find out you've stacked the deck on this trip, I'll leave you high and dry and walk out. Am I understood?"

Ian chuckled. "'Course I understand. You'd have good reason to. But why would I want to put my niece's man in the ground before he becomes her husband? I don't think we'll have any trouble. I'm sure not looking for any."

"All right, then, we'll leave it at that. Just remember, I'm not getting Skip into any shooting war."

"Don't worry. Besides," Ian said, "where would you go? You don't know Alaska like I do."

"I know me and that's all I need to know. I can find my way out of anything, anywhere."

Ian smiled and put his hand on Zac's shoulder. "I believe you could at that. Well, don't worry. Apart from a bear, a pack of wolves, or an occasional mad moose, we ought to get through okay. There ain't much in the way of people where we're going. Most of the trappers there look kindly to strangers, 'cept for the occasional irritable types that hate people no matter where they are."

He looked up at the women circling back their way. "We best kiss the women folks good-bye and hightail it out of here. We got a lot of water to cross and a lot of pretty country for that boy of yours to see."

Jenny stepped over and started to help Skip into the boat, but Zac held her hand back. "Here," he said. "I've got to say my good-byes to you." He pulled her aside.

She held onto his arms and Zac brushed back the lock of hair that had fallen over her face. "I want you to be careful while I'm gone," he said.

She nodded. "This is a switch. Usually when you go away on a trip, I'm the one who worries about you."

Zac smiled in understanding. "Yes, I know, but all the same, you be careful."

She gripped his arms tighter. "I'll look for the next ship sailing. I'll feel so much better when we're all headed south."

"Me too." Zac looked back to where Ian was kissing Risa good-bye. "I didn't like the way he took Van's death, either. The man wired his jaws shut on it like a clam in mud."

"It worries me having you and Skip with him. If someone is trying to kill him, you'll both be in harm's way. I want you looking out for yourself no matter what happens to Ian. Do you understand me?"

Zac smiled. It was always touching for him to have her worry about him. This was different though. This wasn't his business with Wells

Fargo, it was her family. He figured that fact alone bothered her the most. She'd feel totally responsible. There would be no Wells Fargo to blame, no job that he had to do.

Zac stroked her hair. "Don't worry. I can take care of me and Skip both. I'm worried more about you, though. If I am taking the man somebody wants to kill with me, more than likely you have the one who wants to do it close by you. You be careful and find out what you can."

"I will. I'm going to spend some time asking questions. I want to find out who would profit from his death. From what I know already, the list is a long one."

CHAPTER 17

+ + + + + + +

THE BIG MAN WALKED SLOWLY DOWN the street. Sleeping in town had never agreed with him. He liked the sound of the birds in the morning and the noise of the rain on the leaves. It made him feel like a part of the land. Many people in Alaska were like that. They didn't belong in town.

He passed by the window of the cafe and stopped, looking inside. Several people were seated at a table, enjoying bacon and eggs. He could smell the food. They looked up at him through the window, and he could see the fear in their eyes.

He walked on, without smiling, in the direction of the Crystal Palace.

Toquah Kanstanof had been a part of Alaska since childhood. His father had been a Russian trapper and his mother an Athabascan Indian. He was raised with the wolf and the bear and had come to know them well enough to call them brothers. He prided himself on hunting like the wolf and killing like the bear in such a way that was cunning and silent. No one could survive his power—no human at least.

He walked through the batwing doors of the saloon and stood in them for a moment, surveying the room. Just his size and the look on his face was enough to bring several conversations to a complete stop. He'd had that effect on people for years. It was something he enjoyed. Fear was a stew to be savored.

The man behind the bar stopped wiping the glasses and put down his cloth. He watched closely as Toquah approached him. "What'll it be, mister?"

"The name is Kanstanof, Toquah Kanstanof. I'm here to see the ice princess."

"She's in the back room. Just hang on a minute and I'll get you in." Hank moved quickly to the door and cracked it open, addressing the woman who was sitting in the office. "I got a big feller out here that says you sent for him, Miss Kathryn."

145

"Kanstanof?" she asked.

"I think so. Calls himself Toquah."

Quinn put down his mug of coffee. "That's him. Send him in."

Hank backed away from the door, and Toquah stepped in and pulled off his heavy fur gloves. He was broad at the shoulder and thick with muscle. His trim waist was covered with a loose-fitting caribou shirt. His high, lean cheekbones betrayed his native heritage. His clear brown eyes gleamed like bright pebbles in a stream, and his smooth face had a lantern jaw that was marked with a small scar that cut across his chin. He rubbed his hand over his cheek. He had shaved that morning, in anticipation of seeing Kathryn.

Quinn got up from his chair with a sudden squeak. "Been waiting for you, Toquah, ever since Kathryn said she'd sent for you. You drinking anything?"

"Just coffee."

"Fine." Quinn motioned at Hank. "Get the man a hot mug of java." He turned back to the other people in the room. "This is the man we've been waiting for. He'll be going with you, but he keeps to himself. You won't have to worry about him, and it's for darn sure he won't be concerning himself with you."

Toquah listened to Quinn, but his eyes were glued to Kathryn. The woman got up from her chair and stood erect. She was beautiful—sharp, crystal blue eyes, her blond hair piled on top of her head, showing off her long, silky, milk white neck. He stepped toward her, extending his hand. "This is the woman I work for today." His booming voice silenced Quinn for the moment. Toquah had made his point.

Kathryn smiled and took his hand, holding it. "I'm so glad you could make it. We have been needing you."

Quinn cleared his throat. He pointed the other men out in the room. "The man with the red beard here is Smitty. This thing has become sort of personal with him."

Smitty smiled and gave a small salute.

"And this is Puka. He's a Tlingit. He knows that country you'll be in."

Toquah looked the two men over. The redhead was big enough but looked like a hundred other white men he'd seen in Alaska, clumsy and much too reliant on size alone. The Tlingit had the look of the hawk about him, sharp eyes and a silence primed for the kill. He would do nicely. Toquah nodded at the two of them. He held onto Kathryn's hand.

"Normally, this wouldn't be a problem," Kathryn said, "but the man we want has someone else with him that could be. He's from the States, and has the look of a gunman about him."

Hank stepped back through the door with the steaming cup of coffee in his hands.

Quinn walked over and took it. "That'll be all, Hank. You go tend to the bar." He turned and, taking a few steps, handed the cup to Toquah. "I understand you're no longer wanted in Canada."

Toquah dropped Kathryn's hand and reached for the cup. He cradled it in both hands and held it to his lips, breathing in the aroma. "They want me. They just don't want me there. Too many Mounties and too much law."

"Well, you don't have to worry about that here. In Sitka the law is what you make it. Isn't that right, boys?"

Smitty nodded. "Pretty much."

"So you will have a free hand in dealing with our problem."

Toquah sipped the coffee and watched the two men who had been selected to go with him. It was a bad mix and he knew it. The Tlingit would be all right on his own, but the big redhead would no doubt just get in the way. They'd be useful for one thing, though, they'd have to point out the men for him to kill. When that happened, he'd act on his own. He motioned with the cup in the direction of the north country. "I'll need a free hand out there, nobody to answer to and nobody to look out for."

Kathryn moved over next to him. "And you will have it." She curled her hand around his arm. "You can have anything you need. Quinn here has a steamer ready to take you north. It's at the docks now. There is a supply of food and coffee on it."

"Good, then let's get to it."

+ + + + +

The black carriage wound its way up the hill, its brass lights swaying slightly as it rounded the steep curves. Kathryn Jung was determined to pay her respects to the new Mrs. Ian Hays and meet the man's niece she'd heard so much about on the *Northern Star*. What little Zac had said to her on the boat always seemed to have Jenny's name or thoughts about her tagged to it. It was seldom for a man to be so devoted to a woman, and Kathryn was anxious to see the kind of woman who could have that effect on a man.

The rain was falling lightly, beating a steady drumbeat on the leaves of the trees and splattering the mud with dark eruptions of falling drizzle. It would only get worse and Kathryn knew it. She smiled. It would provide a nice excuse to stay longer than just to deliver a polite greeting.

She curled her long fingers around the package on the seat beside her. It was a silver teapot, a wedding gift. It had been wrapped in brightly colored pink paper with a white ribbon and bow. Such a thing was seldom seen in Sitka, but the western custom would make the young bride beam with pride. It would be something she'd remember. Kathryn hoped that would pave the way to learn more about Risa, and still more about Ian Hays and where he got his money.

The carriage pulled up outside the doors of the big house. Having a lumber mill had allowed Ian to spare no expense when it came to building the structure. It was like a palace, three stories surrounded by balconies. It didn't have the normal Russian look that many of the houses in town had. It was more along the lines of a colonial structure. The only reason it didn't attract attention was because it was so hidden up the hill and on the bluffs. There was an air of mystery to the place. The two massive doors that led inside were shaped with an oval archway. The Indian driver got down and went immediately to the house. He lifted the heavy iron knocker and rapped two times on the door.

Soon, Bubba Dean appeared at the door. He blinked at the Indian driver and then at her. Reaching behind the door, he found and opened an umbrella. He tiptoed through the mud and stood beside the carriage, offering Kathryn his hand. "Y'all comes wif me, missy. We don't want to get you wet none."

Kathryn gave the man her hand and stepped down. She straightened her dress and looked up at the empty balcony above the doors. Picking up the package, she clutched it under her arm. "Thank you. I brought a gift for your mistress."

The man smiled. "And she's gonna be mighty happy to have it, ma'am, and to see you too." He held the parasol high over her head while the rain beat on his ebony face. Moments later, he swung the door open for her. She stepped inside.

There, setting the table for lunch, was the Indian woman, Umqua. Kathryn knew her only by sight. Umqua stood up straight, hands on her hips, almost as if she were warding off some intruder. She was in a bright yellow full dress with an apron that covered almost all of it. She pushed her dark hair away with the back of her hand.

"I'm here to see the lady of the house," Kathryn said. She pulled off her gloves and pushed them into her purse, noticing how the words struck home to the woman. Obviously this was a position that she thought belonged only to her. No doubt she viewed Risa as an invader in her domain. Kathryn tucked the notion away in her head. Perhaps she could use it at a later date.

"I have a gift for her, a wedding gift." There was an expression of pain from the woman. *Perhaps her resentment went much deeper than just the house*, Kathryn thought. This was an encounter she was enjoying all the more. The woman seemed incapable of hiding her feelings. "I'm sure she'll want to see me."

Umqua wiped her hands on her apron. She signaled to the man. "Bubba Dean, you go up and get Mrs. Hays. Tell her she has company."

While Bubba Dean silently went through the room and up the stairs, Umqua continued to wipe down the table. It was plain to see that she thought activity, any activity at all, would drive whatever thoughts she had from her head. Kathryn was determined not to let that happen. This would be too good to pass up.

Kathryn stepped up to the table. "Are you Mr. Hays' cook?"

Umqua stopped her wiping. She looked up, glaring. "I take care of the whole house, not just his kitchen."

"And you do such a fine job. It's a job any woman would be proud to do for her man." The last words hit home. Kathryn could see it. No woman liked to slave for something that wasn't her own, and this Indian woman was no exception.

Umqua bent down and rubbed all the harder. It was as if her activity could minimize the pain. "My man works for Mr. Hays."

"Really, and who might that be? Have I met him?"

Umqua continued to look busy, even though the table already sparkled. "He's the man who brought you in."

"Is that so?" Kathryn narrowed her eyes and a faint smile crossed her lips. She had to try very hard to sympathize while not cutting too deeply into the woman's soul. "And I'm quite certain he's been a faithful servant to Mr. Hays. I'm sure Ian takes good care of him."

"He takes care of us." Umqua slurred the words in an almost contemptuous fashion.

"I'm certain he does. Just by looking at you, though, I can tell you were meant for bigger things. You seem so industrious."

The woman lifted up her head and her eyes widened. "Why, thank you." It was the first hint that Umqua could be expected to respond to the promise of success.

"Perhaps you and I can do business some day. You look like the kind of person who could be counted on." In Kathryn's thinking there was nothing like tearing someone down and then building them up again. It made the person's head swell twice as fast and also gave rise to the notion of Kathryn's power.

Risa appeared on the balcony overlooking the great room. She was wearing an unpretentious buckskin dress.

Obviously, the woman has no sense of place, Kathryn thought.

Risa started down the stairs, followed by a blond woman in a very pretty blue dress. The woman had a striking figure and her chin was held high.

This has to be the woman the Cobb man is in love with, she thought.

"Miss Jung," Risa said, clearing the bottom of the stairs, "how nice of you to call."

Kathryn held out the brightly wrapped box. "I brought you a wedding gift. I was in California and just didn't have time to bring it before. I'm sorry I missed the wedding."

Risa took the box. "It was a small family wedding." She stepped back. "I should introduce you to my husband's niece Miss Jenny Hays."

Kathryn extended her hand. "It's so nice to meet you. I feel like I know you already, though. I came up with your fiancé on the *Northern Star*."

Jenny smiled and shook her hand. "That's funny. Zac didn't mention you."

The words struck Kathryn's mind like a slap across the face. It wasn't often that a man didn't take notice of her. She smiled to stifle the pain. "Well, I'm quite sure a man who's engaged doesn't make it a habit of talking about other women. He did discuss you quite often, though. Were you expecting him?"

"I was surprised to see him."

"And a pleasant surprise, I'll wager." Kathryn looked around the room. "I don't see him here."

"He's gone to the woods with Uncle Ian for a few days. He took his son, Skip, with him."

It was the first time Kathryn's conscience bothered her. She hadn't counted on the boy being with them. She looked at Risa. "Go ahead, open the gift. I hope you like it."

Jenny smiled, watching Risa fumbling with the ribbons. "Fortunately, I don't have to worry about Skip if he's with Zac. He can take care of himself as well as our boy."

"I'm sure he can. He seems to be quite the capable man. What does he do for a living?"

"I'm surprised he didn't tell you."

There it was again. The implication was that Zac didn't trust her or even have much of a conversation with her. "Zac's a rancher in California," Jenny went on.

Kathryn's jaw tightened. She wasn't used to dealing with capable, secure women, especially when it came to the matter of their men. "Oh yes, he did say that. I just thought he might have something else he did." She waved her hand in the air. "You know how men are, so many irons in the fire they're hard to keep track of."

Risa held up the teapot and turned it around in her hand. "It's very pretty," she said. "It's silver."

"It's a teapot," Kathryn added even though she knew it was likely the woman knew what a teapot was.

Risa didn't respond. She sat the teapot down on the table. "I am pleased you came by with your . . . teapot." She said the word with emphasis.

"We don't see many teapots in Sitka. When I saw it in San Francisco I hardly recognized it myself," Kathryn lied. "I knew I had to get it for you, though. I'm looking forward to us becoming good friends. I know the pressures of marriage are always easier to bear when there's someone you can talk to." Kathryn smiled. It was a crease on her lips that widened as her eyes sparkled. "I've had three husbands myself, and these things are never easy. But a woman has much to gain from a marriage if she's wise."

Jenny interrupted. "And I'm quite certain you've gained a lot from yours."

Kathryn bit down on the inside of her cheek and forced a passive look. Her eyes glared at Jenny. "I'm sure you mean that well. Yes, I did gain quite a bit from my marriages, and if that man of yours is a successful rancher, I'm sure you'll gain a lot too."

Jenny stepped around Kathryn and walked over to the window. She looked outside into the gray sky. "I see it's stopped raining." She turned around, facing Kathryn and Risa, then spoke up. "You have no idea what had to happen for Zachary Taylor Cobb to love anybody. The amount of trust it takes to build a place where love can occur is enormous. I gained everything I could possibly want when that man decided to trust me enough to love me. I couldn't possibly want anything more. I'm afraid I don't share the view of this being a temporary thing where if a woman plays her cards right, she can walk away from it with more than what she had when she came in. I'm much more of a person now, loving Zac, than I ever imagined I could be."

Kathryn reached into her purse and took out her gloves. "Well, this has been an interesting conversation. I always enjoy talking about love and romance." Blinking her eyes, she stared at Jenny. "And you have such proper ideas on the subject, my dear. I suppose I once shared them as a girl."

Jenny and Risa walked her to the door. "It's too bad you lost them," Jenny said. "I'm a Christian myself. I learn so much about love from what I know about God. Once it's given, it's never taken back. There are no second choices."

Kathryn patted Jenny's arm. "That's sweet and quaint, almost like something a little girl would learn in Sunday school. I do hope you and your man are very happy." She looked over at Risa. "I'm certain you and Ian will be, my dear. If there's anything I can do, anything at all, please don't hesitate to call."

"Thank you again for the teapot," Risa said.

Kathryn opened the door and nodded to her driver. He helped her into the carriage. "Let's get out of here," she said.

The man cracked the small whip, sending the team around the trees that stood at the center of the loop in front of the house. As they started to clear one of the outbuildings, Umqua stepped into the middle of the road, waving her hands in the air.

"Stop!" Kathryn shouted at the driver. "Stop at once."

Umqua stepped up to the coach and leaned her head inside. "Did you mean what you said about doing business with me?"

Kathryn scooted over in the woman's direction and took her hand. "Of course I did."

Umqua looked back at the house, trying to catch sight of anyone who might be at the window. It was empty. "I have something you'd be interested in knowing."

"About what?" Kathryn beamed.

"About what Ian Hays keeps in his basement."

CHAPTER 18

+ + + + + + +

THE WATERS NORTH OF SITKA were a mass of small islands that seemed to litter the sea and form waterways it would take an expert to maneuver. Fortunately, Benny was such a man. He swung the wheel and reached back adjusting the throttle. "Maybe I can get the boy there to keep stoking the engine when I give the word," he said.

Zac looked down at Skip. "I don't think there's anything he'd like better, unless it was steering."

Benny laughed. "We'll have to see about that. There might be a few spots where he could man the tiller."

The islands fanned out in front of them, rocky except for the large stands of trees that stood at their tops. They passed one of the larger ones. It stood like an anvil, with a leg of rock separated from it and wading in the water. The arch formed a small opening that sent the tide rushing through it. The trees on top were straight and tall, reaching for the summer rain that continued to fall. They could see a wall of rain sweeping in from the sea. It soon hit the awning over the small boat, a steady sound of beating and raking water.

The gray mountains stood in the distance with a hint of the summer sun behind them. The shower soon passed, and once again they could see the small islands littering the inland passage. In front of the small boat, a number of dorsal fins broke the surface and rolled the water behind them in gentle swells. "Killer whales." Benny pointed them out.

Skip opened the door to the steam engine and threw in a couple of chunks of wood. "Do they kill people?" he asked.

"They kill something," Benny replied. "Otherwise they wouldn't carry the name, now would they?"

Skip cast a quick glance back at Zac. "Zac says that sometimes people put a name on themselves so they won't have to do anything about it."

"Oh, is that so?"

"Yes, he says if a man calls himself 'Bad Bob,' then people won't try and figure out just how bad he is."

Benny leaned back and scratched his stubbly chin. He broke into a smile. "That's a point. Just maybe I should go about callin' myself 'Bad Benny.' How would that suit you?"

Ian chuckled. "The only thing bad about you is your cooking. What that would do is keep folks away from your fire at night."

"Might not be such a terrible idea then. More food for me."

Skip pointed as a large bird swooped near them. It had a snow white head and flew near the water, pulling a fish out with his claws. "That's an eagle."

"Sure 'nuff is," Benny said.

The bird flapped its wings and rose in the sky, the fish dangling from its sharp talons.

Since the rain had stopped, Zac walked toward the bow of the small boat, watching the small pod of killer whales play on the surface. Ian stepped up next to him, eyeing the fur hat he'd given Zac to wear. "Feeling kinda naked without that hat of yours, aren't you?"

"Kinda."

"You must have done yourself a fair bit of fighting during the war, am I right?" Ian said.

Zac looked off in the distance. "More than I care to remember."

"Couldn't have been very old, either, I'd wager." Ian peeled open his fur coat and put his hands on a pair of red suspenders, pushing them out. "I was a blockade runner myself. I guess a man finds it hard to get the sea out of his innards."

Zac gave Ian a glance, a fixed stare. He didn't think all that highly of people who made a profit on the blood of others and saw most every runner as just that type of man.

Ian pushed his red braces out. "I s'pose fightin' men like you don't hold too kindly to men like me, but what we did was necessary."

"I'm sure it was." Zac looked back off at the mountains.

"We had our share of danger. I myself had to dodge many a Yankee bullet."

"Looks like you did a good job of it," Zac sneered.

"You don't like me much, do you?"

"I don't know you. I don't make it a habit of liking people just because they're kin."

"And just what do you think I do?"

Zac turned up his fur collar. "I see you as a user."

"A user?"

"Yes, you use things and people." Zac could tell his blunt speech was something that interested Ian. Around Sitka, he was no doubt so well off that most people didn't feel right about crossing him. There were probably very few men who felt comfortable enough with him to tell him their mind, and the one man that might have was dead.

"How do you figure I use people?"

"You used the war to get yourself wealthy."

"That was war. If I hadn't done that somebody else would have. I'm more of a practical man. When I see a dime on the ground, I bend down and pick it up."

"Even if it belongs to someone else?"

"A dime's a dime, no matter where it lays. Besides, I treat folks with respect."

Zac ran his finger over the base of his heavy mustache and stared off at the rocks of a small island. "You use the Indian's forests and use them to cut it. Instead of sending Naomi to California, you dangled her like a piece of bait for Jenny to come to you. In that way, you used a young woman." He looked back at Skip. "And I can't pass over the thought in my head that you want to use me and that boy back there to squeeze some measure of revenge, or at the very least give you some cover."

Ian shook his head. "You must be more than a rancher. Most ranchers and farmers I've ever known trust people, and it's plain you don't. That war must have left some deep scars on you, boy."

Zac knew there was a lot of truth in what Ian had said. He'd come back from the war with nobody's shoulder to cry on, not yet a man and no longer a boy. He'd always had the quiet detachment of someone who lived close to death, and his job with Wells Fargo only added to it. He had watched the deepest parts of his heart and soul erode in the sewage of the lower segments of society, the places where men had no hearts, no conscience, no soul. It was only Jenny and the soft touch of her smile and fingers that had begun to rebuild him as a man. Her love had made him begin to trust again, and the fact that Skip looked up to him caused him to summon up whatever remained of his dreams. "I've seen more than my share of death and dying," he said.

"I'll just bet you have. Bet you dished a bit of it out, too, in your day."

"I held a Yankee boy in my arms that I shot in the wilderness. Wasn't no more than murder. I cared more what happened to him than the people who ordered him to go. He wasn't no older than I was, and looking into his dying face was the same as looking at my own."

"That's hard. Takes a hard man to think on it and makes a hard man out of it."

"Sometimes a man has to be hard to go on breathing," Zac responded.

"You ever wonder if breathing is all that worth it?" Ian asked.

"I used to, then I'd remember my mother's words and what she'd read to us from the Bible. She'd tell me God had a purpose for me, even though sometimes I'd have to fight to believe it." He motioned back in Skip's direction. "Then I came across that boy. I had to bury his father, and he started to look to me. When someone gives you a mark to live up to, a man has to do it."

Ian nodded and looked back at Skip. "He's a fine boy too."

"And then there was Jenny," Zac went on. "The woman loves me like I am. There's no notion there of holding back until I become something to her liking. Some women draw a line through a man and love only what's on the one side of the line. Jenny drew a circle around all of me and decided to love everything inside the circle."

Ian swallowed hard. His eyes widened. "She's a good woman."

Zac looked him right in the eye. "She's better than that. Much better."

Benny spun the wheel sharply, sending the small boat chugging toward the shoreline. He yelled at Ian on the bow. "The camp's through them rocks. You best hang on."

Up ahead they could see the narrow passage of water that carried a surging surf into the shoreline. What had been a placid sea turned into a boiling mass of foam, spitting anything afloat out the other side. Ian stooped down, grabbing onto the side of the vessel. Zac took a quick look at Skip as the boy hugged the dog and, bending down, duplicated the man's posture.

The eyes of the small boat stared directly into the swift current. Benny held the wheel steady, and soon they were surfing on top of a wave that shot them through the rocks. It seemed to pick them up with an unseen hand, pushing them past the rocks and the trees on top of the small islands on either side. The camp came into view. Small canoes and a cluster of kayaks dotted the shore. Fires smoked and strings of fish lay exposed to the smoldering open pits. Several Indians pointed to the boat. They soon formed into a swarm of curious men along with a few women.

"Them's some of Risa's people," Ian said. "The land around here belongs to me now, but I let 'em fish same as always. I figured to stop here and buy some smoked salmon to take with us." He grinned, his eyes twinkling. "It never hurts to do business with folks you want to stay friendly with."

Benny swung the boat around and killed the engine. It coasted to the rocky beach and finally nudged itself onto a spit of sandy pebbles.

Ian clapped his hands, sending Hobo bounding out of the boat, and waved toward the camp. "Okay, we don't have long to be here. I'll make the buy, and you and the boy can look around for a spell. Benny's gonna stay with the boat. No sense in giving these people any temptation. We want to leave here with everything we got."

A short time later, Zac, Skip, and Hobo were prowling through the longhouse that was serving as a store. Makeshift tables were filled with hides of every description, and behind a wooden plank there were shelves littered with scrimshaw, the carvings the Indians created out of whalebone and various ivory tusks. Zac stood behind Skip as the boy turned the ornaments over in his hand.

"Look at this," Skip said. "A shark."

Zac looked down at the carved picture of a man in a kayak fighting a large shark. "It took a lot of patience to do that, I'd say."

In the corner, a man was hacking away at a shaved fir log. He sat on the log with both legs straddling it, creating a series of carvings in the pole, faces of animals and men. The hatchet he swung looked more like a small hoe that had been sharpened to dig deep into the wood. Chips were flying as he sent the thing biting into the log, one sharp blow at a time. Both Zac and Skip walked over to watch.

The man was old, with white hair and a wrinkled face, but his arms were strong. They looked to be just as solid as the wood he was working on and shined with sweat in the dim light of the overhead lamps. "I can see you've been doing this for a while," Skip said.

The old man stopped and looked back at Skip. "Since I was six. Some men spend whole life finding out what's inside him. I found out when I was young."

Skip's eyes widened.

The old man turned the tool over and nudged Skip's belly. "What's in here for you?" he asked.

Skip shook his head. "I don't really know yet."

The man lifted his chin, looking into Skip's eyes. His face was wrinkled and the smile made the lines deepen. "You ought to know. How you gonna find out?"

Skip shrugged his shoulders. "I don't know. Maybe by trying out a few things."

The old man got to his feet. He backed up, pointing at the portion of the log he hadn't started work on. "What you see when you look at this?"

"A log," Skip replied.

"Nothing more?"

Skip shook his head. "I'm afraid not."

"Then you not a carver. You something else." The old man looked up at Zac but continued to talk to Skip. "What your father do?"

Skip looked up at Zac, turning the idea over in his head. "He's a rancher."

"Then when he looks at land he sees animals, grass, and water. A man sees what he is inside." He stepped back and pointed to the bare wood. "When I look here, I see bear, eagle, and fish, standing on head of my grandfather."

"You do?"

"I do, and more, much more. I see whole world in this log." The old man held out his hands. He shook the tool in his right hand. "I see world in log and in my hands."

An older woman peeked over the table full of firs. She shook her finger at the man. "Show them what you have," she screeched.

The old man waved at her as if he were swatting a pesky housefly. "I show them." He nudged Skip. "Come on." He chuckled. "I gotta show you what I got or not get my supper."

"Well, we wouldn't want that," Zac said. "You better show us."

The man stepped over the log and led them to the back of the house. There the tables were filled with carved wooden animals. They were painted in brilliant colors, each depicting one of the animals they had seen.

Skip ran his hand over one of the black killer whales. The paint made it shine, almost as if it were wet.

"You like that?" the man asked.

"Yes, I saw some of these today."

"Good. They guide you to us then, show you where to go."

"You do nice work," Zac said.

"Thank you. This is all me. It's all I am."

Skip moved down the table and reached out for a beautiful bald eagle on a carved perch. The thing screeched and flapped its wings, and Skip jumped back as if he'd been shot. Hobo backed up and barked wildly.

The man roared with laughter. "That not carved," he laughed.

Skip held back his hands, crossing them under his arms. "I can see that." He reached down to comfort the dog.

The old woman came running around the table. She grabbed Skip and pulled him back. Turning her head, she shot the old man a scolding look. "You scare the boy. You ought to get yourself a dog like that boy has."

The old man was still chuckling. "I am sorry not to warn you. That's my spirit guide. He stays there to tell me what I do right and what I do wrong."

"He does?" Skip looked back at Zac with a look of doubt. Zac knew that superstition was something Skip had seldom encountered in the States.

"Oh yes." The man reached over and held his hand under the bird. It stepped into his wrist, locking his claws around the old man's hand. "He watches close. You have something that watches you?"

Skip looked at the man and stuck his hands in his pockets. Zac could tell he was almost afraid to touch anything else. "My guardian angel, I suppose."

The eagle began to flap his wings, and the old man reached over and sat him back on his perch. "And you see this angel?"

"No, but I know he's there all the same."

"And how you know what you not see?"

The question seemed to take Skip by surprise. He looked at the man and blinked and then looked back at the log the man had been carving. Taking his hands out of his pocket, he pointed over to the log. "I suppose I know that the same way you can see things in that log over there the rest of us can't see. I know it because the Bible tells me so, and I see it in my heart."

The old man reached over and put his hand on Skip's shoulder. "It is good. You answer well." He looked over at Zac. "You have good boy here. You take care of him. He will be a wise man some day that people will listen to."

"Thank you," Zac said. "He is a fine boy."

Reaching over to the table, the old man picked up a small carved bear. It was standing on its hind feet, with paws outstretched. He placed it in Skip's hand and wrapped the boy's fingers around it. "You take this. You remember me when you see it, and you think about what you going to be."

Skip looked down at the bear. "It's pretty." Looking back up at the man, he smiled. "How much does it cost?"

The old man waved his hands. "It costs too much for you to pay. It cost me my life. You take it and think about what you're going to make." He stooped lower, pressing his face close to Skip. "If you think about it hard enough, it will cost you your life too."

"It will?"

"Yes, when a man know who he is and what he is to do, it cost him his life."

Skip looked back at Zac and Zac nodded.

"Thank you," Skip said. "I'll think about that."

The old man laughed and laid both of his hands on Skip's shoulders.

"Yes, you think about that and I will think about you."

It was a short time later when they walked back to the boat. Ian had made a purchase of reindeer jerky and smoked salmon. He loaded the bundle in the boat.

Skip clutched the bear in his hands. He looked back at the longhouse and then up at Zac. "I sure like that man and those people."

Zac nodded. "Good folks."

"When do you think I'm going to know what I'm going to be?"

"That's hard to say. First a man has to know what he is now, in order to know what he's going to become."

"And what about you? Do you know what you're going to become?"

The question wasn't a new one to Zac's mind. It was something he'd been wrestling with since the war. The fact that Skip would ask it caught him off guard. He put his hand on the boy's shoulder. "Right now the thing I want to be is the best father you could ever have. I know you weren't born to me, but you were brought to me all the same."

"Do you think my guardian angel brought me to you?"

Zac smiled. "It was either yours or mine."

CHAPTER 19

✦ ✦ ✦ ✦ ✦ ✦ ✦

THE DAY PASSED WITH THE UPHILL CLIMB over-looking the deep waterway. Ian forged ahead with the heavy backpack he was carrying, stumping over the rocks with a large walking stick he had cut. Zac had one that was only slightly larger. The heavy fur mukluks seemed out of place to Zac since he was used to wearing boots, and at first they felt like large, awkward moccasins. But they were comfortable, and he was getting accustomed to them and the way he could feel the ground he was walking on. Skip maintained his pace with a small rucksack strapped to his back. It bounced as he walked, but it didn't cut down his curiosity over the small group of weasels that ran across their path.

Even Hobo was carrying a small pack strapped to his back. The dog barked furiously at the weasels and chased them into the stump of a tree. He stood there growling.

"That's all right, Hobo," Ian said. He looked over to Skip. "You watch out for them things, boy," Ian said. "They'll get into our packs and steal us blind. First thing you know, our breakfast will be their supper. That's why when we camp, we hang these packs of ours high."

"I thought that was because of the bears," Skip said.

"Them too. 'Course, I'd much rather face a horde of weasels than one angry, hungry bear."

They walked the tree line with the soft wind blowing through the trees like a whispering choir. The mountains appeared to be much closer, almost touchable, and colder. Below them they could see the river. It snaked its way to the north and wound through the green canyons below.

"There's gonna be plenty of fish in that water," Ian said. "A man could reach out and find his supper in his fingers." He smiled. "'Course, we got all this lazy man's grub we been feedin' on, but I speck you'll be want-ing something fresh off the fire tonight."

Skip's eyes brightened. "That would be good. I can almost smell it now."

Ian chuckled slightly. "You ain't seen nothing till we get to Lilly's cabin. The man learned to cook during a year he spent beached in Hong Kong. He could open himself up a mighty fine restaurant in town and lay away the money hand over fist."

"Then why doesn't he do that?" Zac asked.

"You'll find folks up here a mighty curious lot. They come up here to fight shy of people, not to be beached with a lot of dirty strangers. I suppose Lilly's a lot like that. He doesn't say too much to people unless he needs the money to get by on."

They found a trail along the side of the hill and started down it toward the river. It switched back a number of times and looked to be used by game, given all the grazing they saw along the way. "I got my canoe at the bottom here," Ian said. "It'll take us all the way to Lilly's cabin, and I think you'll find the going a whole lot easier than over the tops of these ridges."

Zac watched as Hobo froze in his tracks and looked back up the hill, listening to a distant grunt.

Ian paused and stood up straight. "It's them same two that have been following us since they smelled our breakfast," he said. "They figure to tag along to get our leftovers, I speck."

"Bears?" Skip asked.

"Yep," Ian answered. "I suppose they're going to be plenty disappointed when we leave them on the river. Sometimes those things trail you like hungry dogs when they smell a man's cooking."

They started back down the trail at a faster pace, stepping over rocks and around the nibbled-over buck brush. Hobo ran on ahead, sniffing at the brush and the smell of game on the trail. They hadn't covered more than fifty yards when Zac turned around and caught sight of the two bears. He stopped stone still. "They seem more than a little curious," Zac said.

The bears had started down the hill in their direction. They stepped gingerly over the rocks, working at keeping their footing.

"At least we have them uphill of us," Zac said. "Makes me feel a little better."

"Why is that?" Skip asked.

"A bear has some powerful hind legs. They're built for going uphill but can be kind of unstable going down one. When a man's being chased by a bear, it's always best to find a steep hill and head down it fast."

Ian smiled at him. "You been figuring pretty good, I'd say, for a rancher." He looked at Skip. "Old Zac here is right, boy. You get on a steep slope and hunker down and them things are more than likely to go tumbling down over you." He pointed down to where Hobo was blazing their trail. "We best follow old Hobo there. He seems to have the right idea."

They picked up their pace and broke out into a trot, keeping an eye over their shoulders at the bears that were working their way down the hill behind them. It took them only a short time before they were beside the fast running stream. Ian swung off his pack and pointed to some brush. "My canoe's under all that. We best get to digging it out—and in a hurry."

The three of them moved over to the clump of brush and started picking up the loose limbs and branches, tossing them aside. In a few minutes they had the canoe turned upside down and were shaking the debris out of its bottom. Hobo had gone back to the trail and was barking at the bears coming their way.

"Only got two paddles, so, Skip, you'll have to ride in the middle with Hobo," Ian said.

They placed the canoe in the water and loaded the gear into it. Ian clapped his hands for the dog. "Come on, boy. We're gonna pick on something more our size." With that, Hobo turned and made his way to the water. Ian scooped him up and placed him in the canoe. "I'd say we made it just in time," he said.

Zac stepped into the canoe with Ian pushing off from behind. The two bears were nearing the bottom of the hill. One of them stood up straight and growled as they slipped off into the middle of the stream and caught the current.

Ian laughed. "Yes, just enough to get a man's heart pounding without breaking out into too much of a sweat. That big Sharps of yours would have done the job on them, though."

"Maybe so," Zac replied, "But I don't like to use it unless I have to." Ian dug hard with his paddle. "You just keep it close all the same."

It took them the better part of the day to travel down the canyon. The winding stream had several places where the water ran through rocks and seemed to hurl them onward. Hobo was placid, though. It was as if the dog was born for water. He sat in the middle of the canoe with his tongue hanging out and was the only member of the group not to show panic.

Paddling around a bend, they saw the cabin. It was a large log structure with grass on the roof. The smoke rose from the chimney in wisps. "There it is," Ian shouted. "Pull for the shore."

Both Zac and Ian dug hard at the water with their paddles. They glided up to a sandbar, wedging the canoe deep into the sandy soil. "Here we are," Ian said. He cupped his hands to his mouth and yelled out, "Lilly, you in there? It's me, Ian, and I brought along some friends of mine."

The heavy wooden door opened up and a short, squatty man with balding red hair stepped out. He wore moccasins with a buckskin shirt and pants and a string of bear claws around his neck. Zac noticed the small windows. They were slats that made the place easy to defend, almost rifle pits. The sneer of his face also showed that he didn't take kindly to strangers, even if they were with a friend.

Hobo jumped out of the canoe and went racing along the shoreline, smelling the brush. Ian stepped out and helped Skip, and Zac climbed out the back. Ian jerked his thumb in Zac's direction. "This here's Zac Cobb. He's my niece's intended bridegroom, so you treat him real nice, ya hear?"

Lilly grunted and put his hands on his hips. The man's fair skin was almost a glowing red from being near the fire, and he had a red beard that tried to cover it as best it could. His blue eyes shone.

Ian looked back at Zac. "The man takes some warming up to get almost civil, but you'll get along just fine."

They started to walk up the path to the cabin, but Lilly stepped aside and held up his hand to stop them. "Don't come no closer." He pointed to the ground where a bunch of small branches were spread out over their path. "I got me one of my deadfalls here. You step on that and you ain't getting back to Sitka."

The three of them edged up closer to the branches, and Lilly reached around and took a long pole. He shoved it into the branches and moved them slightly. Zac held Skip close and they looked down. The man had dug an eight-foot pit and embedded into the bottom were sharpened spikes. "Don't pay to be under cautious 'round here. I got me a couple more on either side of the cabin." He lifted his eyes and looked at Hobo. The dog was still playing by the stream. "I'd say you don't want to lose that dog, you best keep him inside."

"I'll do that," Ian said. "I'll walk him around the thing."

Lilly looked at Skip. "Ain't no place to play either."

"Why do you have that here?" Skip asked.

"There's bad things hereabouts, bad bears and bad people. They try coming up on me unawares and they is gonna be stuck in the bottom of one of these here holes." He stood up straight and smiled. "And I do mean stuck."

Zac and Skip stepped around the deadfall and made their way to the cabin. Ian fell back and took Hobo.

The inside of the dimly lit cabin was like nothing Zac had ever seen in the wilderness. Lilly had a large cooking stove with a pile of kindling on the side of it. There were four plates for cooking and an open pit for barbecuing. Two blackened ducks were hanging over the smoldering fire, and over the stove hung a vast array of cookware. It was something Zac had seen in very few restaurants. A large set of shelves were filled to capacity with every ingredient known to man.

Lilly noticed the way Zac and Skip were eyeing the cooking arrangement. "I do cook to pleasure myself," he said. "Jest 'cause a man's out in the woods don't mean he has to eat like an animal."

Ian stepped into the cabin behind Hobo. He straightened himself up. "See, Cobb. What did I tell you? We're gonna eat mighty fancy here, just like the best places in San Francisco."

Ian walked casually around the stove and looked over a large table. It was made from shaved, rough-cut timber, pegged and spliced to make it sturdy. He placed his hands on one end and leaned down, testing it. "You made this since I saw you last."

"Sure did," Lilly said. He crossed his arms with pride and leaned back slightly. "I got myself a partner too."

"A partner . . . you?"

"That's right, Joe Juneau."

"Juneau! He ain't much of a partner, I'd say. The man will steal you blind and blame you for losing it. Besides, you're already partnered up with me. I don't intend on giving him any kind of split, unless it's from your share."

Lilly moved over to the stove and took down a large, shiny wok. "I figured that. But a man gets plumb tired of just talking to himself." He took down a large spoon with holes in it and shook it in Ian's direction. "You may be a partner, but you ain't here with me. You're up there in that warm house of yours."

"I thought that's how you wanted it."

"I did, but that was then and this is now. Now make yerself useful and set that there table."

Ian looked dumbstruck. Zac could tell the news about Lilly's new partner had hit him hard. Ian muttered to himself as he got down the tin plates and set them out on the table. "Set the table," he murmured. "Why not put out a flower arrangement?"

Lilly overheard him. "That might be a fine idea. You think you could pick something that wasn't a weed?"

The remark got only a cold hard stare from Ian. Jokes were fine as long as they weren't at his expense.

Lilly began to chop meat with his large cleaver. Zac and Skip had taken a seat in the makeshift chairs beside the table, and Skip was giving Hobo all the attention he could take and then some. The dog leaned his neck back under the boy's scratches.

"I ain't got no pork or chicken," Lilly said, grinning. "But I make do with game. You're gonna find that elk and bear do real nice when they're cooked just right." He poured a dark liquid into the wok and dropped the pieces of meat in with a sizzle. The room was filled with an instant aroma.

A short time later the door to the cabin swung open. A man in furs and a leather cap stepped inside, rubbing off the bottoms of his mukluks on the bottom of the doorway.

"There you are," Lilly said. "You know Hays here."

The man nodded. "Yeah, I do."

Lilly waved a wooden spatula in Zac's direction. "This here is the man that's gonna marry up with his niece, and his boy."

Zac watched the man as he took off his coat. He was stocky with broad shoulders. His beard was black, the color of a raven's wing. His thick eyebrows were joined over the bridge of his large nose, and his beard and hair hung down to the base of his neck. He looked at Zac with small black eyes.

"Name's Cobb," Zac said. "This is Skip."

"Nice meeting up with you." He hung his cap on a small round peg driven into the wall. "I'm Joe Juneau." He looked over to where Lilly was stirring the meat with the green clippings of what appeared to be a vegetable. "I found some more today."

"You did?" Lilly asked. "Where?"

" 'Bout two miles downstream, lying there as big as duck eyes."

The news got Ian to his feet. "You got them on you? I want to have a look."

Juneau reached into his pocket and pulled out a small leather bag. He tossed it at Ian.

Ian carefully opened the drawstrings, then poured part of the shiny contents into the palm of his hand, his eyes widening. "You did," he said. "You did sure enough."

Zac knew what they were talking about without even having to look. He'd seen the look on men's faces in California when they found gold. It was like they'd been transported into some fairyland where a man never had to worry or work. Nothing could be further from the truth, though, and Zac knew that well.

"You want to take a look here, Cobb?" Ian asked.

"I've seen it before."

Skip looked up at him. "What is it?" he asked.

"Gold," Zac said.

"I'd sure like to see," Skip said.

Ian laughed. "Why not?" He stepped over and held his hand out under the boy's face. "It's the stuff dreams are made of. A man could do right well for himself on this river."

"Wow!" Skip pushed several of the nuggets over in Ian's hand with his finger. "Is it really gold?"

"Sure enough," Ian said.

"And there's more of it?"

Ian scooted the nuggets back into the bag and drew the string tight. "There's a whole mountain of it, and we're sitting right on top of it."

"And who does it belong to?" Skip asked.

Ian tossed the bag back to Juneau. "This is my land now, so I guess you could say it belongs to me."

"All right," Lilly said, "you boys set yourselves down and we're gonna eat. I think you'll like this."

The meal did have a scent of game to it, but mixed with the flavors that Lilly had concocted, the blend was something to remember. They ate their meal with delight, Skip poking though it curiously at first, but then diving into the mixture.

Near the end of the meal, Ian looked over the table at Lilly. "You did yourself proud again here, partner."

Lilly poked his fork at the tin plate, giving off a sharp, metallic sound. "Man has to fare well for his ownself," he said. He smiled at Skip, obviously enjoying the way the boy was taking to the new experience. "And I'm glad you had the hanker to drop by and show the place off."

Ian stabbed another piece with his fork. "Well, that wasn't exactly the reason I came."

Lilly put down his fork and Juneau stared at him, holding a bun in his hand. "It wasn't? Well, what was it? You figure I'm cheating you?"

Ian waved at him, grinning. "Nah, I don't have any thoughts that way." Suddenly, his look turned sober. He wiped his mouth with the back of his hand. "I came here to warn you."

"Warn me? About what?"

"You remember that nugget you gave me?"

"Of course I do."

Ian picked up a bun from the plate and broke it in two. He took one piece and swirled it in the plate. "Well, I gave it to Fleetwood, just to show him we needed to buy us some property in town."

"And?" Lilly was obviously interested.

Ian put down the bread. He slumped his shoulder over, a long look drooping over his lips. "Fleetwood turned up dead on the glacier. He still had his money on him, but the gold was gone."

"What?" Juneau exclaimed. "You tell him where it came from?"

Ian lowered his head still further. "I did tell him I got it from Lilly here. But I know Van. He wouldn't have said a thing."

"You sure about that?" Lilly asked.

Zac cleared his throat. He'd heard enough. It became clear to him now just exactly why Ian was on this trip and why he'd invited them along. His face flushed. "He did look like he'd been tortured," Zac said.

"Tortured?" Juneau pushed his plate back. "A man will break given enough call."

"That's why I came to warn you. You need to keep a sharp eye out for strangers."

"If you ask me, we need to keep a sharp eye out for partners who can't be trusted," Juneau said.

Zac stood up quickly. He reached down and pulled Ian to his feet. "You and I need to talk."

Ian looked at him, his eyes fluttering.

Zac pushed him slightly in the direction of the door. They walked over and Zac opened it. There was a growing twilight in the forest. The stream cut through the silence with a rippling sound. Zac gently shoved him down the path. "You lied to me. You said you were going to visit a friend, but all the while you knew there was danger here."

"That's not quite true. I'm here to prevent any trouble."

"Yeah, sure, and with my gun to help you if we should find it."

Ian looked around and held both hands out in the direction of the water. "Well, you can see that there's no trouble here. We may have just stopped anything from happening."

"What I see is a man who doesn't care who he uses, a man who would put a child in danger just to save his own hide." Zac grabbed Ian's coat and pushed him forward, holding him over the branch covered pit. "Now, we are leaving tomorrow. Is that clear?"

Ian's face had a look of panic. He nodded his head.

"If you put Skip into any danger, you see this pit? I'm going to drop you in there myself. You won't have to worry about those people who are trying to jump your claim. It's me you're going to have to deal with. Have I made myself understood?"

"I understand." Ian's voice was a whisper. "We leave tomorrow."

At that moment they heard the booming voice of a man across the stream. "Hello the cabin," the man shouted.

Zac could make out the dim figure of a man stepping out of the woods, a big man with a rifle.

"You got something a feller could eat?"

CHAPTER 20

+ + + + + + +

THE TWILIGHT WAS COMING SOMEWHAT earlier this far north, but Jenny still couldn't get used to the long hours. It made her drowsy and somewhat cranky. She seated herself in the chair opposite Naomi and looked at the walls around the girl's room.

"They have tried to make me comfortable," Naomi said.

Jenny glanced at her but couldn't help the frown from spreading over her face. "But have they tried very hard to find us a ship going to Seattle?" She shook her head. "I'd just feel more comfortable if we were gone from this place."

Naomi sat back in the oversized chair and nervously swung her legs back and forth, barely brushing the carpet with her toes. Her shoes made a soft sweeping sound. "In a way it's hard for me to go, and I think it's doubly hard for Uncle Ian to say good-bye. I think he expects he'll never see me again."

"Why is that? He could come and visit you anytime. No one's going to hold you prisoner." She traced her eyes over the walls of the room. "At least not in California."

"I know." Naomi bowed her head, staring at the motion of her shoes as they continued to sway beneath her. "I just think Ian doesn't think he's going to live that much longer."

Jenny moved closer to her. "Why would you say that?"

"He seems nervous lately, and he was so anxious to get you here. He never used to be this way. He always seemed so happy and laughed a lot. Now he just broods at times." She stopped the motion of her feet and scooted closer. "Plus, like I told you, someone took a shot at them on their wedding day."

Jenny thought back over the conversation she had had with Naomi on the second day of her arrival. There were so many things they had talked about, but she wouldn't have forgotten that. "Is there anything else you haven't told me?"

Naomi sat back and once again started to swing her feet. She stopped and, crossing her ankles, held them straight out. She stared at her shoes.

Jenny suspected it was because she didn't want to look her in the eye.

"I think there are things he's not telling me, not telling anyone."

"Like what?" Jenny asked.

Naomi slid off the chair and walked slowly to the window. She turned around, studying Jenny from a distance. Raising her shoulders, she gave out a big sigh. "Like the basement."

"What about the basement?"

"He's keeping something down there," she wrung her hands, "or someone."

Jenny had seldom seen Naomi look more nervous. The days since she'd been in Alaska the two of them had talked of nothing but the hidden years between them, of dresses, dances, books, and places. It was Naomi who had refused to discuss much about her life in Sitka. She'd always been careful to change the subject, although Jenny had sensed there was something that needed to be said. The years apart required time to trust. Jenny knew that. She wasn't about to let this moment pass, however.

Jenny got up from her chair and walked over to Naomi. "Tell me," she said, putting her hands on the girl's folded arms. "Tell me now."

Naomi shook her head. "I don't know." She hung her head. Her voice sounded almost teary. "I'm too afraid to go down there again."

Jenny shook her slightly. "Has he frightened you?"

Naomi continued to shake her head, "No, but Umqua caught me down there." She tightened up, ramrod straight. "I wasn't doing anything. I was just looking around."

"Did she threaten you?"

Naomi bobbed her head. "She told me never to go there again."

"What did you see?"

Naomi's face turned almost a parchment white. She dropped the tone of her voice to a whisper. "I saw a room, a locked room. I think someone lives there, someone they never want to come out."

"Who knows about this?" She gripped Naomi's arm tighter. "Who knows besides Uncle Ian?"

Naomi pulled herself free from Jenny's grasp and paced back to the chairs. "I don't know. I'm not even sure Umqua knows. I couldn't ask Uncle Ian. He had told me not to go down there."

Jenny stepped closer. "Bubba Dean must know. If someone is down there, then they must be fed. Who would do it if Bubba Dean doesn't?"

"Yes," Naomi said, "he must know, but he's totally loyal to Ian. He wouldn't say anything."

Just then footsteps sounded in the hall. Naomi looked toward the door. "That's him."

"I know. I'd recognize that shuffle anywhere."

They listened quietly as Bubba Dean passed their door. He stopped, and they both heard the sound of the door to the basement open. It closed moments later.

"I think we should follow him," Jenny said. "There's no use in keeping secrets. I won't have it."

"How do we know what's down there?"

"We don't, but we ought to find out." Jenny reached out and took Naomi's hand. "You're safe now. I'm here." Jenny pointed to the candle on Naomi's bedside table. "Now, pick that candle up and bring some matches. We're going to discover what Bubba Dean seems to already know."

Jenny opened the door and the two of them stepped out into the hallway, closing the door behind them. They moved down the hall to the large door that led downstairs. Naomi reached into her pocket, took out a match, and struck it against the wall. She touched it to the candle, sending a sliver of flame crawling up the slender wick.

Jenny took the candle from Naomi. She led the way down the dark basement stairs, and Naomi stepped down and closed the door behind them. Jenny stopped several steps later and looked back at her. She could see the girl was almost shaking. "It's okay but let's not talk. Just stay right behind me. I want to hear what's being said, if anything."

Naomi nodded her head.

They got to the foot of the stairs and Naomi pointed to the open door across the room. "The hallway is over there," she said.

It was obvious that Bubba Dean didn't think he would ever be followed.

Jenny lifted the candle and walked toward the cracked open door and pushed it wide open. At the end of the hall she could see the far door open. The light from the sunset cast a pink glow over the walls. She also saw the silver candlestick that Bubba Dean had carried. It was standing unlit on one of the boxes next to the open door. She turned around and looked back at Naomi. "That looks like it goes outside."

"Yes." Naomi bobbed her head. "That door leads to a small garden. Maybe he's out there enjoying the sunset. It does face to the west."

Jenny turned and moved down the dark hall. She held out her hand, lightly brushing it against the wall. The boards were rough and dark, which made the sun outside seem even more inviting. They passed a door with a brass handle, moving ever closer to the opening at the far end of the hall. As they stepped closer, Bubba Dean passed by the open door on the outside. He had a tray in his hand, and his lips were moving as if he were talking to someone.

Both Jenny and Naomi moved to the side, up against the wall. They wanted to keep out of sight as much as possible, at least until they could tell what he was saying and just whom he might be talking to.

Stepping back into the middle of the hall, they walked cautiously forward, moving their feet carefully. It was then that Bubba Dean once again passed the open door. He looked down the dark hall in their direction. Jenny jumped once again to the wall beside her, afraid he had seen the candle.

Naomi was behind her now. She whispered, "Do you think he saw us?"

"I'm not sure."

Moments later Bubba Dean stepped through the door. Jenny quickly blew out the candle as the man closed it. "Who's down dere?" he yelled out.

"It's us, Bubba Dean, Jenny and Naomi."

The man stepped closer to them and held up his candle. "Is you? Miss Jenny and Miss Naomi?"

Jenny walked closer to him. "Yes, we just came down to take a look around."

"Y'all ladies ain't suppose to be here. Miss Naomi know 'bout dat."

Jenny could see the man's face. There were great drops of sweat beading on his wrinkled forehead, but he forced a smile.

"I shouldn't think there would be anything that needs to be hidden from family," Jenny said.

"Dis here is a private area, private only to Mr. Ian. He don't want nobody traipsing 'round dis place."

Jenny stepped forward. "Why not, pray tell?"

"He jest don't, dat's all. You best be taking dis here business up with him."

Bubba Dean stepped closer. His fist was clinched. Jenny could never remember the man looking more nervous nor more intimidating.

+ + + + +

Zac watched the man walk clear of the trees. Even in the gathering darkness, he could see he was a big man, and he relaxed his grip on Ian. Ian stepped aside of the deadfall and glanced back at Zac and seemed to shudder. Zac couldn't tell if he was more afraid of him or the intruder.

Zac moved closer to the water and motioned the man forward. "Come a little closer so we can see you."

The man moved down to the banks of the stream. Zac could see he had furs on, which may have made him appear larger, but he was still good sized. He had a clean-shaven face, which was in itself rare in Alaska.

"You can cross easily about a hundred yards downstream," Ian yelled. "We do have some food that's still hot, and you're more than welcome to it."

He gave Ian a small salute and moved off in the direction Ian had indicated. He carried a rifle in his hand and a small pack on his back.

"He seems to be a hunter," Ian said. "Maybe he wants to set up trap lines."

Zac kept his eyes on the trees on the far shore, looking for others that might be with the man.

"What's wrong?" Ian asked.

"Do you think he's alone?"

Ian swatted a hand in Zac's direction. "Of course he is. In Alaska, men travel alone. It's part of why they come here in the first place."

"Then why would he want food from us?" Zac looked up at the clear skies. "And on a clear night when he wouldn't have to worry about the rain."

Ian looked up. "You've got a point there. We'll keep our eyes on him."

A short time later they spotted the stranger trotting up the riverbank. He ran easily, almost as if he hadn't traveled far that day. Zac wondered if the man hadn't been here for some time, just waiting for them, waiting for them and the darkness.

"Found the spot," the man said. "Might be a place for fish just below it."

"Yes," Ian responded. "Might be at that. Come on into the cabin and rest your back a mite."

The man unslung his pack from his back, opened the door, and stepped in with Ian behind him.

"Found a wanderer out there," Ian announced. He looked at the man. "I never got your name."

"People call me Tom. I'm Athabascan."

Juneau got to his feet. "You're a little far south, aren't you?"

The man nodded. "I guess I am. I just wanted to see this place for myself."

Ian slapped the man on the back. "I've heard your people are good hunters. You down here for bear?"

"Might be."

Ian motioned to Lilly. "Bob, give this man a plate of that fine grub of yours. I doubt he's had anything like it."

Ian's dog, Hobo, had gotten to his feet, growling menacingly. He circled the man, eyeing him.

"Here, Skip," Ian said. "You better take Hobo out for a while. I don't want him running around loose out there. When he finishes his business, bring him back." He glanced over to Zac. "That's all right, isn't it?"

"Yes, I suppose so." He held the door open for the boy. "Just make sure you don't stay out too long. We'll have to get to sleep if we're going to get an early start come morning."

Skip nodded and walked over to the dog. "Come on, boy. Let's go for a walk."

Skip motioned for Hobo at the door, and the dog reluctantly joined him and stepped outside. Zac followed him just out the door. "You watch those deadfalls," he said. "Did you see where the others are?"

"I can find them, no problem."

"Just don't run," Zac said. "Walk."

"Yes, sir."

Skip led Hobo around the first of the traps and down to the stream. The dog stepped into the water and took a drink.

"Come on, Hobo," Skip said. He took a few steps up the river. "Let's go up here for a ways."

A short time later, Skip looked back to see the cabin. He had gone farther than he had intended. The black cabin seemed small, with slivers of light streaming out of the slitted windows. Hobo was still playing along the stream, sniffing at any vegetation that attracted his attention.

Skip clapped his hands. "Come on, boy. Let's go back."

Looking around at Skip, Hobo took a few small steps toward him, then turned and ran in the opposite direction.

Skip gave chase, determined to catch the dog before he got too far. He rounded a bend in the stream, and suddenly a man caught him by the shirt.

"What are you doing here?" the stranger growled.

Skip swung his arms to try to shake himself free. It did him no good. The man's grip was firm. "Who are you?" Skip asked.

"Never you mind who I am. Who are you and what are you doing out here?"

The man had a flaming red beard. He was large and broad at the shoulder, and his blue eyes were staring fiercely at Skip. "My name is Skip

Bond." Skip was shaking slightly. "I'm here with my father and my uncle."

"And just who might that be?"

Skip tried to pry the man's grip loose. "Let go of me."

The man just pulled him tighter. "When I know what I want to know, then I might let you go." He grinned at Skip, leaning down into his face. "Otherwise, I'll just skin you right here and be done with it."

"My father's name is Zac Cobb."

"How can he be your father?"

"He's not my real father. He's just my father now."

"And who might your uncle be?"

"My uncle is Ian Hays and he owns these woods, so you just better get out of here."

"Nobody owns the woods in Alaska."

"Well, he does." Once again, Skip tried to pry the man's hands off him. "And when I tell them what you've done, they're going to be out here to get you."

The man tightened his grasp on Skip and pulled him to his toes. "You just answer my questions. Who all is in that cabin back there?"

"More than you can handle, that's for sure." Anger was starting to take hold of Skip. He could still feel the fear that had shot through him, but the irritation he felt toward the man holding him was taking over.

The man reached into his belt and drew a long, glimmering knife. He held it to Skip's throat. He softened his tone to a menacing, low growl. "Boy, you better listen to me and listen real good." He ran the blunt edge of the knife over Skip's throat in a sawing motion. "I could carve you up right here and leave your bones to the wolves if I wanted to. You better tell me what I want to know or I'm going to do just that."

"There's two other men," Skip gulped, "and a stranger just walked in."

"A stranger? What did he look like?"

"Tall, big man with black eyes. He said his name was Tom."

"Tom, huh?" The man held up his knife in front of Skip's face. "You see this knife, boy?"

Skip nodded.

"You say anything to anybody about this little talk of ours and I'm going to find you." His eyes gleamed into Skip's, almost laughing at him. "Some night when you're asleep, you won't be watching for me, but I'll be watching you."

He lifted Skip off the ground and took the point of the knife, jabbing it slightly into the fleshy part of Skip's neck. "I keep this here knife real sharp."

Skip's legs shook. He could feel the chills running up his back.

"You keep that yammer of yours shut tight. You understand me?"

Skip nodded.

"That's a good little boy. You don't say nothing and maybe I'll let you grow up to be a big boy."

Just then Hobo burst out of the brush upstream. He spotted the man and started to growl. Then he gave a sudden rush on the two of them.

The man let go of Skip, dropping him to the ground. Skip reached out to Hobo and wrapped his arms around the charging, barking dog. "Wait, Hobo," he called out. "Don't go!"

He held on tight as the dog continued to bark. Looking back at where the man had been standing, he saw nothing but moving tree branches. He had disappeared.

CHAPTER 21

+ + + + + + +

SKIP CREPT IN THE DOOR BEHIND HOBO. He was shaking as he closed the door behind him and stood with his back to it, still breathing hard.

"You all right?" Zac asked.

Skip looked around at the other men in the room. He noticed the hard stare from the stranger. This was a man he didn't know and didn't like. He nodded his head.

"Then you better get yourself some sleep," Zac said. "We'll be leaving at dawn."

Skip walked around the glowing fire in the fireplace and took his place on the cot in the corner. He peeled back several layers of furs and scooted his feet beneath them. The fire was glowing and several lit candles made the walls come alive with flickering shadows. Skip's eyes were wide as he watched the shadows dance on the bare wood.

Zac walked over to the boy. "You must be tired," he said. "Usually you don't go to bed without some sort of fuss."

Skip said nothing. He looked up at Zac with his big eyes, just hoping Zac could read that something was wrong. Right now he wanted to talk to Zac in the worst way, but he wanted to talk to him alone.

"All right." Zac bent down and, smiling, scrambled the boy's hair. "You close your eyes and try to think about the sunshine."

"The boy's had a long day," Ian said. He got to his feet and walked over to Skip's cot. "Tramping around these woods takes a lot out of a feller." Ian patted Skip's feet. "You sleep tight, son."

The men began settling down for an after-dinner conversation, but Skip couldn't take his eyes off the newcomer. Tom was hunched over his plate at the table. He finished the last of his meal and straightened himself up. "That was good. What you call it?"

"I call it Mandarin Elk," Lilly laughed. "Ain't no such thing, but it's mine all the same."

Zac pulled out his pipe and the bag of tobacco he carried. From where Skip lay, he could see the stranger's profile against the fire. Skip watched Tom as Zac filled the bowl of the pipe. He noticed how the man took notice of where their guns were positioned. It was as if he were sizing them up. Tom also took careful note of the position of the small windows.

Skip's mind raced. The man with the red beard had seemed pleased when he said a stranger had come to the cabin. It made him wonder if the two of them weren't working together. It was the reason he hadn't said anything when he came in. He wanted to wait until Tom left.

Zac struck a match and held it over his pipe. The mixture sizzled as he puffed it into a cloud of strong aroma.

The stranger sat back slightly and took in a deep breath. "That smells mighty fine. Where does a man get a tobacco like that?"

Zac tossed the bag over to the man. "I get mine in California. It's whiskey-soaked Kentucky leaf."

The man opened the bag and stuck his nose into it. He breathed in deeply and smiled. Handing it back to Zac, he caught sight of the buckskin bag that held Zac's rifle. "What you got in there?" he asked.

"That's his cannon," Ian said. "It's quite a gun, I'd say."

"Can I see it?" The man held out his hand.

Zac reached over to where the gun was leaning against the wall. He picked it up and, turning the bag over, handed it over to the man, butt first.

Skip watched as Tom undid the rawhide strings. He slid the gun out, his eyes growing wider. "It's a Sharps, but not like one I've ever seen before."

Tom hefted the gun in his hand. "This is a lot bigger than your normal Sharps. Weighs more too."

"It's a Sharps Creedmore. It gives me a distance advantage."

He held the gun up to his cheek and pointed it at the candle hanging from the ceiling. "You got sights on it." Pulling it down from his face, he looked across the table at Zac. "You must do some distance shooting with it."

"Some," Zac replied.

"How far?" the man asked.

"Eight hundred to a thousand yards are no problem. Farther than that takes some adjusting." Zac puffed up another cloud of smoke. "The Indians used to call that gun, 'shoot today, hit tomorrow.' I guess because it would hit a target so long after it was fired. Most of the time it finds its aim before the victim can even hear the shot."

Tom lowered the gun in Zac's direction. "How hard does the hammer pull back?" He eased the hammer back into position until the familiar cock of the gun registered. Then, to everybody's surprise, he pulled the trigger. It slammed down on the empty chamber with a loud crack. He smiled. "Sorry, didn't mean to do that."

Zac reached over and took the gun from the man's hand. "If I'd had it loaded, I'd be a whole lot sorrier."

"I guess you would at that."

Zac eyed the man. He reached back and took a cartridge from the bandoleer hanging on the wall. Breaking the gun open, he planted the round into the chamber, then snapped the big gun shut. "Well, it's loaded now and it's in my hands, and that's where it's going to stay."

"Good plan," Juneau said.

Skip was getting more nervous as he watched the stranger. He didn't believe it was an accident the man had pulled the trigger, not for a minute. He didn't think Zac did either. Now he didn't dare turn his back and try to sleep. Sleep was far from him at the moment, and that's exactly where he wanted it to stay. He kicked back the furs that were covering him and slowly got to his feet.

"What do you need, boy?" Ian asked.

"Just a drink of water is all."

Ian picked up the bucket and hit the bottom of it with the tin ladle hanging over the side. "We appear to be fresh out." He swung the bucket in Skip's direction. "Why don't you go out and get us some?"

Skip shook his head vigorously and backed up to his cot. He sat back down. "It's okay. I can wait until morning."

"You go ahead, boy. Somebody might just wake up in the middle of the night thirsty, and besides, you're still dressed."

Going out that door and into the darkness was the last thing Skip wanted to do. He looked over in Zac's direction. He was hoping Zac would see the fear in his eyes, even though he couldn't very well explain it in front of the stranger.

"You want to take Hobo with you?" Zac asked.

"No, sir," Skip replied. "He might run off and then I'd have to chase him."

Ian held the bucket in Skip's face. "Then go on, boy. There's plenty of moonlight and no rain. A man couldn't want much better than that." He looked over at Zac. "I swear I ain't never seen a boy more skittish about work."

Zac just watched as Skip walked slowly to the door. Skip gripped the bucket handle, sweat forming in the palms of his hands, and took one last look at Zac.

The moon was bright, filtering through the trees. It gave a yellow tint to the blackness of the woods. Skip walked along the path, listening for anything that might seem out of place. If the man he had seen earlier was anyplace close, he wanted to hear him long before he saw him. He looked off toward his right. That's where the man had been before, downstream. He was thankful they wouldn't be leaving that way in the morning.

It wasn't until he heard the crunch of the first branch that he froze in his tracks. He backed up with one small step and looked down at the brown patch of twigs that had almost been his doom. Taking a step to the side, he moved around the trap. The sudden bolt of fear had almost made him forget why he didn't want to get water in the first place.

He hurried down to the flowing stream, winding his way past several trees that stood in his way. The moonlight made the water sparkle and the deeper patches in the middle of the river picked up the reflection of the northern lights overhead. He'd never seen anything more beautiful.

Skip looked down to make sure of his footing. Moving out onto a rock that stood in the river, he lowered the bucket. The water surged into it, cold and crisp. He dipped his hand into the stream and held it to his mouth. He sipped from the palm of his hand and dipped it again for another drink. Slowly he got to his feet. Holding the bucket with both hands, he walked the path in the direction of the trees.

"Hey, kid."

Skip heard the man's voice before he saw him. It made his blood run cold.

The red-bearded man stepped out from behind the trees to Skip's far right and pulled out his knife. "You keep your mouth shut like I told you?" he asked.

Skip edged his way up the trail, keeping his eyes on the man.

The man signaled toward him. "Come over here to me. Don't make me have to come and get you."

Skip turned and began to run toward the cabin, the water spilling out of the bucket. He could hear the man moving through the trees now, behind him but gaining.

Running almost up to the deadfall, he stopped in his tracks and stepped aside. He turned around. "What do you want?"

The man stopped a few feet away and smiled. "I just want to talk to you. That's all."

"Okay. Stay right where you are and talk."

The man moved closer and smiled. "Now, since when do buddies stay so far away? I want to know how many guns are inside that cabin." He pointed with his knife in the direction of the cabin.

Skip stepped around the covered pit and then back to the other side of it. "I can't tell you that."

"Well, you better, boy." The man stepped closer.

Skip edged closer to the branches on the ground to a spot where he could feel them under his toes. "I ain't got nothing to say to you. I think you should just turn around and go back to where you came from."

"Now, boy, don't make old Smitty mad." He stepped closer. "You wouldn't want to do that. I just want to tell you something, boy. Something secret."

Skip glanced at the man's feet. He was almost on the branches that covered the pit. One more step would be one step too many. Of course, if he moved too slowly, he might just feel the give in the branches first. Skip didn't want that to happen.

"You told me everything I need to know. Now, just turn around and go away from here. This place is dangerous for you."

"For me? Oh, I don't think so." The man looked down at his knife and turned it over in his hands. "I got me this here knife. What you gonna do to me, boy, hit me with that bucket of yours?"

Skip looked down at the bucket. It was only half full now. He knew he had to take the man's mind off of where he was stepping, just for a moment. There might be no better way to do it. Leaning over the pit, Skip swung the bucket in the man's direction.

Smitty jumped back, fire in his eyes. "Why, you rascal, you. I'm gonna teach you a thing or two, boy."

Running toward Skip, the man's feet hit the branches and he fell in. Skip heard the loud scream, followed by a bellow.

The door to the cabin flew open and Zac stepped out, the rifle in his hand. Ian and the others followed Zac as they ran to the open pit. Zac grabbed Skip, pulling him into his arms. "You all right?"

Skip nodded. "Yes, I'm fine." He cast a glance over his shoulder. "He isn't."

Zac pushed Skip behind him and peered into the pit. He could see the faint outline of the man at the bottom, and they could all hear the continued moans. He turned back in the men's direction. "Somebody go get a lantern. Let's see who's down here."

Zac stooped down and got on one knee. He held Skip. "What happened here, son?"

Skip looked up at Tom who was standing over Zac, looking down into the pit. He was listening to the cries that came from the bottom of the spiked pit, shrill wails accompanied by low, mournful howls. "I can't tell you right now."

For the first time Zac seemed to understand. He looked up in the man's direction. "All right. We get this settled and you and me will go for a walk. That all right with you?"

Skip nodded his head. "Yes, sir," he said.

Moments later Lilly and Juneau returned with the lanterns and held them over the pit. There at the bottom, with spikes driven through him, was the man with the red beard. He was still alive, but Zac knew he wouldn't last long.

"That's Smitty," Ian said. "What's he doing here?"

Zac got to his feet. "You know darn well why he's here," Zac said. "He came to finish the job he started out to do at the Crystal Palace. The only thing I'd like to know is, did he come alone?"

CHAPTER 22

+ + + + + + +

"DO YOU HAVE ENOUGH MONEY for both of us?" Naomi asked.

"Yes, don't worry about that," Jenny answered. "I have enough for the both of us, Zac, and Skip too. Let's just hope we can find passage on the next boat." She looked up at the sky. It was overcast. Anyone who had been in Sitka for any length of time knew it would rain, it was only a matter of when and for how long.

They continued walking. Jenny had been determined not to let anyone know where they were going. She was also convinced that they weren't going to just sit around and depend on Ian's good graces to find them a southbound boat.

"This is quite a walk, isn't it?" Naomi asked.

"Yes, I just didn't want to have Bubba Dean saddle a horse for us. There's no sense in telling them where we're going."

Naomi lowered her head and continued to march. She looked over at Jenny and smiled. "I was just thinking about the walk back. If it rains then, we'll be uphill in the mud."

Jenny laughed. "Yes, ought to be a good excuse for a bubble bath when we get back to the house, I expect."

"Do you think Bubba Dean told Umqua we were in the basement?"

Jenny nodded. "I don't doubt it. Did you notice how polite she was to us at the breakfast table?"

"Yes, she even smiled at me."

The two young women walked along for some time. Jenny looked over at her sister. They were so much alike. "I've got an idea. Maybe we could quote poetry or scripture to each other while we walk."

"I'd like that," Naomi said. "Where should we start?"

"How about the sermon on the mount? I've always enjoyed that."

Naomi grinned. "I'm afraid I've got you at a disadvantage on that. I memorized it for school."

Jenny laughed. "Now, just what makes you think a girl has to have a school assignment to memorize something? Some things are best given to the heart if you love them."

The two of them spent the better part of the next half hour going through what they could remember of the book of Matthew. Each took turns, helping the other out with spaces that had appeared in their memory. Suddenly, the sound of a carriage in the distance behind them drew them up short.

"Who do you think that could be?" Naomi asked.

"I don't know," Jenny said, pulling on Naomi's sleeve, "but I'm not going to stay here in the road to find out."

The two of them moved off the side of the road and crouched in the bushes. Jenny pulled the branches apart slightly to get a better view. Moments later the carriage wheeled by with Umqua, Risa, and Dolly in it. Dolly sat in the front seat laughing and slapping her hands to her knees, as if her actions could affect the speed of the two horses.

"Where do you suppose they're going?" Naomi asked.

"Shopping, I imagine." Jenny got to her feet.

Naomi planted her hands on her hips. "If we'd waited we could have ridden with them."

"And have them know our business? I think not."

It took the two of them some time before they reached the edge of the town. The rain held off, although it threatened to drench them at any time. Baranof Castle sat in the harbor, its gun ports bristling with long-ago threats. Jenny could see a large steamship sitting at anchor. "Maybe that ship will be leaving soon," she said. "Isn't that the one Zac came in on?"

"Yes, I think so. I don't know why it would be back here. They don't appear to be very busy, though."

They walked along the street and Jenny pointed to the shipping office. "Let's go there right away," she said. "I want to get buying these tickets out of the way." She looked out at the harbor where the large black steamship sat idle. "We might even go on that one, if Zac gets back in time."

The office was a white building with peeling paint. Red shutters surrounded narrow windows and the words "Sitka Shipping Office" were painted in a bright green over the door. The people had obviously taken the trouble to keep the sign in good shape, no matter what neglect the rest of the building was suffering from. Jenny grabbed the brass doorknob and twisted it. As the door opened, a bell hanging above it rang softly.

The man behind the counter wore a dirty white shirt with garters lifting his sleeves above his elbows. The green shade that sat on his head was more for effect than anything, Jenny thought. It made his bald head shine all the more. His face was chubby and milk white, and as he smiled he looked like a piece of dough one might be getting ready to slide into the oven.

"Good day to you, ladies. How may I be of assistance to you?"

"We'd like tickets on the next ship sailing for Seattle," Jenny said.

The man reached around to where he had a broken clipboard hanging on the wall. He pulled it down and picked up the stub of a pencil. "That would be the *Blue Goose*. We've been expecting it for a day now."

"What about that ship in the harbor?"

"Oh, that's the *Northern Star*." The man scratched his head. "I don't rightly know what Zubatov's schedule is for that thing. The man comes and goes as it pleases him, and frankly I would have expected it to be long gone before now. You get on that and you could wind up anywhere."

"Well, what about the *Blue Goose*? Any idea of when it will be heading back once it arrives?"

The man lifted the back of his shade as he scratched his head. "Hard to say for sure, but I'd say it ought to be here for three days." He grinned at them. "You know how sailors are. They'll be wanting to tie one on before they start loading for the trip south, plus it will take a day to unload what they've brought us."

"Will that give us enough time?" Naomi asked.

Jenny looked at her and then back to the man behind the counter. "When is your next ship due to arrive?"

"Not for another two weeks."

Jenny bit her lip thoughtfully, then asked, "Can we buy tickets on the *Blue Goose* and then switch them for the boat to follow if it doesn't work out?"

The man leaned down on his pencil. "I suppose so, but most folks that think about it want to leave earlier rather than later when they have their minds set on going. The late boats fill up quite a bit." He stood up and waved the pencil. "People want to beat the cold sea, you know."

"Yes, I can imagine. Well, put us down for four tickets. We'd like two rooms, if you have them."

The man scanned the ledger. "I think I can find you two on the earlier one, but the late boat might be another matter."

"Fine," Jenny said, "then four tickets and two rooms on the early boat, and we'll take what we can get if we have to switch to the later one."

"We shouldn't forget Dolly," Naomi said. "You did promise her."

"Yes, I know. The wedding's not for a while, though. That's a long time for Ian to allow her to be gone. I'm sure he'll put her on a ship in plenty of time to make our wedding."

"I'll just need the names and a deposit," the man said. "You can pay the rest on the day you board the ship."

"Good." Jenny gave the man the four names and opened her purse.

"That will be two hundred dollars," the man said.

Jenny produced a wad of bills and counted out the money. "I would like a receipt," she said.

"Of course," the man replied.

It was then they heard the bell over the door and a fresh breeze followed by the sound of falling rain. Jenny turned around and saw Dave Cormia. The man was in brown corduroy pants and a matching jacket. His white shirt was pressed and his hat pulled down over his eyes. It was the look on his face that was troubling, though. His brow was wrinkled, and the worry written across his face was unmistakable.

"I saw you walking down the street from my window and then watched you go in here," Cormia stated.

Jenny held out her hands. "Don't try to talk us out of this. I need to get back home. I have a wedding to prepare, and Naomi," Jenny reached out and grabbed her sister's hand, "has been here long enough."

Cormia stuck his hands in his pockets and edged next to the hot stove. "Oh, I'm not going to try to talk you out of anything." He bowed his head, staring at his shoes. "Frankly, I'm sorry I was a part in bringing you here in the first place." Raising his head, he stared into her eyes. "I have something else you should know about." He looked over her shoulder at the clerk. "But we can't talk here."

Jenny turned around and picked up the receipt the man had written out for her. "Is that all I need?" she asked.

"Yes, ma'am. Just have your bags packed when we get to loading. You'll know when that is. This place can have quite the party when a ship comes in."

Jenny folded the receipt and put it in her bag. "Yes, I can imagine." Turning around, she walked over to where Cormia continued to warm himself. "Now, where would you suggest we go?"

"Let's go up to my office. I can best explain it there." He stepped over to the door and opened it, ringing the bell once again.

The three of them stepped out onto the boardwalk. Cormia led the way past several shops, and coming to a set of stairs, he pointed to an outside office on the second floor. "It's up there. I'm sorry I don't have an umbrella to offer you."

"That's all right," Jenny said. "We've been wet before."

They came to a landing and he fished in his pocket for a key. Jenny noticed that the lock appeared to be new. It was made out of brass, and Cormia slid the shiny key into it and turned the tumblers. He opened the door and stood aside as the two young women brushed past him.

He bounced the key in his hand. "A man shouldn't have to lock his door, not in Sitka." He dropped it into his pocket and walked to the pot-bellied stove in the back of the room. Lifting up the grate, he picked up some small pieces of kindling and tossed them in. A woman's fan with Chinese writing was hanging on the wall. He reached for it and began to fan the flames inside the stove. Soon there was a growing blaze; he added more wood before shutting the grate.

Turning around, he held his hand out in the direction of a faded green couch. "Please, ladies, make yourselves comfortable."

Jenny and Naomi sat down. "What's this all about, Mr. Cormia?" Jenny asked.

He began to pace back and forth in front of them, glancing in their direction with every pass. "I am glad you've decided to leave Sitka, and if you'll take my advice, you'll leave just as soon as possible. I'd suggest the early boat."

Jenny and Naomi exchanged worried glances.

"You both know I'm your Uncle Ian's attorney?"

"Yes," Jenny said, "we know that."

"And as such I am the executor of his estate."

The women watched him march back and forth across the room. Jenny was wondering where all this was leading.

"I also drew up his will." He stopped and pointed at an oak filing cabinet. "A will that I kept in my files." He resumed his pacing. "I just think there's something you should know, something that may place the both of you in danger.

"Perhaps I should explain something first. Until Ian's recent marriage, his daughter, Dolly, was his only heir." He looked at Naomi, nodding at her. "Of course, he did have something drawn up for your education." He waved his hand. "And something to see you settled."

"I don't need anything," Naomi said. "He's cared for me for years."

Cormia stopped and looked at her. "Nevertheless, he wants you provided for. His new will does more than that, though." He looked in Jenny's direction. "For both of you."

"For me?" Jenny asked the question, pressing her fingers to her chest.

"Yes, the man has great confidence in you." He shook his head. "He also has a great concern for Dolly. The girl is incompetent, and his fear is that she will come into a great deal of money only to have it stolen from her. From what I've seen he may be right."

"What does this have to do with me?" Jenny asked.

Cormia pulled up a chair and sat down. "Your uncle has growing assets, and the property he now has control over has the potential for great wealth. He has three dependents and views at least two of them as incompetent." He pointed his finger at Jenny. "And he wants you to look after their welfare. He has made you a trustee." Bowing his head, he added, "Of course, there is compensation in it for you—ample compensation, I assure you."

"You said three dependents," Jenny said. "I assume you mean Bubba Dean."

"No," Cormia shook his head, "and I'm afraid I'm not at liberty to disclose any more, not while Ian is alive. His servant is well taken care of, though. I think both he and the man's wife will be amply provided for during the remainder of their lives."

Jenny was genuinely puzzled. The numbers didn't add up. "Then why are we in such great danger?" Jenny asked.

"Because the legality of his marriage to Risa might just be challenged should he die any time soon."

"He seems healthy to me," Jenny said.

"That may be, but you know there have been attempts on his life. Some of them have been near misses. I think he's genuinely afraid. Given the new will he just signed, if your role was known and something did happen to him, you would be in an awkward position."

"Why would his marriage to Risa be challenged?" Jenny asked.

Cormia glanced at his shoe tops. "That's something I cannot discuss."

"And what if I refuse the terms of this will?" Jenny asked.

Cormia looked her in the eye. There was a plaintive, almost pitiful look of despair on his face. "I sincerely hope you do not do that. If that were to happen, then I, as the executor of Ian's estate, would have to care for the young woman. Her opportunities here would be most limited, and I am not a young man. I'm afraid the thing that Ian has feared the most would be upon us in a very short time."

"I see," Jenny said.

"If you were to leave and something unfortunate were to befall Ian, I think it would be better if you were beyond the reach of his enemies." He shook his head. "No, I'm afraid that boat for Seattle will be the safest place for you to be, at least until things settle down here."

Naomi stared at Jenny. "We should go right away then."

Jenny nodded and then looked at Cormia. "But why didn't you tell me this before I came?"

"This will is very new. I think Ian wanted to meet you first. That was why he was adamant that you come. He's just looking after the welfare of the people he loves."

"Without much regard for me, I take it."

"Oh no, with great regard for you."

"Something I could live without," Jenny added.

"You will ultimately be in control of his property, with the power to sell it or use it in any way you desire."

Jenny shook her head. "I just don't see why Risa can't have that responsibility. She is his wife."

"Yes, but she is not a white woman. As such, she will never be recognized by the court."

"Amazing," Jenny said. "Her land can go to Ian in a dowry settlement, but she can't have it back."

"That's about the size of it," Cormia said.

Jenny got to her feet. "Then we will be on the next boat south. You can be assured of that."

Naomi stood up. "I think I should start packing right away."

Cormia walked them to the door. He took hold of the new brass doorknob. "One thing you should know. My office was broken into." He looked back at the filing cabinet. "And I think someone rifled through my files. I have reason to believe this new will of Ian's was disturbed. I do hope I'm wrong, but if I'm not, it does put you into immediate danger." He shook his head. "I blame myself for that. I just never thought anyone would break into my office. I mean, I'm not a bank. I don't keep money or a safe."

The two women left the office and started back down the stairs. The rain had slackened to a drizzle and was breaking apart. As they stepped onto the boardwalk, they saw the carriage tied up in front of the general store across the street. Jenny backed up under an awning.

"I see they're shopping," Jenny said. "Maybe you'd like to have a part of that and see if we can ride back with them."

They watched a large wagon roll by. Its wheels mashed into the mud with a squashing sound, and the hooves of the horses sent a small geyser of mud in all directions with each step.

Naomi smiled. "That sounds like a great idea."

They started to move out from under the awning, but Jenny stopped Naomi. Umqua had just stepped out of the store. She didn't have any packages in her hands and moved right past the carriage, walking down the street in a hurried fashion. She was moving quickly, almost running.

"I wonder where she's going in such a hurry?" Jenny asked.

"I don't know," Naomi said, "but I would have thought she'd make the most purchases."

Jenny and Naomi watched her. Rounding the other side of the Crystal Palace, she darted into the side alley. They looked at each other, puzzled.

"Now, why would she be going there?" Naomi asked.

"I wouldn't have the first idea," Jenny said. "But I'm going to find out." She nodded in the direction of the store. "Why don't you go shopping? I won't be long."

Naomi watched her walk away. "You be careful now, you hear?"

Jenny gave her a wave.

It took her a few minutes to cross the street and cover the distance to where they had seen Umqua disappear. Just walking past the smelly saloon gave her the chills, but she held her head high and paraded past it all the same.

Rounding the corner into the alley gave her a start. The stench was overpowering. Fresh garbage had been thrown into piles, and a number of very large rats were burrowing their way through the mess. Jenny stepped sideways, giving the rubbish a wide berth.

As Jenny stepped lightly down the alley, occasionally she would pass a window. She moved closer, tiptoeing to get a better view inside. Several windows down the alley, she got up on her toes and looked in. There was Umqua, talking—or rather listening—to the animated Kathryn Jung. The blond woman seemed to be lecturing Umqua, shaking her finger.

What are they doing here? Jenny wondered. Behind Kathryn stood a tall man with a bushy black beard and dark piercing eyes.

Suddenly the door beside Jenny opened, but there was no place to run. All she could do was stand flat-footed, look out of place, and just hope that whoever was coming out to throw the garbage away not only didn't recognize her, but didn't throw their slop on her.

The large man smiled at her. He held a stained can of garbage in his hand. "You must be Jenny Hays," he said. "We were just talking about you."

CHAPTER 23

+ + + + + + +

THE RIVER WAS RUNNING WIDE and that suited Zac just fine. It did bring out the bears, but with the river fanning out, they could keep the canoe away from them and have enough room to get by without attracting too much attention. By the time the burly bears looked up from their fishing, they were already by them and down the river. Zac was glad now that Lilly had convinced them to leave Hobo at the cabin. The dog could easily provoke a bear attack.

The sun was shining brightly, and at several spots they passed clumps of ripe berries, both bright red and dark black. All in all it made for a day to remember, especially with the snow-capped mountains overhead.

"Benny's gonna have the boat ready for us when we get to the passage," Ian said.

Zac was quiet. The only one of the three of them who had done much talking was Ian. Skip tried to present a normal face, but Zac could tell the boy was still deeply troubled by what had happened at the cabin. From what he'd told Zac about his two encounters with the man, it was plain to see the boy didn't have much choice. As far as Zac was concerned, Skip had done the right thing.

"Would you like to take a turn with the paddle?" Zac asked. He knew that a little work might take the boy's mind off the man killed at the cabin.

Skip's eyes brightened. "Sure, can I?"

Zac motioned to a sandbar along the edge of the river. "We'll put in over there and I'll switch with you."

Ian looked back from the front of the canoe. "If you're going to let the boy paddle, I'd feel a whole lot better if he was doing it from up here. That rear paddle controls a lot of our steering."

"I'm sure he's up to it," Zac said.

"No, it's all right," Skip said. "I'd kinda like to be up front and see more of where we're going."

"That's a good lad," Ian added. "We'll pull for the shore now."

Both men dipped their paddles in the water and pulled hard for the shoreline. In a matter of moments they had nudged the bow of the canoe into the sand. Zac and Ian got out and tramped ankle deep in the water, pulling the canoe farther up on the beach. Zac watched as Ian reached in and shuffled through his equipment. He took out a large shiny pan, and Zac could see right away it was one used for panning gold.

"What do you aim to do with that?" Zac asked, although he knew full well what Ian had in mind.

"I thought as long as we were stopping, I'd try my hand at this sandy spot. Looks to be a likely place to me." Ian nodded toward Skip, who had found a blackberry bush and was picking off several of the ripe ones that hadn't fallen yet. "It looks like the boy would like a stop too."

Zac looked back upstream in Skip's direction. "I suppose so. I just want to put as much distance as possible between us and what we left."

"You mean that stranger, Tom, at the cabin?" Ian asked. He squatted down beside the river and lifted a pan of rocky soil from the stream.

"That's right."

"I wouldn't worry too much about him. This here river carries us a whole lot faster than he can walk."

"If he followed the river," Zac added. Zac looked up at the hills to their north. "He left hours before we did, and if he cut off across those hills, he might be waiting for us up ahead."

"Man's got to sleep," Ian said. He sloshed water over the sides of the pan, moving the thing in a circular motion.

"We've slept on the river for two days now. A man that's driven can sleep in patches and keep on moving."

Ian lifted his head in Zac's direction. "You seem to know a lot about driven men, for a rancher."

"I know what there is to know," Zac said. "Also seems to me that it's taking us a mite longer to go this way than if we just walked out where we came from."

"That's true, but this way we get to ride. I just didn't want us to back-track, and besides, I told Benny to meet us down here."

Zac stood up, watching the tree line. "All the same, a man is easy to find as long as he stays on the river."

"You worry too much, Cobb."

Zac watched Skip. The boy had found a second patch of blackberries farther upstream and was picking them. Some went into his hat while most of them went into his mouth. "I have more to worry about on this trip than you do."

Ian looked up at him. "You know, most folks take some time before deciding not to like me."

"Liking ain't got nothing to do with it. I like you. I just don't trust you."

Ian held up the pan with a grin on his face. "Got me something here." He reached his fingers into the pan and pulled up a gold nugget. "It ain't big, but it's here on my land."

Zac looked around to try to find Skip. The boy was continuing upstream, following the blackberries. "Don't go too far, Skipper," Zac yelled. "We'll be leaving directly."

Skip looked back in Zac's direction. "Yes, sir. I won't."

Reaching into the canoe, Zac pulled out his buckskin-wrapped Sharps. He unwound the rawhide strings he used to tie the thing and slid it out of the case. Picking up the ammo belt, he slung it over his shoulder. He then hung the empty gun bag around his neck.

Ian dipped his pan back into the river. "You figure to do some hunting?"

"I just plan on being ready," Zac replied.

Ian sloshed more water around in the pan. "That's fine. You just be ready. We'll leave in a bit."

Suddenly Zac spotted two cinnamon brown humps coming over the hill. The hair on the back of his neck rose. He looked quickly back upstream to try to spot Skip. The boy was gone, no doubt following the blackberries up the river. He stepped back a few paces in Ian's direction, all the while keeping an eye on the hill. "You better quit your panning and go get Skip," he said.

Ian looked up. "Why?"

Zac nodded in the direction of the hill. "We got company, big company."

Ian got to his feet. "We may be in their fishing spot."

Zac readied his Sharps, slinging the thing to his shoulder. "And just as soon as you get Skip, we'll be leaving their spot."

Ian sprinted past the canoe, dropping his pan into the bottom. It landed with a series of bangs on the slats of the boat, and as Zac watched the two bears, he could hear Ian's feet digging through the sand. *At least the man is running*, Zac thought.

The two bears cleared the top of the hill and stood there watching him. It was almost as if they were making up their minds as to what their next move was. They swayed their bodies back and forth, eyeing the downhill slope. They began to run down the hill in Zac's direction, bellowing as they came. There would be no stopping them now, Zac was sure of that.

He looked back upstream, back to where the river snaked out of view. He could hear Ian calling out for Skip, a series of plaintive cries that were going unanswered.

He turned his attention back to the running bears. Both of the creatures were several hundred yards away and coming on like runaway locomotives. They might be at his feet in a matter of moments. There was no time to lose, certainly not nearly time enough for Ian to get back with Skip.

He lifted the rifle to his cheek and took aim on the lead bear. He would try to break the animal's shoulder. That might put him out of action. The Sharps erupted in his hands, bellowing smoke and fire and dropping the bear into a slow tumble.

Pulling down the rifle, he broke it open, ejecting the hot shell casing. He pulled out another round from the bandoleer and rammed it home. Snapping the rifle shut with a jerk, he raised it once again to his cheek. He fired again, dropping the second bear into a slow downhill spin. The animal tumbled head over heels, growling and howling with each flip.

The first bear had gotten to his feet, and Zac shook his head at the tenacity of the thing. It opened its mouth and roared, showing a set of polished teeth. Then it once again started on its run in Zac's direction. It was a slow, methodical gait, determined and angry. No doubt the beast's anger and adrenaline were carrying it forward.

Zac broke open the rifle once again and took out another round. He slid it into position and closed the weapon with a snap. There was no time for a heart shot, and his attempt to break the animal's shoulder had failed. Raising the rifle, he tracked the beast as it came down the hill. He sighted in on the bear's head and the snowy teeth he showed when bellowing. Zac took a deep breath, letting out the air in a slow, deliberate fashion. He squeezed the trigger, ever so slowly, and the rifle once again exploded. He watched as the beast jerked aside and then skidded to a stop at the bottom of the hill. A cloud of dust rose up at Zac's feet.

He lowered the rifle, staring at the dead animal.

Zac turned around and saw Ian running with Skip in tow. The boy was still being careful not to let the berries fall from the full hat he was carrying. They skidded to a halt near where Zac was standing. "It's too late now," Zac said.

Ian looked at the bear that was lying close by. "I can see that. Mighty close, I'd say."

"Too close."

Zac started to walk up the hill. He could still hear the sounds of the second bear he'd shot, a series of low moans.

"Where you going?" Ian asked.

"I'm not going to let that thing lay there and suffer. You both get in the boat, and I'll be along directly."

He walked slowly up the hill to the spot where he'd taken the second bear. It lay on the ground, its eyes blinking open. Zac planted another round into the Sharps and fired, wishing he didn't have to put an end to such a magnificent creature.

A short time later he pushed the canoe off the sandbank and settled into the spot between Ian and Skip. He opened the Sharps and replaced the spent cartridge with a fresh round.

"You figure on doing some more hunting?" Ian asked.

"No, but I'd say if someone is waiting for us downstream, they know we're here by now. Noise carries a long way down the river, and there's no mistaking what a Sharps sounds like."

The river narrowed and a number of fish flashed by the surface. The water tumbled over the rocks and the canoe dropped down a series of small falls. Zac balanced himself in the middle and tried to make sure it stayed afloat.

The boat went through a series of large rocks in the stream. Each one could have done considerable damage. Zac could see Skip pushing off the rocks ahead with the paddle and then digging deep at what he saw as the main current. "Good work, Skipper," Zac said.

The canoe bounced down a series of waves, and Skip dug hard to try to keep it in the current around a bend. Suddenly, they found themselves in a peaceful stretch of water. It was deep and smooth, the color an azure blue.

The stream fanned out into a flat, still surface, almost as quickly as it had become a boiling cauldron. Several trees stood along the edge and one had become the perch to more than twenty bald eagles. The birds sat in the branches, like a convention of lodge members; they turned their orange beaks slowly, following the canoe as it went by.

"I'd hate to be a fish in here," Skip said.

"I reckon you wouldn't last long," Ian laughed. "They seem to be just waiting for supper."

Both Ian and Skip pulled their paddles hard through the water. Zac was at least thankful for that. This calm stretch of water meant they were traveling at a slower speed, and there were very few obstructions to give them cover. It made Zac hold the Sharps all the tighter. He scanned the sides of the hills on either side, watching for anything, especially movement.

They heard the whitewater up ahead long before they saw it. Zac looked back at Ian. He assumed the man had made the trip through this part of the river before, but it was always difficult to tell with Ian.

"You know this river?" he asked.

"Sure I do," Ian said.

Zac knew it was dangerous to assume anything when it came to whitewater. "You've been down this part yourself?" he asked.

Ian shook his head. "Didn't say that. Benny and Lilly have said lots about it, though. I figure I learned all there was to know from those fellas."

"Great," Zac mumbled under his breath. "You been 'round the horn?" Zac knew that if Ian was a seaman, Cape Horn would be something he would know well. It was the most treacherous stretch of sea in the world and a graveyard to many an experienced sailor.

"Sure have, several times."

"And did you think you learned all about that from the men who told you what it was like?"

"The horn's something a man has to see for himself to believe. But this is just a river. It ain't the horn."

"I've been on rivers that make Cape Horn look like a bubble bath," Zac said. "Let's just hope that what you heard is true."

The noise of the river grew louder. It was already too late for Zac to change places with Skip. No amount of second guessing would make it otherwise. He spread himself out in the middle of the canoe and prepared for the worst.

Around the bend they spotted the first set of rapids. They were rising and falling some three to four feet. Even at that height, Zac knew the water would be dangerous for a canoe. "Pull hard," he shouted. "A canoe's got to be going faster than the water it's in to stay stable."

Skip and Ian dug hard in the water, shooting the canoe over the swells in the river. It bounced when it hit the bottom of the waves, rising up to catch the next set of swells. Zac picked up a small bucket and began to bail out the water.

Up ahead, two large boulders stood in the stream with the water roaring through between them. There was no other way around the gap. Zac knew it had to be done, no matter what was on the other side.

It was then that he heard the first shot. The bullet buzzed past his ear like an angry bee whose nest had been disturbed. Zac dropped the bucket and picked up the Sharps. "Keep paddling!" he yelled.

CHAPTER 24

+ + + + + + +

BOTH IAN AND SKIP BENT LOW and kept the paddles churning. Zac took aim at some movement he saw on the northern slope and squeezed off a round. The gun bucked in his hand, its report booming over the water. The acrid smell of the gunsmoke curled over the glassy river.

Just then there was a shot from the south side of the river.

"They're on both sides!" Ian yelled.

Zac pointed ahead. "Make for those two rocks," he yelled. "We're sending this canoe down without us."

"We're what?" Ian roared out the question, not believing what Zac had just said.

"You heard me. We're getting off at the rocks." Zac nudged Skip and pointed to the left rock. "Put us in there. When I pull you out, you find a piece of that thing to hang onto. I don't want you going down river with this canoe."

Skip nodded and pulled his paddle in the direction of the rock. Another series of shots boomed out from the trees on the hill to the south of them, followed by a shot fired from the north side of the river. That shot hit the canoe, creating a hole only inches from where Zac was sitting.

The rocks foamed at the base of the two boulders, water racing around them and over a series of falls below. Zac only hoped the spray of the water would make them harder to see. He knew it wouldn't make for an easy shot on his part either. He checked his sidearm, hooking the rawhide strap over his Colt. Picking up a handful of shells, he dropped them into his pocket.

He looked back at Ian, pointing at the rocks. "When we get in between, you jam your paddle into the one on the other side. Give us time to climb out, then we'll hold it for you."

Ian's eyes were wide. He started to speak but Zac cut him off. "Just do what I say. They have us in a crossfire, and if we go any farther, we're all dead."

Skip rammed the canoe directly into the rock, and Ian swung his paddle over to the other side, wedging it hard up against the boulder. Zac looped the sling of the rifle over his head and shoulder and tumbled over the side. The frigid water bit into him like the jaws of some great beast. Grabbing Skip's arm, he yanked him into the river. It was chest deep on Skip but only up to Zac's waist. Even then, it was hard for Zac to keep his footing. He stumbled, holding the boy against the current, then bracing himself against the rock. Wiggling his foot under the water, he found a crack and wedged his toe into it. He strained, picking Skip up and slamming him against the rock. "Hold on tight," he yelled.

A shot from the south slope glanced off the rock, sending fragments in all directions. Zac knew it was only a matter of time before the men would find a better position. The empty canoe coming down the stream would tell them all they needed to know. He shouted at Ian, "Now jump!" Zac held out his free hand. "Jump for me."

The old man let go of his grip on the paddle and, turning in Zac's direction, threw himself into the water. He landed with a splash, churning the water with both arms. The man looked like a water-borne windmill in a tornado, splashing and working at keeping some sort of forward movement.

Zac reached out and grabbed for his hand. He clamped onto it and hung on as Ian's body curled around the rock, next to Skip.

Suddenly, the canoe spun in the rocks and then, turning over, went squirting between them and down into the chilly foam. It landed on the rocks like a water-soaked drum with a series of bangs. Zac watched it surge down the river, banging on the rocks and bouncing in the water.

Zac heaved back, hauling Ian toward him and fighting the surging current. He braced the rifle more securely around his shoulder and, reaching down now with both hands, pulled hard. "Kick," Zac shouted. "Fight to get your feet under you."

Ian's face was pure white. He blinked back the water from his sky blue eyes and grit his teeth. He fought to get his feet under him, then reached for the slippery rock. He tried to find a grip on the watery surface but kept sliding back into the current.

Zac pulled harder, and Skip reached around and with a free hand grabbed Ian's coat. "Pull hard, Skip," Zac yelled. They both yanked, struggling against the cold and the swift water that was threatening to take Ian downstream. Between the two of them, they hauled the old man to a spot where he could get his feet under him.

Ian blinked back the water from his eyes. "Can you see them?" he yelled.

Zac nodded his head. "They got good position."

Another shot boomed, taking out another piece of rock over Skip's head. Bits and pieces peppered Zac's face, stinging his cheek.

"One thing's for sure," Zac said, "We can't stay here."

Ian shook his head, agreeing. "No, we can't."

Zac looked off to their left. A small part of the stream was surging past them on that side—not enough for a canoe to pass, but more than enough to carry a man downstream. There were smaller rocks on that side of the river, forming a barrier against the bank, and a stand of trees slightly behind them. "Do you think you can make it over there?" he asked.

Ian leaned back slightly, looking around the boulder. "I might be able to."

"Might won't do it. You get over there, and I'll keep shooting to the north. You make it that far and whoever is on that south slope won't be able to see you. I'll pass Skip over to you, and we'll hunker down in those rocks for a while."

Though Zac spoke with confidence, he knew it was a long shot. Ian would be exposed to shots from both directions for a short time and, after that, so would Skip. To make matters worse, after Ian got over that portion of the stream, they'd know which way to look for Skip and be waiting for him.

Zac peered around the rock, looking downstream into the main channel. There was another stand of rocks in the middle of the river, the water pouring through and around them. His mind raced. He looked back at Ian. "When you get safe on the other side, I'm going down this way."

"You're what?" Ian asked.

"Look," Zac said, "when you make that crossing, they'll know where to aim for the two of us. I'm going to give them something else to think about."

Ian nodded grudgingly. "It might work."

Zac grabbed the man's shirt collar and twisted it, pulling him close. "Only thing is, when you hear me shooting from down river, you come back out there for the boy. You understand?"

Ian nodded his head. Zac could see the fear rise in his eyes.

"I've pulled your fat out of the fire more times than I care to think about. If you don't get yourself out in the open to help Skip across that part of the stream, you better hope they kill me."

"I'll be there," Ian said. "You can count on that."

Zac looked over at the stream to their left. "Now, get ready. When you hear me shooting, you get over there." He pushed Ian around the rock and into position. They both knew he'd be open to fire from the south bluff.

Moving around to where Skip was still hanging onto the rock, Zac put his hand on the boy's shoulder. "Skipper, it's important that you move fast when I start shooting down there, but I want you to be careful most of all. Keep your feet under you. I don't want to see you go flying down this river. You understand me?"

"Yes, sir. I understand."

"Now, you get ready to go. Watch where Ian steps and learn. When he gets there, you let me know. This first group of shots is to give him cover, then I go down river. When I start shooting again, you make a beeline for those rocks on Ian's side."

Skip nodded.

"There's one thing I want you to remember most of all though, Skip."

"What's that?"

"Remember I love you."

Skip wrapped both arms around Zac's neck and hugged him tightly. "I love you too," he said.

"I'm sorry about this, son." Zac wasn't sure if it was tears in the boy's eyes or just water from the river. Either way, it was hard to look.

He pushed Skip around the boulder to a spot behind Ian. Moving back to the other side of the rock, he raised his rifle and waited. He thought perhaps the men in ambush were going for better position. It was obvious they hadn't exactly planned on letting loose so soon, or at least one of them hadn't. If they were on the move, this might be the perfect time for Ian to go. There was only one way to know for sure.

Leaning out, he drew a bead on a stand of trees on the north side of the hill facing the river. He fired.

Ian began his run through the water as Zac reloaded and fired again. The stream was up to his hips in the deepest part, and he struggled forward against the swift current. He was almost to the bank when the first shot was fired in his direction. It landed to the right of him, tearing through the water. It had come from the north side, the side Zac was firing on.

Zac thought he saw movement in the trees before the shot was fired. It was a blur of white and tan, like the sheepskin coat Tom had worn. It would make a target, though. Raising the rifle to his cheek, he squeezed the trigger. The rifle bolted in his hands.

Ian splashed his way to the rocks and dived for cover behind two of them that were hugging the ground. He laid there for a few moments before turning around to catch Skip's eye. He gave the boy a small wave.

Skip yelled at Zac. "He's there!"

Zac slung the rifle over his head and shoulder and pulled it tight. He watched the water roar by for just a moment and then jumped into the swift current. Zac caught sight of the rocks ahead and swam. He strained and kicked to keep the current from flipping him over. His lungs were practically bursting. With one hard kick, he broke the surface and sucked in the air.

A shot rang out. The bullet slammed into the water close by. They knew where he was. That was one thing he'd actually been hoping for. Taking sight of the rocks once again, he dove under the water.

The current carried him up to the rocks, pushing him into the crack that had formed between them. Placing his hands on the bottom, he lifted himself up out of the water. The force of the river on him was enough to take his breath away. He unslung his rifle and crammed it between the two rocks. It would make a bar to haul himself out of the water. Slowly, he lifted himself up and got to his feet.

Now he had to find the shooter, or at least the one on the north side of the river. They had been watching him, and he knew they must be waiting for him to show his face. He crouched low, holding the rifle close. He didn't want to show it before he could shoot. He edged his way close to the north side of the rock. There was no time to waste; Skip had to get to the shoreline. Zac pulled out four rounds of ammunition from the bandoleer and stuck them in his mouth. There would be no time to pull cartridges from a wet leather belt, and his cold fingers might fail him just when he needed them most.

Zac took quick aim. He would have to fire and reload instantly. He pulled the trigger, sending the huge load into the trees. Breaking the gun open, he extracted the shell and pulled one from his mouth, jamming it into the breech. He snapped the gun closed, lifted it to his cheek, and fired again, repeating the procedure several times.

He could see the fire was having its effect. A number of branches were being broken in the trees he was firing into, and if the man there wasn't injured or dead, he was certainly plenty scared. He could only hope that Skip had made his break for the shore.

He moved back behind the rock and pulled out four more rounds. His heart was throbbing faster now. He could almost see his wet shirt rising and falling with each beat. A bullet buzzed past him from the south side of the river. While he'd been keeping the man north of them busy, he was sure Skip had easily made his escape from the water.

Now thoughts of Jenny and Skip flashed through his mind. He thought about what it was like to hold Jenny in his arms and look into her eyes. He thought about Skip's smile, a smile that said he was safe with Zac's love.

He rounded the south side of the rock and took a quick scan of the bluffs overhead. He searched it, ready to fire at the slightest sign of movement. What he saw surprised him. He saw a tall man running down river along the bluff. Then he heard a shot, but it was a shot from a different gun.

Zac quickly moved back to the north side of the rock. He could see the man he'd been shooting at clear the trees and make his way over the top of the ridge. They were obviously leaving, but why?

Placing the cartridges back in the bandoleer, he slung the rifle over his head and shoulder. He edged his way to the south side of the rock and dove in, swimming hand over hand and kicking for all he was worth. In a matter of minutes he was climbing out of the water and onto a rock. The sunshine felt good, but he was shaking like a willow tree in a high wind.

Skip came running in his direction, followed by Ian. The boy climbed the rocks where Zac was standing, not bothering to look for the best footing. When he got to the top, he threw his arms around Zac.

Zac hugged him. "You all right?" he asked.

Skip looked up at him. "I was worried."

"So was I."

Ian stood at the base of the rocks and pointed up the hill. "There's somebody else up there. Who do you reckon it might be?"

"I don't know, but I think we better climb up and give that man our thanks."

It took the three of them some time to scale the bluff that overlooked the river. Zac got to the top first, unslinging his Sharps. Bending down, he gave first Skip and then Ian a hand.

Ian got to his feet. "You see anybody?" he asked.

Zac pointed down river. "No, but I smell a fire."

They began their walk, winding their way through the trees. Zac went ahead, his gun in hand. Soon, they stood in the trees on the edge of a clearing. There in the middle of it was a roaring fire. Small pieces of wood had been sharpened and driven into the ground, and on each one a piece of fresh meat hung. A coffee pot bubbled over a portion of the fire, the brown mixture running and foaming down its sides. It smelled good.

"Hello, the camp," Zac yelled. "Anybody here?"

"Come on ahead," a voice roared back.

The voice was a familiar one to Zac, but he couldn't place it. He held his hand back. "You two stay right here until I find out who it is," he said. He stepped into the clearing, his rifle at the ready.

"You might as well put your gun down, Cobb," the voice said. "I've already killed all the fresh game you're going to need." The man stepped out of the woods from across the clearing and smiled. It was Mike Wass, the man Jenny had come up with on the *Tiger Lilly*.

"It's you," Zac said. "I wasn't expecting to find you."

Wass laughed. "Neither was the fella who was up here. He took off like a scalded dog. I bet you're glad to see me, though."

"Those are the truest words ever spoken."

Wass gave hand signals to Ian and Skip, who were still standing on the edge of the clearing. "Come on in. I've got hot food and a warm fire." He looked at Cobb. "Took you long enough to get up here."

Zac smiled. "Can't say we're in the best of shape."

He looked over Zac's shoulder at Ian and Skip. "You better get out of those clothes and dry off. We'll hold them over the fire with some branches I cut and have you back together in no time."

"We sure appreciate this, Wass," Ian said. He started unbuttoning his shirt. "When we get back to Sitka, I'll have to throw you a party."

"What did you see?" Zac asked.

"More like what I heard. I've been hearing that big Sharps of yours up and down the river for a couple of hours now." He pointed back into the woods that ran up the mountains to the south of them. "I was looking to run trap lines there when I heard the shooting. Figured I'd come and see what it was all about. I can't have people scaring all the game away. Man's got to eat. The closer I got, the more shooting I heard."

He motioned in the direction of the bluffs. "I saw a tall Indian over there. He was shooting down into the river." Shrugging his shoulders, he smiled. "Just figured I'd join in, that's all."

CHAPTER 25

+ + + + + + +

As THE SMALL BOAT TURNED THE BEND around one of the islands, they spotted the castle that stood in the middle of the harbor. It was a welcome sight even though it was designed to have the opposite effect. They could see a large steamship that was being loaded by men swinging booms that were filled with boxes and bales of fur. They could also see a second ship. This one was at anchor. It wasn't being loaded and looked dark against the sky.

"Wonder what the *Northern Star's* doing here still?" Ian asked. "It ain't had time to get to Seattle and back, and I'd think Zubatov would be wanting to do that before the ice closed in." He shook his head. "Man don't make money by sittin' in the harbor."

Sea birds swooped down over the water, and the smell of fish was in the air. It was a strong odor, even from where they were. They could feel the rain even before they saw it, a chilly cloud that swept down from the mountains and then rippled over the water.

Zac pulled Skip back under the awning just as the first drops hit it. "You glad to be back?" he asked.

Skip looked up at him. "Some, I guess."

"I guess you like the outdoors."

Skip nodded. "I like it lots."

"We'll have to spend more time outdoors when we get home."

As they approached the docks, Ian stared at the man who was standing there, a man in a suit. "Wonder why he's here? That's Dave Cormia, my attorney."

"Maybe you're being sued," Zac teased.

Ian chuckled. "I doubt that. Folks 'round here run from the law, not toward it."

Benny swung the wheel, easing the boat next to the dock. Zac and Ian jumped out, and Zac held out his hand for Skip.

"I'm afraid I have some bad news for you," Cormia said.

205

"Bad news?" Ian asked. "Couldn't be any worse than what we've already gone through."

"I'm afraid it is. Jenny is missing."

The words snapped Zac's head around. He stepped closer to the man, Skip at his side. "When did this happen?" he asked.

"About three days ago. The women were in town shopping, and she was supposed to ride back with them. When she didn't make it, they thought she'd decided to walk. It was another day before your niece, Naomi, came and talked to me about it. I did organize a search, but they haven't turned up anything yet."

"Did they search the hills?" Ian asked. "She might have gone for a hike and got lost."

"I doubt that. She was in a dress. She and Naomi had come into town to buy steamer tickets. I saw her and we spoke in my office. I wouldn't think she was even thinking about a hike."

"Who was the last one to see her?" Zac asked.

"We've been asking around town, but so far haven't turned up anything." He scratched his chin. "I suppose Naomi would have been the last."

"We better go see her then," Ian said.

Zac lifted his rifle and slung it over his shoulder. Skip slipped his hand into Zac's. "We'll find her," he said. "I'm sure she's all right. You know Jenny. She knows how to take care of herself."

Cormia pointed to the end of the dock. "I have a carriage. We'll get there quicker."

Soon they were rolling up the road that would take them to Ian's house. It was also one of the few times Zac had seen Ian quiet. The man obviously had a lot on his mind; Zac was hoping at least some of it involved where to find Jenny. He sat in the front with Cormia, and even though the carriage wasn't his, the reins were in his hand.

Cormia looked back at Zac. "I encouraged them to take the early boat, but now I wish they'd taken the one that left a week ago."

The carriage rolled through the garden. Bubba Dean was tending his bees. They buzzed around his face in a halo of yellow specks. His face was covered with a net and long padded gloves were pulled up to his elbows. In his mouth was a white clay pipe. He grinned, clenching his teeth around the thing.

Ian pulled up on the reins. "Is Risa in the house?"

"Naw, sir, she ain't. She done gone to dat Injun village. She's trying to get dem folks to hep her look fer Miss Jenny. I speck she'll be back b'fore long though." He looked at Zac. "Got me a pipe, too, but I use it for my bees."

Skip looked over at Zac, puzzled.

"Tobacco smoke stuns a nest of bees," Zac said. "A man can use it if he wants to get honey from a natural hive."

Ian slapped the backs of the team, sending the carriage farther along the path to the door. They pulled up outside the house and Ian dropped the reins, stepping down. When they opened the door, he called out to a quiet house. "Hello, the house!"

The sound of giggles erupted from the kitchen. The door swung open and Dolly stepped out, holding both hands in front of her face. They were covered in white flour and were a match for the smears of chalky flour dust on her face. "Look," she said, "I'm making biscuits." She looked back in the direction of the kitchen. "Umqua is showing me how."

Ian took her in his arms and lifted her, twirling around the room. She hugged him, squealing and leaving her hand prints on the back of his shirt.

"I'm so glad to see you, Daddy. I missed you." She dropped to the floor, her eyes turning suddenly serious. "Jenny ran away though. We looked everywhere for her."

"Where's Naomi, darling?"

Umqua stepped out of the kitchen, wiping her hands on her apron. "I think Naomi in her room. I told her it best place for her."

There was a hardness in the woman's face that Zac didn't like. One would have thought her to be a prison guard who had confined someone to isolation, and from the things Jenny had already told him privately, that might well have been the case.

"I'll go talk to her," Zac said.

Ian spoke up. "Hang on. I'll go with you."

Zac stopped in his tracks and pressed his fingers into Ian's chest. "I better talk to her alone first. You stay here and catch up with your daughter."

Zac could tell it didn't suit the man to be left out of whatever Naomi might say, but he wanted her to be free to talk. Jenny's situation was for the most part a product of Ian's predicament, and if the man was in the room when Naomi was trying to explain it, she might not be as talkative. Right now, he wanted to find out everything she knew, and more than that, he wanted to know what she suspected.

He walked down the stairs that led to the lower level of the house and marched down the hall, stopping in front of Naomi's door. Lightly, he rapped on it.

"Who is it?"

"It's Zac, darling. Can I come in?"

Naomi flung open the door and fell into his arms, weeping. "Oh, Zac, I'm so sorry. If you'd been here this wouldn't have happened. I know that." She clung to him, sobbing. "I should have gone with her," she said, shaking her head. "I never should have let her out of my sight."

Zac patted her back and stepped into the room with her still clinging to him. He closed the door behind them. "Don't blame yourself, sweetheart." He pointed to a set of chairs beside the fireplace. "Now, why don't you tell me what happened."

"I thought she'd decided to walk. I didn't really want to walk, but she did. . . ."

Slowly and deliberately, Zac began to unwind the story out of Naomi. She told him about the boat tickets, making sure he knew they'd now been canceled. It was hard for her to relate everything that Dave Cormia had said about Ian's will and Jenny being made a trustee, but she let it be known the man had advised them to leave as soon as possible.

She shook her head. "I don't know why he thought it was dangerous for us to be here, but he did."

"I'll talk with him about it," Zac said. "Where did she go when you left her?"

Naomi looked up at him, her eyes growing larger. She spoke deliberately, making sure he got every word. "Umqua came out of the store, and we watched her go into the alley behind the Crystal Palace." She shook her head. "That seemed strange to us." Scooting forward on the chair, she stared into his eyes. "Why do you think she'd be going there?"

"And that's where Jenny went?"

Naomi took out a handkerchief and dabbed her eyes. "Yes, that was the last time I saw her." She paused before adding, "If something bad had happened to her, they'd have found her. Don't you think?"

Zac got to his feet. He reached over and put his hands on her head, smoothing her hair. "We'll find her. Don't worry." Stepping over to the door, he turned back. "If anything else comes to mind, you let me know."

She nodded. "I will."

Zac made his way up to the great room where the group was still gathered. Umqua had gone back to the kitchen, but the rest seemed to be waiting for Zac's report. Ian stepped toward him. "Did you find out anything?"

"Some."

"What did the girl say?"

"Did Jenny hide from us?" Dolly asked. "Is she playing hide-and-seek?"

Ian patted her hand. "Something like that." He looked at Zac. "What did she say?"

Zac looked over at Cormia. "She told me about the visit to your office, about how you told her she was in danger."

"You told her that?" Ian's attention was diverted to Cormia.

"I had to." Cormia stepped away from Ian and paced across the room. "You put her in a dangerous position." Turning back around, his face was almost pained. "I didn't say anything that shouldn't have been said. I just told her that I thought she should get back to California as soon as possible. If someone is trying to kill you, she's a likely target."

"I don't understand," Zac said. He stepped toward the lawyer. "Why don't you explain everything for the rest of us?"

"Ian here has made Jenny his trustee. She alone is responsible for the protection of his dependents and the disposal of his property. If that land of his is as valuable as he thinks it is, somebody might put great pressure on her to sell it to them, or give it away for that matter."

"What about his wife?" Zac asked.

"That's a complicated matter. His marriage could be disputed by the court, and Risa has no legal standing before the authorities here in Sitka. She's an Indian."

Zac began to pace the floor, his hands behind his back. "Then I'm going to need the names of anyone who might profit from getting their hands on this property."

Ian sat down in an overstuffed cowhide chair. "That might be anyone, Cobb."

Zac shot him a hot stare. "You know, I'm plumb wore out of being in the middle of your war. You knew all this before you dragged Jenny up here."

"No," Ian said. "I can assure you I didn't. I just wanted to be sure she was someone I could trust if anything were to happen to me."

"Then you could have asked her before you put her in this position."

"I thought she'd be honored."

"You're a lying fool, Hays! You didn't say anything about this to her because you knew she'd turn you down."

Zac looked over at Dolly. The girl had backed herself into a corner, and he could see she was frightened by his attitude and the harshness of the way he was talking to Ian. "We would have gladly cared for your daughter if anything happened to you. But this money and property of yours—as far as either of us is concerned, that's a burden that belongs to somebody else."

"I just thought—"

Zac cut him off. "You thought other people would be as interested in your wealth as you are. Well, that's where you're wrong."

Cormia stepped forward. "What do you propose to do now?"

"I don't see where I have any choice in the matter. Jenny is missing, and we've got to do everything we can to find her."

"What do you suggest?" Ian asked.

"Naomi said that Jenny was following Umqua when she disappeared. She was following her around back of the Crystal Palace. I suppose we're going to have to find out what she knows and who it is in that place that wants all your gold."

Ian got to his feet. "I'll go get her."

Moments later he followed Umqua back into the room.

"You want to see me?" she asked.

"Yes," Zac said. "When you were shopping in town the other day, Naomi says Jenny followed you around back of the Crystal Palace. What were you doing there?"

It was obvious Umqua was troubled by the question, troubled and surprised it was being asked. Evidently it was the first she had heard about being followed. She took a step back and nervously twisted her apron.

"I—I shopping," she stammered.

"What were you shopping for in that alley?"

She looked back at Ian.

"Please answer the man, Umqua."

"I looking for a woman to do laundry for me."

"You don't do your own?" Zac asked.

Umqua glanced back at Ian, bowing her head. "I do laundry, but all these new people here. I need help. Lots company means more work in the kitchen and everywhere else."

Ian cleared his throat and dropped his hands. "And we do appreciate all the work you're doing, Umqua."

"Do you have the name of this woman?" Zac asked.

"What name?" Umqua almost shouted. "They no have names, not that I understand."

"But we'd be able to find her if we looked?" Zac asked.

Umqua threw up her arms. "Maybe, but the woman not there, so I still doing all the clothes." She pointed at Zac. "Even the ones you wearing now."

"I think I'll do my own." Zac was getting irritated, but he wasn't through yet. "Did you see Jenny following you?"

"No, I see nobody."

"So I suppose Risa could tell us just when you got back to the store."

Umqua began to pace with short steps. "I not know what she can tell you. I just know what I did. I sorry she ran away from you, but not my fault." Umqua threw her hand in the air, as if to brush away a pesky fly. "You do what you like. I tell you all I know. You not find that woman that be your fault. It not mine."

"Where do you suggest we go from here?" Ian asked.

Zac motioned in Umqua's direction. "We go looking for a laundry woman and see if there's one even in that direction."

"I'm sure Umqua's telling the truth," Ian responded. "She's telling us all she knows."

"You can afford to be sure," Zac shot back. "I can't."

Ian stuck his hands in his pocket and walked to the window. He looked out into the bright sunshine to where Bubba Dean was working. "I just trust my servants, Cobb. They've been with me a long time." He turned around. "If I can't trust them, who can I trust?"

Zac scratched his chin. "I'm not sure you should be so trusting. But if you have that much confidence in them, you should have made them your trustees, not Jenny." Zac blew out his breath and prayed for patience.

"Right now you and I have got to pay a visit to that saloon. Someone wants to get their hands on that land of yours, and I suspect we'll find them there."

"I suppose you're right. I'll get my hat and we can go."

"Not just yet," Zac said. "I want to go when I know we can find everyone there."

"You mean tonight?"

"Yes, tonight."

Ian stepped over to where Zac was standing and pulled him aside. "Listen, Cobb, I'm more sorry about this than I can begin to tell you. I know this is all because of me, and I'm going to do anything I can to help. Whatever it means and whatever the cost, I'll pay it. I just want Jenny back, same as you do."

Zac accepted Ian's apology. Feeling a new surge of adrenaline in him, Zac clapped his hand on Ian's shoulder. "I'll tell you one thing, though, whoever it is that's decided to go to this length to bring you down is going to be sorry they ever messed with Jenny."

✦ ✦ ✦ ✦ ✦

The hallway was quiet with only the sound of padded feet moving across the floor. The footsteps stopped outside of Ian's study door. The brass knob on the door had a hasp, but it sat ajar without a lock. A hand turned the knob.

Ian was lying on a small daybed that sat in the corner of the room. He'd been exhausted when they got in, and he wanted to make sure he was more alert when Risa returned. He turned his head at the sound of the door opening and his eyes widened. "What are you doing here?"

The intruder tossed a beehive into the middle of the room and closed the door. Outside, the brass hasp was closed and then secured with a padlock.

Ian watched the combative bees as they circled around the room. An angry galaxy of stinging insects, they began to swarm, landing on the ceiling and the furniture. They especially liked the bright yellow of the upholstery on the daybed. They began to assemble on it, crawling over Ian as he tried to shield his face. He fought them off, swatting at them with his bare hands.

"Help!" he screamed. "Anybody, help!"

It was then the stinging began. Ian jumped. First one bolt of pain surged through him and then another. Large welts began to appear over his hands and head. The bees gathered in droves.

Ian got to his feet and began to swing his arms in the air. He felt the soft bodies of the flying insects on the palms of his hands as he swung, accompanied by sharp, painful stings. He backed up to the door and turned the knob. It opened a crack but stopped where the padlock held it. Ian pressed his face into the tiny space. "Help!" he yelled into the hall. "Please help me!"

There was no answer. He swung wildly at the bees, backing up to the balcony. His movements only made the bees more violent. The fierce stinging continued, sending Ian into a wild, frantic attempt at escape. Reaching the balcony, he swung furiously at the swarm. Stepping back, he went over the side.

CHAPTER 26

+ + + + + + +

RISA CAME THROUGH THE BACK DOOR in the kitchen. Assuming it would be empty, she was surprised to see Dolly there. The young woman had her hands in a large bowl of dough, kneading it and then spreading her fingers in the air to watch how the dough spread between them. "What are you doing?" Risa asked.

Dolly grinned, her faced covered with smears of flour. "I'm making a cake for dinner. Umqua said I could. She said it would keep me in the kitchen and out of trouble."

A warning bell went off in Risa's head. Umqua rarely turned her kitchen over to anyone, much less Dolly.

Dolly's face turned down, suddenly sad. "Naomi doesn't feel much like playing with me now. I guess she's missing Jenny and it makes her feel sad."

"Did Ian and the men make it home yet?"

Dolly nodded her head up and down.

"Yes, they came back, but that Mr. Zac went into town." Dolly dropped off the stool she was sitting on. Her eyebrows drooped in the middle. "He was talking bad to Daddy. I think he's angry."

Risa hung up her coat on a hook beside the door. "He has a right to be. The woman he loves is missing."

"I think he means to cause trouble."

"Why would you say such a thing?"

Dolly lifted her chin with confidence.

Risa stepped over to her. Putting her hands on Dolly's shoulders, she spun her around. "Tell me. Why do you think he wants to cause trouble?"

"'Cause he had his pistol around his waist. I saw something else too."

"What?"

"He has a little gun." Dolly lifted up her arm and then patted her underarm, leaving a smudge of flour on her dress. "It's right here that he carries it. He didn't think I saw it, but I did. He put some bullets in it before he started walking into town."

Risa dropped her hands from Dolly's shoulders and took a step back. "That does sound like trouble."

Dolly nodded her head vigorously and smiled. "See, I told you."

Risa laid her hand on the girl's shoulder. "We have to think of some way to help him."

"Maybe Daddy can help him." The sudden smile on her face turned into an instant frown. "But he was mad at Daddy."

There was a pounding on the front door. The sound of the brass knocker was hard to miss. "I wonder who that is?" Risa asked. She left, and Dolly followed her through the doors into the great room. She looked around. "Umqua must be gone."

"I think she's napping," Dolly said.

Another series of knocks sounded at the door. She walked over and opened it.

Cole Pressley stood in the door, his hat in his hand. "Excuse me, ma'am."

Risa stepped back. "Please come in, Mr. Pressley."

Dolly grinned, as was her habit with most single men. She motioned her hand forward. "Yes, come on in. I'm making a cake. You can have some if you want."

"That would be nice. Maybe a little later." Pressley was wearing a red-and-yellow plaid shirt, stuffed down into worn jeans. His smooth face and square jaw normally had a broad smile on them, but just now there was a somber frown.

"You must be here about the search we're organizing," Risa said.

He clutched his hat in his hand. "That was why I came, ma'am, but it's not why I'm here now."

"It's not?"

Pressley looked around the room. "Is Mr. Hays' man servant around? I didn't see him."

"You mean Bubba Dean?"

"Yes, ma'am, Bubba Dean."

"Well, I just got home myself. I haven't seen him. Why do you need to find Bubba Dean?"

Pressley looked over at the still-beaming Dolly. "Ma'am, there's something I need to tell you, but I would like to have you alone for a moment."

"Of course." She turned back toward Dolly. "Why don't you go and finish that cake of yours? Mr. Pressley and I have things to talk about."

Dolly grinned at Pressley. "And when I bake it, will you eat some?

Daddy says I can cook real good, sometimes."

Pressley nodded his head. "I'd love some. A little later though."

Dolly backed up, her hands behind her back. "You stay right here until I get it fixed."

Pressley forced a smile. "I'll be right here."

As Dolly left the room, Risa broke into chatter about what was on her mind. "I'm glad you're here, Cole. We need to organize a search for Jenny, and I'm afraid her fiancé is getting into more trouble than he realizes. Dolly told me the man's gone to the Crystal Palace and he's armed."

Pressley motioned toward the cowhide sofa. "I need to talk to you about something else first. Would you please take a seat? I'd feel a lot better if you did."

Risa backed up and sat down. "Of course, what is it?"

"Ma'am, this is hard for me to say . . . very hard."

"Please, go on." Risa felt tiny pricks of fear work their way down her back.

"I found Mr. Hays outside his study window. He's dead."

Risa jumped to her feet and ran out the door. Pressley followed her.

She ran around the corner of the house and spotted the body in the flower and rock garden. He was sprawled out on it, looking like a rag doll fallen off the shelf. She carefully stepped over the rocks and, kneeling where he lay, picked up his head and laid it in her lap.

Pressley stepped over to her. "I didn't want to say anything with Miss Dolly in the room."

Risa began to cry, rocking Ian's head in her lap. She nodded at him. "You did right."

"I was just coming up to the house and I saw him like that. He wasn't breathing. I'm not sure what those things are on his face and hands. They look like stings to me."

"Bee stings," Risa said.

Pressley looked up at the window. "How did they get up there? A swarm, you figure?"

She continued to rock the man in her arms, crying softly.

"I better go get Bubba Dean. We can take him into town, to the undertaker's."

Risa didn't look up. "We were warned," she murmured. "We were warned."

+ + + + +

Zac walked into town just as dusk was settling over the harbor. He could see an old woman on the road ahead of him. She was stoop shouldered and walked with a cane but moved along the road like she was late for an important appointment. The woman's stamina impressed him.

He overtook her just as they got to town, and she stopped to greet him. A smile crept over her face and her eyes twinkled. "Good evening, sir," she said.

Zac tugged at the brim of his hat. "How are you, ma'am? Nice evening, isn't it?"

"Yes, it is." She turned and walked off across the street, leaving him wondering who she was and just where she might be coming from. To the best of his knowledge, Ian's house was the only one up that hill. Still, she might have been part of the hired help he hadn't seen before.

A smoky fog poured over the docks and crept along the street. He could still see the steamship that was taking on cargo. It would have been the one they were to travel on, the one that Jenny had purchased tickets for. The sailors would be drinking tonight. It would be a busy night for the Crystal Palace. He could also see the dark outline of the *Northern Star*. The vessel was still riding at anchor. It was dark with lights on in the lower cabin.

Zac stopped outside the saloon and pulled out his Colt. Opening the cylinder, he dropped a sixth round into the empty chamber. Normally he carried an empty cylinder under the hammer. It was safer that way. But when a man had a feeling he might be needing it, that was the time he ought to have a sixth round in place.

Zac looked in the window and spied several women dancing around the room in colorful dresses. The bar itself was crowded and very few tables had seats still remaining.

Zac circled around the saloon and stepped into the muddy alley. As he made his way over a garbage pile, he saw a form lying beside it. The man had a beard matted with wet mud. His eyes were closed, and what little of his face that could be seen was covered with dirt. The fingers on his gloves were missing, and the old coat he wore was torn in several places. It was hard to recognize the shoes he was wearing because of the cakes of muddy ground wrapped around them like soft overshoes.

Zac stooped down beside the man and gave his chest a gentle shove. "Uhhh . . . what?" The man blinked his eyes open.

Zac was surprised to find him still breathing. "Who are you?" Zac asked.

"Name's Horace." The man spat out the words, drops of dark spittle trickling over his lips and down his beard.

"Here, you better get to your feet and get some fire in your bones."

Zac wrapped his arms around the man and lifted him to his feet. Placing the man's arm over his shoulder, Zac walked him over to the blazing barrel. He straightened him up and stepped aside. "Your feet going to hold you?"

Horace looked down at his feet, almost surprised they were still there. "I think so."

Reaching into his pocket, Zac pulled out several pieces of jerky left over from the trip. He handed them over to the man.

Horace held them in his hand, looked up at Zac and then back down to the meat. He blinked his eyes furiously.

"Go ahead," Zac said. "Eat it. You look like you could use it."

The man cupped his hand together and began to chew the meat. He kept his eyes on Zac.

"How long's it been since you ate?" Zac asked.

"I don't rightly know anymore."

"Where do you live?"

The man looked back at the alley. "I guess I lives here."

"You seen any local women around here that take in wash?"

The man took another bite. He chewed the meat slowly. "You lookin' to get your clothes washed?"

"No, I'm just trying to find the woman who does it."

"Well, there ain't none, least not to where I would know about it. Sure ain't none 'round here. If there was, she'd be runnin' me off."

"All right," Zac tugged on the brim of his hat. "Much obliged." He turned to go but then stopped and felt down in his pocket. There were two more pieces of the dried meat left. He pulled them out and shoved them in Horace's direction. "You better hang on to these and find yourself someplace warm."

The man reached out and took them. "All right. I'll sure 'nuff do that."

"Do you know anybody in town?" Zac asked. "Anybody you can stay with?"

"I got me an old pardner. He's here sometimes to see one of them wives of his."

"One of his wives? That wouldn't be James MacGregor, would it?"

"Yeah." The man's eyes brightened. "Mac."

"Well, I know Mac. I came up on the *Northern Star* with him. Why don't you look him up? I'm sure he could get you a decent meal and a hot bath. Say, Horace, what's around the other side of the alley?" Zac asked.

"Nothing back there but the back door to the Crystal Palace and a few places I don't know much about. Folks at the palace has me haul some of their stuff away fer a drink once in a while."

"Next time tell them to pay you in cash." Zac tipped his hat in farewell and made his way down the dark back alley. It was just like the man had said. There was little sign of life, certainly no laundry. He walked toward several of the dark windows and looked inside, then made his way to the one bright spot that lit the alley. It was the office window of the Crystal Palace. He could see Kathryn Jung standing inside, talking to the man Ian had called Quinn. She had a cash box in her hand and was counting out the ongoing proceeds of the evening. The smile on Kathryn's face told him business was good.

Zac made his way back to the boardwalk and then walked to the batwing doors of the saloon. He pushed them open slowly.

Pushing his way through the noisy crowd, Zac stepped over to the bar. He recognized the man Ian had called Hank, though Hank refused to catch Zac's eye.

The man standing next to Zac began to pound on the bar. "Hey, barkeep, how 'bout a little service? I want me another beer and I want it now!" The man was burly and looked like he'd had a few beers too many already. His eyes blazed and his beard quivered as he continued to yell. "Bring that beer over here."

"Hold on," Hank yelled. He picked up a glass and held it under the barrel, filling it with the amber liquid. Walking over to the man, he set it on the bar. "That'll be a dollar."

The man pulled a silver dollar out of his jeans and slapped it on the bar.

As Hank turned to walk away, Zac grabbed his shirt sleeve. "Hold on a minute. Not so fast."

Hank straightened himself up. "What can I do for you?"

"You go back in that office and tell Kathryn that I want to see her."

"She ain't here." He turned to walk away, but Zac grabbed his shirt once again.

"Don't give me that. I saw her back there and I want to talk to her out here."

"Look, I can't do that. You see how busy I am. You just come back some other time."

Zac pulled the man closer, then suddenly jerked his arm and sent his head slamming into the bar. He reached under his arm and pulled out his gun. Cocking the hammer, he pushed it into the man's face. "I don't think you're too busy for this," Zac said. "Now, are you going to get her?"

"Yes, sir. I'll get her."

Zac let the man up. Hank tried to stand tall. He was shaking, but his eyes caught something over Zac's shoulder. "Maybe there's somebody you should see first," he said.

"And who might that be?"

Hank pointed to the front door.

Zac turned around. Standing in the door were Bubba Dean and Skip. Zac walked over to the two of them. "What are you two doing here?" he asked.

"We come to fetch you home," Bubba Dean said. "Miss Risa done sent us. She figured you'd come if I brung your boy."

"What's wrong?"

"It's Mr. Hays, sir." Zac could see the man's eyes were tearing up. His lower lip was quivering. He pulled Zac aside, lowering his voice. "We done found him dead, sir, and you gots to come."

Zac's heart dropped to his feet, and he immediately turned back to face the nervous bartender. "I'll be coming back, and when I do, you tell Kathryn that I want to see her."

Bubba Dean had the carriage tied up outside, and after everyone was settled in, he whipped the horses as they bolted out of town.

"How did it happen?" Zac asked.

"We ain't rightly sure jest yet. Feller that worked at the mill found him. Looks like he fell off the balcony from his study, but he looks mighty peculiar."

"How is that?"

"He done gone and got stings over his face. I works with bees and they look like bee stings to me." Bubba Dean shook his head. "I ain't never known a swarm to come into the house. Can't figure out how a thing like that would happen."

Zac looked down at Skip. "You all right?"

"Yes, sir. I was staying with Naomi. Risa said she thought Naomi would feel a lot better if I was with her."

"Yes, I think so." Zac put his arm around him.

When Bubba Dean pulled the carriage up outside of Ian's home, Zac hopped down and said, "Why don't you show me where they found him?"

"Yes, sir." Bubba Dean stepped down from the carriage, and Zac and Skip followed him around the side of the house. The light was dim; just what Zac would call a fingernail moon hung in the sky. Bubba Dean pointed up to the balcony. "That there's his study up there." He shook his head. "The man wanted lots of them balconies. He said he didn't like to always feel cooped up, even when he was indoors."

"Where do you have him?" Zac asked.

"He's on the sofa in the great room for now, at least until we can get the undertaker to pick him up. I stopped off at the man's place before I come to look for you."

"What made you come to the Crystal Palace?"

"Mrs. Hays thought from the way you was talking that you might go there. I thought so too."

Zac looked up at the open doors to the balcony. "I guess a man could die from a fall like that."

"Yes, sir. He sure 'nuff could."

They walked back around the front of the house and came in through the front door. Risa was seated on a chair across from the sofa. Ian was laid out on it with his hands crossed over his chest. He looked like a man sleeping, except for the red marks on his face and hands.

Zac walked over to Risa and put his hand on her shoulder. "I'm sorry about Ian," he said.

She looked up at him, tears in her eyes. "I know he brought you and Jenny here against your will, and I'm sorry about that."

"That's behind us now, and it's nothing you should fret over."

"I did talk to my people today. I think they will help you to look for Jenny. There's a good man coming tomorrow who knows the country. You won't go wrong with him."

Zac walked over and stooped beside the body. The stings were evident and numerous. He looked up at Bubba Dean. "Can you show me his study?"

"Yes, sir. You just follow me. It's up on the top floor."

The study was located on the topmost floor, one floor above the upper bedrooms. Ian had wanted it built to give him a better view of the ships that came in and out of the harbor. Bubba Dean walked down the hall with Zac following him and stopped at the door. There was a lock on the door and the door was ajar, pushed up against the locked hasp.

"That's mighty peculiar," Bubba Dean said.

Zac shook the lock. "Do you have a key to this thing?"

"I have some keys, but Mr. Ian always kept the key to the lock he used for this room with him."

"Did he have a habit of locking it?"

"Jest when he was gone. He didn't like for folks to go lookin' 'round in this study of his."

Zac thought it was strange. There was no way a man could put a padlock on the door to a room he was using. It had to have been put there by someone else. "Did you or anyone else lock the door here after the body was discovered?"

"No, sir, not to my recollection. I don't think nobody's been up here. Didn't think to do such a thing."

"Maybe you better try the keys you have then. It might be one of those."

Bubba Dean took out the ring of keys. "It ain't one of these here keys. I'se sure of that. Mr. Hays keeps that key with him at all times, keeps it in his pocket, and there ain't but one of them."

"Try them anyway. I've known some padlocks to open."

Bubba Dean shook his head and pulled a ring of keys out of his pocket. He began to go through them one at a time. Finally, one of them sprung the lock open. Zac watched the man's eyes widen in surprise. "Well, I be darn."

Zac took the lock off and handed it to Bubba Dean. He swung the door open. "Maybe you better light a lamp."

"Yes, sir." Taking a match from his pocket, he struck it and walked to the desk where a lamp was sitting. Lifting the globe, he pressed the match to the wick and turned it up. There on the floor was a beehive. A number of bees were still crawling over the thing.

Zac drew his knife from his belt and stuck it into the hive. He walked it carefully over to the balcony and dropped it over the side.

"That sure is a queer thing," Bubba Dean said.

"Yes, it is."

"I handles them bees my own self. Mr. Hays won't come near 'em. He says the stings is bad for him."

"Anybody else handle bees?"

Bubba Dean looked off in the distance and then at Zac. It was obvious the question had registered a memory in his mind, but he slowly shook his head. "No, sir, not anymore. Just me now, that's all."

"Well, you better think a little harder. If you're the only one that handles bees and you have the key to the lock on the door, it looks bad for you."

Bubba Dean hung his head. He continued to shake it, almost as if he were unwilling to believe anything that had happened.

"Hays was murdered, I'd say," Zac went on. "Killed by someone who knew what they were doing."

Zac's statement hit Bubba Dean hard. He shook his head and turned the padlock over in his hand. "I guess it do look bad." He continued to look at the floor where the beehive had been. "I don't understand this. I don't understand it at all."

"Well, we'll find out," Zac said. "Let's go down so I can check one more thing." He reached over to turn out the lamp, but a thought struck him. He opened Ian's desk drawer. A padlock was sitting in the drawer and Zac picked it up. "Looks like we found his lock."

Bubba Dean's eyes brightened. "Yes, sir. Dat's it all right."

Zac handed the lock to the man. "You better lock this up when we leave. If you're right, I think I know where we can find the key."

"Yes, sir. I sure 'nuff will."

The two of them stepped out into the hall, Bubba Dean closing the door behind them and snapping the lock down on the hasp. Zac was still holding the man's ring of keys. He pressed his fingernail into the brass key Bubba Dean had used to unlock the padlock on the door, raking a small scratch on it. When Bubba Dean turned around, Zac handed him the keys.

They walked down the hall and the stairs to where Risa was still sitting with Ian's body. "Has anyone touched the body?" Zac asked.

Risa looked up and shook her head. "No. This is just like he was when we found him."

Zac bent over the body and started pulling things from the man's pocket. He took out his watch, several twenty-dollar gold pieces, and finally a key. He handed it over to Bubba Dean. "Try this," he said.

Bubba Dean was still carrying the lock taken off the door. He snapped it shut, then inserted the key. Zac watched him as he turned it. It didn't open. "That's mighty strange," he said.

"Yes," Zac said. "It is."

CHAPTER 27

✦ ✦ ✦ ✦ ✦ ✦ ✦

ZAC WAS UP AND GONE LONG BEFORE Umqua had set the breakfast out on the table. At first, he didn't much like the idea of having to find Kathryn during the day. The woman would no doubt be sleeping after a long night of taking the sailors' money. But on second thought, the idea grew on him. *It might not be that bad after all*, he reasoned. *Someone in bed is much easier to find.* He also took some comfort in the fact that her thugs would no doubt be sleeping in as well. A woman like that would have plenty of protection any other time of day.

He passed a group of dwarf dogwood trees. They were in full bloom and the scent from their small white flowers pleased him. It reminded him somewhat of Jenny's perfume, and a sob caught in his throat. Ian's death only magnified the need to find Jenny quickly. Rounding the bend in the road, he once again spotted the older woman he'd seen the night before. *She must work for Ian in some way*, he thought. *Nobody else would be climbing the long hill up to the big house without a good reason.* He wondered if she knew about Ian's death.

The lady was clad in black, a long dress that kicked around her ankles when she walked. Her cane was black with a silver tip, and she was hunched over singing a tune that Zac recognized. It was the familiar hymn *Amazing Grace*.

He stopped in front of her and touched the brim of his hat. "Morning, madam."

The lady ground to a halt and flashed him a bright smile. Her blue eyes shone. "Good morning, young man."

"Are you going up to the big house?"

"Yes, I am."

"You know of Mr. Hays' death?" he asked.

The lady grinned. "Yes," she cackled, "I do." She gently pushed at her hair. The gray bun was in place, but it was a feminine, almost girlish thing to do.

Odd, Zac thought. *For a woman dressed in mourning to be in such good spirits doesn't seem appropriate.* He wasn't about to challenge her, however. "Well, I hope that doesn't put you out of a job," he said.

"Mercy no," the old woman laughed. "That's a rich one."

"Well, I'm glad to hear that." He cast a glance back up the hill. "I'm sure those folks up there will be needing your help."

Her eyes twinkled. "Yes, they will." She laughed. "I'll be a big help."

"Well, you take care walking up there."

She set off, shouting over her shoulder. "Oh, I will, young man, I will."

When Zac made it to town, he wondered if word about Ian's death had already spread. News had a way of traveling. He didn't like it, though. He was hoping to catch Kathryn completely unaware. He was operating on a hunch, a feeling that the woman knew about Jenny's disappearance. Though she probably wasn't holding Jenny herself, it would be an easy thing for her to send a man to do her dirty work while she kept her hands clean.

Zac continued his walk and cleared the section of trees that were hiding the harbor. The steamer at the dock was continuing to load the last of its cargo along with a handful of passengers, but the *Northern Star* was gone. It had slipped anchor and gotten underway during the night.

The smell of fish was in the air along with a mixture of soot, a constant aroma in Sitka. He stepped up to the door of the Crystal Palace and pushed it open.

He immediately spotted Hank. The man was seated over at the potbellied stove with a cup of coffee in his hand. Next to him was the man in the denim shirt Zac had seen when he'd been in the place with Ian. The sight of Zac at the door almost made Hank choke on his coffee. He sputtered and got to his feet.

"You again," he said. He backed up, then swung around behind the bar. "Look, I don't want no trouble."

Zac stepped forward. "There won't be any trouble, not if I find Kathryn and she tells me what I need to know."

Hank signaled to the man still seated by the stove. "You better go up and get Quinn. Wake him up and tell him to get down here fast."

The man got to his feet and edged his way to the stairs. His hands were spread out and his feet moved deliberately. He had a six-gun on his hip, and Zac could see the temptation to use it forming in his eyes. Still, he did just what he'd been told. He rounded the bottom of the stairs and took them two at a time in a race to the rooms above the saloon.

Zac stepped closer to the bar. "I don't need Quinn or anybody else you've got in mind. I just need to talk to Kathryn. She knows me."

"Maybe she don't want to talk to you." Hank was moving slowly down the bar. Zac wondered if he didn't have something else on his mind.

"Then she can tell me that herself."

Hank took another step to his right. "You're outta luck 'cause she ain't here."

Zac stepped closer. "You told me that last night. It wasn't true. I saw her before I ever came in here. I'm not in the habit of asking for something that I can't have."

Hank took another small step to his right. Zac saw him glance down below the bar. "Well, this time it's true. She ain't here. If you know what's good for you, you'll leave well enough alone and go back to where you came from."

Zac pulled back his buckskin coat, exposing his holstered Colt. "I guess I'm not in the habit of doing what's good for me." He pointed to the bar. "Now, if you have a scatter-gun under there, I'd suggest you do what's good for you and take a step back. I can plant a .45 slug in your forehead before you ever bring that thing up, and don't think I won't, either."

"You wouldn't do that."

Zac stepped closer. "Don't bet your life on that. A man who pushes his last chips into the middle of the table better know for sure what the other fella is holding. The plain truth is, you don't know me. I've done it before. You wouldn't be the first."

Hank took a step back from the bar and held his hands up. "Don't go to doing anything fast. I'm not armed. I got no stake in what you want."

"That's smart. Now, you just move around from behind that bar. I'll breathe easier and you'll keep breathing."

Hank moved quickly to his left, clearing the bar in a matter of moments.

"That's fine," Zac said. "Now, you just relax, and I'll get my business over with when I see Kathryn."

"Like I told you, she ain't here."

Zac heard the clamor of footsteps on the stairs and turned his head in time to see Quinn, followed by the man in the denim shirt. Quinn had his gun belt buckled on, and the man following him looked to be ready to use his. They obviously felt that the advantage of numbers meant safety for them. Two or three to one usually meant danger for the one. Zac knew that wasn't necessarily true, however. Quinn was just a big man, and that made him a rather inviting target. If the other man knew how to use that revolver of his, Zac would take him out first. For a man to be dangerous with a gun meant two things, a proficiency with firearms and a determination to kill. Zac had both.

"Here, here," Quinn said. "What do you mean coming in here and threatening my employees?"

"No threat," Zac said, "just an ultimatum."

Quinn stepped off the bottom stair and walked over to the door. This made him an even more inviting target. He was framed in the light. It also told Zac that while the man may have been good with his hands, he was of no account when it came to fighting with a gun. The other man rounded the stairs and stood beside him. He was closer. It made him the first target.

"You've got no right to be issuing an ultimatum, not here in my place. Now, why don't you just go back to that old man you're staying with? He'll tell you what you need to know."

Quinn obviously hadn't heard about Ian's death. If the news had gotten out, he would have thought Quinn would have been among the first to know. Zac played on his ignorance. "I'll talk to him just as soon as I'm finished here."

"And just what do you want to know from us?" Quinn asked.

"I don't want to know anything from you."

"Just let me take care of him," the man in the denim shirt said. "He's just a farmer. He ain't got that rifle of his to club people with neither."

"No call for that, Jasper," Quinn said. "I'm sure our friend here can listen to reason."

"He just needs to be taken down the street to old man Palmer's place and laid out." Jasper was obviously making a reference to the undertaker. "He'll listen to reason then."

Quinn smiled. "My associate here fancies himself as quite the gunhand. I'm sure you wouldn't want to give him a try."

"I've tried more than my share," Zac replied. "He'd be no different. They're all dead now."

"You hear that, Jasper?" Quinn inquired. "The man here's a rancher who knows how to handle that gun of his."

"Yeah," Jasper's grin spread over his face, exposing blackened teeth. "I heard. That's better in my book. I don't want to go up against some sodbuster."

"I'd suggest you back off," Zac said. "I just want to talk to Kathryn."

"What about?" Quinn asked.

"The matter is between me and her."

Jasper motioned in Quinn's direction. "Just let me do it. We ain't got no call to waste time with this man. I seen what he did to Smitty with that rifle butt of his, but that don't prove nothing to me. I'm gonna send him out of here feet first."

"No need for that," Quinn said. "He just needs to be satisfied with no, that's all."

"I'm afraid that's not all. I'm not leaving until I hear what I came to find out. I need to hear it from Kathryn Jung, that partner of yours. When she talks to me, then I'll be out of here." He looked over at Jasper. "Then you and your lapdog here can play quick draw."

The last insult was too much for the man. He slapped his hand to his holster. Zac simultaneously drew his Colt and fired. Just as the man cleared his holster, the slug met him at the third button, spinning him around. He collapsed to his knees. The gun dropped from his grip and clung to his trigger finger, then slowly fell to the floor. The man gazed for a moment at the sight of Quinn standing in the door. Quinn was frozen, suspended in the fear of what he was seeing. Opening his mouth as if to say something, the man dropped to the floor.

Zac had turned his revolver on Quinn the instant he'd fired the first shot. From where he'd hit the man, he was certain there would be no need for a second. He wanted to be ready if Quinn had any idea of following his friend's lead.

Quinn held his hands up high. "Don't shoot," he said. "That wasn't my idea."

"Maybe not, but the man was your associate. You're armed, same as him."

Quinn slowly reached down to his gun belt. He unbuckled it and let it drop to the floor. Lifting up the toe of his boot, he kicked the rig in Zac's direction. "All right. I'm unarmed now."

Zac looked back at Hank. The man was quivering at the bar, holding onto it with both hands. Zac motioned at him with his revolver. "You go take your seat by the stove. Stay there so I can see you."

Hank nodded vigorously and began to move toward the chairs. "Yes, sir, I'm moving."

Zac looked back at Quinn. "Now, let's get back to my question. Where is Kathryn?"

Quinn shook his head. "You are a determined sort, aren't you?"

"That I am." Zac waggled the barrel of the gun in Quinn's direction.

"She isn't here." He began to motion with his hands, easing them back and forth in midair. "I know Hank said she wasn't here last night and she was, but she's gone today."

"Where is she?" Zac asked.

Zac could see the hesitation in the man's eyes. He knew exactly where Kathryn was. He just didn't want to say. Zac was going to make sure that he did, though, no matter what it took. He had a feeling that if he could find Kathryn, he'd find Jenny.

"I'm not sure," Quinn said.

Zac cocked the revolver. "You better make sure."

Quinn gulped. "She left on the *Northern Star* early this morning."

"Where was she going?"

Quinn pulled back. Zac could see that he didn't want to say another word. He'd already said far too much.

Zac took another step toward the man. "You know what I'm looking for. My fiancée is with that woman, and I aim to get her back."

Quinn's eyes practically bulged out of his face. He swallowed hard. "You don't know that."

"I do now." Zac pushed the revolver up to the man's forehead, burying the muzzle of the Colt into the man's skin. "Now, where is she?"

"I can't tell you that, and I don't believe you'll shoot me down in cold blood."

Zac looked back at Hank. The man was still seated in his chair, his fingers clinging to the table. "You back there," he yelled out. "Make yourself scarce."

Hank shakily got to his feet and moved quickly to the office door. He opened it and bolted in, slamming the door behind him.

Zac turned back to Quinn. "Now it's just you, me, and the dead. You don't tell me what I want to know and I'll drop you where you stand. I'll buckle that gun around your dead body and this will look like self-defense. Only thing is, you won't be around to dispute my word."

Zac leaned into the man, driving his point and the barrel of the gun home. "Do you know how important it is to a man to find the woman he loves? Well, I'll tell you. It's a matter of life or death. Only thing is, in this case it's your death. Now, I mean business. Don't doubt my word."

Quinn gulped. His Adam's apple rippled.

"I'm gonna count to three," Zac said, "And three is the last word you're ever going to hear. One. . . ."

"Okay, that's enough! I'll tell you. They've gone north to Mount Fairweather Bay. Your woman is with them. They're just trying to make a business deal, that's all."

Zac relaxed, pulling the gun away. "You better be right. If I get up there and what you say isn't true, I'm coming back for you. I won't be counting either. You won't even hear the number one. Am I clear on that?"

Quinn nodded his head.

+ + + + +

It took Zac almost a half-hour before he found Palmer's undertaking parlor. The place was off a side street with a barn door entrance that held the man's hearse, a solid black carriage with plumed black festoons set in silver. The windows were etched with the figures of angels playing harps.

Zac stepped through a door off to the side of the carriage house and into a sitting room with a red velvet settee and chair. A picture of Jesus stared him in the face, Jesus with a lamb nestled in his arms.

"May I help you?"

The voice was sudden, almost startling. Zac turned around to face a rather thin man with white mutton-chop whiskers and sharp features smiling at him.

"You Palmer?" Zac asked.

"Yes, indeed I am, Ezra Palmer. How may I help you?"

"Do you have anyone working for you?"

The man shook his head. "Not at the moment. But I have no need for help, if that's what you're asking. My assistant left for Seattle to get supplies. He should be back in three weeks' time."

"No, I'm not looking for work. I'm looking to give you some."

"Is that right?" The man could hardly conceal a smile.

"Yes, if you go down to the Crystal Palace, you'll find your morning's work waiting for you."

"I see."

"But I need to ask you another favor, one that I'm willing to pay for."

"And what would that be, sir?"

"You have Ian Hays here?"

The man bowed his head. "Yes, I have the dear man in my back room now."

"And you haven't told anyone about his death, have you?"

"No, sir, I haven't. It is my usual practice to inform the paper though. I was going to do that this morning."

"Fine." Zac reached in his pocket and took out two twenty-dollar gold pieces. He laid them on a marble table next to him. "The only thing you have to do to earn that is to keep Hays' death quiet for the next three days."

"Three days is a long time. The family will want the man buried before that."

Zac pulled out three more of the coins. He stacked them. "Make an excuse. Just keep things quiet until then."

The man reached out and raked the gold coins into his hand. "I won't ask you the reason for this unusual request, but I don't see what harm it will do. I'm not sure I can keep it quiet for three days, however. Two might be the best I can do."

"Do what you can and we'll just keep this matter to ourselves."

"Why of course, sir. My lips will be sealed—like the dead."

Zac brushed the brim of his hat to the man and walked out the door. He hoped Palmer was the tightlipped sort. Right now, he was looking for any kind of an edge he could get. Three more days without anyone learning of Ian's death might give him that. Jenny would be having a hard enough time without the news of Ian's death. When word did hit the streets, her plight might just become serious.

The thought of the old woman he passed hit him. He'd seen her the night before. She'd obviously spent the night in town, and it was just as plain that Palmer hadn't been talking to people about deliveries he'd received during the night. *How did she know?* he wondered.

He started his walk back down the street. If nothing else, Quinn could be expected to try to get word to Kathryn and whoever else might be with her that Zac was on to their location. He just needed to make certain he got there first.

The sky was clouding up, which was a usual occurrence. He would need supplies and some warmer clothing. He knew he'd also need to find Benny. The man's boat might be the only thing he could hire to take him to this Mount Fairweather Bay. He glanced across the street at the shipping office. Taking big strides, he crossed over.

The bell rang over the door, and a man behind the counter turned to face him. "Can I help you, sir?"

Zac walked over to the counter. "I'm looking for a private charter."

"We can help you there, sir."

"Actually I'm looking for a skipper and a small boat I already know. He works for Ian Hays sometimes."

"You mean Benny McGill."

"Yes, that's right. Do you know where I might find him?"

"He's got a room at the Cosmo." The man laughed. "You'll find him in bed till noon, I imagine."

"All right. Thanks very much." Zac walked back to the door, ringing it as it opened. He stepped out into the street and made his way in the direction of the Crystal Palace. He walked past the place slowly and made his way around the corner and into the alley. He didn't see Horace.

Maybe the man had taken his advice. Zac hoped so.

As he rounded the corner, he felt a solid blow to the head. Stars burst in his brain—his mind tumbled over and over. He fell to his knees. One more blow to the back of his head made everything dark.

CHAPTER 28

+ + + + + + +

ZAC'S HEAD BUZZED. HIS ARMS were heavy, leaden and unable to move. His eyes fluttered open with the feel of a warm spoon on his lips.

"You better eat your soup." It was Mac's voice. Even though it seemed faint, Zac could recognize it. "Dimple Cheeks here fixed it for you."

The room was still turning in a soft spin. He blinked his eyes. The woman was seated on the bed next to him. She smiled, showing a full set of white teeth and the dimples in her cheeks that gave her the name Mac was given to call her. She pushed the spoon into his lips, and the broth trickled down his throat. It was warm to the taste with a salty flavor.

"Where am I?" he croaked.

"You're at my place, old buddy."

Zac turned his head to look around the room. A number of trophy heads were hanging over the mantel with an enormous bearskin sitting in front of a roaring fire. Blankets were hung on the walls, and the furniture was homemade from spruce knitted together with rawhide. It was simple but homey.

"How did I get here?"

"I drove off the man who slugged you," another voice said.

Zac barely recognized the man's voice, but it was hard to mistake the man as he stepped up to the bed. He was still disheveled and covered from head to foot with dirt. It was Horace, the man in the alley, whom Zac had given the meat to. "Hank's the man that done it, the bartender over to the Crystal Palace. He was whopping on you pretty good with one of his beer keg mallets. Lucky thing he didn't kill you. He would have, too, if I hadn't come along."

Mac laughed. "That was probably the first time Horace has been on his feet in days."

"I just held my arms out this a way." Horace held both arms up, doing his best imitation of a bear. "Then I yelled and said, 'You get away from that man.' Durndest thing I ever saw. He done just that. Lit up and ran away."

"You did good." Mac swatted the man on the back.

Horace coughed at the blow to his back, then straightened himself up. "I heard you say you knew Mac here, so I brung him over to get you. We both had to tote you over to his place here." He shook his head. "You weren't movin' none at all."

"We had the sawbones come over to look at you," Mac said. "He said there weren't much he could do that we couldn't, so we just let you lay."

"I appreciate it," Zac said. "What day did you say it was?"

"I don't know." Mac scratched his head and looked out the window as if he expected it to be written in the sky. "But you been here two days now."

Zac threw the edge of his covers off. "I got to get going." He started to get up, but his head throbbed.

"I don't think you ought to move around for a few days yet," Mac said. "You took yourself some kind of whops on that head of yours. Now, I know you're kinda thick-skulled, but a man can take only so much."

"I don't have any time to spare. Jenny's been kidnapped and I know where she is. Quinn confessed she's being held on the *Northern Star*."

Mac leaned back. "Well, I'll be. I wouldn't put anything past that man." He leaned forward, glaring at Zac. "What's he gonna do, white slave her?"

"No, but I've got to go get her and I've got to leave today."

Mac looked back at the window. "That servant of Ian's brought your rifle yesterday. We got word to them what happened, and he run it down here with his carriage. I speck he thought you'd be takin' yerself some measure of revenge."

"I've got no time for that. I've got to get a boat and get underway for Mount Fairweather Bay."

"That where they took her?" Mac asked.

"That's what I hear, and I need to get there."

Mac smiled. "Me and Horace know that place pretty well. We trapped there for two years or better."

"I wanna go with you," Horace said.

Zac swung his feet off the side of the bed. Each movement he made was labor, coupled with pain. "I'm afraid you wouldn't be up to it."

Horace leaned over so he could look Zac in the eye. "Right now I think I'd go a mite further than you could."

Zac wove a bit, sitting up. He looked up at the man. "You probably could at that."

"Then it's settled," Mac said. "Both Horace and me are going with you. I doubt you could find your way a hundred yards across an ice field, and when you get there you're going to need some help, probably way more than we got to offer."

Zac looked up, first at Mac and then Horace. "Do you know what you're getting into?"

Mac grinned. "Sure. Anything I can do to give Zubatov a black eye, I'll do in a minute. Plus, you got a wedding to go to—yours. You know how much I love weddings, and I'm gonna insist on being invited to yours."

"Yes, I know." Zac pointed at Horace. "Only thing is, I want *you* to get a bath before we go, a bath and some clean clothes. If I'm going to be sleeping next to you, I don't want your lice or fleas."

Mac began to laugh holding his stomach. "Boy, that will be the day. We all call old Horace here, Grubby. It's kind of a pet name." Mac looked at him. "Well, what do you say, Grubby?"

"If that's what it takes, then I'll do 'er," he gulped.

Mac slapped him on the back and grinned at Zac. "Maybe something good will come from this after all. Nobody's been able to get this man in a tub for as long as I've known him. He must really want to go bad."

"Mac, you got to go find Benny McGill. It's his boat we're taking. I'll try to get our food together." He looked at Horace. "And get Horace here cleaned up."

It took Mac more than an hour to locate Benny and get him started on getting the boat ready. Horace was putting on some clean clothes Dimple Cheeks had rounded up for him when Mac got back. He stood there staring at the man as he buttoned an old checkered shirt. "Horace, you do clean up well."

Dimple Cheeks giggled. "He even washed out his beard," she said.

"I can see that. It's brown too, not black."

"He'll need to be armed," Zac said.

"No problem there." Mac walked over to a large steamer trunk and, lifting the lid, began to rummage through it. He held up a revolver and holster. "Here's my old Smith and Wesson." He tossed it over to Horace. "You buckle that on. I've got some ammunition for it." He pointed up at the gun rack. "You can take one of my Winchesters down off the rack. There's ammo in the boxes over there. Take a box."

"You planning on a war?" Horace asked.

Mac looked back at Zac. "I just figure as determined as our friend is over there, we better be ready for whatever comes."

Dimple Cheeks fixed them a hot meal of soup and steak. All three men knew it might be the last hot food they would have in some time, and they ate it like there would be no tomorrow. Horace had a big grin on his face as he pushed a piece of steak into his mouth with his fingers and pulled at it, ripping the piece off and chewing vigorously.

"At least you wiped your mouth," Zac said.

"Man can't be expected to make too many changes so fast," Mac added. "It makes his head swim."

"Didn't your mother teach you to use a fork and spoon?" Zac asked.

Horace frowned. "I got taught lots of things, and all of them I left in the States when I come up here. I figure a man ought to be left to shift for himself in these parts."

Mac grinned at Zac. "That's the way of a man in Alaska. That's why I come here and that's why Horace here stays. You don't got to impress nobody. You just got to make do."

Zac broke a piece of bread and deliberately picked up his knife. He buttered it smoothly. "I don't think of it that way. No matter where a man is or who he's with, he's still the same man on the inside."

"Is that why you killed that man in the Crystal Palace the other day?" Mac asked.

Zac bit off the buttered end of the bread and thought as he chewed. "There's lots of reasons for a man to kill and be killed. In the war, you marched off into battle with people you grew up with. If you turned and ran, it would be like turning your back on everything and everyone you knew. So you went on. You walked into cannon fire with canister that was like buckshot laced with fire. And you killed because you had to. I suppose I do that now for the same reason, only because I have to. I don't find any pleasure in it."

Mac leaned over the table. "He did deserve it, didn't he?"

"With a man like that you figure that it's only a matter of time before he kills someone else. He's the type that's always on the prod. He doesn't do it for the money, he does it for the pure pleasure of proving himself."

"So you figure you saved some other fool's life," Mac replied, "somebody like me?"

"That's about the size of it."

"Well, me and all the other fools around these parts surely do thank you. Can't help but wonder, though, if the doing of the thing doesn't leave its mark on your insides. It would me."

Zac put down the bread. "Then maybe I should do this thing alone. It's been my experience that when you go up against dangerous men in desperate situations, you have to be ready to pull the trigger." Zac lifted his finger in the air to make his point. "You can't do that and he'll pull the trigger on you. One flinch, one moment of indecision, and you're the dead man folks are grieving over."

He got to his feet and walked over to where Mac had hung the heavy fur coat he was loaning him. Lifting it from the peg in the wall, he stuck his arms in. "It's one of the reasons I usually like to go alone. I know what's in my head. I may not know what's in somebody else's. If I can't trust a man to shoot, then I have to look out for him."

Mac got to his feet and shrugged on his coat. "I ain't never shot a man before, but I killed me many a bear that aimed to have me for dinner. I reckon I can just think of it that way." He paused, looking at Zac. "And I don't miss."

Horace got up from the table. He reached over and took another piece of meat, cramming it into his mouth. He was chewing as he spoke, but the words were not lost on anyone. "Don't make no never mind to me. I can tell you one thing, though. I didn't go through all that bathing and scrubbing to be sitting here by the fireplace. I ain't gone that soft in the head, not just yet."

Mac slung his rifle over his shoulder and picked up his pack. "There you are. Looks like you got yourself a posse."

"Looks like I have," Zac replied.

It took the three of them the better part of an hour to load their supplies aboard the small boat. Benny had the boiler fired up and a fresh supply of wood piled beside the engine. "You're going up to Fairweather Mountain from what I hear," he said.

Zac nodded.

"Well, don't let that name fool you none. We're gonna have ice in the sound there and lots of it. We'll have to pick our way around it. Ought to be a real mess."

He dropped the gate on the firebox and, turning several valves, threw the engines into gear. The small boat chugged away from the dock and into the harbor. "That Jung woman's steamer left this morning," Benny said. "It was headed north."

"Did you see who was on it?" Zac asked.

"Sure did. Hard to miss. That woman's partner, Quinn, was on it."

✦ ✦ ✦ ✦ ✦

Jenny crouched down in front of the small stove. She opened the grate and poked at the coals with one of the few remaining sticks of wood she had left. The air had turned bitterly cold, and the howl of the wind seemed to rip by the outside of the ship. She poked at the glowing embers and then, getting down on all fours, began to blow gently on them. A small flame sprang to life. Tearing at the piece of wood with her finger-nails, she pried several splinters loose. She then laid them ever so care-fully on the small flame and stood up.

The cabin they had put her in was small, but it did have a bed and warm blankets. She imagined the bed was the only warm place on the boat and was perhaps their way of keeping her there during the night. She had been kept in the cabin as long as the ship remained in Sitka har-bor, but today they had allowed her on deck. The ice field the boat had sailed into was large and treacherous. Even if she could manage to get away, there was no escaping the freezing water.

She bent over the small wash bowl and picked up the piece of soap, dipping it into the water and rubbing it on her hands. Peering into the mirror, she massaged the small bit of suds onto her face.

She still didn't know why she was here. It had been almost a week and no one had asked her anything, except what she needed in the way of some small comfort they might offer. She hadn't even met the captain, though there seemed to be no one in charge, just a group of underlings who were doing their best to keep her under lock and key. When they had rowed her out to the waiting ship in the harbor, it was under the pretense that Zac was there and needed her help. She should have known better.

She looked over at her purse, sitting on the small table. It still con-tained the bantam .32 caliber pistol she carried. The men hadn't even bothered to check it. Perhaps there was still some politeness, even in the worst of men. Going through a lady's purse could never be construed as manly, and few would guess that she even carried a pistol. She had been tempted to use it for several days now, but the men who cared for her had always come in groups of three or four, and they were heavily armed. Besides, there was no place to go.

She heard footsteps outside her door and squeezed the soap in the palm of her hand. Turning around, she faced the door and watched as the small brass knob turned.

A lanky man with a dark blue coat pushed the door open. He had a black beard and piercing eyes. His curly black hair was neatly parted and tucked behind his ears. "Good evening, Miss Hays. I'm Captain Zubatov. I'm sorry I wasn't here to greet you when you came on board."

"Why am I here?" Jenny asked. "This is kidnapping."

He shook his head slowly. "No, I assure you that we have only your best interest at heart." He lifted his hand and motioned around the room.

"We've given you one of our better cabins, and my men have been standing guard over you."

"To keep me a prisoner."

"Why no, to protect you."

"From what, the comfort of my own room?"

"I can assure you, that will be explained in good time, all in good time."

Just then Kathryn Jung entered the room. She was wearing a fur coat and hat, and a smile on her face.

"You," Jenny said, "I should have known."

"I'm sorry about all of this, Sitka is not safe for you just now. We feared if we tried to explain this all to you that you wouldn't listen to us, and I couldn't see you come to harm. I like your bridegroom-to-be. How could I let something disastrous befall the woman he loves?"

"I can take care of myself. Just take me back. I demand that you take me back this instant."

"You have no idea of the danger that awaits you there, does she, Captain?"

"No, indeed she doesn't."

"There are people there who want to kill you," Kathryn said.

"Why me? I don't know anyone here."

"You have control over a piece of land that used to belong to the Tlingit Indians. It was property that was the dowry your uncle received when he married Risa. Now they want to kill him for it, and we have knowledge that he's given that property to you. Don't you see? What you do now can not only spare your uncle's life, but yours as well. You really must divest yourself and your uncle of this land. You'll be well paid, of course."

"I know about this trusteeship. My uncle's lawyer told me everything. He also told me someone broke into his files and may have seen Uncle Ian's will." Jenny looked at the both of them. "I would say the chances are that burglar was the two of you."

Kathryn shook her head. "Heavens no. We just want to protect *your* life." She held out a piece of paper. "All you need to do is just sign this and sell the property. We're prepared to compensate you generously."

Jenny turned her head from the woman and the paper she was holding. "Then why would you keep me a prisoner and take me up here?"

"For your protection," Zubatov said. "This area is far away from those who might try to kill you, and we were afraid you wouldn't listen to reason."

"And now you think I will if you keep me prisoner and hold a gun to my head."

"There is no place to go up here," Zubatov said.

"You just read over the papers we've had drawn up," Kathryn said. The woman had a calm smile on her face, one that Jenny detested. "I'm certain when you see the wisdom of what we propose, you'll understand the absolute foolishness of doing anything else."

It was the woman's air of superiority that really got Jenny's anger aroused, and once again she turned away.

"Here, I'll put them here on the bed. You take some time and read them carefully. It will be safe to take you back once you've signed them."

Jenny wadded the small piece of soap in her hand. She would have much preferred to have Kathryn alone, if only for a moment. She shuddered, her hands shaking. She had to get control of herself. She had to take control of the situation. She turned her head around and watched Kathryn leave the room.

"Is there anything else you'll be needing?" Zubatov asked.

Jenny shook her head and stepped over to the door. She had an idea. It was something Zac had told her about from one of his trips. A man had made a successful escape from a jail, and he'd done it with a bar of soap.

Zubatov started to close the door, but Jenny stopped him. "There is something, Captain."

He opened it wider. "What would that be?"

She reached into the brass latch area of the door and pressed the small piece of soap down into the mechanism. There was no key to the door, only a locking device on the outside that froze it into place. A small spring inside the door would push the latch into position. She had seen it when the men who brought her food had come and gone. It was that latch that she wanted to hold in place. She only hoped the piece of soap would do it.

"I'd like something hot to drink in the morning, some coffee." She pressed the soap harder and deeper into the latch and wiped the area clean with her fingers, making sure the packed soap would not be visible when the man shut the door.

"Why of course," Zubatov smiled. "I'll bring it to you myself."

With that, he closed the door.

+ + + + + + +

CHAPTER 29

JENNY BACKED UP TO THE DOOR, listening for the latch to engage. It didn't. The man twisted the lock on the other side and then walked away.

She stood there for some time, breathing heavily and listening for the sound of footsteps. All was quiet. Turning around, she slowly pulled the door. It opened. She reached around, unsnapping the lock, and closed the door.

Now she had to get prepared. She raced over to the table and picked up the box of matches lying there. Putting on her fur coat, she stuffed the few remaining pieces of dry wood down into the pockets. She picked up the slab of cheese she hadn't eaten and stuffed it into her purse. Then looking around, she spotted the papers Kathryn had left for her to read. They would made a good fire starter. She wadded them up and crammed them into the pocket with the wood.

Moving back to the door, she opened it slowly. The passageway was empty, and it was doubtful that on such a cold night anyone would be on deck. It was a chance she had to take. She made her way down the dimly lit passage to the stairs. Slowly she climbed them, one at a time.

The passage and stairs led out onto the rear deck of the ship. This was good. Even if someone was moving around, they would most likely be at the bow of the ship.

She hurried across the open deck. Reaching the rail, she spotted a coil of rope. She tied one end to the railing and threw it over.

The ice field covered the entire bay, and even though the ship still sat in the water, somehow she knew there must be ice nearby. She only hoped it would hold her. Climbing over the side, she lowered herself down the rope. A small wooden ledge stood out from the hull of the ship near the water line. She touched it with her toe and then gently released her grip on the rope. It was slippery. One foot gave way and slipped beneath the ledge. She grabbed onto the rope and it burned her hands.

Her heart was beating faster now, and the cold wind felt good against the heat of her body. Lifting up her foot, she scrambled to get it back on the ledge. There, she had it. It made her shudder to think of falling into the water.

She looked down. A small floe of ice brushed up against the *Northern Star*. She could see it bobbing on the water, the slight tug of the current rocking it up and down in a slow, rolling motion. But she could see that it was moving. There was no time to waste.

Turning her back to the ship, she looked down at the ice. It was hard to measure just how far she had to go, but she could hear the ice rubbing against the ship. No doubt the piece next to where she was would be thin; perhaps it couldn't hold her. It certainly could never take the force of her landing. She would have to jump farther, jump into the spikes that seemed to protrude from the top of the flow. Right then it wasn't the thought of pain that bothered her, it was the thought of staying locked up on the boat.

She leaned back, pressing her spine up against the cold oak planks of the ship. With one mighty shove, she leaped into the darkness. Her hands spun out in front of her and she landed on the ice, sliding forward.

The ice beneath her shivered with the blow of her body. It rocked in the water. Daggers of pain shot through Jenny's arms and knees. The fur coat had protected her some, but it couldn't shield her from the hardness of the ice itself.

She reached out with her hand, grabbing one of the peaks of ice in front of her. Slowly, she pulled herself up, away from the edge of the ice. Moving one knee forward, she placed a foot underneath her. She shook all over as she climbed to her feet.

The ice was moving now. The force of her jump had caused it to get some separation from the ship. She watched as the black hull slid slowly away. There would be no turning back now even if she wanted to. She was alone, by herself on the ice.

She looked out on the white, snowy field. From where she stood, it had the appearance of a solid blanket of ice, but she knew that wasn't true. It was more like a series of small movable islands and rocks on an inky black sea.

Another thought shot terror through her. She had only been told about the polar bear, the white monster of this land. One thing she did know was that they did their hunting and feeding on the ice fields at night. Right now, she was a part of its food chain. She might even make a complete meal for a family of these creatures.

She inched her way to the other side of the flow. Her ice raft was about the size of her bedroom at home. It wasn't thick enough to hold her though, and just now her weight was beginning to cause the black water to lap over its edges.

She watched as the ice made its way to yet another snowy island. This one appeared to be larger, but she knew that looks could be deceiving. The shelf surrounding it might be very thin, and she didn't have the advantage of a ship to push off from when she made her jump. She could easily hit it and plunge into the water. No one had to tell her that someone who was wet would never survive the night. It was doubtful a swimmer, even after spending only moments in the water, could make it through an hour.

Lord, please, Jenny thought, *I am here and you are here. I am never far away from you, and your eyes never leave me. Please, Lord, direct my steps.* It was a simple prayer, but one she knew would be heard. The Lord always was and always would be with her.

She got up as close to the edge as she dared. The water was almost up to her toes. She knew the ice would give when she made her jump, she just hoped it didn't give so much that she would fall short.

Suddenly, she changed her mind. A standing jump would never work. No, she'd have to back up and take a running leap across the dark finger of water that separated her from the ice beyond. That was her only chance.

She took a few steps back, judging the distance, then a few more. This would have to be it. She hoped the thing wouldn't buckle under the impact of her steps. Taking a few deep breaths, she ran for the edge and jumped.

She hit the island of ice on the other side of the water, but her fears were well founded. The portion of the ice under her feet gave way, sending her up to her ankles in cold water. Grabbing the ice in front of her, she pulled herself up.

Her purse had landed a few feet from her, close to the edge of the ice. She scrambled over to where it lay and picked it up. The last thing she needed was to lose her purse. It held the only means she had of defending herself. Even though the little .32 didn't stand a chance against a polar bear, it was sure to put fear into any man who might chase her.

The mukluks on her feet were soaked. She could feel the cold as it inched its way through her toes and up her legs. There had to be a way to dry off. Opening her coat, she reached under her skirt and pulled down the slip she was wearing. She stepped out of it, then sat down on the ice and pulled the mukluks off, shaking the water onto the ice. She waved them back and forth, trying her best to get the last of the water out of them.

Her bare feet on the ice stung. The cold was like a sharp knife being jabbed into her toes and feet. She tore half the slip into strips and crammed them down into the mukluks. With the other half, she quickly dried off her feet. Grabbing one of the sealskin boots, she pulled it on. She could still feel the dampness, but the portion of slip she had stuck in there was doing its part to soak up the moisture. She only hoped her body heat would do the rest. It was a heat that was fast disappearing. Quickly, she pulled the other boot on and got to her feet. She stamped at the ice, furiously trying to beat life into her toes. It was hard to imagine what would have happened if more than her feet had gotten wet.

She began her walk around the small isle of ice. It was larger than the first, but not by much. It had carried her farther away from the ship, however, and she was grateful for that. "Thank you, Lord," she whispered. There was a long way to go before she reached solid ground, though, and she knew it.

She made her way around and was surprised to see how close the next patch of ice was. Backing up slightly, she jumped for it. She hit the thing, sliding forward again on her elbows and knees. She wouldn't complain about it, though. A little pain was far better than the water of the bay.

From far away she heard the long, mournful howl of a wolf. It was followed by a chorus of baying wails, like some collection of lost souls in torment. There was a loneliness to the cries, and right now she could understand it completely. There was also a danger and it sent sudden shivers down her back. She didn't want to meet up with a pack of wolves. She had never felt more defenseless.

Suddenly in the distance she heard a cracking sound. It was like the noise of a thousand trees being felled by an ax, a slow, ripping reverberation followed by a thunderous boom. Jenny looked out over the water and saw a large shelf of ice drop into the bay with a crash. The massive glacier was giving birth to more ice on the water. That was what she was standing on, what the glacier had produced the day before.

She circled the patch of ice and jumped for the next one. It was no more than a step away, and she was grateful she hadn't been forced to land on her shins and elbows once again. She was moving north, into the teeth of the glacier. She knew it was her best move. There would be more ice there, more stepping stones to the shore.

One thing did bother her, however. It would have been natural for the men on the ship to assume she'd go south. That was the direction of

Sitka. Her rope had been lowered on the north side of the ship's hull, though.

Looking off in the distance, she could see a larger mass of ice. It towered over all the rest, dwarfing the small floes of ice that swam around it. She would try to make it there. From the top of the thing she might even be able to see where she was going.

She jumped onto the next piece. It shivered under her, unstable and rather thin, she would guess. The much larger piece was quite close now and she made a quick leap, swinging her arms for balance. She landed with both feet under her, and her footing held. It was good to stand on something more stable, even though she knew it wouldn't last long.

She looked over the large island of ice. It had a peak that she couldn't see over and a number of jutting edges that picked up the light of the night sky. This wasn't merely a piece of ice floating in the water, it was an iceberg. She had heard about them from the captain that brought her into Sitka, and now she was standing on one. Ships dreaded them, and she could see why.

Kicking at the slope with the toe of her mukluk, she pounded out a foothold and stepped into it. She repeated the process with her left foot. Slowly, she inched her way towards the top to get a look around the area. It took her some time, but she neared the very peak of the berg. It was a place she didn't want to stay, however. The large berg was very top heavy, and she'd already been told how they rolled over when the ice underneath them melted away. If she stayed on top of this much ice, she might soon find herself swimming for her life in the freezing water. Still, it would provide her with a good view for a short time, only a moment, and that was what she wanted.

As she neared the peak of the berg, a sound sent shock waves of fear into her. It was a growl, followed by another more distant reply. *Bears!* she thought. *Polar bears.* It was the last thing she wanted to hear, the very last thing. She had no way of defending herself against such creatures. One of them was close by, that was plain by the level of the roar. Just how close, she didn't know.

She laid flat against the ice and pulled herself forward. Now she was thankful she had decided to climb the thing rather than walk around it. Had she done that she might be face to face with the terror making her heart pound.

Pushing her head up, she looked over the edge of the peak. Now she could see it, the huge white outline of the bear running over the top of the ice floe nearest to hers, sniffing at the air and growling. She hoped it hadn't picked up her scent. Pulling her head back, she noticed the wind direction for the first time. It was coming from the south, right over her, and toward the direction of the bear. No doubt it was catching her aroma, and the smell she was carrying was driving the thing wild with anticipation.

Once again, she heard the roar of the beast. It seemed to be right on top of her. She began to shake, but for the first time it wasn't from the cold. It was from the sheer panic of soon being on the same iceberg as the bear. The beast would make short work of her, pistol and all.

She watched as the beast made his way to the edge of the ice. He was going to jump now, jump and swim, but where? She could only hope that it wouldn't be in her direction. He dropped himself into the water and began to paddle. Then he went under and she lost sight of him. She couldn't wait. She knew that. She would have to make her jump onto the ice the bear had abandoned. He might not come back to it, and at least she would be downwind. Her scent would disappear.

Climbing over the top of the peak, she scooted down the thing on her back. Several rocks tore away at her spine as she went over them. It was like sliding down a huge washboard. Her feet hit the bottom and she bounced up. She backed up slightly and jumped for the ice in front of her, landing on all fours.

Quickly, she scrambled to her feet. There was no time to lose. If the animal came back, there was nowhere to go. She spotted a spit of ice to her left, but that was the direction the bear had taken. She would go the way the animal had come from. She stepped over the ice and onto the edge that looked out over the dark water. There was another ice floe. It looked to be only about three or four feet away. On dry land such a distance would never bother her. She could easily jump it. But this was a different matter. Here, if she missed, there would be no second chance. She took two steps back and ran, jumping near the edge of the ice. It bounced under her feet as she flew into the air.

She landed on all fours, sending another series of jabbing pains into her elbows and knees. There was no time to even think about the pain; she had to keep moving. Getting to her feet, she continued to pick her way over the ice. The floes were closer together. They made for easy jumps, but she was getting colder. The air raced by her with howling wails.

It must have been more than two hours before she could recognize anything she thought might be land. She could see several small trees jutting out over the water in either direction. It was much too far away for a jump, however. It looked to be more than twenty yards.

She took several steps back and stared at the blackness of the water.

She was tempted to simply lower herself and make a swim for it. She could swim and it wouldn't get her head wet, but a jump might plunge her into the deep water. She would take that chance though. She'd come this far, she wasn't about to hold back now. She took a couple of very deep breaths. "Lord, please be there to catch me . . ." she whispered. Then she ran for the edge and jumped into the cold air, her arms spinning wildly.

Her feet hit the water with a splash and she fell forward on her hands and knees. The water was only a couple of inches deep at this point, although in the darkness it had seemed much deeper. She must have landed on a sandbar. She was wet though, very wet.

She got to her feet and began walking very quickly to the trees. Soon, she was climbing up a large group of boulders. The trees were above her, and they would offer her some protection from the wind. They also might conceal any fire she could get started. The aroma of the smoke would give her position away to any animals in the woods, but as long as she could keep the fire bright, she wouldn't send up a column of smoke to the men on board the ship. That was the last thing she needed to do, tell them where to find her.

The trees made it difficult to see. They were thick and blocked out what little moonlight was left. When she came to a slope in the hill, she darted around the back side of it, pulling the smaller trees apart and crashing her way through the undergrowth. It was dense here. It would make good cover. Plus the noise she was making gave her some assurance that no one would be able to take her unawares.

She pried two trees apart and stepped into a small clearing. She could see the outline of a large tree. Even in the dim light she could tell that it had been hollowed out by a fire, most likely caused by a lightning strike. This would be the perfect place.

She set her purse down inside the tree and began to look around for wood. What she needed now was a bright, hot fire made from dead branches. She began to gather what she could find and soon had an armful. Stepping over to the tree, she dropped her load there.

Jenny fumbled in her pocket for the agreement Kathryn had insisted on her reading. It would give her great pleasure to use it to start the fire. There was some justice in that. Pulling it out, she wadded it into a loose ball. She brushed the ground clear of the pine needles and snow and set the paper down. Reaching into her pocket, she produced the small pieces of kindling she had taken from her cabin. They were remarkably dry. She bit into the end of one of the pieces, peeling it back. Right now, she needed small pieces, and these few that she carried would make excellent starter if she could nurse them along.

She began to lay them over the paper in teepee fashion, circling the paper with a small pyramid of kindling. This would make a hot flame fast, and she'd have to capitalize on it with what she'd picked up from around the clearing.

She got down on all fours and pulled out the box of matches. Taking one out, she struck it. It burst into flame. Even the small flame of the match gave her fingers some measure of warmth. They shook as she pressed the match down into the paper.

It only took her a few minutes to nurse the flame into a hot fire. She continued to add to it, building it higher. The flames lit up the small part of the forest she'd decided to hole up in. Their shadows and the reflection of the crackling fire played off the branches and limbs that hung around her.

She sat down and wrenched off the mukluks, laying them down so their openings would be pointed at the flame. Tonight, or what was left of it, would be a time to dry off and get a small amount of sleep. It would be morning before they noticed that she was gone, and by then she'd be moving on. If they were going to find her, they'd have to look long and hard.

CHA30PTER

+ + + + + + +

THE MORNING BROKE OVER THE ICE-FILLED bay with a soft pink glow bathing the ice with a rosy hue and illuminating the water. It was black no longer, but a brilliant and deep blue, the color of a sapphire sparkling in the crown of a queen. An eagle looped over the water in slow, easy circles and then dived. It skimmed the surface of the water and then was airborne once again, a fish struggling in its talons.

Sergei Zubatov stepped out of the galley and signaled for two men to follow him. They formed a single line walking directly to the room where their female prisoner was being kept. Sergei knocked. "I have your breakfast, Miss Hays." There was no answer.

He snapped the lock and pushed the door open. The room was empty. Dropping the tray on the floor with a crash, he shouted, "She has escaped! The woman is gone."

Several minutes of yelling ensued and Zubatov inspected the room, barking out orders. He rushed onto the main deck and looked out over the ice fields. They were bare and pink with the morning sun. Soon Kathryn joined him.

"Where is she?" The woman was angry. It showed by the flushed expression on her face.

Zubatov continued to survey the ice. "She's out there somewhere. I'm having the men search the ship now, but she's out there."

"How could you have been so careless? I told you the soft treatment you were giving the woman would be wasted. I've spoken to her before. She's hardheaded and can be spiteful." Kathryn snapped.

Sergei held out his hand. In it were the pieces of the bar of soap. "The Hays woman is smart. She pressed this into the lock while we were talking last night."

"You fool. Haven't you ever learned that a woman can be the most treacherous when she's smiling and talking?"

Their conversation was interrupted by one of the sailors. "We found a line tied to the rail. It's on the aft deck. Must have got off the ship that way."

Zubatov and Kathryn followed the man to the rear deck of the ship. The sailor reached over and hauled in the rope. "Here, Captain," he said. "She went over this way."

Toquah Kanstanof emerged from below deck. He wore a tan shirt, open to the cool breeze, and his long black hair had been smoothed into place. "I'm glad we waited for Toquah to return before we sailed," Kathryn said. She watched the man as he walked toward them. It was obvious from the expression on her face that she liked what she saw. "If you'd had it your way, Sergei," she continued, "we'd have been here without him, and now it appears we will need an expert tracker."

"I understand you have a problem," Toquah said.

Kathryn smirked at Zubatov. "You might say that. It seems our captain's escape-proof cabin was anything but." She pointed to the rope still tied to the railing. "She went over here last night."

Toquah stared out at the glacier to the north of them, in the direction of the escape route.

"She wouldn't have gone there," Zubatov said. He pointed to the other side of the ship. "The woman would go south, toward Sitka. We should start our search there."

Toquah looked up at the blue sky, trying to imagine the darkness of the night before. He shook his head. "I don't think so. The moon is new. There is little light. The woman would not know north from south. She just wanted to find land. She not care which direction she was going. She not care until now, in the daylight when she can see."

"Then where should we begin to search?" Kathryn asked.

"Did the woman take matches?" Toquah asked.

"I'm not sure," Zubatov shook his head. "I'll have to look."

Toquah continued to scan the treeline around the bay and the slopes that led up to the hills and mountains that surrounded them. "If she did, then she may have a fire. I see no smoke. This woman is smart."

"Or dead," Zubatov countered. "She may not have even made it. We may be here for days looking for a body that can't be found. I know I wouldn't try to walk across that, not even in the light."

Toquah seemed to ignore Zubatov. He pointed to the glacier. "We go there," he said. "If the woman made land last night, then she will see where she needs to go today. She will have to cross the glacier. We will see her there against the snow and we will catch her." He pointed to one of the sailors. "Take your looking glass and keep watching that shore over there. The woman may come back to see if we follow."

"And if she doesn't make it to the glacier?" Zubatov asked.

"Then we will camp along the side of the thing, in the woods. She will come tomorrow, if she doesn't come today."

Zubatov wandered off to talk to the sailors who would accompany them. Kathryn curled her arm into Toquah's. She smiled at him and began to speak in low tones.

+ + + + +

Jenny's sleep was ended by a group of low flying geese. Their honking brought her straight up into a sitting position. There was another sensation that awakened her. She was freezing cold. She looked over. The fire had gone out hours earlier and she had no intention of starting another one. Smoke could be seen for miles. It would be nothing but a flag to signal her presence. She was shivering, though, and her teeth were chattering.

She crawled over to the ashes and picked up her mukluks. They were dry. Getting to her feet, she stamped them into place. She would have to move fast, but first she would go back to the water's edge and look at the ship. She wanted to know if they already had men on the ice looking for her and which direction they were going. Then she would head for the glacier. Night would be best, though. There was no sense in showing herself on the ice in the light of day. That would make it too easy for the searchers. If she could make it to the edge of the river of ice, she would wait for darkness to cross.

Walking slowly to the rocks, she kept her head down and her profile low. She crept up behind one of the largest ones and poked her head around it. Zac had told her many times that the way to see people when you didn't want to be seen was to look around an object, never over it.

The ship hadn't moved. The smoke from the stack curled up over the ice, snaking its way into the blue sky. *Maybe they think I'm dead*, she thought. Of course if they had reached that conclusion, they would no longer be at anchor in the bay. They were still waiting, however, waiting for her.

She backed away from the rock. There was no sense in giving them a head start. If they were going to find her, they would have to do it the hard way. Jenny wasn't about to make it easy. It would be tougher going through the woods, but at least she'd be out of sight. She had no intention of following the shoreline, no matter how far away from the ship it seemed.

Turning, she walked back into the trees and then climbed in the direction of the glacier. The hills were hard. They were rocky and scattered with small trees. In less than an hour, she was on top. Moving a patch of trees, she peeked through them. There was no movement from the ship. She breathed a sigh of relief.

It took Jenny most of the day to get to the glacier's edge. The thing was impossible to miss. It covered the entire head of the bay, and the periodic cracks and explosions that came from it indicated the birth of yet more of the pack ice and bergs that filled the bay.

She backed off the edge of the glacier and walked for some distance into the trees. There, she found a small fir tree. Its branches were hanging low. There hadn't been any sign of rain and that was unusual in itself, but if it did rain, this place might offer some protection.

Stepping over to another tree, she began to break off its low branches. This was another thing Zac had talked about. The branches would become a bed. They would keep her off the ground and just a little warmer, even without a fire.

Jenny laid the first set of branches under the fir tree's limbs, stretching them out. The second layer of limbs were reversed, keeping the bed fairly even. Zac had called this "mother nature's feather bed," and Jenny was hoping he was right. Reaching back into the pile, she worked at breaking off the smallest of the fronds and separating them from the larger branches. She leaned over the bed and pushed them in, creating a third layer of the softest needles.

Jenny had to have some sleep. This night would be a long one. To cross the glacier under cover of darkness would take hours. It would be a slow and rigorous hike, and she would have to take care not to fall into a crevasse. Then after crossing there would be no stopping. She would press on. There had to be as much distance as possible between her and the men of the *Northern Star*.

She nestled on the bed, curling into a ball. It was just as Zac had said. It was the most comfortable bed she'd slept in the entire trip. It didn't take long before she was fast asleep. Hours later Jenny's eyes snapped wide open and she stared into the darkness. A noise had awakened her this time, the noise of an animal close by. She rolled over and froze at the sight of a large silver-haired wolf.

She reached over and grabbed her purse. Sticking her hand inside, she pulled out the bull-pup pistol. It was something she wanted to avoid using at all cost. The noise of a gunshot would carry for miles. Getting to her feet, the thing backed off, growling at her. Reaching down, she picked up one of the branches that had been stripped clean and swung it at the wolf, a quick strike that whistled in the air. Again the beast backed up. It was alone and that was good; it was also rare. From everything she'd been told, wolves hunted in packs. Jenny had no doubt that if she did manage to drive the creature away, he would be back. He would follow her and he wouldn't be alone.

She swung again, striking and dancing forward like a swordsman. The wolf jumped back, cocked his head as if looking her over, and then loped away.

Turning, Jenny ran in the direction of the glacier. She wanted to put as much distance as possible between her and the wolf and the reinforcements he would no doubt summon. Maybe her trail would grow cold on the ice. It was a faint hope, but one she clung to.

She came to the edge of the glacier just in time to hear another crash in the water. Stepping out onto the ice, she made her way across it, swinging her arms to keep her balance.

The ice was rocky, and she worked at spotting the rocks on the surface. No doubt they would be on top of the most solid parts of the frozen river, and that was where Jenny wanted to step. Making her way over to them, she would pause and look for the next safe landing place. She stopped and looked down. The darkness of the night made it impossible to gauge how deep the crevasses were. All she could do was try to avoid them.

It took most of the night to cover the glacier. It was time that was hard on her. She constantly felt the compulsion to look back for the wolf pack that might be following. There was another feeling, too, an unsettling feeling. She couldn't shake the sensation of being watched.

When she finally stepped out onto the ground, she breathed a sigh of relief. She was free, free of the ice and hopefully free of the wolves. Turning into the trees, she heard a voice.

"Hello, Miss Hays. It's good to see you." It was Zubatov. He stepped out from the trees. "We thought we had lost you. You had us worried."

Reaching into her purse, she pulled out the pistol. "You stop right where you are. I'm not going back with you, not now, not ever."

The man stepped closer. He held his left hand in the air. "You wouldn't do that, not to someone trying to save you."

"You come closer to me and I'll shoot you." She backed up into the trees, but the man kept coming.

"I don't believe you'd do such a thing, not a nice lady like you."

"Don't you test me." She held the gun out ramrod straight, using both hands and trying her best to keep them from shaking. "I've fired a gun before, Captain, and I hit what I aim at."

The man dropped his right hand to the holster at his side. Jenny could see that it held a large revolver. He stepped closer. "I mean you no harm.

I'm just trying to ensure your safety. You'll die out here from cold or starvation."

"I'd far rather do that than die at your hands. You don't really expect me to believe that once I've signed those papers I'll ever make it back to Sitka, do you?"

"Why shouldn't you believe that? When we get what we want, you can have what you want." His voice was warm and soothing. "A warm home and a new husband."

"If you do kill me, do you really expect Zac to let you live? You don't know him like I do. You kill me and you're a dead man. You may be dead already."

"You just let me worry about that." His smile was chilling. "I'm going to lead you back to my ship or carry you. The choice is yours."

Jenny held the gun steady. There was no way she was going to go back after what she'd already suffered. If it was going to end, it would end here. She cocked the hammer on the gun and took one more step back into the trees. "I promise you, Captain, you take one more step forward and I'm going to put a hole in you that you won't recover from."

He began to raise his gun. "You don't want to die. You have too much to live for." He stepped toward her and she fired.

The man was stunned. His revolver fell to the ground and he clutched his chest, looking into her eyes. He dropped to his knees and then fell forward.

Jenny felt sick inside. Suddenly, a pair of strong hands grabbed her arms from behind, shaking the revolver loose. She was spun around and slapped across the face, and she dropped to the ground.

Jenny looked up. She saw a big man with long black hair and a smooth face. He glared at her. "You going back with me."

"Who are you?" she asked.

He sneered at her. "Toquah Kanstanof. I come to take you back."

"H-h-how long have you been standing there?" She stammered.

"Long enough to hear the whole thing."

"Why didn't you—"

"What? Keep you from killing Zubatov?" He smiled. "You needed to speak your mind, and he needed to die."

✦ ✦ ✦ ✦ ✦

Benny eased the small craft around the bend and immediately caught sight of the plume of black smoke from the steamer. He killed the engines. "This is as far as we'd better go," he shouted.

Zac pointed to an icy beach next to the entrance of the bay. "You'd better put us in there. We'll take it from here."

Benny spun the wheel and started up the propellers, chugging the small craft in the direction of the point Zac had indicated. Minutes later, he beached the boat on the sand. "Okay boys, the rest is up to you. I'll wait right here and put my fire out."

Zac climbed out of the boat, lifting the pack that contained the ammunition. Mac scrambled out, followed by Horace. The group lifted out their supplies and waved good-bye to the skipper as they sauntered up the hill and into the woods.

"How you reckon we're gonna get out to that ship?" Mac asked.

"I don't have any idea," Zac said. "I was hoping you did. When it comes to this area of the country, I'm making this up as I go along."

They rounded the top of the hill and moved along the tree line, doing their best to keep out of sight. Zac and the group stopped to look. Not only was the *Northern Star* there, but the steamer that had left Sitka the day before they did was anchored next to it. There was also a smaller boat. It was being rowed from the north end of the bay.

Zac dropped his pack and took out the brass spyglass Mac had stored. He opened it up and peered at the smaller boat. Then he handed the thing to Mac.

"There's three men in that thing and they've got a woman," Mac said, peering through the glass.

"Yes," Zac replied, "it's Jenny."

Mac handed the spyglass to Horace. "Whatever we do will have to wait till nightfall. I don't hanker on stomping over that ice while folks is shooting at me in the broad daylight."

Zac nodded in reluctant agreement.

"Let's just hope they don't decide to leave before then," Horace added.

Zac pulled the pipe out from his jacket pocket and stuffed it with tobacco. He struck a match and lit it. The thing would help him to think, and right now, it was what he needed most.

+ + + + +

The small boat glided toward the *Northern Star*. It edged its way to the side that had the lowered gangway. Toquah stood up, pulling Jenny to her feet. He pushed her up the rope-suspended series of planks, prodding her as she walked in front of him. When they stepped through the open rail, Kathryn was there to meet them, along with Quinn. She was smiling. Toquah held on to Jenny's arms.

"Mr. Quinn here has some news of Sitka for us," Kathryn said. She looked at Jenny, her face turning sour. "It seems we have less time than we planned for, and no time at all for your stubbornness. Your uncle Ian is dead."

Jenny pulled hard, trying to wrest herself free from the man's grasp. "You're a murderer, too, then." She spat the words in Kathryn's direction.

Kathryn's voice was calm but chilling. "I didn't do it, but I can't say I'm sorry it happened." She looked over at two of the sailors standing by. "Take her below to the hold. We won't be giving her any more special treatment. We'll see how she likes life in the cold darkness."

The two men grabbed Jenny and led her away while she continued to struggle.

Kathryn looked back at Toquah. "And where is our beloved captain?"

Toquah reached into his pocket and pulled out Jenny's gun. "I'm afraid the captain will no longer be with us. She did just like you said she would."

Kathryn bounced the gun in her hand. "I'm glad I left this where I found it. I knew she'd use it sooner or later on the man. That's why I kept sending him down to care for her." She grinned and dropped the pistol in her pocket. "The man was ignorant when it came to women."

"One less partner you have to share with," Toquah added.

"Yes, and one more ship." She smiled at Quinn. "Isn't that right, Mr. Quinn? Our supplies will be so much less expensive."

The big saloon owner smiled and nodded.

"We do have one more thing to worry about, however," Kathryn said. "And we'll have to leave here tomorrow and find another spot to anchor." She paused, making sure she had the man's full attention. "Miss Hays' intended knows where we are. Even now he is no doubt headed in our direction."

CHAPTER 31

+ + + + + + +

ZAC WAS AT THE EDGE OF THE CLEARING. He had a small fire going directly under a small spruce tree. The slight smoke was filtering through the branches and a coffeepot hung on the fire. The three men had dozed off and on through the early evening, but Zac was eager to get to Jenny.

Zac bent over and poured a cup of coffee. "You better drink this down," he said. "We'll have to get moving soon. It's after midnight."

Mac took the cup and held it to his lips. He let the aroma circle his face. "How you plan to get to that ship?" he asked.

"I've taken care of that." Zac pointed to the side of the hill that ran down to the bay. "I built us a raft."

Mac sent out a spray of hot coffee. "A raft? You expect us to make it on some rickety old bunch of stumps you piled together?" He swung around and pointed in the direction of the bay. "That ship's in deep water. Don't be fooled about that. You get us swimmin' in that water and we're gonna be dead."

Zac smiled at the man. "Trust me."

Mac took another drink of coffee. "Trust you? Who in their right mind would trust a man in love?"

Zac poured himself another cup of coffee. "That's the problem with you, Mac. You don't understand what love means. If you did, you wouldn't have five wives. A man who loves does his best because he has a reason to beyond his own miserable hide. It's something I've been learning."

Mac sipped on his coffee, studying Zac. "You been learnin' that?"

"I'm a Christian now. Didn't use to be, although I'd heard enough about it since I was a boy. When God loves a man, He does something about it. He doesn't just sit around and think pretty thoughts."

Mac and Horace exchanged glances. "So we're supposed to trust your judgment on frozen water because you're in love," Mac said.

Zac sipped his coffee and a small smile creased his face. "That's about the size of it. I'm not going to let you boys get your feet wet. I need you too much."

Mac looked over at Horace. "Well, I guess we know what there is to know about this man. He ain't no preacher, but he sure is a deacon, a deacon that more'n likely kills folks for a living."

Horace nodded and sipped his coffee.

"I am a rancher," Zac said, "But I also work for Wells Fargo. I'm a special officer."

"What's that?" Horace asked. "Is that like a bounty hunter?"

"Something like that." Zac looked off in the direction of the bay. "Only thing is, I'm working for the woman I love now. I'm kinda counting on that to bring out the best in what I do."

"I feel better about that," Horace said.

Mac snapped his head around. "Why is that?" he asked.

"Least we ain't gonna get ourselves killed by some tenderfoot fool."

"Nah," Mac agreed, "Just some bounty huntin' deacon in love." He looked over at Zac. "All right, where do you have us crossing the Red Sea?"

Zac sat down his cup and picked up his rifle. "Follow me."

He led the two men down the hill. They moved through the trees and frozen brush. The biting wind was stronger now; it was coming from the north, over the ice, and right into their faces. They could feel its full effect when they cleared the trees.

They could see the ship and the small steamer. It appeared that the ship had a fire going in a container on deck. No doubt it was to keep the guards warm who were assigned to keep watch.

Zac led the two men between the rocks and down to the water's edge. On the beach was the raft. Zac had used a number of large deadfalls and tied them together with a coil of rope. The raft was at least eight feet long and six feet wide.

Zac pointed to the ice. "We won't have to go all the way, only as far as the ice."

"That stuff is bad," Mac said. "It can't be crossed by just anybody." Mac had spent his time on some of the ice floes in Alaska but never this early in the season. "You never know what's on the other side," he went on, "and you never know if that ice is gonna hold you up, especially with three of us."

"That's a chance we'll have to take," Zac said, "even if we have to go one at a time." He stepped onto the raft and picked up one of the long poles he had cut to shove them off with. "I'm going. You can stay if you like."

"Count me in too," Horace said. He stepped onto the raft and picked up a second pole.

The distant boom of the glacier brought their heads around. A large shelf of ice and rock was separating from the face of the icy river. It fell into the bay, shaking the ground.

Mac held up his hands. "All right, I'm going." He pointed his finger at Zac. "But when we get on that ice, I'm gonna do the leading. You on that stuff is gonna be like a hog on a greasy dance floor."

Mac stepped onto the raft and picked up the third pole. Together, they turned and pushed against the mud, floating the raft free.

"So far, so good," Mac said. "We managed to get off without soaking ourselves to the bone."

Zac had found several pieces of wood that could reasonably serve as paddles. They were cumbersome but provided some resistance against the water. Moving slowly through the darkness, they made their way toward the ice. The raft bumped into the first of the islands. Zac wound the length of rope that was left around the pole he was carrying and drove it into the ice. Taking the second pole from Horace's hand, he jumped onto the ice.

"Now, just you hold on," Mac said. He followed Zac, jumping onto the ice. The small island shook under his weight. "I said I was going to lead and I meant it. You wait right here with Horace. I'll feel my way across with this thing and tell you if we can get over it."

"Sounds dangerous," Zac said.

"It is," Mac grinned, "but I'm with a man in love."

It took the three of them more than an hour to cross the ice field and get anywhere close to the ship. As promised, Mac went first, picking his way over the ice and using the pole to probe the depth of where they were stepping. He turned back to Zac. "Those pieces up close to the *Star* are too measly to hold us up." He pointed at the smaller steamer. "But the boat over there is backed up to some good-sized ones."

Zac nodded and the man hopped the small finger of water that led to the smaller boat. He scrambled up the side of the small berg next to the boat and flattened himself on top of a small peak. Zac followed and then Horace brought up the rear. The three men lay side by side, watching for any movement on the deck.

Mac looked around at Zac. "Might be better to take this one first anyway. Fewer crew members."

Zac looked into Mac's eyes, then over to Horace. "All right, but remember, no shooting here, no matter what. Use your knives. I don't want any noise. Jenny's still on the *Northern Star*."

Mac and Horace nodded their heads.

They moved around to where the ice floe ran up to the steamer's aft deck. The smaller boat was much closer to the water, and Zac jumped for the rail. He caught it and pulled himself up. Looking around, he could see that the deck was dark. They had no one to guard, so there was no one walking around. Zac knew that more than likely there was only one man on the bridge.

He bent over and grabbed Horace's hand, pulling the man up. He stood on the deck, shaking. Reaching down, he helped Mac climb aboard.

"Look," Zac said, "there's probably only one man in the wheelhouse on watch. You two watch the forward hatch and I'll go up there. When I'm done, I'll come back for you."

Zac scampered off around the wheelhouse, bending low to avoid the windows. He rounded the bridge and stuffed his hands in his pockets. It was doubtful everyone on this boat knew all the sailors on the large steamer. He'd just have to take that chance. He straightened up, tipped the fur hat he was wearing down over his eyes, and walked up the stairs.

The man on the bridge had a candle lit. He was bending over it and eating a cup of soup with a spoon. "Who are you?" the man asked.

"I'm on the *Star*," Zac said. "Just thought I'd check on your food supplies."

"You getting low?" The man stepped over in Zac's direction. In the darkness, there was no way they could see each other's faces. Zac reached under his coat and felt for his revolver.

The man stepped closer. "We got some dried meat below, if you'd like to try your hand at that."

In a blur, Zac pulled out his revolver and sent it crashing up against the side of the man's head. The man fell backwards, hitting his head against the bulkhead. Zac bent down and turned the man face down. He picked up a length of cord sitting on the chart table and tied him up. Looking around, he spotted an oily cloth. The man had obviously been using it to wipe down the brass. He placed it in the man's mouth and tied it tight.

Zac went back down the stairs, rounding the deck. He spotted both Horace and Mac as they crouched beside the hatchway. "Shut this up tight," Zac whispered.

Mac dropped the iron bar over the hatch door. It was designed to keep the storms out, but tonight it would keep the steamer's crew in.

"All right," Zac said, "let's get over to the *Star*."

The three of them walked around the bridge and onto the forward deck of the steamer. They crouched behind the rail and watched as a guard was circling the deck of the *Star*. "This is going to be a mite tougher," Mac whispered.

Zac nodded. "I better go over by myself and take care of that one. Then you two come over. They already have a fire going on the forward deck. We'll just help it along. You two can be at either end of the cabin and keep anybody away that tries to come around. I want that whole crew on deck putting out the fire. I'll go down the aft hatch and look for Jenny."

"Sounds like a plan," Mac agreed. Horace nodded.

Zac watched the man circle the deck once again. He wanted to be below it and climb aboard just as he made his next turn. Then he'd wait for him to come back around. He looked back at Mac. "You signal me when he comes 'round again."

He watched as the man made his turn, then scrambled over the rail and lowered himself onto a small piece of ice swaying between the two ships. It was small and Zac held onto the steamer, watching the ice bob in the water. He looked up and waited for Mac's signal.

Moments later, Mac leaned over the rail and motioned to Zac.

Zac leaped from the small ice floe and grabbed on to the *Star*'s rear deck railing. His rifle banged against his back on the strap. He hauled himself up and threw his leg over the side, pulling himself onto the deck. Crouching low, he drew his knife. He circled to the shadowy area beside the rear hatchway and waited.

A few minutes later he heard the man's footsteps, a pacing of shoes on the hard, wet deck. The man turned the corner and Zac sprang at him. He wrapped himself around the man and rammed the blade home. The man's rifle spilled onto the deck, and Zac lowered the man next to it.

Minutes later, he could hear Mac and Horace as they scrambled onto the deck. They both ran to where Zac was waiting by the body.

"You two take your places," Zac said. "I'm gonna keep this man's watch." With that, he stood up and unslung his rifle. He didn't want anything to appear any different. He would continue the man's circle around the deck. He'd be a little late, but anyone on the other side wouldn't even lift their heads at the sound of his footsteps.

He sauntered around the cabin, spotting two men who were warming themselves beside the glowing fire. Their backs were to him. They didn't even appear to take notice as he stepped in their direction. The fire was in an iron drum and the men were feeding it with a fresh supply of wood, warming their hands as they stuffed the blaze.

Zac walked calmly over to the two of them. The man with his back to him who held the rifle would be his first target. He'd have to move fast. He was in plain view of the bridge now. A sudden movement on his part would no doubt attract attention. He just counted on the fact that the man up above would be too startled to move very fast.

He rammed the butt of his rifle into the head of the first man. He could hear the crack of the skull as his head rocked beneath the sudden blow. Swinging the barrel around, he caught the second startled man with a vicious rap across the face. The man dropped to his knees, and Zac came down hard on the top of his head with the rifle butting, sending him sprawling onto the deck.

He reached into the flaming barrel and pulled out a burning piece of wood. Leaning over, he began to touch it to the other wood boxes scattered around the deck.

From the bridge behind him, Zac could hear a man open the door. "Hey, what's going on down there?" the man shouted.

Zac drew his revolver and turned. The man was carrying a rifle and shouting. Zac aimed the Colt and fired. He cocked the hammer and fired a second time, sending the man tumbling down the stairs.

He had to move fast. Zac quickly reached back into the flames and pulled out a second piece of burning firewood. Stepping over to the railing, he climbed up and touched the flame to the small, rolled-up sail. In seconds it erupted into flames.

Jumping down, he ran for where Horace would be stationed. He reached the man and pointed behind him. "That ought to keep them busy, but you shoot anybody who tries to come this way."

Horace nodded.

Zac stepped over to the rear entrance of the cabin and threw the door open. A sailor was coming up the stairs and Zac kicked the man in the chin, sending him back down. He was on the sailor in seconds, rapping the rifle into his head with brute force. Stepping over the man, he rounded the corner in time to see a door open. He drew his knife just as Quinn stepped out. He was heading forward.

Zac caught Quinn by the collar and jerked him. He drew his knife, placing it against the man's throat. "Where's Jenny?" Zac growled.

Quinn turned his head slightly. "You!"

"Yes, me, and you know I mean business." Zac dug the knife in deeper to the fleshy part of the man's throat. "Take me to her, now."

Another door opened, and Zac pulled Quinn back around his own still-opened door. They listened as a number of men ran down the corridor in the direction of the fire. Zac knew it would take them some time to get it extinguished, and if they tried to go aft, they would get the surprise of their lives. He pushed Quinn back into the corridor. "Take me to her."

"Let up a bit," Quinn squeaked. "I can't even move."

Zac relaxed the knife gently, pushing Quinn forward. The big man stepped down the corridor and came to a set of stairs right below the stairs that led up on deck. "She's down there," he said.

Several lamps were hanging along the spine of the ship. They swayed with the movement of the water, sending their shadows back and forth over the rough timber walls.

"You'll never make it off of here," Quinn said. "We have too many men."

Zac pushed him. "Right now, they're busy fighting a fire." He jerked Quinn by the collar and pressed his knife in. "Where is she?"

Quinn pointed to a door. "She's in there, but I can't vouch for the kinda shape she's in."

Zac pushed the man up against the wall, next to the door he had indicated. "You stand right there. Don't move a muscle."

He raised the rifle and delivered a hard blow to the brass lock hanging on the door. It sprung open. He opened it and shoved Quinn inside.

Jenny was huddled on a wooden bench next to the wall Quinn fell against. The light fell on her and she looked up. "Zac, is that you?"

Zac reached out and grabbed her hand, pulling her towards him. "It's me, darling. I'm here."

She fell into his arms. "I hoped and prayed you'd come."

Jenny was wearing only a thin dress. She was shaking, and Zac could feel the goose bumps all over her body. He placed his hand on her face. It was puffy around one eye, almost closed. Her left cheek was marked with a cut.

"Who did this to you?" Zac asked. He looked over at Quinn, glaring at the man with hatred. "Did he do it?"

Jenny shook her head. "No, it was a man named Toquah, Toquah Kanstanof."

A burst of gunfire from the deck above startled Jenny. Zac looked down at her. He knew she'd never make it outside in the cold.

"Take off your coat," he shouted at Quinn. "And those mukluks of yours."

Quinn unbuttoned his fur coat and shimmied out of it. He threw it at Zac's feet.

Zac picked it up and handed it over to Jenny. "Put this on."

He watched Quinn as he pulled off his fur-lined boots. They would be much too large, but right now fit was the last thing on Zac's mind. They would do, at least until he could find something more suitable for her.

Quinn kicked them in Zac's direction, and Zac reached over and raked them under Jenny. The gunfire continued. "You better put these on. We've got to get back up on deck."

Zac pointed the rifle at Quinn. "If I see your face again, I'll kill you on sight. Your only chance is to stay right here until you hear nothing. Is that understood?"

"I hear you," Quinn said.

Zac and Jenny backed up outside the door and Zac closed it. He picked up the broken lock and, closing the hatch, wedged the thing into place. It wouldn't hold a determined effort to break free, but Zac was counting on the man's natural cowardice to keep him from being too energetic.

They moved down the hall and walked up the first set of stairs. What they saw shot fear through the both of them. Jenny looked at Zac. The fire had flared.

CHAPTER 32

+ + + + + + +

THE GUNFIRE CAUSED KATHRYN TO BOLT upright in her bed. Outside, she heard the man tumble down the stairs. The stairs that led up to the bridge were just outside the corridor, and given the fact that her cabin was the closest to the deck, she could hear almost anything that went on.

She threw off the blankets and fur comforter and yanked a pair of britches off the bedpost. The hardwood floor was cold and clammy. It curled her toes just to stand on it. She yanked her shirt onto her bare arms, and stuffed her feet down into the furry mukluks beside her bed. She couldn't get them on fast enough. Lifting up her pillow, she pulled out her pistol and moved to the door.

She could hear the sound of running outside her door, followed by the men yelling on deck. There evidently was a fire, but that wasn't what this was all about. Zac Cobb was on board. She knew it just as sure as the world turned. *How could one man cause so much trouble?* she wondered.

She opened the door in time to watch several sailors run by. One of them with a bucket in his hand came to a halt next to her, panting. "You be careful, ma'am. We got us boarders with guns. There must be a dozen or more." The man pointed in the direction of the stairs and the door that led out onto the forward deck. "They started a fire on the fore deck and we got to put it out." He looked back in the direction he had just come from. "Don't try to get out back that way. They got armed men back there, already killed one of us."

She followed the man up the stairs and stopped, looking out. The fire had spread to the front of the ship. She watched a man close to the rail. He was hauling up a bucket of water when a shot rang out from behind the cabin area. He collapsed on deck, his bucket of water spilling. Just the sight of the fire sent a rush of terror through her, and the idea that

265

the men who were trying to put it out were being shot at made her queasy.

She stepped down the stairs to the corridor below. Getting back to the steamer Quinn had come north on was out of the question. It was anchored behind them and the men who were shooting were in that direction.

She looked up in time to see Toquah striding down the hall. He was dressed warmly, with a fur hat and gloves. He had his rifle in hand. When he caught sight of her, she could see the look of worry written across his face. This was not his type of fighting, closed up on a ship. She knew the man preferred the open spaces.

She grabbed onto his coat as he stepped up to her. "What are you going to do?" she asked.

He shook the Winchester rifle he was carrying. "I'm going to kill me some men."

"I'd feel better if we were away from here," she said. "Is there somewhere we can go and wait until we know what happens here?"

He swallowed hard and stared at her. "That boat we used is tied up off the bow of the ship. We could reach it, but what would be the point? We got a war going on here."

"Good, why don't you get it ready, then?"

He shook his head slightly. "There's fighting to be done," he said.

"We don't know how many men are up against us. Cobb may have brought a posse with him. Anyway, the ship has more than enough men to handle the situation. I just don't want to be on board if that fire keeps spreading."

She could see him thinking the matter over. He hadn't yet seen the flames.

"I'll do it, if that's what you want."

She nodded her head. "Yes, that's what I want. I'll go get my warm coat and my rifle and meet you on deck in a few minutes."

He turned and stepped up the few stairs to the door. When he opened it, she could see the flames. They had spread and the shooting was still going on.

Turning around, she ran back to her cabin. Everything was going wrong. Jenny would die in the belly of the ship, and she needed the woman's signature. There was no time to think about that now. She only knew she had to get away, and as far as possible.

✦ ✦ ✦ ✦ ✦

Zac pulled Jenny along the stairs that led to the rear deck. He made sure he was in front. The last thing he wanted was a surprise. Turning to her, he took out the short pistol he carried in his underarm holster. A liquid pallor bleached Jenny's tight skin. He could see the blue veins that normally gave color to her cheeks, and her teeth were chattering. She tried to stop it, but each time her jaw would slack, the knocking of her teeth would begin again. "Here, you better take this," he said.

She shook her head in a jerky motion. "No." Her breath was short and she had her arms wound around her for warmth. "I don't want it."

"You might just need it before we're through." Zac could see the look of panic in her eyes. He couldn't understand it. He'd seen her shoot before. It couldn't be fear.

"I've done enough killing. I have no desire to take another man's life."

He crammed the gun back into his holster and took her hand, rubbing it with both if his. "Let's hope we've both done enough."

They started up the final set of stairs and then Zac heard movement, followed by muffled talking. He held Jenny still and drew his Colt. He motioned for her to stay right where she was, moving his open hand up and down. She nodded.

He moved up the steps slowly, then stood still. There were three men standing at the door with their backs to him. Their guns were drawn, and obviously they were waiting for just the right moment, a time when the shooting on deck started back up and they could be sure that the men they were after were preoccupied.

Zac cocked the pistol. The sound froze the men in place. "Just stand right where you are and drop those guns," he said.

One man started to turn around. Zac yelled, "Don't move. Just do what I say."

The man to the right dropped his revolver to the floor, but the one on the extreme left of the group swung around, his hand flashing a six-gun. Zac fired, the smoke filling the corridor. He fired a second time before the man in the middle turned and fired in Zac's direction. The bullet flew wildly past him.

Zac dropped into a crouch and took aim, firing into the man's midsection. The shot crumpled the man over, spilling the gun from his hand.

The third man, who had done as instructed, bent over with his hands tucked behind his head. He positioned himself like a duck in the midst of a shooting gallery, still refusing to even turn around. "Don't shoot!" he screamed. "I ain't got no gun."

Zac stepped over to the man. He picked up his revolver and then the other two guns left by the men he had shot, dropping them into his coat pocket. "Stand up," he said.

The man slowly got to his feet and edged his way in Zac's direction.

Zac stooped down to the second man he had shot. He held his hand to the man's neck. "This man's alive." He looked up at the older man, then got to his feet. "You take him to a cabin and get him some help." He waggled his revolver. "Do it now."

The man stepped over and, putting his hands under the wounded man's arms from behind, lifted him up. He began to drag him down the corridor.

Zac turned and walked down the stairs to where Jenny was standing. He took her hand. "We've got to get out of here."

She nodded and followed him back to the door, staring at the man on the floor and shaking.

He opened the door and poked his head out. "Horace! Mac! It's me." With that, he stepped out the door, holding Jenny's hand and pulling her after him.

Horace was lying in the shadows on his stomach. His revolver was still in his hand and Zac could see his head move. He stooped over the man, then looked up and fired at several sailors trying to work themselves into position.

"I'm hit," Horace groaned. He let out a slow, mournful note of pain. "They got me in the belly. Durn fool I was too. I stood out there when I shoulda been in the shadows."

Zac turned the man over and, scooting forward, held his head in his hands. "We'll get you out of here. Don't you worry." He dragged him over to the side of the cabin, behind a storage barrel.

Horace smiled and coughed as he tried to laugh. "You really think you're dragging me back across that ice field? Ain't likely. This is as far as this old boy is going to go."

Zac took aim and fired once again at the forward deck area. The men there were keeping their heads down and from what he could see, they were frantically trying to put out the fire.

"We stung 'em a good one, didn't we?"

"Yes," Zac said. "We did."

"You get that gal of yours?"

Zac looked over at Jenny. She was huddled against the cabin wall next to the door. He signaled to her. "Yes, I got her. She was cold but alive."

"I'm glad." Horace's eyes rolled slightly.

"We got to get you out of here."

"You just put that nonsense out of your head." His eyes drifted to the stern of the boat. "You fix me up over there and load my rifle. I'll keep them off of you fer a spell. Give you time to get away without them folks shooting down at you."

Jenny walked over. She stooped down next to where Zac had the man in his lap.

"This is Jenny."

"Pleased to meet you, ma'am." He looked back at Zac, then once again at Jenny. "You got yerself a fine man here. He sure loves you a whole lot. Been mighty fine to me too. Treated me like regular people and got me cleaned up for the first time in years. You better get your-selves gone b'fore them fellers get that fire under control and head this a way sure 'nuff," Horace said.

Zac looked up at the masts. The flame was climbing, and he could see that one of the masts had fallen onto the deck, starting a new series of fires. "I don't think they're anywhere close to that."

"You just pull me back there," Horace said, "and go get this here lady warm. I'll keep 'em off you."

Zac laid down a number of shots from his position into the forward deck. He wanted the men there to think twice before they ventured in their direction. He then took several minutes to put Horace in position.

Horace waved them off. "I can shoot at either side from here. Now you folks get. Don't let me stay here for nothin'. You get long gone, ya hear?"

Zac reached down and patted the man's shoulder. Then he grabbed Jenny, motioned to Mac, and the three of them lowered themselves over the side and climbed up onto the forward deck of the steamer. They moved to the rear of the boat.

"There's a dory hung over the stern," Zac said. "We'll take that. It'll save us from taking Jenny across that ice."

Quickly, they untied the dory and lowered it onto the ice flow next to the steamer. They could hear shooting now from the *Northern Star*. Horace was doing his job.

The fire from the *Northern Star* was glowing in the night sky. They were sliding the small dory across the ice, and they could tell the men on board the *Star* were losing their battle for the ship. It wouldn't be long before the situation turned desperate. Almost all of the masts were on fire; they watched as another of the forward masts fell to the deck with a shower of sparks.

"I don't think that whale oil I saw on deck is gonna help them none," Mac said.

"I wonder where Kathryn is," Jenny said. "I'd hate to see anyone die like that, even her."

Mac pointed to a spot north of them. "I think I spotted her," he said. "She and a man are off on that whaleboat the ship carries. Hate to see her get away neither."

"I'll go after them," Zac said.

Jenny reached over and grabbed his arm. "Why? Why do you have to do that? Haven't you done enough already?"

Zac held her hand and looked into her eyes. "Those people are reckless. They won't stop. I don't want to get to Sitka and have to look over my shoulder wherever I go, and I sure don't want to have to worry about them coming after you. You're a witness against them."

"The man knows what's best," Mac said.

"Be careful. Toquah Kanstanof will be with her," Jenny said. "He's the one that hit me."

"You watch out for him," Mac said. "I've heard of that man. The Mounties want him real bad."

"I don't suppose there's any way I can talk you out of this," Jenny said.

"I'll be careful." He pulled his glove off and ran his fingers over her cheek. "I won't take any unnecessary risks. If I can't catch up with them tonight, I'll come back."

"You do that," Mac said. "Old Benny will be waiting for us with that boat of his in the morning."

Once again they started to push the dory over the ice and soon came to the place where the raft was tied.

"You take the dory," Mac said. "I'll pole her and me over to the spot to where we left the fire. Won't take me no time at all to get it started again. I'll put her in one of the bedrolls and get some hot food in her."

Zac pushed back a strand of Jenny's hair and gently kissed her forehead. "You'll be all right. Mac will get you warm."

"I won't be all right without you, and neither will Skip. You think of us when you're out there. Don't do anything foolish."

"I won't." Zac kissed her. "I'll be with you shortly."

He waited until Mac had placed Jenny on the raft and then slid the dory into the water. Dipping his paddle in the direction he'd last seen the whaleboat, he glided through the cold water.

Soon, he caught sight of the whaleboat. Toquah was rowing around an ice floe, pulling away from the ship and in the direction of the shore. Zac paddled harder. He wanted to place himself in between the boat and the open water that led to the rocky beach. Kathryn turned her head around and spotted him. Zac could see that she was talking to Toquah. The man dropped the oars and picked up a rifle. Taking aim, he fired. The bullet whizzed by Zac's small boat, thudding dully in the water.

Two can play that game, Zac thought. *Let's see how you take to this*. He reached for the Sharps and raised it to his shoulder, lifting up the rear sight. Killing the man outright was something he didn't want to do. He fired the big gun, the sound booming off the ice. The slug went directly into the hull of the whaleboat, and in the distance Zac could hear the sound of the glacier, a deep, muffled rumble. The shots from the rifles were having their effects on the fragile ice.

The shot from the big gun swung Toquah into action. He dropped his rifle, sat down in the boat, and once again started straining at the oars. He was pulling hard now, in the direction of the glacier. Evidently he wanted to lose Zac in all the ice. He pulled the big boat around a large berg and slipped out of sight.

Zac picked up the paddle and followed. Rounding the berg, he lifted the paddle and drifted. The ice seemed solid against the night sky, and in the distance the light from the fire rippled over the white frozen walls. Zac had lost sight of the whaleboat. He dipped the paddle in the water and pulled hard. His muscles strained against the black water, but the warmth of the work was comforting.

When he rounded the next gap in the large icebergs, he spotted the boat. He strained to see more clearly. Now he could see only one figure in the boat. It was Kathryn. She was at the oars, pulling the boat steadily in the direction of the glacier.

Zac swung his head from side to side. Toquah might have hidden in the stern of the boat, just waiting for him to approach, but that wasn't likely. Kathryn wasn't the kind to ever row unless it was absolutely necessary. The other possibility was that Toquah had gotten off the boat and was waiting for him in ambush.

Zac paddled the dory over to the large berg the whaleboat had just passed, nudging it up onto the edge of the thing. Scrambling out, he pulled the dory up. The wind was beginning to pick up. That wasn't going to help the men putting out the fire on the ship. It sent a ripple of icy spray down Zac's back. That was good. He wanted to be alert. He needed to be ready. He dug his mukluks into the side of the rise that led up the peak of the berg. From there he would be able to see better. One step at a time, he climbed the peak. Reaching the top, he slid forward on his belly.

His first thought was to look over the ice, but he saw nothing, only the barren blankness of the ice as it spread out over the bay and Kathryn still pulling at the oars of the boat. Then he looked down. He saw the man, crouching with his rifle and waiting for Zac to clear the berg in his dory.

Zac got to his feet and jumped. He sailed through the black air, his rifle out from his body. He hit the man at full force with his feet, sending him spinning across the narrow shelf of ice that surrounded the large berg. Toquah had been separated from his rifle. He gingerly got to his feet and flashed a cruel sneer in Zac's direction. The man was large and formidable. He took a step forward and then sheer panic raced across his face. The thin ice underneath him was breaking.

"Get down," Zac yelled. "Flatten out."

Toquah seemed helpless, suspended in time and the fear of the moment. He took another step forward, hoping against hope that the thin ice would bear his weight. Suddenly, the ice gave way. It broke off right where the man was standing, sending him down into the icy water.

Zac stepped closer to the edge. He'd come as close as he dared. Toquah was splashing furiously, and the look of terror written across his face told Zac all he needed to know. The man didn't know how to swim. Every furious splash, every effort, seemed to be carrying him farther away from the berg.

Zac bent down and held the barrel of the rifle in Toquah's direction. "Grab onto this. I'll pull you up."

Toquah reached for the end of the rifle, but missed. He went under and came up sputtering and coughing, scattering the dark water in flying masses. The near rescue sent him into further panic. He splashed at the cold, frigid black water, fighting it. The cold was having its effect now. Each of the man's furious splashes became weaker and slower. They sounded like splats, landing on the surface with a thump that echoed over the ice. Zac held the rifle out as far as he could, then watched as Toquah slipped under. He watched for a few moments, waiting for any sign of life. There was nothing there, only the black, frozen bay.

Zac got to his feet and skirted the edge of the berg. It would be easier to bring Kathryn in now. He got to the dory and, pulling it into the water, stepped in. He paddled hard to make up the distance. As he rounded the next berg, he was surprised to see how far she had gone. She was very close to the glacier, much too close, and still pulling on the oars. Zac paddled harder. Kathryn could see him now. That was apparent. He watched her as he paddled. At a distance she might mistake him for Toquah, but not for long.

Suddenly she put down her oars. Zac laid down the paddle and carefully stood up. He cupped his hands to his face and yelled. "It's all over now, Kathryn. Come back in my direction."

He watched as she slid forward in the boat. Then she stood up, a rifle in her hands.

Zac waved his arms. "Don't do that. The ice."

She fired a shot, the echo sounding out over the bay.

Zac froze. The glacier was stirring. The rifle shot had done it. The glacier rumbled to life, and a large shelf tore apart from the frozen river. Kathryn saw it too. She turned around and watched as the icy ledge slid off and dropped toward her. It took only moments, but the roar of the ice seemed to fill the entire bay. It hit the whaleboat and capsized it, sending Kathryn over the side. Zac watched as the ice continued to slide downward. Mountains of rocky frozen river rumbled down and crashed into the water, filling the bay with choppy water, floating ice, and fresh-peaked bergs.

CHAPTER 33

+ + + + + + +

THE BIG HOUSE FELT EMPTY AND BARE even though it was filled with people for the reading of the will. Without Ian it was a lonely place.

Zac watched Risa as she sat listening to David Cormia. She was attentive, but Zac could tell that she wasn't understanding the full implication of what the lawyer was saying. There was a bewildered look on her face, mixed with fear.

Zac sat beside Jenny on the couch. They both turned their attention to Umqua and Bubba Dean. The two of them were setting out trays of food. The plates were piled high with fresh baked bread, a pork roast, and numerous cheeses.

Umqua was wearing a full dress. It was a dark blue, proper enough to be called a mourning dress, but with enough color to be worn on other occasions. Bubba Dean was wearing a black suit. The man's starched collar was cutting across his neck and he looked uncomfortable. He'd have looked uncomfortable in the thing even if he was sleeping.

The man's eyes darted in Zac's direction, refusing to lock on. It was almost as if he were trying to guess just what Zac was thinking without giving himself away. There was a sheepishness to his movements. He held the tray of cheese over in Naomi's direction and cleared his throat. "'Scuse me, Miss Naomi. Y'all wants some cheese?"

Zac got to his feet and walked over to where the man was circling the room. He was bending over Cormia, giving out his "'scuse me" line, when Zac tapped him on the shoulder.

Bubba Dean swung around. Zac could see almost a flinch in his eye. "I'se sorry. I was jest coming over y'all's way."

Zac took hold of the tray, prying it away. Bubba Dean's eyes widened. Now he was surprised and looked a little puzzled.

"I'm going to take your server for a few minutes," Zac said to Risa.

Risa nodded. She wasn't paying much attention. She continued to listen to Cormia.

Zac sat the tray down on a table between the two chairs. "No need for this now. I need to talk to you."

"Me, sir? Why for? Am I doing something wrong?"

"No, you're doing everything right." Zac pulled him over to the side of the room, to a spot beyond the hearing of the others. He looked back and noticed that Umqua was watching them, and the look in her eyes said that she wasn't the least bit happy about Zac talking to her husband.

"I sure hopes everthin's right. Mr. Ian would want it that way."

"When we get through with this will, it won't make any difference what he wants."

Bubba Dean blinked his eyes and swallowed. If it was possible to look any more uncomfortable, Zac had never seen it.

"One thing, though," Zac said. "Don't you think he'd want us to find his killer?"

The man's head sank, his chin resting on his high collar. "I don't think that's gonna make no difference any which way."

"It ought to. It does to me, and I'm sure it will to the law. Murderers shouldn't go free."

"No, sir. I reckon not."

"Then I'd suggest that we've got a couple of questions that need answering, and I figure you're just the man to do it."

Zac signaled over to Jenny and she got up from the couch, joining the two men. "We're going to do a little exploring," he said. He motioned toward the stairs.

Cormia had just wrapped up his final comment, and few people noticed as they left the room and went up the stairs, but Zac looked down and caught sight of Umqua. The woman hadn't taken her eyes off them. He smiled back at her.

They took the second set of stairs that led to Ian's study and walked down the long hall. The light was streaming in from the window at the end of the hall. Stopping in front of the door, Bubba Dean reached into his pocket for the key.

Zac put his hand on the man's wrist. "Why don't you use the key on your key ring? It worked before."

"No, sir. I done put Mr. Ian's lock back on this here door. Dis is the key you took offa the man."

"Then where is the other lock?"

Bubba Dean shrugged his shoulders. "Don't rightly know."

"I think you do." He held his hand out. "Let me see that key ring of yours."

Bubba Dean swung his arms in front of him like a child who had been asked to play a game when he didn't know the rules. "Dey ain't gonna work here. You done seen that for yourself." He reached into his pocket and produced the ring of keys.

Zac looked back at Jenny. She was watching the whole thing intently. "Now, why don't we just follow Jenny here. Darling, take us to the basement, to the room you and Naomi saw."

He shot a glance in Bubba Dean's direction. He seemed stunned. His mouth dropped open. "Is there a problem with that?" Zac asked.

There was a pause. It was hard for the man to get the words out. "No, sir. There ain't no problem. All that is Mr. Ian's business."

"Fine," Zac said. He motioned toward the back stairway, the one that would take them into the lower areas of the house without having to go back through the great room. "Lead on, darling."

"I'd be glad to," Jenny said. She stepped out in front of the two men, and rounding the corner of the hall, made her way down the stairs.

The carpeted stairs made for quiet walking. Stepping around the corner that led to the main floor, the three of them took the next set of stairs, which led to the lower level. Jenny pointed at the door. "The basement is down there."

Zac could see that there was a new lock on the basement door. He held out the key ring for Bubba Dean. "Which one is it?"

The man scratched his head. "I don't rightly remember."

Pulling out his Colt, Zac tossed it into the palm of his hand, butt first. He slapped the lock with the walnut pistol butt and it sprung open. "Now we won't have to worry about you finding it."

"No, sir." Bubba Dean nervously scratched his head. "I reckon not."

They left the door open, allowing some light to shine on the stairs. At the bottom was a table with several candlesticks. Zac took a match out of his pocket and popped it to life on the end of his thumbnail. He held it to a candle, allowing the flame to crawl up the wick. Picking it up, he motioned to Jenny and Bubba Dean. "After you, folks. I'll just follow along."

They walked across the open basement, and Jenny opened the door that led into the corridor. The hallway was dark, with closed doors on either side. As they passed by, Zac took notice of the handles on the doors. It wasn't until they got to the last door that he saw the lock. It was shiny and brass and it hung on a strong hasp drilled into the door.

Zac pulled the key ring out from his pocket and handed it in the direction of Bubba Dean. "Why don't you open it for us?"

The man swallowed. Zac could see his Adam's apple ripple over the top of his high, stiff collar. "I can't rightly do that."

Zac held the keys up. "Who uses these keys other than you?"

"Just folks 'round here what has need of 'em from time to time."

"Like your wife?"

The words hit Bubba Dean, and he rocked back on his heels. Zac knew he'd struck home. The man's lips trembled. "She might have need sometimes."

Zac handed the candle to Jenny. "Let's just see if I can find the key, then." He flipped the keys over in the ring until he came to the brass key he recognized. It had his mark on it, the mark he'd made to show the one that unlocked the padlock hanging on Ian's door on the day the man died. Holding it out, he inserted it into the lock and turned it. The lock sprung open.

Zac twisted the knob and pushed the door open. The three of them stepped into the large room. Oversized windows with bars on them looked out onto the ocean. A large canopied bed stood in the center with a fireplace and mantel on the wall. A sofa and chair flanked either side of a tall set of shelves, each of which were filled with dolls of every description.

On the floor was a gray-haired woman. She had her back to them and was setting out several dolls around a small table. The plates and cups on the table were child-sized. She seemed to be humming a tune as she lost herself at play.

Bubba Dean looked at Zac and Jenny. "This here's Miss Eva. Mr. Ian keeps her down here soze she won't get into no trouble." He raised his voice to get the woman's attention. "Missy Eva, I gots some company fer you."

The woman turned around, scooting over the floor. It was the grayhaired woman Zac had seen walking along the road both to and from the house. She pointed her bony finger at Zac. "I know you, don't I?"

Zac nodded. "Yes, ma'am. We met."

Jenny was almost too stunned to speak. Her mouth moved, but the words weren't coming out.

"You know this woman?" Zac asked.

Jenny didn't respond at first. She simply stood there, staring for what seemed like the longest time. "That's my aunt Eva," she finally said. "I thought she was dead."

The woman got up from the floor and walked toward them. She sang as she walked. "Oh the moon shines tonight on pretty red wing. . . ."

"You see why we keeps her down here," Bubba Dean said. "Poor woman ain't right, ain't been right for years. Mr. Ian couldn't bring himself to put her away in one of them places. He went and saw one a time or two and didn't eat nor sleep fer days when he gots back home. Said they just locked old folks away in dark rooms where they piled onto one another."

The woman walked up to Zac. "You are a handsome man," she said. She held her arms out. "Would you like to dance with me? The band can play real nice."

"Some other time," Zac said.

"Y'all wants to go out to your garden now?" Bubba Dean asked the woman.

Her face became animated. "Yes." She nodded her head vigorously. "Yes, I'd like that very much. Can I take my dolls with me? They like the sunshine."

"Sure. You fetch 'em and we'll wait for you."

Sauntering back to the tea party, the woman gathered up the dolls in her arms, hugging them tightly. She rocked them gently, swinging her arms back and forth as she walked back to the door. Bubba Dean led the way and opened the door to the garden at the end of the hall, stepping back as the woman walked out. Zac and Jenny followed.

Jenny continued to stare at the woman as she laid her dolls out on the grass in a circle around her. "I remember her from my childhood," Jenny said. "She was always serious, always filled with things to do."

"Well, she's playing now," Zac responded.

Jenny nodded her head.

Bubba Dean clasped his hands in front of him, eyeballing the woman as she played. "Mr. Ian loved her a whole lot. He couldn't put her in one of dem places, and he weren't about to get himself no divorce."

Zac looked over at Jenny. "That's why he was so concerned about Risa's spot in his will. The man was already married."

"Aunt Eva is his third dependent," Jenny added. "It's clearing up for me now."

They watched as the woman was suddenly distracted by the flight of a bee. She got to her feet and followed the thing over to the flowers, bending down and watching it. "I take it you learned about beekeeping from Jenny's aunt Eva here," Zac said.

Bubba Dean nodded. "Yes, she kept them things all the time in Maryland."

Jenny's eyes brightened. "I can remember that now. I thought of her when I first saw your beehives here, but only for a moment."

"I think we've seen enough here," Zac said. "We better get back to the others."

It took them a short time before they soothed the woman back into her room. Bubba Dean closed the door and placed the lock back on it. He caught Zac's arm. "Listen, I ain't sure jest what you intend to do 'bout this, but go easy."

Moments later they returned to the great room. Zac took his seat on the couch beside Jenny. "I sent Dolly and Skip to the kitchen to bake," Umqua said. "They not need to be here." It was plain to see that Umqua was agitated. She had already cleared the food from the table and was pacing the room, doing her best to look busy. She then froze to attention beside the kitchen door with Bubba Dean at her side. David Cormia was busy organizing his documents, and Zac cleared his throat, catching the man's attention. "Let me ask you a question," he said.

"Of course."

"Before Jenny came to Sitka, who was going to have control over the disposition of Ian's property?"

Cormia nodded at Bubba Dean and Umqua. "He was going to leave the administration of everything to his servants there."

"That's what I figured," Zac said. "And what if, for some unfortunate reason, Jenny wasn't around to do that job now?"

"Then I would have to find someone else who could."

"Like Bubba Dean and Umqua?"

"Probably, they were Ian's first choice."

"What you saying?" Umqua spat out the words and stepped forward. She was angry and it showed in the way she clenched her jaws tight. "We always took good care of him."

"And I'll just bet you took care of him on the last afternoon of his life too," Zac said. "I've seen enough to tell me everything I need to know."

Bubba Dean stepped forward and put his arm around Umqua. "Don't you be too hard on her. She was lookin' after things 'round here. Spent a good deal of time taking care of Miss Eva too."

Risa looked alarmed. "Who is Miss Eva?" she asked.

"I'll have to explain that to you in a bit," Cormia said. "Your husband might have been wrong, but he meant well."

"The road to hell is paved with the cobblestones of good intentions," Zac said. "In this case, I think the man's chickens came home to roost." He pointed at Umqua. "You had a plan, although maybe our Miss Kathryn Jung helped you with it. That's who you were going to see on the day Jenny disappeared. When Ian was alone in his study, you unlocked Eva's door and took her out to tend the bees. She brought one of the hives back indoors and you led her up to Ian's room. You had the woman toss the bees into the room and then you made sure it was locked. Stop me if I'm going too fast for you."

Umqua held her hands to her side, her fingers balling up into fists.

"You were doing your part with Ian, and Kathryn was supposed to do hers with Jenny. The problem was Kathryn failed and you didn't. You did exactly like you were supposed to do, and if things had worked out, none of us would be here to question you about it."

Zac looked at Bubba Dean. "I don't blame you. You probably had no idea of this until it had already been done. I do blame you, though, for not coming forward with what you knew. You showed loyalty, but poor judgment." He cast a glance at Umqua. "You've always been loyal, only this time it was to the wrong person."

Umqua reached into her apron pocket and pulled out a small revolver. She shook it in Zac's direction. "Not good for you to meddle in our business. We not ask that woman of yours to come up here in the first place. What right she have? She never take care of the man for forty years like my husband did. She never cook for and care for his wife." She looked over at Risa. "Both of them."

She paused, pointing the gun at Zac. "You got no right. We earned this, we didn't marry it."

Zac got to his feet. He took a step toward the woman. "But you thought you married it, didn't you? You saw Bubba Dean here as your chance to get what you wanted."

"What if I did? Every woman does that with the man she marries."

"I didn't," Risa spoke up. "I loved Ian."

Zac continued to step forward. "You didn't care for people, you just used them to get what you wanted. You used your husband, and you used that woman downstairs to kill the man who trusted you."

Just then the door to the kitchen flew open. Dolly stepped into the great room with a chocolate cake in her hands. Her smile was broad, showing every one of her teeth. "Looky what we made. You can eat it. It's real good."

Umqua took her eyes off Zac and looked back at the girl who had startled her. Bubba Dean brought his hand down on her arm, slapping the gun to the floor. It slid across the waxed oak. Zac raced over and picked it up.

Bubba Dean wrapped his arms around the woman. Tenderly he said, "It's all right, sugar babe. I ain't gonna let nobody hurt you no more. I'll takes good care of you, and you won't have to hurt nobody no more."

✦   ✦   ✦   ✦   ✦

It was several hours later when Zac took Jenny into the gardens. The sun was shining, which was a rarity. Clouds were forming out to sea, and over the mountains gray smoky trails of rain were making their march onto the land. The sunshine would be short lived and right then Zac knew Jenny needed every second of it. "Are you all right?" he asked.

"How did you know Umqua was involved with all that?"

Zac stroked his chin. "I didn't figure it was Bubba Dean. The man had been with your uncle too long for that. I just had to figure out where the lock went that was hanging on Ian's door, and with what you had told me about your and Naomi's little trip down there, I thought that might be the logical place to look."

She swung around, facing him. "But you didn't know it was Eva in that room, did you?"

"No, but that uncle of yours always struck me as the kind of man who was hiding something. Some men live so long covering up a lie, they start to think of it as the truth. Umqua might have gotten away with it, too, if it hadn't been for the lock. I just had to ask about who might gain if you weren't around to carry out your uncle's wishes. Umqua had plenty of reasons, and her story about why she was in that alley when you turned up missing just didn't hold up."

Jenny dropped his hand and walked off. She looked up into his eyes, but it was a distant look. "You know, both you and I thought that the thing we would have to deal with when we got married was the matter of your job and the Wells Fargo company. This changes that, though."

"This changes nothing."

"Yes, it does. Now I have a simple-minded cousin and a helpless aunt to take care of."

Zac pushed her hair from her forehead. "I don't think that's what you're worried about. We'll take Dolly with us and love her like she's our own. Cormia can find care for your aunt. She's comfortable here. As far as Risa is concerned, you can sign that land back over to her and make sure she's well provided for. We'll take care of all that before we leave."

Jenny turned and walked away. It was obvious to Zac that those weren't the things that were bothering her. He followed her and took her arm, turning her around. "Tell me what the problem is."

Jenny had tears in her eyes. "I don't want to marry you, not now."

"Why not? You love me, don't you?"

"More than ever . . . that's why." The tears were rolling down her cheeks.

He wiped her cheeks with his fingers. "You beat all, girl. I've never known you to cry when I had a handkerchief."

Jenny looked off in the direction of the house. "I don't want to turn out like those other Hays women and have you worrying about me. I don't want to be kept in your basement. I love you too much for that."

"You don't know that's going to happen. You're different and I'm different. Jenny, I've learned something from you. You don't just love the part of me that everybody likes, and there ain't much of that. You love all of me. And I love all of you. That ain't ever going to change."

EPILOGUE

✦ ✦ ✦ ✦ ✦ ✦ ✦

THE CHURCH IN CAMBRIA WAS FILLED to overflowing. Hans had been preparing the food for days, and Dolly had insisted on having a hand in the baking.

The sun was shining brightly, forming a golden haze in the dry grass. There seemed to be no clouds to speak of, only wisps of white streaky smears from the day before. The grass waved across the hills, and all the hitching rails at the small white church were filled with the reins of horses. Buggies formed several lines behind them, anchors of lead holding the reins to the ground as the animals fed.

Jenny sat in front of a mirror in the small side room with Naomi fussing over her hair, making sure it flowed down her neck and back in a smooth texture.

"Are you nervous?" Naomi asked.

"I'm nervous for Zac," Jenny smiled, "but not for me."

Just then there was a tapping at the door. Naomi stepped over and opened it. A big man in buckskins and a full beard tramped in, followed by a large woman with curly black hair. She was grinning and hanging on to the man's arm.

Jenny spun around in her chair. "Mac! I'm so glad to see you. Have you seen Zac?"

"Not yet. I figure the man got the skitters and done run off." He leaned forward and flashed a smile. "If you need me to, I'll hunt him down. I'm a pretty fair tracker, you know. Bring him in here at gun point if I have to."

Jenny laughed. "I don't think that will be necessary. He's probably out back cutting the watermelon."

"Well, you never can tell about men folk when it comes round to marrying. They're liable to do most anything." He glanced at the woman on his arm. "This here's my wife Emma. Brought her along from Seattle, her

285

and our three young'uns. They'ze most likely with Zac and the watermelons by now."

Jenny nodded. "Pleased to meet you."

Mac straightened himself up to his full height. "Let me move on to say that Emma here's my only wife now. She was number two, and since number one's dead and gone, by all rights she's all I'm entitled to. That man of yours didn't make me none too proud of what I was up to."

He pulled Emma closer to him, grinning at her. "I 'splained things to Emma here and she done forgive me. She's a mighty good woman to do that. Most would cut me loose with the business end of a frying pan, I reckon."

"I expect so," Jenny agreed.

"Well, I'm walking the straight path now." He crossed his heart. "That man of yours and the way he loves you taught me a whole lot."

"I'm glad," Jenny said. "God always meant for two people to become one."

Mac nodded. "That's right, two, not four or five."

Emma nudged him in the ribs with her elbow, smiling as she did it. "He's learned his lesson," she said.

"I sure have." Mac nodded.

"I'm happy for you," Jenny said, "You and your family."

"Well, we'll be running along to our seats now. Just wanted to bring Emma in and have her see the lady that Zac is so caught up with."

Naomi held the door and closed it behind the couple. She looked at Jenny, and they both began to laugh. "Men learn slow," she said.

"Yes, but men do learn," Jenny replied.

Suddenly, the sound of the organ brought both of them to attention. They looked at each other. "I think it's time," Naomi said.

Naomi walked over to the side door and opened it. She held it as Jenny walked through, bending over to pick up the bridal train that followed her dress. They would have to walk around the church and come through the front entrance.

Moments later they stood at the front door. Dolly held a basket full of flower petals. The girl had busied herself with plucking petals all morning, and she grinned and held up the basket. "You think this is enough?"

"Yes." Jenny nodded. "That will be fine. You go in first and I'll follow Naomi."

Dolly ran her fingers through the flowers, smiling and filtering the petals. "I just love flowers and weddings. They both smell like love."

The tune on the organ changed, and Jenny signaled for Dolly to go.

They watched her as she sauntered up the aisle, dropping petals on the beaten carpet. Naomi smiled and followed.

Jenny's heart was beating faster. She could see Zac standing at the altar. The dark suit made him seem even taller. Jeff Bridger was at the front, and alongside Zac was his best man, Skip. From where she stood, she had never seen Skip looking better or with a cleaner face.

The minister rocked back and forth on his heels. He smiled as he looked over the packed church. Jenny watched him as he surveyed the crowd with a broad smile on his face. It was when he spotted Zac's Aunt Hattie on the front row that he stopped stone cold. His jaw dropped.

Hattie had worn a bright red dress with puffy sleeves that would have looked out of place at a Fourth of July picnic. She had on a pair of lace white gloves that she kept pulling on. Her flat white straw hat was cocked to the side of her head. A yellow daisy stuck out of a red hatband and drooped over her nose, looking like it had been picked that morning. She blew on it, sending the thing bouncing to the side.

She spoke up in words that could be heard over the music. "You ain't gonna ask that fool question 'bout folks objectin' to this here weddin', is you?"

The preacher dropped his chin and with a somber look shook his head. It was hard for Jenny to tell from where she stood if the man was answering her question or expressing his disapproval. In any event, Hattie took it as an answer she agreed with.

She grunted. "Good, never much cared for that. 'Sides, with this here bunch you could never tell what might come out."

Jenny watched as Dolly reached the small platform at the front. She dropped a fistful of petals and took her place, grinning all the while. Naomi swung sweetly into position, staring back down the aisle at Jenny.

The music stopped and Zac reached over and picked up his violin, the instrument he always used to express the deepest feelings of his heart. He lifted it to his chin and began to play the sweet melody of *Ode to Man's Desire*. The music seemed to fill the church, and it filled Jenny's heart as she started down the aisle toward the man who had decided to draw a circle around her and love everything inside it.